To Arthur Yanofsky Q.C.

With admiration
and appreciation,

Jeannette Moscovitch
August 17, 2010.

The Expatriate

A Docunovel by Jeannette Moscovitch

Published by

CULTURAMA PRESS

The Expatriate

A Docunovel by Jeannette Moscovitch

Published by Culturama Press

Legal Deposit, 2010, Bibliothèque Nationale du Québec
National Library of Canada

Printed and bound in Canada

Library and Archives Canada Cataloguing in Publication

Moscovitch, Jeannette
        The expatriate / Jeannette Moscovitch.

ISBN 978-0-9813074-0-4

        I. Title.

PS8626.O825E96 2009   C813'.6   C2009-905430-2

This book is a docunovel: all locales are authentic and exist. Most incidents occurred. All characters are fictitious.

Copies of this book may be obtained through:
Invisible Cities Network: http://www.InvisibleCitiesNetwork.org
Or telephone: 514-937-7937

DEDICATION

To my late husband,
Judge M. Moscovitch

'Justice is conscience. Those who dearly recognize the voice of their own conscience usually recognize the voice of justice.'
Alexander Solzhenitsyn

TABLE OF CONTENTS

THE PREPARATION
DÜSSELDORF, AUGUST 1945

Captain Yanos von Heissel closed the door of his Düsseldorf home, took his usual brisk walk down the pathway lined with rose bushes, but hardly noticed how luxuriantly they had bloomed. He was busy checking his daily agenda of urgent chores.

His wife's passport was renewed in her maiden name, Lara von Stradta, and included their daughter, Brigitta. Second on the agenda was a transfer of one million American dollars, in his wife's name, to the International Bank in Zürich.

He discussed with Lara relocating to her birthplace and residence of her parents in Zürich. She agreed that it would be more comfortable there, until Düsseldorf was rebuilt. Preparations for the move began immediately. Her parents were advised to expect their daughter and granddaughter, but their son-in-law was obliged to remain in Germany for an indefinite period before joining them. There was much to be done: obtaining various official discharges from the German government, selling his father's mansion and paper mills as well as his own home. Because of official delays, censorship and interrupted mail service, communication by mail or telephone would be limited and probably delayed for long periods. The captain was pleased with the clarity and brevity of his communiqués, traits honed and practised during his military service.

To celebrate the last family evening together, he made reservations at their favourite restaurant and arranged for a limousine to drive Lara and Brigitta to the train station the next morning. With great reluctance the captain decided not to accompany them. It would be too much of an emotional strain.

Any disclosure of his secret plans would be irrevocable and risky, something he might regret forever. The less said the better.

He took great pains to buy going-away mementos. For Lara, he had chosen a fine honey-coloured leather suitcase from Italy. It would last a life-time and remind her of him whenever she traveled. For Brigitta, he had chosen a gold cross that was encrusted with a one-carat diamond in the center. It hung on a delicate filigree chain of eighteen-carat gold. The clerk had asked if he should engrave his wife's initials on the suitcase. The captain had declined, but asked for the following to be etched in script on the back of the cross: "To Brigitta from Dad."

He checked the agenda again. Everything pertaining to his family affairs had been taken care of. His obligations to them, as far as he was concerned, had been fulfilled.

Suddenly feelings of regret and apprehension began to break his composure. Never again would he see the lovely Lara with her porcelain complexion, ash-blond hair and blue green eyes. Even at thirty-eight she had a girlish figure, unlike their plump daughter of fourteen. Lara was not to be blamed for what had happened. Secretly he had taken the required training and tests to join the Luftwaffe, passed with great distinction and received the title of Captain. When he had finally told her about this, she objected to the choice. The Luftwaffe, in her opinion, was the most dangerous of all military divisions. She had insisted that he change to a less dangerous one. Due to her efforts and her parents' influential connections, Lara found him an executive position in the German bureaucracy. One of his duties was to pick at random the names of men, women and children over twelve; they would be deported to labour camps and, when they could no longer work, they would be exterminated.

The captain's parents had objected to his joining the Nazi party, specially his father, who had witnessed the disaster of World War I. They had begged him not to volunteer. He refused emphatically, saying "only a coward would decline to serve his country when needed."

During the first years of World War II, both Lara and the captain had been mesmerized by the glamour, the euphoria that accompanied German victories. Unfortunately, it was all over now.

A glance at his watch indicated that he must hurry for an appointment with Dr. Hans Middler, the family doctor. His heart began to beat unusually fast. His forehead moistened. He quickly wiped it with an exquisitely embroidered white muslin handkerchief, a gift from his Swiss mother-in-law.

Düsseldorf, a centre of supplies for the Luftwaffe, had suffered more than its share of enemy bombardments. Even far from the city centre, a few targeted buildings had been bombed. The district was shabby. Some buildings were still standing, half destroyed, and others, in the process of repair, were sorry reminders of their past elegance. The tall edifice where Dr. Hans Middler combined his living quarters and his office was partially wrecked but still standing; one quarter of its rooftop had been blown away by a low-flying plane.

The captain climbed two flights of rickety steps to Dr. Middler's quarters. He used his large bedroom, separated from the library by an elaborate Chinese panel, as a patient's recovery room. The second room was converted into a surgery, and the third was his office.

Dr. Middler's greeting was warm, yet with an undertone of suspicion. "My boy," he said putting a hand on the captain's shoulder, "I haven't seen you since your parents' untimely deaths. What can I do for you? I hope that I can help, but you've probably noticed that I've grown old and somewhat feeble." He sat down and waited for a reply.

The captain had rehearsed the scene many times but was at a loss when it actually took place. He began with the wrong sequence of events.

"Do you remember the Kesselmanns? They owned a large stationery store on Kastanienstrasse? My father's company sold them quite a few products."

"Yes, of course, a nice Jewish couple with an only son." He looked at his visitor blankly. "But what has that got to do with you?"

The captain moved nervously in his chair and quickly plunged into the purpose of his visit. "At the moment, I am being sought by the International Crimes Tribunal, the one that is being set up at Nuremberg. The officers of my department will be put on trial for crimes against humanity."

Dr. Middler emitted a low and mournful sound, but the captain continued resolutely. "One of them has already committed suicide, another escaped. In retrospect, I can't believe that I committed what they accuse me of. We all acted on military orders, which we had to obey. Most of us didn't comprehend the consequences of what we were doing. We were cogs in a large wheel and—"

The doctor moved to the edge of his chair and interrupted angrily, "There are higher laws to obey than military orders. When you signed those papers, sending innocent men, women and children to slave labour, a living death and then to certain death, well, you must have known how evil that was. Yet you agreed to it."

The captain shrugged his shoulders, ignored the accusation and chose his words carefully. "How can you say that? We were fighting for our country. If you really want to distinguish good from evil, look at the rampant corruption in our society. It's—"

The doctor could not restrain himself and interrupted again, "It's society's duty to regulate corruption, but murder—no, murder is an absolute. It's not redeemable."

Disregarding this interruption, the captain continued with conviction. "We were fighting for a united Germany. And I believed at first in Bismarck's concept that Germany must unite under an autocratic ruler with the help of the army, the political machine and the state church. To this, Hitler added the unification of Europe. I hoped that we would achieve this goal, a noble one, and wanted to help."

Captain von Heissel paused strategically to observe Dr. Middler's reaction. The doctor's face had turned gray. He put up his hand to restrain the captain but remained silent. He supposed that, to some, the truth might come late and in various guises. The doctor waved his hand, a sign for the captain to continue.

THE EXPATRIATE

A slight pleading tone crept into the captain's voice, "I want to save my family humiliation and myself the prospect of life imprisonment or the death penalty. My only chance is to leave before the tribunal gets organized. I mean, I want to emigrate to South America with a borrowed passport and a facial disguise; otherwise, I'll be arrested and prosecuted. But look here, I have a passport that could serve my purpose." He handed Jaakob Kesselmann's passport to the doctor.

"How did you get that?" the doctor asked suspiciously.

"Well, it was an amazing coincidence. Remember all those travel restrictions during the War? Trains departed from Düsseldorf at ten o'clock every Wednesday morning. On the very morning that Kesselmann was leaving for a northern labour camp, I was traveling to Berlin for a meeting. A few minutes before the train departed, he spotted me on the platform, called out my name and threw his passport out of the window to me. In it was a note for his parents. He must have hoped that the passport would make it easier to trace his whereabouts."

"Five weeks later," continued the captain, "I returned to Düsseldorf, searched for the Kesselmann stationery store and found it closed. The neighbours told me that Mrs. Kesselmann died first and her husband shortly afterwards." A slight smile hovered around his lips as he continued. "I looked at the passport many times. You see, Jaakob was almost exactly my age. In fact, he resembled me very much, which amused me. So, I kept it. Here it is."

Doctor Middler took a few moments to think, leaned back in his old swivel chair and looked up at the two light bulbs on steel tubes. There was still a shortage of electricity. The first bulb lit up, but the second one was still flickering. He put his hand over his eyes as he bent forward on the desk. Thoughts flashed through his mind.

This man was completely unmoved, he told himself, when orders came from headquarters to send innocent people to be killed. He obeyed without hesitation, understanding his complicity in evil. And why? So that Germany would control Europe. *"There had been many like him, those who had defended their beliefs and prejudices which they hold as truths."*(1) We're living in a twilight zone with no clear demarcation between good and evil. Was Nietzsche right? The doctor was thinking of one lengthy passage in particular: *"The Christian myth has finally lost its redemptive power...God is dead...to recognize untruth as a condition of life: that is certainly to impugn the traditional ideas of value in a dangerous manner, and a philosophy which ventures to do so has thereby alone placed itself beyond good and evil."* (2) Are good and evil really interchangeable? he asked himself. If so, we're like wild animals; the strong overcome the weak and eat them. No retribution, no stigma involved! The supremacy of the strong, who seek power and freedom from the restrictive grasp of morality and the stifling air of compassion, that's one of Nietzsche's *Ubermenschen*. But this man, this captain, he's no superman. He's the weak one now; I'm the powerful one. I can destroy him just as he destroyed others. Is there a greater evil than a crime that remains unpunished?

At this moment, both bulbs lit up and shone brightly. The doctor glanced at Captain von Heissel, who was standing erect, his feet close together. The only sign of angst and despair was the pure white handkerchief wiping his forehead.

Doctor Middler had much to consider. He was an intimate friend of the von Heissel family. Should he now send their only son to an ignominious death? Yanos wants to escape, the doctor thought, but he also wants to save his wife and daughter humiliation. In Zürich, his wife and daughter could live and die peacefully. On the other hand, he'd be helping a criminal to evade justice. Dr. Middler was about to refuse the captain's request, when an anomalous idea occurred to him. Perhaps a just punishment would be to do as requested, to change this man's identity so that he'd have to feel what a Jew—Jaakob Kesselmann—had felt. Being shot to death would be too easy for the captain. But living among Jews as one of those who had once persecuted them would be a fate worse than death.

Finally, he answered. "Well, my boy, I will try to transform your face as a token of my friendship for your parents. But, remember that I'm eighty-one years old. Oh, I'm a good diagnostician. My loyal patients still come to me. But my hands, well, they're not what they once were."

THE EXPATRIATE

The captain had chosen this doctor for several reasons. Doctor Middler had long been a friend of the family. He had always been a skillful surgeon and just as important was his age. He was old and in a few years, he'd be dead, leaving no trace of the captain's record.

"Well, you are the best surgeon around here. And everyone would agree," he added emphatically.

Dr. Middler ignored the compliment. "Please come back tomorrow, after lunch. I'll explain what's involved. Then, I'll give you two days time to make your final decision." Without another word, the doctor shook the captain's hand. "See you again. Till tomorrow after lunch."

Before his appointment with Dr. Middler, the captain had spent many hours pondering his dilemma. To avoid prosecution, he would have to hide somewhere in Europe, which was quite unsafe and dangerous, and he would always be on the run. The alternative would be to stand trial, hoping to be exonerated as a mere bureaucrat. But this possibility had seemed highly unrealistic, considering the journalistic hysteria and the fact that one associate of his team had already admitted culpability by committing suicide. At best, a judge might sentence him to twenty years. Even if his prison were in a foreign country, the publicity would be disastrous for his family.

Considering his circumstance from all angles, he had decided to assume a new identity, despite the pain of an operation and the anxiety that would follow it. With a new face and an escape to South America, he might be able to forget the past or even to enjoy a new freedom. But he had to hurry. Urgent tasks had to be completed before his appointment with Dr. Middler.

Pulling his hat well over his forehead, he sauntered home. His mind drifted back to happier times, as he strolled along the once resplendent *Kastanienstrasse*. Its sculptured bridges had once shielded from the sun the small canals. Along the edges of these canals had grown multicoloured flowers: azaleas, forget-me-nots, pansies and *tausendschon* roses. These blossoms had stood proudly on their stems, facing the sun in full abandon to be admired by strolling passersby. Sidewalk cafés had been filled with gaily dressed ladies and gentlemen chatting quietly, while the rippling water nearby echoed their cheerful mood. Today, all was silent and gray, sharing a mutual gloom. He stopped where the canals ended. Then, as if awakened from a daydream, he walked to *Steinstrasse* and phoned Lara. She would have to be ready with Brigitta, at seven, for dinner to celebrate their departure in the morning for Zürich.

Lara greeted him at home, looking unusually beautiful in a two-toned lilac silk dress. She was wearing the exquisite necklace of large pearls, a gift form her mother. Even Brigitta looked rather charming in a blush-pink cotton dress with tiny organza rosettes covering the bodice.

The captain had made reservations at their favourite restaurant, near the *Konigshalle,* concert hall and then sent gift-wrapped presents there, in advance, to surprise them. This last evening was to prove as delightful as a romantic dream. He forgot both the past and the future. It was sheer joy dancing with Lara, while the orchestra played nostalgic German melodies. The captain even danced a few times with Brigitta. They would be leaving tomorrow morning at nine o'clock, and this evening would have to last forever in his memory. So be it! True to his self-imposed discipline, he never for one moment revealed his inner angst, but Lara noticed that he used a handkerchief to wipe his forehead more often than usual.

In the morning, when finally they drove off in the limousine, he remained standing on the verandah, immobile, as if in a trance. His mind was totally blank. The tinkle of a bicycle's bell jolted him back to reality, and the pressing matters at hand.

All the furniture at home was packed, ready for shipping to Zürich, except for his desk. He had instructed Lara to leave this task because he wanted to check which documents to destroy. In the end, though, he had destroyed all of them. But he checked again, just to make certain that every drawer had indeed been emptied. His knee accidentally touched a side drawer. From the bottom, a thin panel sprang forward. There lay a photograph of his father, Colonel Helmut von Heissel, with the inscription "To Our Proud Patriot, Colonel Helmut von Heissel, from General Klaus von Würtemberg." He wanted it for himself but decided that Brigitta should have a photograph of her paternal grandfather.

THE EXPATRIATE

"My father died a proud patriot," he whispered sadly, "but I will die an expatriate." After putting the picture into the top drawer, he packed the desk for shipping to Zürich and hurried off for his appointment. To be punctual—was inherent in his personality.

The doctor, in a white surgical coat, had just ended an interview with a patient when the captain arrived. Intuitively he knew what the captain had decided to do.

"Yes," said the doctor. "I'm glad that you came on time." He began to shift the photograph in his hands. "I've studied Jaakob's photo, the one on this passport. Strangely enough, you do have similar features." Putting his hand on his own chin, he continued, "I'll have to chisel your chin down a little, heighten your cheekbones and—your nose is about the same length, but his is a little wider. Although I won't touch yours. I'll just raise your forehead a little."

The captain twitched uneasily in his chair and began to wipe his forehead but the doctor continued nonchalantly, "I'll have to tan your face slightly and dye your hair a little darker. Overall, you're going to look just like Jaakob Kesselmann. If anyone examines your passport, all indications such as facial structure, cheekbones, nose, and forehead will be the same. But you are slightly taller." He paused a little. "You probably know that most Jews are circumcised. Have it done as well. The procedure may be painful for a little while, but you'll avoid suspicion in case you are examined." The captain gripped the arms of his chair and was about to object, but the doctor continued. "The operation will last about five hours under complete anesthetic. You look pretty healthy to me, so I don't anticipate any complications except some excessive bruising, maybe, which will take longer to heal than the circumcision itself. Don't worry. I'll examine you completely before you go under the knife."

The captain sat there, attentive but apprehensive, and nodded his consent without uttering a sound.

"Well, then, we'll proceed as follows: I won't receive any other patients for the duration of your stay. That will be about sixteen days, maybe a little longer. During that time, I won't engage a nurse. No one must suspect what I'm doing. The outside door will have a sign: 'Closed for renovations.' For your comfort, part of my large bedroom and the library will be yours for the duration of your stay. Of course, I'll buy food and other provisions. But I warn you. You must not leave until all the bruises have completely disappeared; otherwise, we'd both be in grave danger."

The captain was rather touched by the doctor's precautions. "You know, I really appreciate your careful concern. I'll always be grateful to you."

The doctor continued, disregarding what his patient had said. "My payment will be three thousand American dollars, half of it in advance. Oh, and I'll need one thousand marks immediately to buy special instruments and medicines in Frankfurt. The journey may last several hours. If I miss the connection, I'll be back late tomorrow evening."

"Yes, I agree to all your conditions. But I have only six hundred marks. I'll give you the full three thousand American dollars on Friday morning. That will give me two and a half days to attend to all my business."

The doctor shook his head in approval. "Till Friday, then."

Abruptly, as if automatically conditioned, the captain pulled himself upright, clicked his heels, drew his hat partially over his face and walked down the street. His thoughts were on the future. Closing the door on the past and venturing into the unknown rather excited him—particularly the trip to Buenos Aires, where he planned to establish a paper mill. The captain looked forward with exhilaration to a new freedom: no military commands, no family obligations, no government assignments.

But these repetitive musings were unproductive, he reprimanded himself, because there was so much to do and so little time. He had to get accustomed to his new signature, for instance, because all transactions would be those of Jaakob Kesselmann. Also, should he hire an agent to sell his properties? That could be more dangerous than doing so himself, he realized. If a "wanted list" with his photograph were distributed throughout the country someone could still identify him, but if he dealt with, out-of-town buyers himself, they were less likely to recognize him. Betrayal would still be a risk but he had to take that chance.

THE EXPATRIATE

Scanning the newspapers for property and business buyers, he found a widow with a daughter and grandson who were looking to purchase a large house in a luxurious neighbourhood. He arranged to meet them immediately at the house and sold it for a mere $200,000. It was easy to make this woman believe that all original documents had been lost during the War and that he was the owner's only living relative. Finally, he managed to get all the forms necessary for a transfer from the last owner to the new one. These documents required only the new owner's signature along with that of a notary with whom she had previously done business. How to explain his haste? He decided to say he was merely an intermediary and had to return quickly for the sake of his business in Berlin. It was not unusual at that time for people to sell off the assets of their distant relatives whose fates were unknown. Everyone knew that these intermediaries were seldom well paid, that many of them traveled from far away to finalize sales and had to return quickly, and that some had to put the funds in safety deposit boxes until the owners or their descendants could claim them. Transactions such as these were quite acceptable.

The captain used this stratagem for other transactions, which were accepted without question. In the Frankfurter *Tageblatt*, he found a buyer for his father's paper mill and mansion. Due to the low value of the mark, he had to increase the selling price of the mill. Although the mill had not operated for a year, it still contained both machinery and merchandise. Buyers would also consider the good reputation of this old company, which could begin to function immediately. Given the current shortage of paper, moreover, it would prove very lucrative. The captain asked for cash.

After completing all of these transactions, he converted all currencies into American dollars and deposited them in various sums at different banks, all under the name of Jaakob Kesselmann. Next, he met the new owners of his residence, gave them the keys, picked up his four valises and had a leather printer change the initials from Y.H. to J.K. Finally, he called a taxi and delivered his luggage to the Hotel International, where a suite was reserved for Mr. J. Kesselmann.

Before retiring, the captain decided to take a short walk in the city that he loved so much. The pale sun was sliding away, shimmering through the blue smoky sky. Shadowy figures were laying down their shovels near piles of rubble, where they had worked all day to clear the land for new buildings. A warm, soothing wind whistled through the gray atmosphere.

He walked to the *Altstadt*, birthplace of Heinrich Heine, Germany's most revered poet next to Goethe. High above the house, now used as a pub, hung a dingy plaque: "Heinrich Heine, 1797-1856." Heine had been a Jew. Across the street, a little further down, stood the municipal court, which had luckily escaped the bombs. Its four walls were intact but dilapidated, its façade chipped everywhere. The cobbled street no longer had sidewalks. On both sides were pubs, whose waiters wore brown leather aprons and served *Altbier*. Their customers sat at round tables, drinking, chatting and even singing. The captain would have liked to linger with them, perhaps for the last time, but he was afraid of being recognized and arrested. Besides, it was hard to walk on the slippery cobblestones. He hastened back to his hotel.

Memories of the *Altstadt* faded. His immediate commitments became more urgent. Had he made a wise decision? There was still time to cancel the operation and pay Dr. Middler handsomely while taking his chances with the tribunal. He could still reconsider, but he would have to decide very quickly, one way or another, and then take action without looking back. By the time he reached the hotel, his doubts had disappeared. Tomorrow at nine, he would be at Dr. Middler's.

In his room, however, the coming ordeal began to trouble him again. Movie stars have had facial plastic surgery, he reasoned. Do they hesitate? He would not be greatly transformed, in any case, merely changed superficially. Perhaps his concerns were exaggerated. Then there was the question of learning a foreign language. He already spoke English and French, thanks to parents who had insisted on private tutors for a son who, in the future, would deal with customers in England and France. As for Spanish, he would begin to learn it immediately after arriving in Buenos Aires.

THE EXPATRIATE

To forget the surgery, he began to review his itinerary. First, he would travel by train to Le Havre. There, he would be examined by the Immigrant Aid Association. For that to happen, of course, he would have to present the necessary papers, as a refugee, for a visa to Argentina. What if something went wrong? What would an alternative plan be? He did not know. The busy day had exhausted him. Opening the window for some fresh air, he stood still and gazed out at the city of his birth.

The drizzle had stopped. Below and all around him were a few signs of postwar recovery. At the hotel, the bed-sitting room had Louis XV furniture and was decorated in beige, blue and gold. The bathroom glittered with highly polished chrome. During the War, this would have seemed like a fantasy to most Germans.

Suddenly, sadness, loneliness and fear overcame him. Alone in this world and with obligations to no one but himself, he was free. But was this what Goethe had meant by *Freiheit*? Despite freedom in one sense, after all, he was about to become a prisoner of his fears and his beliefs: a German citizen who sought haven in Argentina, a primitive country by European standards. He looked at the hand-carved mirror over a dresser and hardly recognized himself in the pale and tired image. Constant brooding and questioning, he had always assumed, was a Russian trait. They were expert at useless introspection, he had scoffed. But now!— He peered through the picture window, where the pale crescent moon was disappearing, leaving a litter of golden stars twinkling in a black canopy. He would have to get a grip on himself. Maybe he had been working too hard for too many years. That had never even occurred to him. He had simply assumed this work load, like so many of his compatriots. As soon as the captain put his head on the embroidered pillow cases, he sank into a bucolic landscape and found himself in his maternal grandmother's summer home on the outskirts of *Rüdesheim* on the Rhine. Here was the little garden and the wooden fence that enclosed it. Beyond the fence are ancient trees. Within it are wild roses, red poppies. His family and a few neighbours are sitting around a wooden table for afternoon tea. *Fraülein* Tessie, the Austrian maid and cook, serves her own *Sachertorte* and *Apfelstrüdel*. His mother has teased her, claiming that German *Apfelkuchen* contain less sugar and are therefore much better. *Fraülein* Tessie replies as usual in her Austrian accent: "Never! That's not true!" His father cautions his wife to stop; otherwise, another Austro-German war would break out. In fact, he laughs, this would be the first Austro-German Cake War. Everyone else laughs and tells jokes, which as a child he cannot understand.

The captain then finds himself one warm Saturday night on *Drosselgasse*. There, he sees a pub with open doors. People are singing, dancing into the cobbled street, even hugging each other. Yanos clings to his mother's dress for fear of getting lost in the cheerful tipsy crowd.

Suddenly, the gardens, the flowers, the music, the laughter have all disappeared. The captain's alarm clock was ringing. The pillow was wet from perspiration. What had happened to that innocent and happy world? How had he become a stranger in his own country? He took a cool shower, as usual. Then prepared for his appointment and arrived at Dr. Middler's as scheduled with the punctuality of a fine Swiss watch.

THE METAMORPHOSIS

Dr. Middler, wearing a surgeon's white coat, greeted his patient cheerfully. He showed no signs of fatigue from yesterday's train trip. Fully aware of the captain's anxiety, he began by pointing to a table with carefully displayed instruments and medications.

"These have already been sterilized—" he said, and was about to continue when the captain, eager to satisfy the doctor by paying promptly, handed him an envelope with the three thousand American dollars.

"As for the six hundred Deutschmarks for your trip to Frankfurt, that's a small token of my appreciation."

Automatically, the doctor put the envelope in his pocket and continued. "First, I'm going to examine your heart, check your pressure and do a blood analysis. After giving you a general anesthetic, I'll perform the circumcision. Then I'll work on your face, and after the operation I'll cover it with bandages, leaving openings for your eyes and mouth. The operation will take several hours—four, maybe five—but the bandages will be removed in a week."

The captain put on a hospital gown and lay down on the table. Then the physical examination began, followed by a blood test. When the captain's condition proved normal, the doctor anesthetized him and began to operate. The operation lasted under five hours and was without complications.

Next morning, Captain von Heissel found himself lying on a large bed with a hand-carved headboard. Beige wallpaper with narrow olive stripes matched the silk curtains. One wall, lined with bookcases, led to a large space, previously used as a salon;

now, it was a recovery room with storage cabinets for medical supplies.

When Dr. Middler heard movements in the recovery room, he brought in a tray of appetizing breakfast delicacies. The captain moved drowsily, unaware of his surroundings but anxious.

"Where am I?"

"You're in my recovery room. It's the morning after your operation. You slept well all night. I notice you are examining the décor in this room. I rescued the furniture and even the wallpaper after my house was bombed. Now it's my personal quarters, as well as a recovery room when necessary. Some time ago, I suggested that hospitals redo their bleak recovery rooms to resemble cheerful surroundings, like their homes. But the War sidetracked that idea. Anyway, this is where I sleep, eat and live. I'm still trying to forget the catastrophic ruination of our country. Every time I look up at that shattered chandelier, with its two light bulbs taken from the washroom below, I remember everything we lost. When are we going to learn our lesson?"

Captain von Heissel did not answer. Instead, he looked at the doctor defiantly and ate silently. Dr. Middler thought it best to leave him alone.

The captain fell back on his cushion, looked up at the ceiling. What would life be like, he thought, without the past? His identity began to trouble him: how would he conceal his real self and assume a new one? Was anyone really free of the past? Nonetheless, he began to console himself. Just look forward, and plan a new beginning. Because of his physical transformation, he would have to continue the life of Jaakob Kesselmann. Maybe he could live with a double identity. Maybe most people live that way! They present a façade to society but maintain the real self to themselves. Outwardly, he would be Jaakob Kesselmann, the German Jew. Inwardly, he would still be Yanos von Heissel, the German Catholic. He shut his eyes for a moment but then glanced at the bookcases. Maybe some author had faced a similar dilemma and resolved it with a new insight.

He walked slowly toward the bookcases. Many books were damaged, the doctor had explained, because a bomb had exploded nearby; water had been sprayed indiscriminately to prevent the fire from spreading. The doctor had spent many hours, looking through the books, restoring them with loving care and packing them in waterproof boxes before placing them here in his library.

Prominent on the first shelf were Martin Luther's German Bible, which he had translated in 1534, and the works of Hans Sachs. The latter, from Nüremberg, had lived between 1494 and 1576. A professional shoemaker, he had nonetheless written light poetry and plays. Eventually, he had become the protagonist of Richard Wagner's famous opera: *Die Meistersinger von Nüremberg*. But that name—*Nüremberg*—sounded ominous to the captain. After all, it had recently been a center of Nazi pageantry.

He moved on and picked up a rather badly scarred book, *Der abenteurliche Simplicissimus,* from 1668. Literary historians considered this book, by Hans Grimmelshausen, the first German novel worthy of that name. By describing the wanderings and adventures of its protagonist, Grimmelshausen exposed human folly and the resulting horrors of war. The captain remembered studying it in the *Gymnasium*. In those days, the story and its message had seemed remote, but now he was struck by its relevance and similarity to the present events.

Elsewhere, placed in alphabetical order, the captain found works by the most famous German writers and thinkers. He rolled the familiar names around on his tongue: Friedrich Engels, Johan Gottlieb Fichte, Johann Wolfgang von Goethe, Johann Gottfried Herder, Georg Wilhelm Friedrich Hegel, Ernest Theodor Wilhelm Hoffmann, Friedrich Holderlin, Hermann Hesse, Heinrich Heine, Friedrich Gottlieb Klopstock, Heinrich von Kleist, Franz Kafka, Karl Marx, Eduart Morike, Heinrich and Thomas Mann, Friedrich Nietzsche, Rainer Maria von Rilke, Arthur Schnitzler, Franz Werfel. And then came Gotthold Ephraim Lessing, who had achieved a striking success in 1755 with Miss Sara Sampson. This had been the first noteworthy example in German of a *bürgerliches Trauerspiel, a*s a middle-class tragedy. It had departed from the classical tradition of royal tragedies. But what caught the captain's attention, particularly, was Lessing's last and most famous book: *Nahan der Weise*. It is one of the most beautiful messages in German literature. Lessing shows that the Jew and the Muslim are at least as noble as the Christian. No wonder that this book, about the clash of three religions during the crusades, represents a high point of the Enlightenment: the gospel of tolerance. The captain smiled. In view of twentieth-century intolerance, he thought, this book seemed incongruously juvenile.

But he felt very proud. What other country could boast of so many great authors and philosophers?

The captain picked at random Johann Peter Eckermann's *Gespräche mit Goethe.* He happened to open the book where Goethe says that the *"Germans are a funny people, always making life difficult with their deep thoughts."*(1) A few pages further on, he found another quotation that seemed relevant to his own situation: *"What else can man do after committing a dreadful offense, but pull himself together and start again?"*(2) Evidently, Goethe did not believe that a man should be punished forever. But in the captain's case, society wanted to teach him and all future offenders that the punishment must fit the crime even though some perpetrators had been ordered by higher authorities to kill or be manipulated by social pressure to kill. Whatever minute particles of truth might have rested in these justifications, society now said, the consequences of Nazi persecution proved that its perpetrators were guilty of the most heinous crimes in the history of mankind and the judges at the Nuremberg Court agreed.

The captain brushed aside this dreary thought and tried to remember some of the aphorisms that he had learned by heart at school. In the prologue to Goethe's Faust, the Lord tells Mephistopheles that *"man, in his dark impulses, knows the right road from the wrong...But you true sons of heaven...seek in your minds what is permanent in change."*(3) He nodded approval; nevertheless, he knew secretly what had detracted him from the right road. Faust then continues to question himself. *"What has the world to offer me? Renunciation, you can't do this, you can't to that. This is the eternal refrain that rings and jangles in our ears hour by hour, all our life long."* (4)

He put back the masterpiece and again picked up Eckermann's *Gespräche.* Goethe had believed that *"to complete a great project, one mind is enough for a thousand hands."* (5) How true that was, thought the captain, in Hitler's case. If only the Americans had minded their own business, Europe would now have one government under one ruler. At that moment, the heavy volume that he had been holding fell to the floor with a loud thud. The doctor who had been watching his patient through the slightly opened door entered immediately. He noticed the creased bandages on his patient's face and rushed in to prevent the captain from bending.

"Please sit down," he said, pointing to a chair, "and let's make plans for the next few days. In two days, the bandages will come off your face. Be prepared to see patches of black, blue and yellow all over. They'll disappear bit by bit ever day. I want to emphasize this, because most patients run straight to the mirror. What they see is frightening, of course. They can't imagine that their wounds will heal in a few days. They want to believe their doctor, yet they must believe their own eyes. But you'll see for yourself."

Dr. Middler knew that peace of mind speeds the healing process. He decided to divert the captain's attention. "I've found something for you among my dictionaries. It's an introduction to the Spanish language."

The captain bent forward a little to take the book from the doctor's outstretched hands, genuinely pleased that he was getting so much attention. Compulsively, he began to hug the doctor. "Thanks. Many thanks." Both men settled down for some refreshments. The doctor now tried another diversion: literature. He picked up the German translation of Gogol's Inspector General.

"I'm sure that you've studied this at university. I read it several times, and I must admit that the Russians are the best humorists in Europe."

"Not exactly, Dr. Middler. What could be funnier, after all, than our own Kleist in *Der zerbrochene Krug?* And he wrote that, way back in 1808. But later on, I must admit, the British produced some fine humorists. Think of the stories about Jeeves by P.G. Wodehouse. Anyway, I was quite shocked to find out that both Gogol and Kleist—did you know this?—had very sad lives."

"Well, what about the Poles?"

"No, no, no," replied the captain without hesitation. "Aside from Chopin, the Poles accomplished little in any sphere. No, it seems to me that no country has made more contributions than Germany."

The doctor did not reply. How could anyone argue effectively against prejudice? He knew that the Nazis had also fostered this chauvinistic mentality.

"What you say is interesting, but we have no time for all that right now. Here's some practical advice. Repeat your new name as often as possible and practise the signature on Kesselman's passport. I'll leave you now," the doctor said, putting his hand on the captain's shoulder. "You'll want to look at the Spanish book. Oh, and please eat the fruit that I've left on the table. It will speed up the healing process."

Two days later, Dr. Middler returned to remove the captain's bandages and found him pouring over the Spanish primer. "Spanish is a fascinating language," said the captain. "I like its soft sounds."

"So do I," the doctor replied peeling the gauze off his patient's face. "Have you read any Spanish novels?"

"Oh, yes, I've read translations of Don Quixote and *Miau* by Galdos. I liked Don Quixote. But *Miau*, well, that story could never happen in Germany."

Why not?"

"Because our government doesn't tolerate procrastination. It attends to business quickly and gets things done. Only Spain and a few other countries have governments that tolerate procrastination."

Dr. Middler shrugged his shoulders. What arrogance! Having lived much longer than the captain, he could remember many instances that proved the contrary. Once again, though, he realized that this was no time for arguments about prejudice.

When Dr. Middler had completely removed the dressing, the captain ran to a mirror. Almost immediately, the doctor heard a loud anguished cry.

"God, who am I?"

THE EXPATRIATE

Dr. Middler tiptoed into the washroom as the captain was examining each bruise.

"You're now Jaakob Kesselmann, a good chap, rather reticent but well read, who helped his father to expand the family business. Come, sit down. I know how shocking this must be, but you'll be as handsome as ever in five or six days. Let's have a drink and listen to some German music."

Dr. Middler asked about the captain's plans. "What's on your itinerary after leaving Düsseldorf?"

"As soon as I decided to go through with this, I bought a train ticket to Le Havre. The Immigrant Aid Association there, has Argentine visas for German Jews who fulfill their requirements. In fact, Argentina grants permanent citizenship to those who have enough capital to start enterprises. That's because those businesses will provide jobs for local workers. If I get this document, then I'll book passage by ship to Halifax and fly from there to Buenos Aires. I would enjoy visiting two continents were I traveling as myself, as I was."

Dr. Middler disregarded this remark and continued. "Someone will probably question you about Jewish culture, or at least become suspicious if you don't know anything about Judaism. You should have some basic knowledge of Jews and Judaism. Even I know that their most sacred of holy days is Yom Kippur. That's when Jews repent by fasting and ask God to forgive their sins. I wonder how many of us Germans could do so now and face the creator?"

"We had a task to do, and we did it. We could have established an Aryan society and become masters and benefactors of Europe. No other country has done that since ancient Rome."

"If you're going to cite history, you must admit that the Romans eventually lost their empire as did the Greeks before them and the Mongols after them. And what about Napoleon? As for us, we lost two world wars. It seems obvious to me that creating empires is folly. But getting back to you, let me say this: If someone recognizes you, due to your ignorance of Judaism, then all your suffering will have been useless."

"My parents often mentioned that many German Jews no longer practised Judaism."

"Yes, that's true. But you still need to know something about it."

Terror spread across the captain's face. His hands began to tremble. Dr. Middler gave him a sedative. "What's wrong? You made your choice. Now you must live with the consequences."

"But how can I live such a lie? I'll have to assume their beliefs, and their characteristics. How will I be able to see through all this deception? How can I pretend to be a Jew, when I'm a Roman Catholic?"

Dr. Middler agreed that the captain would have serious problems. But he pointed out that most people live deceptively, albeit not to the same extent. "Many present to the outside world nothing more than a façade. They want people to think that they are better, cleverer, richer, kinder, more learned or more successful than they really are. And I believe that most of our neuroses are consequences of such deception. People can't live up to the images that they present to the world. You believed that you, your party and your country, would bring Europe to a new golden age, but you didn't care about the means or the cost to others. Now that those others have defeated you, they want to punish you. Your only escape is this subterfuge. But you still have some reason to hope for salvation. And that all depends on what you learn and how you adjust. You're a clever man. You might well be able to sort out the confusion. Let's hope that you choose the best from each of your two identities."

The captain moved about nervously. "Yes, yes, but all I know is how to chart a course and follow it. I firmly believed that we were going to win. That gave my life a clear course to follow. And now, well, I don't have one."

The captain bided his time, as if expecting the unexpected to happen. And it did. But it happened several days later, when he glanced once again at the mirror. The discolorations had completely disappeared, and there he saw the handsome face of Jaakob Kesselmann. Dr. Middler, recognizing the captain's smile of satisfaction, approached him with another task. He would have to dye his hair darker than his own burnished gold. The doctor applied a German dye that would take half an hour to dry. Patiently, the captain waited. Then, he ran to the mirror again, stood still and smiled feebly. *"Gut, sehr gut, ganz gut. Wer soll das glauben?"* ("Good, very good, completely good. Who would believe it?")

Dr. Middler brought in some fruit and a fine cognac. "Let's drink to a better tomorrow for both of us."

"I'll drink to that." The captain seemed cheerful as he sipped the cognac.

"I hear that Buenos Aires is a beautiful city, quite rich and full of opportunities. You'll certainly be able to find a job there. Maybe you'll set up your own business."

The captain nodded his head. "My immediate concern is to get the permit for citizenship. I'll have to accept your assessment of the Jews and try to conduct myself as honourably as I always have."

"Well, that sounds reasonable to me. You can't foresee the future. You can't protect yourself from fate. But still—" He paused and continued in a different direction. "Now, according to your schedule, you'll be leaving in two days during the afternoon. I'll be off, then, and let you do your packing."

On the morning of his departure, the captain decided to wander for the last time through the city of his birth. Meticulously dressed, with a wide-brimmed hat pulled down over his forehead, still imagining that he might be recognized, he strolled along Kastanienstrasse. A few cafés were open. Now and then, he could hear melancholy tunes, and continued to saunter along, deep in thought. Unexpectedly, a man came toward him and laid a strong hand on his shoulder. The captain shuddered, took a step backward and stared curiously at the person in front of him. The stranger addressed him, almost choking with joy.

"As I live and breathe, Jaakob Kesselmann!" He threw his arms around the captain and began to whimper. "Don't you remember me? Zoltan Freiberg? We were neighbours. Our parents were friends."

The captain was frightened. This was his first test. He looked intently at this stranger and calmly responded. "Forgive me, Zoltan. I was shell-shocked, during the War. I'm still regaining my memory."

Suddenly, he realized how quickly he had learned to lie so well. This was the stock answer that he had found in reports during the War. Asked about their antecedents, many said the same thing. Of these people, he thought, maybe one per cent had told the truth. At the moment, though, he needed to divert attention from himself to Zoltan. He asked how Zoltan's family fared during the War.

But Zoltan continued without answering. "Let's go for some coffee, Jaakob, and I'll tell you how lucky I was to be saved." Sitting in a darkly lit café, Zoltan told his story.

"A farmer near Düsseldorf, used to deliver eggs, milk and fresh vegetables to our home. Well, this farmer was left helpless. All of his workers were called up, for military service. His wife was weak, and his only son lived in America. So, he asked the Agriculture Department to permit him eight employees. And guess what? He got them. I don't know how, but he got them. He chose four Christians and four Jews. I was one of the Jews. Every six months, he had to renew his permit. That made us very uneasy, I can assure you. Meanwhile, he taught us farming. He was eager to produce more than expected, so that the government, which took a good portion of his produce, would continue to employ us. Our little group of eight was cozy. We all became good friends. And Greunelberg treated us kindly. When the War ended, old Greunelberg sold his farm. He and his wife bought a little cottage in Switzerland and went to live there. Meanwhile, Helmut Burgeschemel and Hans Kraus became my very close friends. They were interested in emigrating with me to Palestine and introducing our new farming and irrigation techniques. I consulted the British authorities in Palestine. They accepted us and we were told to pick up our permits in Le Havre."

The captain moved uncomfortably in his chair, silent and apprehensive. They might all meet, after all, on the train to Le Havre. He'd have to chat with them and fabricate plausible answers on the spur of the moment. At the moment, though, he needed to keep Zoltan talking. "Yes, but what happened to your parents and your wife?"

"Thank God, my parents died naturally. The blasted Nazis permitted them to keep their store as long as they serviced the soldiers, who came to take as much as they could. My wife—you remember Freda—joined the Red Cross and was transferred to Geneva. From there, she traveled to Genoa and eventually, to Palestine as a nurse. I heard nothing from her for a long time. Greunelburg, good man that he was, tried to contact the German Red Cross in search of her. Every reply was the same: Cannot identify. Reported missing. Then, out of the blue, Greunelburg received this cryptic telegram: A nurse is waiting for one of your helpers. Will contact you soon. The signature was F.F. The War was almost over by this time. One day, the Immigrant Aid Association notified me that my wife was in Palestine and had sent money for my passage. That's when I confirmed the presence of my two buddies. Together, in Palestine, we could initiate irrigation projects."

The captain bit his lips. What could he say now? "You're so lucky, Zoltan. I lost my wife. She caught pneumonia, and we couldn't get the proper medication. Both of my parents died, too, and now I'm alone in the world and on my way to Argentina. Where I'll settle, I still don't know."

His remarks were vague. He dared not let Zoltan know how to contact him. "But that's where I plan to open stationery stores and start again." He paused, "Well, it was nice seeing you. I hope that my memory will have improved by the time we meet again. We'll be able to reminisce then. Now, though, I must hurry back to my hotel. I'm leaving this afternoon."

The captain abruptly picked up both bills, but Zoltan grabbed his arm. "Let me pay for this and walk with you to your hotel."

The Captain agreed. "It's nice of you," he said, "to spend your last moments in Düsseldorf with me."

"What are you talking about Jaakob? Considering all that your parents did for me—well, if I can ever help you, please don't hesitate to ask."

In the hotel lobby, the captain tried to shake Zoltan's hand. But Zoltan embraced him. "As my parents would say, "*Sholem.*" (Peace) Good luck. We must forget the past." Without another word, Zoltan turned around to hide his tears and left.

The captain remained standing. By now, he was very agitated. Would he always have to think of lies so quickly? Far away from

Germany, he was unlikely to meet ghosts from the past. But even one more encounter of this kind might be impossible to carry off.

After waiting till Zoltan was out of sight, he headed back to *Kastanienstrasse* once again. It was after the lunch hour. Some people were returning to work; others were walking their well-groomed dogs. For some reason, even the dogs seemed sad. Where was the world that he had known? Why not throw himself into the canal and sleep forever under its soothing, watery canopy? No more destructive urges, no more longing for his wife, no more fear. Suddenly, gray clouds appeared and began to hide the sun's golden orb. Why, he asked himself, does it appear more resplendent now than ever before? Why had he so seldom appreciated the sky's natural beauty? With that thought appeared a ray of hope. We German soldiers fought to the bitter end. But I'll carry on. His melancholy mood disappeared as he planned to start all over again in Argentina. In a more buoyant mood, he began to whistle the German national anthem as he hurried back to Dr. Middler's to pick up his luggage.

Dressed in his Sunday suit of navy-blue serge, Dr. Middler was sitting at his desk in front of a carefully wrapped package. He had grown surprisingly fond of his patient and admired his self-discipline. Here was someone who always combed his hair, even when his face was covered with bandages. His white shirt was always clean, his shoes always shined. He ate on schedule. He recorded neatly on a pad every daily activity—caring for his toiletries, reading, studying Spanish. This was scheduled living. It came so naturally that he was unaware how rigidly disciplined he was. When the captain walked in to say farewell, both men knew that they would never see each other again.

Sadly, the doctor handed him the package. "It's an abridged history of the Jews and Judaism. It is called The Jewish Manual. I think that you'll find it useful and even interesting. As for your new life, I'm certain you will succeed. You have two of the most important characteristics for success: self-discipline and drive."

Dr. Middler squeezed the captain's hand and hugged him warmly. "Good luck. Don't worry. Always be cheerful." These were his final words. When the taxi arrived, the captain collected his valises and drove off. At the station, his cabby ran inside to bring a cart for the luggage. The captain tipped him generously. The cabby thanked him profusely and playfully added, "Bon voyage, capitaine" an expression he had picked up from French passengers. The captain froze. Had this man recognized him? He hurried with his luggage to track three, where he stopped to look around.

Everything seemed eerie, somehow: clean but shabby and still. Years ago, it had been friendly and bustling. He had heard many languages there. The station had been a backdrop for many joyous occasions. When he used to return from Berlin, Lara and friends had met him there. They had been able to sing and drink without any thought of the brutal world at large. Now, all was gray and cold. Those waiting looked weary and anxious. He, himself feared what he knew and what he did not know about his future.

LE HAVRE, FRANCE

As the train for Le Havre arrived, passengers stampeded to get on. But Captain von Heissel remained on the platform till an attendant shouted the proverbial "All aboard." Like the cars of other European trains, this one was divided into cubicles of two benches facing each other, and each bench seated three passengers. The captain wanted to sit in an obscure corner, alone. Unfortunately, only two empty seats were left. He sat down opposite three German soldiers. Once the train started to roll, passengers began to jostle for more comfortable positions, and as it gained speed, they shuffled their parcels to safer places. Then a porter escorted a lady to the last empty seat. Evidently, she was from France because she spoke French.

No one spoke for a little while. The silence felt ominous. Suddenly, one of the German soldiers began to introduce himself and his companions. "I'm Kurt Knabel," he spoke directly to the captain. "This is my friend, Hans Grundig, my fellow assistants, Erik Halhausen and Friedrich Volger. We're going to find out how many captured German soldiers still remain in Le Havre and arrange for their return to our country."

After this explanation, he stared at the captain. "You look familiar. What's your name?"

The captain could hardly believe his bad luck. He had made a great effort to be alone. The die was cast! "My name is Jaakob Kesselmann. Le Havre is my first stop."

"Well," said Kurt, "you look somewhat familiar. The four of us worked in the Statistic Department, where we kept getting lists of deportees to the labour camps from a Captain von Heissel. We did see him once or twice; I do not remember now, how many but we had quite a few telephone conversations with this guy. You look a bit like him, and sound exactly like him. Anyway, your name sounds Jewish. I hear that many Jews are leaving for Palestine. Maybe that's not such a bad idea. I would, probably, if I were a Jew. And some Jews did survive."

"That's enough, Kurt," interrupted Hans. "This crazy War has caused plenty of trouble. Everyone in my family was killed. Who the hell cares if Jews or Turks or Slovaks lived in Germany? The whole thing was all a stupid mistake."

Kurt remained silent. "Right. Forget the War. Can we buy beer on this train? Let's drink to a new future. Jaakob, what kind of beer do you want?"

"I'll have a Heineken."

"So, it's Heineken for everyone. I'm paying."

When the porter brought their beer, toasts in German rang out. The French lady looked at them with dismay and asked the porter to change her seat. "I can't stand the Germans," she said in French. "They're all barbarians!"

"Oh, please remain where you are," the captain spoke in French. "They don't mean any harm."

"Harm, you say. What do you know about harm? You can all go to hell for all I care."

Hans interrupted, "Obviously, she doesn't like us."

"Well," Kurt replied, "why should she?" But he added with a wink, "She probably lost several lovers on account of us. Jaakob, ask her if she wants some refreshments, and if she'll at least drink to peace."

The captain admired her spunk. Moreover, he found her pretty, especially the sparkle in her black eyes. And she was indeed hungry. But she'd never drink to peace with Germans.

Meanwhile, food and drink were having their effects on other passengers—especially the four German soldiers, who began to sing German lieder. During one of them, the French lady, Mlle. Eugenie, stood up defiantly and began to sing "La Marseillaise." Surprised and fascinated, the soldiers stopped to listen. She was a soprano, no doubt a professional one, and she alternated between soft crescendos and slow diminuendos. Most surprising to Hans was the quality of her voice. He asked if she had trained for the opera.

Deciding to answer despite her reluctance, at least indirectly through the captain, she replied that her parents had given her all the training necessary, even sending her to Italy. But she had insisted on joining the Resistance and postponed her studies till after a French victory.

"And guess what," she said directly to the captain, "the Jews were among our very best and most courageous fighters. It was one of them, from my own group, who smuggled himself into England and helped to decipher the German secret code."

The captain had heard about English agents who had cracked this code but did not know that some of them had been Jews. In as few words as possible, he expressed his pleasure to hear this. Nervous, now he shut his eyes and leaned back. Those damn resistance groups, he murmured to himself, had certainly inflicted a lot of damage on Germany. And now, he had to congratulate them for doing so. Whoever heard of victims congratulating their own victimizers?

"Ask her," said Kurt, "why she came to Germany. I mean, if she hates us so much, why come here?"

Her answer echoed what many people had said immediately after the War: to search for missing relatives. The singer's aunt had been on a secret mission. Her niece suspected that it had been planned by the Resistance. In a few months, at any rate, the aunt would have returned to Le Havre via Düsseldorf. A communiqué had confirmed, that she would return soon. But after a reasonable delay, when the aunt had failed to return, her niece decided to travel to find her in Düsseldorf. Replies to letters and phone calls in these chaotic times were hopelessly delayed. Her aunt did leave a message with a mutual friend, saying that her business in Düsseldorf had been interrupted. The niece, having tried unsuccessfully to locate her, was therefore returning to Le Havre.

The captain translated all this into German, adding that he would not ask her anymore personal questions on their behalf. The train had picked up speed and was now rattling on so noisily that conversation was becoming difficult. All remained silent.

Thinking about what they had just heard brought back memories of the sordid brutalities that they had seen or experienced in wartime. But, they tried to convince themselves, it was all over now.

Disembarking at Le Havre station, the passengers entered a world of chaos. People were running around looking for baggage carts, because they could not find porters. The dockworkers were on strike—their union demanded not only a wage increase of three percent but also a reduction in weekly hours from thirty-seven to thirty-four. The dockworkers prevented all the other workers from crossing the picket line. Moreover, they harassed anyone who even tried to establish order. The whole station was inoperative.

Meanwhile, the four German soldiers had left their luggage with the captain and the French lady. When one of them returned with a cart, she grabbed it and dashed out so quickly that no custom inspector could stop her, found a taxi and drove off. Just then, Kurt came running with another cart. All five stacked their luggage on it and hurried off to the custom's desk. But as passengers poured in from other trains, the waiting line became longer and the passengers more impatient. Moreover, the union allowed only two inspectors to work. Things were getting out of hand. At this point, the overworked inspectors decided to stop examining luggage and let everyone through.

As the five men said goodbye to each other, Kurt felt he had to say something cheerful to his Jewish passenger. "Jaakob," he said with his hand on the captain's shoulder, "you're lucky, in a way, to be one of the surviving victims. The man I mistook you for, the captain, he's now being hunted down like an animal for what he did to you, Jews." The four soldiers wished each other good luck, but the captain remained silent.

He hailed a taxi and set out for the International Hotel. This, too, was now being rebuilt in the latest American style. Glass, steel, marble, gold accessories, everything conveyed modernity and luxury. A clerk at the registration desk asked for his passport, his home address, the length of his stay, and in which currency he would pay. Handing over his passport, he replied that he would pay with American dollars and that his house was on a street which was still being rebuilt and might be renamed. He added that at the moment, he did not know exactly how long he would stay. These answers sounded plausible enough. Actually, he had forgotten the name of the Kesselmann's home address. Because he was planning to pay with cash, his home address had not been very necessary. These anomalies made no difference, not this time. The clerk sent his passport to the general manager, who examined it carefully. It was clearly authentic, the captain knew, because it had once belonged to Jaakob Kesselmann. Someone compared the photo with those on the wanted list but saw no resemblance between the man at the registration desk and any War criminal. A little green light began to flicker at the desk, indicating that all of the captain's documents were in order. The captain prepaid a small sum for his stay and was directed to a very well-appointed room. After unpacking, he had dinner in the hotel's elegant restaurant. Then, exhausted, he fell asleep.

Next day, after breakfast, he called the Immigrant Aid Association. The captain insisted that he needed an immediate appointment, because his ship was scheduled to sail for Canada within a few days; if he were to miss it, he would have to wait for two weeks. And it worked. He got an appointment with Irwin Weidemann for two o'clock that very afternoon.

Promptly at two, the captain entered a room where three gentlemen were sitting. Weidemann came forward and welcomed him warmly.

"You are Jaakob—"

"Jaakob Kesselmann."

"So what is your full name?" The agent said that to rattle his petitioner. An imposter would often carelessly blurt out his real name, probably not both, but at least one.

"My full name is Jaakob Kesselmann. You have it right there on my request form."

The captain suspected that the other three men were recording his answers. At the very least, they were suspicious of him.

"You were born in 1905. So how old are you?

"I was born in 1905, as stated on my documents. It is now 1946. I am forty-one years old."

"Thank you for demonstrating your mathematical skill."

The captain felt stupid.

"What happened to you during the War?" continued Weidemann.

"I was sent to a labour camp near the border between Germany and Poland. I worked there, in the mines, when the camp was bombed, I was shell-shocked. Someone brought me to a hospital. I recovered physically and partially regained my memory."

As he answered questions, the three gentlemen left their desks one by one and entered another room. This was where they kept pictures, letters, passports and other documents. Some of those documents were about War criminals.

Itzak Glisermann was very observant. Verifying Kesselmann's passport, he noticed a vague similarity between Kesselmann's photograph and that of someone on the wanted list: Captain von Heissel. Both had been born in Düsseldorf. Both matched each other, more or less, in height, weight, hair colour and somewhat in eye colour. Heissel's father had manufactured paper, and Kesselmann's had owned a stationery store for paper products. In this topsy-turvy world, thought Glisermann, coincidences do occur. It was his duty to investigate such coincidences.

Moishe Yigdal believed that Kesselmann had answered the questions honestly, and David Gonsher agreed. Kesselmann's calm demeanour spoke in his favour. He had answered without irritation, when asked for his name several times.

"Let's call in Weidemann right away and evaluate Kesselmann."

They reviewed the basic problem: his resemblance to von Heissel, the same place of birth, both more or less in the paper business and so on. These similarities could be coincidences. Weidemann insisted, however, that the applicant's savoir-faire and his calmness were signs of a well-trained German agent or soldier.

"I suspect, I really do suspect, that this man is not Kesselmann. Let's try something else, just to make sure. Tell him that a doctor will have to examine him for a serious or contagious disease. After all, immigration authorities and even some shipping lines require such precautions. The Kesselmanns, according to our files, were quite orthodox, so their son must have been circumcised. It's easy enough to check."

"Yes," Gonsher replied, "but many German Jews don't circumcise their sons. They consider circumcision barbaric."

"Well," Glisermann intervened, "it's too bad that thumbprints weren't put on passports."

The four of them huddled together. Weidemann outlined the procedure. "Let's be clear and simple. First, explain that it always takes a day or two for us to process documents and prepare permits. Next, arrange for a doctor to examine him tomorrow at ten. That will tell us immediately if this man has been circumcised. Even if he has, of course, he could still be an imposter. We'd have to delay him and look for more information on the Kesselmanns. And if the doctor conducts a friendly conversation, an imposter might unwittingly betray some minor detail that doesn't fit."

Weidemann did not see the captain wiping his forehead repeatedly. Instead, he saw someone who looked unperturbed. "All is well, Mr. Kesselmann. But we still need a certificate of good health. You do seem to be healthy. Even so, we've arranged for a doctor to be here tomorrow at ten. His report will be attached to your visa, and you'll be able to buy your air ticket for Argentina."

The reassuring manner was deliberate. Weidemann wanted to keep his applicant from escaping. Fear, he knew prompted some imposters to run away, while others prepared new and well constructed alibis.

Bracing himself, the captain listened carefully. *"Auf-wiedersehen,* till tomorrow at ten." Then he left abruptly.

But he was not taken in by Weidemann's explanation. Why did they want to examine his body? Maybe for signs of physical abuse: scars from beatings or bullet wounds, because they may have documents which stated that a Kesselmann had worked in a labour camp during the War. But he had no scars. How would he explain that? Well, he was still young and recuperated rather quickly. And maybe they wanted to see if he had been circumcised? He returned quickly to the hotel, sat down comfortably, and had begun to sip a glass of white wine when the inner torment returned. Should he pack up and run away? No, of course not, that would almost prove he was an imposter. But if some telltale sign aroused suspicion, he'd be arrested immediately and possibly jailed. He had no physical scars. How could he explain that, if his camp had been bombed? He could say that he was healthy and healed quickly. Or that, suffering from shell shock, he couldn't remember exactly how long he'd worked at the camp before the bombing, and how long it had lasted, or how long it had taken him to recover. After all, the bombing could have occurred early in the War. After recovering, he could have gone to work again outside Berlin. Yes, he repeated to himself, that would be plausible. In fact, for some, it would be true to a certain degree. Relieved by his ability to fabricate answers, he began to practise Kesselmann's signature by copying it from a note that he carried in his breast pocket.

After supper, he decided to continue his preparation by reading *The Jewish Manual* that Dr. Middler had given to him. Since it was first published this manual had grown into a massive tome, a small encyclopedia. It had chapters on everything that anyone might need to know about Judaism and the Jews. The captain had no particular interest in Judaism or any other religion. The chapter that did interest him, though, was on Jewish history. The preface, however, immediately irritated him.

"The Jewish population is small: approximately one half of one percent of the world's population. From a purely statistical point of view, therefore, hardly anyone would ever hear about Jews. And yet, nothing could be further from the truth. Jews have won far more Nobel prizes, for instance, than their statistical presence in fields such as physics, chemistry and medicine that would lead anyone to believe. Moreover, the Jewish contribution to fields such as religion, science, literature, music, finance and philosophy is staggering.

Something else about the Jews is worth noting from the beginning. Unlike some other civilizations of the ancient Mediterranean world—the Babylonians, Persians, Phoenicians, Hittites and so on—that of the Israelites continues into the present and will continue into the future.

THE EXPATRIATE

Only the civilization of India is older. Unlike the Indians, however, the Jews were driven out of their country and had to survive for two thousand years in alien countries while preserving their own cultural traditions. They cared more about ideas that endure than about material objects that do not always endure. These ideas have affected not only Jews, moreover, but also Christians, Muslims and even the non-religious people of our own time. The Chinese, Hindu and Egyptian peoples are the only ones living today who are as old as the Jewish people... Unlike the Jews, they were not driven out of their countries, nor did they face the problem of survival in alien lands. The modern age presents special challenges to Jews: nationalism, industrialism, communism, and fascism with its emphasis on anti-Semitism."(1)

He put down the book and began to look for the author's name. It was Jewish, which suggested a certain bias. Nonetheless, he flipped a few pages and continued to read. This passage began with a quotation from Exodus in the Bible concerning an early attempt to kill Jews.

"Now a new king arose over Egypt. He said to his people, "Look, we have made slaves of the Hebrews, but they still keep apart and may be plotting against us. What shall we do now?"

"Let us pass a Law," said the Wise Men, "that all the boys born to the Hebrews should be drowned. Then the girls of the Hebrews will have to marry Egyptians and become Egyptians like ourselves." The suggestion pleased the King, and he had a law passed that all Hebrew boys should be drowned as soon as they were born." (2)

The captain put away the manual so he could think about what he had read. What should a nation do if forced to eliminate one segment of its population for the benefit of another? He had heard that population explosions had provoked massive adjustments in both India and China, where governments directly discouraged mothers from having girls and, in China, permitted only two children per couple. At first, he considered this a calculated necessity in the interest of collective survival. But then, he began to think of his daughter, Brigitta. She may never be as beautiful as her mother, or as clever, he thought. But he loved his daughter. He loved her little gurgles, her tiny, pudgy hands clinging to his neck. How could she harm society? But then something else occurred to the captain. The notion of a pure race had happened even in Biblical times! But the Egyptians, after all, permitted Israelite women to marry Egyptian men. The quest for a community of pure roots seemed futile in view of history: conquest after conquest had been followed by assimilation at best and mass murder at worst. But the captain was aware that some Jews had resisted assimilation, formed their own little communities, and survived under foreign rule. *The Jewish Manual's* simplistic accounts of Israelite battles began to bore him. He flipped a few more pages and was rather surprised to read that:

> *"Judaism, unlike religions such as Christianity and Buddhism (but like Hinduism), has no single founding hero. It evolved out of pre-history, carefully selecting ideas from the Egyptians, the Babylonians, the Persians and others. To this day, the Jews have one central aim: to reveal and experience the sacred, by studying Torah, in the midst of the profane."* (3)

The Captain became irritated again, especially as too many good qualities were being attributed to the Jewish race. He put away the book and tried to sleep, to be rested for tomorrow's ordeal.

Next day, at the Immigrant Aid Association, Weidemann greeted the captain and ushered him into an examining room. Dr. Spengler dressed in a white surgeon's coat, immediately asked the captain to undress.

"This is a general examination. We just want to know that you're in good health." Had Kesselmann had any childhood diseases? Had any of his aunts or uncles died of heart disease or cancer? And how many aunts and uncles did he have? Ah, that was a problem. The captain hesitated, having forgotten to study about Jaakob's aunts and uncles. He shut his eyes, therefore, pretending not to hear. But Dr. Spengler repeated his question. Weidemann,

THE EXPATRIATE

Yigdal, Glisermann and Gonsher were listening in the adjoining room. This hesitation must have been obvious to all of them.

Most German families, the captain supposed, had two brothers and one sister. With that in mind, he answered the question. "If my memory serves me well, and it's slowly coming back to me, my father said that he had one brother who had immigrated to America. But he had another brother. As a boy, I often saw his son—that is, my cousin—but seldom his father. As for my father's sister—my aunt—she died giving birth to her second child."

It just so happened that the Jaakob's father had, indeed, had two brothers and a sister. The captain's guess was a lucky shot in the dark. As for the death, at birth, of the aunt's second child, an epidemic of puerperal fever had caused many deaths at the turn of the century. The captain believed that all of the Kesselmanns had already died and assumed that few records had survived the bombings. Dr. Spengler expressed sorrow about all of this, but he added that Jewish families were usually very close and celebrated Jewish holidays together. With this remark, he hoped to provoke a description of some festive occasion which would reveal a mistake or inconsistency.

The captain spoke after a brief silence, "I find it hard to remember the past." This response was, indeed, characteristic of amnesia but Dr. Spengler had few resources to verify it. However, there was clear evidence that the captain was circumcised. Then he proceeded to examine the gall bladder, the prostate and the appendix.

"You seem to be quite fit, Mr. Kesselmann, and in good health. Please get dressed now and remain in the lounge. I'll write the report for Mr. Weidemann. He'll complete the necessary forms and inform you of the results. You'll have to wait several hours, so you might want to return later on." The captain decided to wait.

Dr. Spengler discussed the examination and interview with his colleagues. They still insisted on re-examining the facts. Weidemann remained unconvinced, for instance, and had grown even more suspicious.

"Let's consider the facts separately. If he's actually von Heissel, how did he alter his appearance? It's true that a few excellent plastic surgeons remain in Germany, but—"

"But," Glisermann interrupted, "they're aware of the penalty for helping war criminals to escape: losing their licences for life."

"Yes," replied Weidemann quickly, "but von Heissel would surely know of someone who would take the risk."

At this point, Gonsher pointed to the passport. "But how did he get that? We checked very carefully, and it's the real thing. The listed height is within half an inch of this man's height. His eyes are somewhat lighter, it's true, than the ones on this passport. His skin is somewhat lighter. But his hair is about the same colour. And if he really did suffer some physical trauma, we would indeed, see changes in skin colour, hair colour and weight. When we demanded his passport, moreover, the man seemed composed enough. I mean, he didn't even ask when we'd give it back to him."

Yigdal shrugged his shoulders. "Is there any other evidence to evaluate? So far, all the facts prove that this man is Jaakob Kesselmann."

"All we have," Glisermann added, "is Weidemann's suspicion due to some personal contact with von Heissel."

Glisermann then repeated the question, "If this really is von Heissel then how did he get Kesselmann's passport?"

"Listen," said Weidemann, "the most unlikely things happen in wartime. You all know that."

Glisermann, who disliked Weidemann, stroked his chin. "What about the fact that this man has been circumcised? Sorry, Weidemann, your vague suspicion doesn't override all the facts that we do have. Give him the damn visa. Give him the documents. We can always keep him under surveillance in Buenos Aires. As far as I'm concerned, we should give him the benefit of the doubt and get on with our work." And so, the documents were signed and placed in an official envelope. Nevertheless, Weidemann insisted on handing them over, personally, to Kesselmann. Looking straight into the man's eyes, Weidemann would shake his hand and wish him good luck. This was the ultimate test, because he could never forget von Heissel's steel-blue eyes—eyes that lacked even a trace of compassion. One last look, Weidemann thought, might yet convince him one way or another and set his mind at ease.

Weidemann stepped as close to the captain as he could but found himself unable to look into those eyes. The captain gazed steadily at the envelope in Weidemann's hand, thus avoiding eye contact. In fact, he took the extra precaution of wearing gloves to show that he was in a hurry.

"All I can tell you," Weidemann told his colleagues with a sigh, "is that this man is exceptionally smart. He anticipated all of our moves."

The captain left quickly to buy his ticket for an Atlantic crossing. He chose the RMS Victoria. A brochure attached to all tickets informed passengers that the crossing would take fourteen days—unless the ship sailed into fog. Back at his hotel room, the captain ripped open the official envelope. The documents that he found inside were clear and simple, with just a few instructions. According to the passport, he had been born in Düsseldorf. As the bearer of this visa and this permit, he might settle in Argentina, but must always carry both passport and permit on his person due to the wartime loss of his birth certificate. In Buenos Aires, he must report to the Immigration Department every six months."Ah," he said aloud, "there's the catch!" With the exception of this restriction, though, everything was in order. He worried now only about an interrogation when boarding the ship.

Before beginning to pack, the captain walked to the window and looked out at the Atlantic Ocean. The sun seemed to rest uneasily on a pewter sea, which heaved angrily. Below, moreover, the city seemed small and dilapidated. Depressed, he shut the window, finished packing, called a taxi and arrived on time for embarkation.

THE TRANS-ATLANTIC CROSSING

The captain's usual apprehension gripped him as he boarded the *RMS Victoria*. Would the authorities check his luggage? What would arouse their suspicion? Perhaps his fashionable clothes? As for his documents, the captain was confident that all were in order. Nevertheless, he decided to book a cabin in the first class. A canopied gangplank led passengers from the shore directly to the ship. Before boarding, everyone labeled their luggage with names and cabin numbers in large letters and left them on the pier for attendants. Then an official asked for passports and tickets. Once that was out of the way, the captain began to worry about his luggage.

"When and where," he asked meekly "is the luggage inspected?"

"We don't inspect luggage, sir. Custom inspectors will do that when you disembark."

Aboard ship at last, he took a brochure from the purser. It included a map of the ship and a schedule of its social events.

"Please go to the maître d' in the main dining room," said the purser, "to choose your first or second seating for dinner."

The *RMS Victoria* was modern, spotlessly clean and luxurious. It had room for a thousand passengers and a crew of four hundred. Standing just outside its Louis XV dining room, the captain glanced around the huge lobby. It was flanked on one side by a circular staircase of white and gold and on the other by a golden Greek goddess, who stood on a marble pedestal, water gently spraying her feet. The Chinese carpet of pink, blue and beige added a mellow ambience.

According to the seating plan, he would sit next to another German passenger. When the captain arrived at six, his dinner partner was already there.

"I'm Hermann Baumbach from Frankfurt," the man said cheerfully. He was tall, handsome, with clean-cut features, and wore a fashionable suit of navy blue, an immaculate white silk shirt, a tie with navy blue and red stripes. But the captain's eye was attracted to something on his head: a *peau de soie* skull cap. He was surprised, to say the least.

"I'm Cap—" he began to say, but stopped abruptly. He was about to say "I'm Captain von," but, realizing his error too late, he tried to correct it. "I mean, I'm fascinated by your cap. Do you wear it all the time? Oh, but before you answer, I should introduce myself. I'm Jaakob Kesselmann, from Düsseldorf."

"Glad to meet you," Baumbach replied in German. "To answer your question, no. I'm not an orthodox Jew. But I wear my skull cap only at dinner. It's just a custom we followed at home. Listen, we could continue in German if you wish, but I lived in London for a while. I'm really quite proud of my English. How about you? Would you mind if we speak English? I'd prefer that language. And, you know, this is an English ship."

"Oh, yes, by all means," the captain answered in English. "It's my second language."

Focusing on Hermann's headgear, he made a mental note to check *The Jewish Manual*. As Jaakob Kesselmann he should not have had to ask about Jewish headgear. For the time being, though, he would use his favourite strategy: directing attention away from himself.

"Did you have any trouble leaving Germany?"

"No, not really. First I had to get a German exit document and then a Canadian entrance visa. That's where I plan to open a branch of our family business. Someone told me to consult the Immigrant Aid Association in Le Havre. They handled all of my documentation—not just the visa but also my passport, my birth certificate and so on. They did a great job, I must say. The whole process took no more than thirty minutes. A Mr. Weidemann handled all the details. Nice man! Anyway, when I asked if they needed any more information, he just said: 'No, we already have in our files detailed documents of many Jews.' Can you believe that? Just as efficient as our own German system before the War."

The captain sat still—the food in his mouth began to taste like straw. "Yes, yes," he muttered, "it was the same for me."

Now, of course, he realized that his own suspicions had been justified. This Jewish organization had given him the visa because it lacked enough evidence to detain him. The captain wanted to say something about being glad that Baumbach's family had managed to escape, but what he carelessly did say was: "So, some of you Jews got away."

"Hey," Hermann replied, "you sound like, well, a Nazi—a disappointed one. And what's this about 'you Jews'?"

"Oh, no, wait a minute. You've misunderstood me, Hermann. I'm glad that some Jews got away. Did I say 'you'? No, no, no. I meant 'us.' That's what I meant. It's my English, you see. I sometimes have trouble with my pronouns."

Hermann was quick tempered, but he did understand from personal experience that speaking a foreign language could lead to unfortunate mistakes and sometimes even funny ones.

"Yes, of course. Sorry, Jaakob. We German Jews have become very sensitive. Too sensitive. Let's forget it and drink a toast to the journey ahead."

"Sure," the captain was quick to answer. "My treat." The sommelier suggested a wine that both men knew well and liked: *Auslese*, a German Riesling. It was sweet and aromatic. Both men felt soothed not only by the wine but also by the elegant setting. Feeling cheerful, they became very talkative. It was the captain who first realized that they were becoming too giddy. Prudence, he felt, required a quick exit. On the pretext of having some urgent business, he excused himself. Hermann was relieved. He too, was tired, after a long day.

The sun glided down to the horizon as Le Havre's shimmering lights vanished, and the *RMS Victoria* sailed into a vast blackness. Instead of returning directly to his cabin, the captain decided to take a few turns around the deck, while thinking about his situation. His future seemed as dark and fathomless as the sea. Even though the ship had sailed across it many times, repeating the same route over again and again, like the many choices in his life, but now he had chosen a new route. Worse, he had no real sense of direction, his only goal being to get away as far from the Fatherland as possible. Even establishing a new paper mill might have hidden drawbacks. Would Argentina allow foreigners to own businesses? Would he have to recruit an Argentine partner? But he had made his choice. Returning to his cabin, memories of Lara and home haunted him. By now, newspapers would have reported him missing. Maybe she'd already realized that he had escaped. Should he have sent her a postcard, just to let her know that he was alive? A few innocuous words about an interesting journey, and a fictitious signature that no one else would recognize? In retrospect, he felt guilty about making her believe that he must remain in Düsseldorf to settle business—although that was partly true—and then follow her to Zürich. But journalists had just declared that his department was under investigation. What else could he have done but vanish? Besides, he knew exactly how Lara would have reacted. She would have spoken immediately to her parents, who would have used their connections to bribe officials on his behalf. Lara would never have understood that neither money nor influence would work. Not this time. Journalists were vicious and relentless. They demanded justice and retribution.

Lara had absorbed the nineteenth-century worldview of her parents. After graduating from the *Madchenschule*, she was sent to a *Wirtschaftschule*. There, she had learned about being a proper wife and housekeeper. Everyone was charmed by her beauty and wit. Her voice was soft but with a distinct trace of *schweizerdeutsch*. Gracious and suave, she never spoke disparagingly of anyone not even if she despised the person secretly. Lara preferred simple literature with a strong love element. Art, especially modern art, was barely comprehensible to her. Theatre, on the other hand, was everything. As a young girl, she had wanted to become an actress; she still enjoyed watching others perform. Lara loved her parents, her opulent way of life, her husband and her daughter, in that order.

THE EXPATRIATE

The captain loved his wife, even though he could not define exactly what he loved about her. It had taken many years for him to realize that they seldom talked about literature, philosophy or society. He had reserved these topics for his father and members of his club, all of them men. Lara satisfied his physical needs. Vivid recollections of their lovemaking aroused a longing for her, impossible to repress on this exciting night. He slipped into bed and went to sleep but kept waking up repeatedly. Before swallowing a sleeping pill, he had to admit that the company of a woman would relieve at least, some of the tension that he had been enduring for months. He wondered if Hermann felt the same craving. At breakfast, he would try to find out somehow, discreetly, if any available female companions were on board.

Next morning, Hermann's greeting provided an opportunity. "Good morning old chap, as the English would say. You look tired. Didn't you sleep well?"

"No, as a matter of fact, I didn't. But, to tell the truth, you look just as tired as I am." The two men looked at each other, but neither wanted to be first to mention their common problem.

"Do you know what's wrong?" the captain tried to be discreet. "We've concentrated too much over the years on business. We need a little fun now, some relaxation, some company. You know, female company."

Well, there it was. If Hermann was as astute as he appeared to be, he knew perfectly well what this meant. And sure enough, a merry twinkle appeared in his eyes.

"Hmm. Yes, I see what you mean. Well, there are two possibilities. We could ask the maître d' to invite a couple of ladies to join us for dinner. Or one of us could ask his steward about any lonely ladies on board. How about this? I'll ask the maître d' over there. You ask your steward, and after lunch, we'll compare notes."

Hermann learned that it can take a little while to arrange requests of this kind. The captain had better luck. His steward told him that someone on staff hired women as hostesses for social gatherings. These hostesses asked lonely men to dance with them at cocktail parties, and so on. The captain pressed a two-pound note into the steward's palm. In return, the steward wrote the names of three women and their phone numbers, assuring him, of course, that all three were beautiful.

When the two men met on the upper deck after lunch, the captain had some useful information for Hermann. They hoped to find at least one of the women in the lounge and look at her before introducing themselves. Strolling around, Hermann picked up the daily bulletin, which announced a special program in the main lounge during high tea. It would feature several performers: Clarice Honeywell, the ship's director of activities; Solédad Perez, a dancer and singer; and Andreev Slovitcz, a Bulgarian magician. As soon as Hermann saw that two names matched those on the steward's list, he sent a message to the captain's cabin. They agreed to meet in the main lounge at tea time.

Meanwhile, the steward lost no time. He contacted the women, informed them of these two particular male passengers who would attend the performance, and described the men. He knew from many years of practical experience that the men would like these two women. The steward was a very astute businessman, who augmented his income by arranging introductions of just this kind. He always kept a list of passengers, particularly those travelling alone. But he also depended on his stock of coloured contraceptives that he bought in Lisbon. These were expensive but reliable.

The steward's choice was, indeed, prescient. Clarice Honeywell was the ship's social director. Well-trained for her job, she mingled easily among the passengers, smiling and greeting everyone with a bon mot. Solédad Perez was a dancer and singer, one of the ship's prime entertainers.

Hermann and the captain entered early to get seats as close to the stage as possible. Clarice, watching at the main entrance, immediately recognized the pair. She smiled, pointed to the two seats that had been reserved especially for them, and ordered cocktails. Just then, Solédad appeared on the stage to check the microphone. Clarice noticed that the two men were staring at Solédad. Pointing to her, she explained that this performer was going to sing and dance a fandango, one that had probably originated not in Spain but in South America. By now, the lounge was beginning to fill up. Clarice excused herself to greet the other guests.

Both men looked at each other and silently agreed that the women were beautiful and would certainly be acceptable for a few trysts. Speaking in German so that no one seated nearby would understand, the captain suggested that they invite the women for dinner and then for a private nightcap. Hermann smiled and winked approvingly. The waiters were now serving refreshments. The lights dimmed at three-thirty and Clarice stepped onto the stage.

"Good afternoon, everyone. I'm pleased to introduce a distinguished artist. Solédad Perez is well known to European audiences for her extraordinary singing and dancing. She was born in Malaga, Spain, but she's proud to be international. Her mother is Spanish, and her father Greek. She speaks and sings not only in Spanish and Greek, but also in English. Her dancing career took her to Paris, where she was highly praised for her innovative style. Time doesn't allow me to mention her many prizes. Miss Perez will be followed by our magician, Andreev Sloevitcz. He's Bulgarian and well known in professional circles. After his performance, we'll have a short question-and-answer period for those who hope to find out just how Mr. Sloevitcz performs his tricks."

Clarice did not refer to anything personal about the performers. She might have said, for instance, that Andreev was Solédad's former husband. Clarice knew that Solédad had insisted on a divorce, claiming that Andreev was unbearably jealous and had no patience for any job. Or that he had convinced the ship's entertainment department to hire him so that he could support their child.

Andreev had been born in Plovdiv, Bulgaria, of Greek parents. He spoke not only Bulgarian and Greek but English as well. Even as a boy, he had loved to hang around the Gypsies. It was they who had taught him about magic. Tall and handsome in a distinctly virile way, he wore a dramatic magician's cloak. It was made of heavy ribbed silk and trimmed with a narrow white collar and cuffs. Although women pursued him now, as they always did, he showed little interest in them and continually stalked Solédad.

Solédad's performance lasted thirty minutes. She walked out onto the stage, clacking her castanets and whirling her chiffon skirts of blue, green and soft orange. The spotlights followed her around closely, forming a rainbow of many colors. Suddenly, the music stopped. Solédad began a haunting song about unrequited love, concluding with a soft moan. Silence followed, awkward moments of utter silence, and then came the applause. Solédad bowed several times and wafted off just as Andreev appeared.

A young boy followed the handsome magician and set up a small, square table. The tricks were familiar to almost everyone: pulling a rabbit from a hat, demonstrating that a box was empty even after the magician had thrown many articles into it, and so on. One trick, the final one, was more unusual: swallowing the flame of a candle. But the applause, some thought, was far in excess of its merit.

With perfect composure, Clarice thanked the performers and called for questions. When no one had any, she proceeded to announce the next day's activities. The show was over, and everyone began to leave.

Hermann and the captain rushed backstage and introduced themselves to Solédad, congratulating her for a splendid performance. She was hardly surprised, so the two men realized that someone had told her to wait for them. In no time, Clarice came backstage. The captain, seasoned in etiquette, invited both women for cocktails and dinner. Immediately, Hermann added his own invitation. The ladies accepted with pleasure, of course. As the four of them walked away they saw Andreev without his cape, peering around the empty hall. He was obviously looking for someone. Hermann stopped to thank him for a performance that really had intrigued him. Solédad showed no sign of knowing or even recognizing Andreev. Both women remained silent until Solédad broke up the foursome. She had to change her dress and wanted to rest before dinner. The others followed, promising to meet in the main dining room at six-fifteen.

Back in his cabin, the captain made plans. He preferred Clarice, but Solédad could teach him a few basic Spanish expressions which would be useful. To avoid any unpleasantness with Hermann, he phoned to explain the reason for his preference but also to say that the choice was up to Hermann, who said much the same thing.

"Then it's settled," the captain replied, "Clarice will sit near you and Solédad next to me. But I have a suggestion. Let's ask Solédad to recommend a Spanish dinner and a Spanish wine to go with it."

"Yes, but remember to bring our own bicarbonate. A few years ago, when I was in London, a group of us went to a Spanish bistro for paella. Sometimes, even now, I think that it's still in my stomach. Let's hope she'll pick something else. Oh well, I'm just joking. It doesn't matter. Whatever she chooses will be fine with me."

"Good. And you know what, Hermann? You're really an agreeable chap."

"Until this evening, then."

The captain smiled while putting down the phone. For the first time in many years, he was beginning to feel a warm sentiment for another man—and a Jew at that. This Hermann, he really is a fine fellow.

The captain still had some time to wile away. With less reluctance than previously, he picked up *The Jewish Manual.* Opening it at random, he came across something about Seneca, a Roman senator of the first century and a great admirer of the Apostle Paul. According to Seneca, (3BC-65AD) *The Manual* reported that:

> *"many Romans admired the Jews for their sobriety and spirituality. By the first century, in fact, over ten percent of the population of the Roman Empire was Jewish, seven million out of seventy million. Even more Romans would have converted to Judaism, had it not been for the requirements of following rigorous dietary laws and (for men) submitting to circumcision. When the early Christians dropped those requirements, pagans flocked to the new community. Some of them resented Jews, however, for having failed to welcome them. Others resented Jews for looking down on Roman culture. Still others resented Jews for refusing to intermarry with Romans." (1)*

The captain found this interesting, but had to put the book away and dress for dinner. When he and Hermann met at the dinner table, it was clear that they had at least one opinion in common: no matter how trivial the occasion, dress elegantly for ladies. As for the women, they always dressed as exquisitely as the occasion required but neither one wore a wedding ring.

The captain immediately assumed his role for the evening: master of very formal protocol. He pulled out a chair for each woman, for instance, and told her where to sit.

"Both of you look beautiful and well rested," he said with a polite smile, "after such an arduous afternoon." The women were accustomed to lame compliments.

"Well," replied Solédad, "we are used to our work." The captain looked at Hermann, thinking he might have liked to take over for him. But Hermann sat still and motioned for the captain to proceed.

"Solédad, why don't you choose an aperitif as well as some Spanish food and wine to go with it?"

Before Solédad could answer, Clarice interrupted. Her job involved public relations, convincing passengers that the management would satisfy the specific needs of every passenger. "Oh, that's a good idea. On the other hand, maybe you gentlemen would like to taste our *gefilte fish*. It's made by our kosher chef, you know, the best on either side of the Atlantic. Did you know that he had won a blue ribbon from the Swiss Culinary Academy? Our Jewish passengers often tell me how much they enjoy his kosher specialties. His *Süssigkeiten* are tastier than anything from the French patisseries and—"

Both men almost burst out laughing when they heard the English pronunciation of *Süssigkeiten*.

"Well," Hermann said at last, "that's very thoughtful of you, Clarice—trying to make us feel at home." He noticed that Jaakob seemed lost in thought for the moment. "We certainly will tell our Jewish friends about all this. But we've been eating Jewish food for many years, so I agree with Jaakob. We should try some more exotic—I mean foreign—food. And, well, who could make a better choice than our new Spanish friend?"

THE EXPATRIATE

The captain listened for the special intonation in Hermann's voice. Clever bastard, he thought. He could hardly have said it better himself. Of course, he had no idea that Hermann had always hated his mother's or anyone else's *gefilte fish*. As for the captain, he had never eaten it in his life.

"Yes, let her choose the menu. We'll leave the kosher chef in peace for a few more evenings."

"Well, our national dish is paella. It's usually made with chicken, shrimp, scampi and rice. It takes quite a while to prepare. Yes, I do know that Jews don't eat shrimp and scampi but paella tastes just as good with beef. What else? Oh, the wine. I've spoken to connoisseurs who say that *Pesquara*, from *Rebera.*, is a good red wine."

"Oh, that sounds great," said the captain. "But first, let's have our cocktails and dance. I hear the orchestra tuning up."

After they had toasted each other's health, the captain took Solédad's arm and led her to the dance floor. As soon as he put his arm around her, she pressed herself as close to him as possible. He began to feel the warmth of her body. Her cheek barely grazed his, but it came just close enough for the slightest movement of her mouth to touch his face. The captain was taken aback, surprised at such unabashed boldness, but he responded by tightening his grip around her waist. He felt her breasts responding to him. His cheek boldly touched hers. All this while dancing to a sentimental Strauss waltz. Their dramatic twirls attracted the attention of other couples. Oblivious to their surroundings and unaware that most couples were leaving the dance floor to watch them, the captain and Solédad danced on and on. Each clearly understood the other's body language. When only two couples remained dancing, the orchestra leader announced a forty-five minute break. Holding hands, looking elated, the captain and Solédad reluctantly returned to Hermann and Clarice.

While the others were dancing, Clarice and Hermann had been discussing the peculiarities of their respective cultures. Clarice's parents had always complained that the Germans had no sense of humour.

"Evidently," Hermann replied, "they had never met my uncle Fritz. He could turn any situation into a comedy and prance about like Charlie Chaplin. Anyway, let's make a deal. You don't say anything negative about the Germans, and I won't say anything negative about the British.—Deal?"

"It's a deal. And it goes into effect immediately."

"Come to think of it," Hermann said, breaking the deal, "I once heard that Churchill smoked Cuban cigars, not English ones."

They were laughing at each other's jokes as Solédad and the captain returned.

"*A su salud et felicidad, amigos.*" (To your health and happiness, friends.) This was Clarice's attempt at Spanish. Solédad almost spilled her wine.

"Oh, Clarice, that sounds terrible. Spanish sounds soft and many words have tonal endings."

The captain remained silent, reluctant to antagonize anyone. It was Hermann who came to Clarice's defense.

"Well, listen to the two of you! I don't think that an accent matters so much. Anyway, it certainly doesn't matter as much as vocabulary and grammar. Think about it. How many people can capture tonality and accent without living in a foreign country for many years? I had no trouble understanding Clarice."

At this point, the captain decided to support Hermann. "Please, Clarice, speak as much Spanish as you like. I have to start learning it soon, you know, but I doubt if I'll ever lose my German accent."

Solédad realized that she had been justly rebuked. Even so, she was angry. Whenever they went out together with men, Clarice assumed the dominant role and made her feel inferior. Besides, Solédad's immediate situation seemed uncertain. She was sexually attracted to the captain, true, but she preferred Hermann. He seemed more solid, somehow, more stable. Long bored by living alone, she felt the need for companionship. And if she was going to find it on this trip, she'd have to act quickly. But Clarice was Hermann's partner, and they seemed to like each other. That settled it. She would concentrate on Jaakob. He was exciting, to say the least. What a physique! He still walks like a military man. But that, of course, was the problem with him; his stiff posture made him vaguely arrogant. Well, who could figure out what men were really like? Do they ever tell women the truth about themselves? She smiled at Clarice and tried to mollify her with flattery.

"You poured the wine beautifully, Clarice. It's quite an art to pour wine properly, Anyway, I hope you'll like the paella."

Clarice did, and so did everyone else. After the main course, a waiter brought the dessert menu. Before anyone could choose Solédad interrupted.

"How about a simple Spanish desert? I know a really good one." After the paella, everyone had confidence in Solédad. "It's made of fresh strawberries floating in orange juice."

Then coffee was served with thin English biscuits and everyone was beginning to feel mellow. The orchestra had returned, so the captain asked Solédad to dance. Later, he hoped, they would take a stroll on the promenade deck. With that in mind, he turned to Hermann.

"*Wiedersehen,*" he said with a wink. Hermann winked back at him, as he took Clarice's arm and led her to the dance floor.

The orchestra played popular American songs, but the captain knew very few of them. It made no difference. He held Solédad tightly and kissed her cheek. After a few dances, they left for the promenade deck. In the darkness, they could hear the waves heaving with the regularity of a beating heart. Their ship, with its ribbon of shimmering gold electric bulbs, was an intruding speck on the vast, raging black infinity.

The captain let go of Solédad's arm and stared down at the sea. Alone, he thought. I'm alone in a hostile universe! For a moment, his mind drifted back to Lara. Where was she now? What was she doing? Something was happening to him! Maybe he should just jump over board, feel those waves pummel his body, slip into the abyss and find some kind of eternal peace. Even the delightful woman standing beside him could never truly satisfy him. Nothing made any sense.

Solédad nudged his arm, then grasped his hand, as if she had read his mind. "Jaakob, *mi querido*, your face has changed—just now. I saw it change. What's wrong? Is it what happened in Germany? I read how much you Jews suffered during the War. Do you know what we always say? We say that Jews are the wise ones. That's what we say where I come from. It's because, maybe, Jews know how to face adversity. Is that right, Jaakob?"

His face softened, his shoulders sagged. How lucky to have a sympathetic companion near him at this moment. Unable to speak, he just put his arm around her and kissed her. She responded tenderly, startled by this rush of emotion.

"I know what you need, Jaakob. Let's go to my cabin and have a drink."

"Oh, yes, that's just what I need." He replied.

Solédad had been given a palatial top floor stateroom with a door that opened onto the deck. She needed space to house her extensive wardrobe as well as to practise her dance steps. In addition to a bed and some chairs, she had a refrigerator, a radio, a telephone, a writing desk, and several cupboards for clothes. The curtains and linens were pale lilac and light pink. Solédad assumed that the captain would be impressed by all this, but he merely observed that Germany had recently refurbished one of its old ships with lots of gold and glitz. With all due respect to the British, he added, the German ship was now more luxurious than this one. Ignoring this remark, Soledad took out a bottle of champagne and opened it quickly.

"Help yourself, while I change into something relaxing. Make yourself a little more comfortable, take off your jacket and put on this bathrobe." The captain smiled and obeyed.

When Solédad reappeared, she was wearing something sheer and flimsy, revealing her firm breasts, flat long torso and long legs. She turned off all but one light. He suddenly realized how much she was trying to please him.

At the moment, though, he could not think clearly. He moved closer to her and unobtrusively touched her breast. She lay back on the bed. As he bent over to kiss her, she put her arms around his neck and drew him even closer.

"*Te* quero," she said sleepily, "*te quero.*"

THE EXPATRIATE

He presumed that she meant, "I love you," and tried to say the same thing to her, but the words stuck in his throat. He remained silent while feeling the warmth inside her body. After a sudden release of tension, each drifted into a dreamless sleep.

Next morning, streams of light filtered into the cabin. The captain woke up, but Solédad remained fast asleep. Looking through the porthole, he saw the heavens looming above and an orange golden ball gliding over the horizon, casting shimmers on the silvery waters. He dressed silently and left a note near the phone. "You're a lovely lady. See you soon, Jaakob."

The captain tiptoed out into the deserted corridor and reached his cabin at the stroke of five o'clock. Unable to fall asleep, he resorted to his usual remedy: reading *The Jewish Manual*. The bookmark had fallen out. By opening it at random, he lost the historical continuity.

"In the fourth century, Emperor Constantine the Great in the year 324 made Christianity the official religion of his empire. This meant that Christians suddenly acquired imperial power. Their Church was now an arm of the state. When it adopted the Nicene Creed in 325, therefore, all had to approve its principles. Those who refused to do so became heretics. This was the new pattern: enforced uniformity. According to Edward Gibbons, Christians killed more of their own in the first hundred years after coming to power than the Romans had during the previous three hundred years.

After dealing with pagans and heretics, Christians turned their attention to infidels—that is, Jews. For not recognizing the Messiah that their own prophets had predicted, many Christians, believed these people were evil. Anti-Judaism became a respectable form of Christian fervour, although theology was not its only motivation. Christians, who had steadfastly endured relentless persecution under the pagan emperors, used their power to persecute a minority that resisted just as steadfastly."(2)

59

Suddenly the book fell from his hand. He woke up late, tenderly recalling his tryst with Solédad but little of what he had read. Too late for breakfast, he took a brisk walk on the promenade deck. The cool fresh air and tranquil sea revived his hopes. An old motto came to mind: Never dwell on the past. He began to look forward to establish a new business in Buenos Aires. After all, paper and paper products were universal necessities. But then, as usual, he succumbed once more to anxiety. Would being a Jew restrict his progress? Would people always be inquiring about his past? And was he, in fact, guilty as charged of crimes against humanity?

The captain answered that last question with a categorical no. He had acted on orders and in accordance with the belief that a united Europe, governed by Germany would inevitably be in everyone's best interest. A few passengers walked by, greeted him and interrupted his train of thought. Irritated, he found a deck chair in a secluded corner.

An inveterate note-taker, he took a small pad from his jacket pocket and began to list his daily activities. Once, in London, a friend had confessed that he began every day with the acronym "COP," that is, "Coordinate, Organize, Prioritize." Since then, the captain had been doing just that.

Today, his priority was to show Solédad some token of appreciation. But he had to discuss it with Hermann, who might want to do the same for Clarice. He shut his eyes, relaxed, and tried to feel the luxury of total forgetfulness. Just then, Hermann saw his friend reclining in a deck chair. He playfully poked the captain's head. The captain jumped up with a fearful look in his eyes, turned around and stood up straight.

"You know, Jaakob, you had such a frightened look just now, as if you were confronting—I don't know—the Gestapo or something. Come on, now, it's a beautiful day."

The captain relaxed and smiled wanly. "Well, how was last night?"

Before Hermann could answer, both men began to laugh.

"Oh, Hermann, I had a tigress."

"Well, I had a gentle dove."

"Shouldn't we buy them something? You know, to show our appreciation?"

"Yes, that's a good idea."

"Well, then, what do you suggest?"

"I went to one of the ship's stores and saw a few small leather evening purses, some red and some stamped with gold designs."

Hermann gestured with his hand. "I'd rather not buy purses, which are used mainly for money. The *goyim* (Christians) believe that we Jews think only of money."

Hermann's interpretation surprised him. Lara always wore a purse, but that was where she kept her handkerchief, her compact and some money. He wanted to show Hermann, however, that he knew about this Jewish fear.

"*Mea culpa,*" he replied with a shrug. "So, what would you suggest?"

"For Clarice—I don't know. She wore some sort of perfume that smelled like lilacs—rotting ones. God, it nearly asphyxiated me. I could buy the kind that my sisters use. It's Chanel No.5 or 6 or something like that. She can always exchange it. As for Solédad, she wears colourful clothes. Maybe one of those silk scarves. But that could be expensive."

"*Herrlich, mein Freund.* You're a genius."

He could hardly keep from smiling. Hermann must have had a lot of fun last night. Cheerfully, they headed for the stores. As soon as they entered, two saleswomen put on their welcome smiles. When men came in without women, experience had proved over and over again, they were easy targets for expensive gifts—and not necessarily for their wives.

"May I help you, gentlemen? Looking for something special?"

Unlike most customers, these two came directly to the point. Hermann spoke first. "I'm looking for a good perfume, and my friend is looking for a silk scarf." One woman took out a few perfume bottles, describing the virtues of each.

"Chanel No. 3 is heady, No. 4 is woody, No. 5 is clean, No. 6 is sweet."

She stopped. Hermann thought for a while. Eventually, he asked a surprising question. "Is this store British or American?"

"Neither, sir. We're independent. Our stores are on many luxury liners. We sell mostly British, French, American and Spanish products."

"Jaakob did you hear that? This is a new trend in business: going international."

"Yes, but I'm not sure that I like it. Were you ever on the old *Bremen*? I mean, before it was refurbished? Now there was a ship. On the *Bremen*, you could buy the very best products. Most of them German, of course."

"Oh, forget it! Not everything German is so good. National socialism wasn't so good either. Anyway, let's get back to business. I'm going to buy this Chanel No. 5. It's the most popular, and my sisters use it."

The captain's choice was a little more difficult. He saw square scarves, oblong and triangular ones. All had bizarre but colourful designs—flowers, squares, circles—and yet the general effect in each case was harmonious. He chose an oblong one and asked for the price in American currency. It was expensive at one hundred dollars, but the captain was feeling good. The two men received wrapped packages, each with a little card that was attached by ribbons. The friends smiled at each other and looked forward to another enjoyable night. At the captain's suggestion, they sent messages with invitations for dinner.

That evening, when Clarice and Solédad approached the table, they found two exquisitely wrapped packages. Hermann's card was laconic: "To a pleasant friendship." The captain's was even more so: "Best Wishes." Clearly, both men wanted to emphasize that these relationships would be casual and fleeting. The women understood that. The same thing had happened on every voyage, although they wished that one liaison of this kind would lead to marriage. At least these two men, they assumed, were not married. That gave them some hope. Each decided to open her gift later on, and privately.

This time, Clarice chose the main course and the wine to go with it. She ordered a partly British dinner: roast beef with

THE EXPATRIATE

Yorkshire pudding, mixed vegetables and some horseradish sauce. For desert, she chose the chef's *gâteau aux pommes et pistaches,* followed by assorted cheeses and a special cognac.

Despite the dubious reputation of English cooking, everyone enjoyed dinner. And Clarice felt completely at ease this time, because she knew that Hermann would join her for the night. Solédad, however, began to feel anxious, and was the first to suggest dancing. On the dance floor, she snuggled close to the captain—presumably to teach him a few new steps. He understood the maneuver. After a few unsuccessful tries, he suggested that they go to her cabin.

As they entered the cabin, he sensed how painstakingly she had prepared a seductive atmosphere. The lights were pinky dim, near two lounging chairs stood an elaborately hand-painted lacquered coffee table on which were placed two Bacarrat gold-edged champagne tumblers and a carafe of an exotic champagne. The captain concluded that Solédad was taking this escapade too seriously. For him, it was a temporary escape from stress and anxiety; he had no intention of continuing this liaison after disembarking. If only he could explain how complicated his life had become. Besides, she probably was aware that affairs of this kind were occupational hazards for anyone who worked as a shipboard dancer.

Solédad sensed that something was wrong. As they crossed the threshold of her cabin, he should have taken her in his arms, kissed her and whispered a few endearing terms. His reticence began to trouble her. But she hid her disappointment.

"Let's have a drink."

The captain enjoyed his. He found it soothing. So soothing that he almost forgot where he was. The room became shadowy, his mind hazy. He felt her sitting near him, almost naked, stretching her arms out to remove his clothes. His hands gripped her shoulders, just as her soft breasts caressed his chest. He felt ripples going up and down his spine. In the dark, he penetrated her perfumed body. Neither spoke. The soft lights dimmed and disappeared.

Much later, when he opened his eyes, pale sunlight had already begun to seep through the porthole. A happy and peaceful expression on her face, Solédad was sleeping. The captain slipped happily and quietly into the dimly lit corridor and headed for his own cabin.

As he approached it, he heard footsteps behind him. A heavy hand, reaching from behind, suddenly gripped his shoulders.

"Stop, you Jew Kraut!"

Startled, the captain stood very erect and still. He lapsed into German due to stress. *"Was wollen Sie?"*

"Listen, Jew Kraut. I'll say it in English so that you'll understand me clearly."

Before the assailant could utter another word, the captain almost blurted, "But I'm not a—" but did not finish the sentence, "—a Jew."

"Listen," said the stranger, "if you don't stop fooling around with my wife, I'll blow your head off."

The captain recognized Andreev, the magician, and regained his composure. "She gave me the impression," he whispered hoarsely, "that she wasn't married. Otherwise—I mean, I would never—" It was not gentlemanly to accuse a woman, true, but it was not ladylike to use a man.

Although the captain did not know it, Solédad had at least two reasons for keeping her marriage secret. She knew that Andreev was watching her and wanted to show him that their marriage was over by going out with other men whenever she pleased. Besides, many single male passengers looked for single women and paid generously for their company. But the captain wondered why she had not admitted the simple truth to him. She could have said that her husband wouldn't give her a divorce. She could have said that, being Catholics, they could never get a divorce. Even at dinner that night, he had noticed her wistful mood. Andreev had probably threatened her, and she must have insisted on continuing the affair. The captain would never know the whole truth but, he realized that he would have to avoid Solédad at all costs.

Shaken, the captain entered his cabin, flopped on his bed and immediately fell asleep. He slept so soundly, that he got up very late the next day. Near the door, he found an envelope and assumed that it was from Solédad.

But it was from Hermann, who was worried when his friend missed breakfast and lunch. For his part, Hermann was delighted with Clarice. Moreover, he was able to discuss with her his future business plans in Canada. Finally, what were Jaakob's plans for dinner? Nice guy, the captain thought, but how many Jews were like that? He kept thinking about that while shaving and abruptly had a flashback, by no means for the first time: Lara. How could he have forgotten Lara so quickly? But even that thought faded.

Looking into the mirror, he whispered, "Jaakob Kesselmann, you're a handsome Jew!" He wasted no time and immediately sent a note to Hermann. "Sorry, couldn't join you for lunch. Will explain later." He felt no obligation to send an explanation to Solédad. If he failed to show up for her performance, she would assume that their affair was over—which is to say, that Andreev had carried out his threat.

The captain took a stroll on the promenade deck. Maybe he could find a nice woman amongst the passengers there. Finally he settled down in a deck chair, and took *The Jewish Manual* from his pocket. He lost his place again, as usual, but did remember Seneca's revealing statement about St. Paul: that other Jews resented his approval of intermarriage. He smiled. Even the Jews wanted a pure race! But what kind of man was Paul? He flipped a few pages and found the following passage.

> *"Like Jesus himself and many other religious leaders, Paul has been interpreted in very different and often opposing ways throughout the centuries. For Friedrich Nietzsche, he was sly and superstitious. For Martin Luther, on the other hand, he was a rock of strength. For Ernst Renan, he was an "ugly little Jew." (3)*

> *"Paul's encounter with Jesus on the Damascus Road, in approximately the year 45, led to his conversion. And that led to his new career: converting others. Unlike many other Jews, Paul saw no reason for pagans to become Jews first, in order to become Christians. God had established covenants with both Jews and non-Jews in the*

past, so it seemed reasonable to conclude that God had established yet another one with the coming of Christ. In any case, most Jews did not want to become Christians. At the same time, more and more Romans did. They found the idea of Christ's atoning death very powerful. What Paul did was to include redemption from sin among the defining features of a messiah. In effect, Paul's theology marginalized Jews within the Christian community. Roman Christians outnumbered Jewish Christians. Within only fifteen years, Christianity was no longer a Jewish sect; it was a separate religious community with no ethnic identity. By the time of Paul's death in 62 A.D. in Rome at the hands of Nero, Christianity was spreading quickly throughout the Roman world." (4)

The captain slipped *The Jewish Manual* back into his pocket, reclined comfortably and looked up at the sky. The ship was sailing slowly but steadily. Shutting his eyes, he began to think about the two parallel religious separations: first Christians from Jews and then Protestants from Catholics. Yet all believed in one God, all expressed themselves through myths. If God had anything to do with order and justice, why was there so much chaos and injustice? Unwittingly, he was asking questions that Jews and Christians had always asked. But the captain was thinking of an answer that would have shocked his ancestors. Given all the chaos and injustice, he asked himself, why not allow the wisest and fittest people to rule? That, he still believed, was really what Hitler had wanted. This was interesting, so he picked up *The Jewish Manual* once more and read another passage: *"Man can find redemption from sin only through Christ, the first atoner."* (5)

Shutting his eyes, he thought about some Christian beliefs. Could a surrogate expiate sin? More important, was he himself a sinner? According to all Christian theologies, everyone without exception was a sinner. He must therefore be a sinner, true, but surely not for what he did during the War—not for obeying the orders of those with authority over him. Brought up as a Catholic, he had believed most of its doctrines and practised them before joining the Nazis. It would be hard to abandon what he had learned as a child. As an adult, though, maybe he could deepen his understanding of those doctrines.

A strong breeze distracted him. Opening his eyes, he saw a woman at the rail, looking down at the lower decks. The wind had blown her voluminous skirt over her head, revealing black underwear edged with red lace. Smiling, he crept up to her and bent over the rail to see what she was looking at.

"What's so fascinating down there?"

Instantly, she stood up straight and looked menacingly at him. "Le Boche," she screamed and then spat into the ocean. It was his German accent, no doubt.

"You are mistaken, mademoiselle. I'm a German Jew. My name is Jaakob Kesselmann."

She paused to scrutinize him. Before her stood a handsome, distinguished man, probably in his mid forties. She immediately adjusted her skirt. A faint blush spread over her cheeks as she realized that he had seen her underwear. They looked at each other in surprised silence. She was very pretty, he thought, especially the angry flash in her brown eyes.

"Sorry. I'm Catherine Bourgogne." She paused, looked at him, then continued, "I'm an art historian. My specialty is restoration. I restore damaged paintings, and am interested in paint, as well as paintings. That's why I was looking at the workmen down there, painting those lifeboats. Such thick white paint! Have you noticed how spotless this ship is? Someone keeps painting over the dirty spots as soon as they appear."

The captain looked down and waited for a few moments. Catherine looked at him and smiled, suspecting what he was going to say.

"You know what? I'm getting hungry. Why don't we go to the lounge for some tea and crumpets, or whatever the English call those things?"

"Well, why not?"

Waiting for tea in the lounge, the captain focused on her profession. "You must have a lot of work now. I mean, because of the War. People on both sides must have hidden countless masterpieces in dark and dusty places—too little humidity, not enough—"

"Yes," she replied with a laugh, "after all, people aren't the only victims of War. But not all of my work is with artistic casualties of the War. I'm on my way to the National Gallery in Ottawa. Some paintings, including a Rembrandt, need cleaning. And after that, I'm off to the National Gallery in Washington."

The captain was not a connoisseur of paintings, but he found himself interested in how professionals cleaned works of art—how they rejuvenated paintings or statues, restoring them to their original state. It represented rejuvenation and efficiency. That was also needed in business.

"I'm on my way to South America to open a paper mill in Buenos Aires, and—" He stopped momentarily to observe his companion. She had both attractive and unattractive features. Her slightly thick nose, brown hair and eyes were somewhat ordinary, but she had a small waist and a clear complexion. Moreover, she was interesting.

"Does your work often keep you away from your family?"

"I have elderly parents," she replied after sipping her tea, "who live outside of Paris." With a smile, she added, "But to answer your question, I've never been married." The captain smiled back at her.

"But," she asked, "how about you?"

"My wife and family died during the War. I want to start a new life somewhere else."

Catherine was clever enough not to pursue the matter. If he had wanted to elaborate, he would have done so without being asked.

"Well, then," he said, "shall we dance?"

"Sure, but I must warn you that I haven't had much practice."

Catherine was not quite as awkward as she pretended, but she preferred not to continue dancing. Back at their table, they chatted aimlessly for a few minutes about American movies. Then, the orchestra suddenly stopped playing. They turned to see what was going on, and the captain spotted Solédad. Of course, thought the captain, she works in this lounge as well. How stupid of me to forget!

Solédad sang from her Spanish repertoire for half an hour and then left the stage. Looking around, she spotted the captain with Catherine and quickly walked over to them. "Hello amigo. I saw you on deck with—"

"Solédad," the captain interrupted stiffly, "this is my friend Catherine Bourgoyne. She's from Paris." The two women greeted and appraised each other discreetly.

"Solédad," the captain broke the awkward silence, "I bumped into your friend Andreev. He told me that you'll have dinner with him this evening." Alarm and dismay crept into her eyes. Andreev had carried out his threat and revealed the truth. Her liaison with the captain was over.

Catherine sensed immediately that Solédad and the captain had been intimate. But this made no difference to her. The captain would be free at least for this evening. Solédad excused herself, and left. The captain remained with Catherine, who waited a few minutes and then slowly explained.

"Every night, I sit at a table for six: three women and two men. There's room for one more. Would it be possible for you to join us this evening for dinner? By the way, one of the men at our table is another German passenger, Helmut Müller. He speaks English beautifully, but he's probably just another Nazi. It would be nice if you come and, well, put this chap in his place."

The captain kept sipping his drink, showing no outward sign of anxiety. He needed time before answering. How would this Helmut react? What if he had seen the wanted lists? What if he, too, was from Düsseldorf? On this Ship if, Müller were to report his suspicions to one of the officers, he would have no concrete evidence to support his allegations. Besides, the captain wanted to spend the evening with Catherine. Apart from anything else, it would force him to learn self-discipline, in circumstances such as these.

"Thanks," he answered hesitantly, "but I'll have to speak to my dinner partner. I'll call you as soon as I get back to my cabin."

That evening, Catherine introduced the captain to those who had already sat down at her table: Edward Peterson from Canada, Irene Huslav from Yugoslavia, Greta Milosovici from Hungary, and—facing the captain—Helmut Müller.

"Strange, isn't it, Jaakob? You look just like someone I saw in Berlin during the War."

"Maybe," the captain replied. "Berlin is a big city. I must look like lots of people there. Precisely where did you live in Berlin?"

"Near the Reichstag," Müller answered and without hesitation he began his tirade. "The Allies bombed so many streets. They were merciless, you know. They deliberately destroyed as much as they could. And the Russians, in particular, are still looting our museums. They might not even recognize a few masterpieces, but they'll take anything back home to the Hermitage or the—"

"Sure, they will," the captain interrupted. "And why not?" he asked, trying to hide his real feelings.

"That," Helmut returned angrily, "is because you're a Jew."

"Helmut," said Edward in a huff, "we agreed to forget the War during this trip."

"You Canadians suffered less than any other people," Helmut answered with cool contempt, "all you did was send a few battalions to fight against us. Now you boast, as if you were responsible for winning the War. One good thing you did, I must admit, was to give refuge to some of our soldiers who were falsely accused of crimes against humanity."

"First of all," replied a livid Edward, "we're a small country, at least in population. We sent over too many men, in my opinion, for a War that had nothing to do with us. We sent them over, in any case, for an altruistic reason. Otherwise, Hitler would have destroyed Western civilization. At least we helped to get rid of him. As for war criminals taking refuge in Canada, well, I don't know anything about that. But I'm sure going to find out as soon as I get back home."

Irene, who had hardly spoken at all, was suddenly unable to restrain herself. "Stop it, all of you! We'll never have peace if you keep this up. Haven't you learned anything from the last two wars? There is a God. Yes, and He'll forgive all of us. He'll show us the light." Everyone suspected that Irene was a nun. No one knew why she was going to Canada.

It was Catherine who restored peace. "The War is over, let's forget it, for now." Before anyone else could continue, she asked the waiter to fill their wine glasses and began to focus on a problem that deeply interested her.

"I wonder if divorce is as common in America as it is in France and what happens to divorced women there?" It was the beautiful Hungarian Greta who quickly answered in a heavy accent, "I was divorced, and then I lived with a married man for ten years. We were young, so we didn't care what people said. We had a child. He promised from the very beginning to divorce his wife and marry me, but he never did. I sued him for breach of promise and support. The judge dismissed my claim for breach of promise but ruled that he would have to pay for child support. Nothing for me. I wonder about the laws in other countries."

"I don't know about other countries now," Catherine responded, "but I do know something about Holland in the seventeenth century. That's because I've studied Rembrandt. In 1633, he married Saskia van Uylenbruch. When she died in 1642, Rembrandt hired Gaertje Direx to take care of his house and son. She was a young and penniless widow, so she really needed a job. Gaertje worked there for several years and became, well, more than a housekeeper. Rembrandt gave her Saskia's rose diamond ring and promised to marry her. Meanwhile, they lived together. But in 1646, he hired Hendrickje Jegher to help with the increased household work and soon fell in love with her. When he dismissed Geertje, she went to court, charged him with breach of promise, and demanded that he either keep his promise to marry her or support her for life. The court dismissed her first demand but awarded her two hundred florins annually for life. Now, just imagine this. Saskia had left an estate of about forty thousand florins to Titus, her son, and to the children that he might have. As for her husband, she had left him the use of her house—provided that he would not remarry." Human nature does not change. Everyone smiled, that is, except Helmut.

"If a man remarries, he should assume the responsibility of looking after his new wife and their children. Yes. But not with the assets of his previous wife. Saskia was right. She did the right thing. This provision in her will, merely made it necessary for Rembrandt to support his new wife on his own but not with the assets of his dead wife. Besides, it would prevent him from marrying a fortune hunter—"

"I must tell you," Catherine interrupted, "Rembrandt died bankrupt."

"I wouldn't be surprised," said Greta to Helmut, "if you still believe in the old German saying—you know, that women are only for the three, *Kinder, Küche and Kirche.*"

"Well," Helmut was quick to reply, "it was certainly less confusing when each sex had clearly defined functions."

"Yes," said Greta, "but that was in the past. Things might change, now, because of the War. After all, women have worked in munition factories. They've taken jobs that men had to leave because of the War. Whether you like it or not, things are always changing. Even laws keep changing. That's the way life is."

"It's true," Catherine added. "I think that legal equality will mean a new way of thinking about marriage, as well."

The captain began to think about his own marriage. Lara had been a meticulous housekeeper, a good mother, a gracious hostess, a partner who had helped him in every way. She had been happy. He had been happy. What more could anyone want? The old ways worked. Why change them now?

"Catherine," he said, "you have a good education and a good job. And do you know why? Because so many men died in the wars and women took over for them." Helmut said nothing, but he agreed.

The captain began to observe Catherine more closely. She was far from beautiful but attractive all the same. A strong personality! He recalled a remark that his mother had often made: "We Germans prefer the English to the French." But he now knew that remarks of this kind didn't mean very much. Consider Hermann, he's a good Jew and a good German. Suddenly he felt a hand squeezing his arm. It was Catherine.

"Stop daydreaming, Jaakob. The waiter wants to know if you want liqueur in your coffee."

THE EXPATRIATE

The captain nodded. "Oh, yes, of course. I was just thinking about something else for a moment. But now, I think that I'd like to dance. How about you?"

The captain held her close, putting his cheek against hers. She pressed closer to him. The vital spark was not there.

"You look tired, Jaakob. Let's take a short walk on the deck and then relax a little in my cabin."

He could hardly believe it. She was propositioning him. "Oh, yes, certainly. That would be pleasant."

On the promenade deck, the captain noticed a flock of petrels, against the darkening sky. As if heeding these harbingers of storms, he and Catherine held hands tightly. A rough sea made the ship sway. Walking became difficult, and they went directly to her cabin. It was bigger than he had expected. Catherine quickly explained that all single cabins had been booked, so she had been assigned this double one. She threw a bathrobe to the captain, who began to undress as she went to the washroom to change into a sheer nightgown.

She returned, sat on the bed, beckoned the captain to come near her and turned off the light. Her scent wafted over him, reminding him of Lara. The ship continued to sway, but it now did so to the rhythm of their bodies. Later, exhausted emotionally but relieved of tension, they found comfortable but separate positions on the bed.

The captain dozed off quickly. In a dream, shadowy soldiers appear. So does Lara, crying and then laughing as he makes love to her. A thick pigtail of yellow hair falls into his hand. He kisses her neck and murmurs, "Lara, where are you?" He woke up suddenly and looked anxiously at Catherine. She was fast asleep on the other side of the bed.

After a few hours, the ship's heaving began to rattle everything in the cabin. Everything on a table fell to the floor. Cupboard doors opened and shut. Even with all that noise, everyone could hear the loudspeaker.

"Passengers will dress warmly and proceed as quickly as possible to the main dining room. Do not take the elevators, but walk slowly down the staircases."

JEANNETTE MOSCOVITCH

Catherine and the captain dressed quickly. He kissed her and said that he had to get something in his cabin; he would meet her in the dining room. Catherine seemed surprised but did not question him. After all, it was none of her business.

In his cabin, the captain quickly took his passport and entry visa, and put them in a waterproof envelope. Then he attached the envelope to a string, so that he could wear it around his neck. Putting on a warm coat, he rushed to the staircase. It was already crowded. Passengers were trying their best to walk steadily on a wobbly, unsteady staircase. Most tried to be polite at first. Eventually, though, they found it hard to resist pushing and shoving.

In the dining room, all the tables had been removed and the chairs arranged in rows. In front of each row was a heavy rope, a makeshift banister for passengers who might slip. On both sides of each row were enormous posts to hold these ropes in place. As soon as most passengers had found chairs, an ominous silence chilled the room. But then a cheerful voice replaced the stillness.

"Ladies and gentlemen, this is Captain Johansson speaking. As you are aware by now, a hurricane formed last night. It originated in South America and is moving northward. My officers have inspected our engines and found them in perfect condition. They've inspected all stabilizers, and found these functioning properly. Even so, I've ordered a check of the lifeboats and had them lowered from their davits. And I've alerted officials in nearby countries. They inform me that helicopters are ready to come for us immediately, if necessary. These are precautionary measures. We're sailing northwest to avoid the storm's path and should be out of harm's way within a half hour. There's no immediate danger. But we must, of course, be prepared for any emergency. The pounding and splashing are caused by waves reaching the lower decks. These will subside soon. Please remain calm. Our staff will pass around Dramamine for those who feel seasick. I'll inform you every fifteen minutes of our situation. Meanwhile, I want to thank you all for cooperating."

The captain looked for an empty seat but instantly, felt an inexplicable need to find Hermann first. At their last meeting, Hermann had looked pale. He would probably be seasick by now. After walking around the dining room twice, the captain found Hermann sitting near the exit of the dining room, next to an elderly man. Hermann was helping old Imre Landau to sit securely. The captain's immediate instinct was to hug his friend, but Hermann spoke first.

"I called you several times last night and sent a message to your steward. You probably didn't get it. It was to warn you that I expected a storm. I saw petrels flying around. Maybe it's just a superstition, but I've heard that they fly ahead of storms." After pausing, he continued. "By the way, Solédad came looking for you. She was worried that you'd be seasick and wanted to give you her special remedy."

"Where's Clarice?" The captain wanted to know if she was still Hermann's friend.

"There are ten children on board, so she went to help at the nursery."

"Ah, good woman!"

"And a good companion as well."

Imre began to groan and slip off his chair. Both younger men helped him back into his seat. But the captain looked at him and thought of what a Nazi might say. This man was old and sick; society would be better off without him. Why keep him alive, a burden to himself and to others? The Nazis never euthanized anyone just for being old, but they did euthanize people for being mentally handicapped. And many Germans had protested. But the Nazis certainly hadn't invented euthanasia. In one form or another, many societies—including the universally respected ancient Greeks had practised it.

Meanwhile, Hermann's thoughts were far from euthanasia. He wanted only to revive Imre. With that in mind, he asked the captain to find the ship's doctor and get some coffee. Hermann was still helping Imre to sit in the chair, when the captain returned. Imre swallowed a few pills prescribed by the doctor, and Hermann gave him coffee, one spoonful at a time. Gradually, Imre regained his colour and even his equilibrium. Surprising himself, the captain found this very satisfying.

"I'll go now. I promised Catherine to meet her. But I'll be back soon. I'd like to stay with you until the storm is over."

He found Catherine chatting with Irene. Catherine spotted him immediately and pointed to an empty seat next to hers. As soon as he sat down, the lights went out. The ship no longer heaved; it jolted. Panic ensued. Loud screams of help, what's happening, filled the dining room in a shrill cacophony of confusing cries. The calm voice of Captain Johansson came over the microphone.

"Ladies and gentlemen, we're sailing through some very turbulent water. Our officers are trying to stabilize the ship and keep heading northwest as quickly as we can. The helicopters have arrived for anyone with a heart condition. Everyone, please, remain seated. The lights will go on as soon as possible. We'll keep you informed. We're in no great danger, so please keep calm."

They sat in silence and gloom. The captain held Catherine's hand. After a few minutes, he explained that he had to look after an ailing friend. He found his way in the dark by walking in a straight line and turning right at the last row of chairs. Hermann was standing up. With one hand, he held down Imre. With the other, he held a finely crafted Star of David, which he sometimes wore under his shirt.

"What were you murmuring just now, Hermann?"

"I was praying."

"Do you mean that you still believe in a god?"

"Yes, I think so."

"Well, he didn't do anything to stop the Nazis."

Hermann smiled. "In the concentration camps, I hear, they used to say that God had taken a leave of absence."

The captain stood still, surprised and puzzled.

"Well, we can discuss this later. If there is a later."

As the darkness deepened, so did the silence. Every few seconds, they heard waves rolling across the deck. And then the lights began to flicker a little. Everyone applauded.

"Ladies and gentlemen, this is Captain Johansson again. We're out of the storm's path now but not completely past the turbulence, which will continue for a little while longer. I'll ask you to return to your cabins, as soon as all the lights are fully functioning. Thank you for your patience."

And after a few minutes, the lights did grow brighter. A few passengers thanked God, but most attributed their safety to modern technology. And then, as expected, the captain's voice resounded:

"Our situation is normal once again. To maintain order, please go slowly to the elevators, one row at a time."

As a row of passengers left, the captain caught sight of Solédad and waved to her. Instead of joining either her or Catherine, he remained for a few minutes with Hermann and Imre. This nightmare, at any rate, was over.

Opening his cabin door, the captain found a mess. Everything had fallen on the floor. Although it was almost dawn, he put on his pyjamas and before crawling into bed, he gazed out of the porthole. The dark sea was calmer, but treacherously calm. A gray haze rippled over the ocean and a mournful darkness spread everywhere. Some turbulence still persisted, but slumber overcame him quickly. "Yes," he whispered to himself, unconsciously dreaming. "I'm Captain Yanos von Heissel, awaiting your orders. All documents are here. I will attend to everything immediately."

The ship rolled again. A heavy brush and a bottle of cologne encased in a hard metal holder fell to the floor. The clatter startled him. He got out of bed once more, picked up what had fallen, entered the washroom, glanced into the mirror and bitterly whispered, "You're a Jew, Jaakob Kesselmann. And don't you forget it. But," he added with a smile, "you're still a handsome fellow."

Before returning to bed, he gazed once more through the porthole. They sky was clearing. A pale moon floated just above the horizon. The captain paced back and forth, recalling his childhood home. Back in bed, sleep eluded him. He picked up *The Jewish Manual* which would certainly put him to sleep and began to read.

"The Jews might have been grateful to the Romans for treating them leniently after three rebellions. In the second century, though, the Jews rebelled once more.

This time, the emperor Hadrian chose a different policy. He banished them. Only a few years later, Antonius Pius allowed them to return. He admired Jews and offered them a great deal of freedom. The Sassanians, who had inherited the Persian Empire in the third century, offered Jews even more freedom. Conditions changed once more with the advent of Islam in the seventh century. Over the next century, the Muslims carved out a huge empire. The problem was that this empire included many Jews and Christians who refused to become Muslims. Christians, who had never understood Jewish resistance to Christianity, now resisted Islam with the same strength. What had been a Jewish fault in their eyes became a Christian virtue. "(6)

Drowsy at last, he slipped a bookmark into *The Jewish Manual* and fell asleep. Next day, in mid-afternoon, a knock on the door woke him up. It was the stewardess, come to tidy up his cabin. She handed him the daily bulletin, which announced a masquerade for the following night. Four participants with the most original costumes would receive prizes. The notice advised passengers to use the simplest materials available. Anything would do: hats, baskets, paper masks, bedspreads, clothes and so on.

The captain phoned Hermann immediately to ask if he wanted to participate as a team and discuss their plans over dinner. Hermann was punctual, as usual, and stood up when the captain approached. He greeted his friend in German, but the captain smiled and answered in English. When the waiter came to take their orders, the captain taunted Hermann.

"Shouldn't we at least try something German? How about *Sauerbraten?*

"Well, I would like to see how they cook it à *l'anglaise.*"

As it turned out, the meat was roasted to perfection. The waiter brought a German wine, with the compliments of Captain Johansson.

"You know something? I'm glad that we lost the War to England," Hermann joked. "At least they learned a few recipes from us."

THE EXPATRIATE

The captain remained silent. He could not show how such words of defeat stirred him.

"Now," the captain asked, "about the masquerade. Have you thought what you're going to wear?"

"As a matter of fact, Jaakob, Clarice called to let me know that she could provide us with material from the ship's stockroom. I've been thinking that I could come as Stalin and Hitler."

"And precisely how," replied the annoyed captain, "will you do that?"

"Oh, I'll just get two big pieces of cardboard. Clarice said that the stockroom is full of them. I'll cut them up into placards, so that I can hang them on my shoulders—one for the front and one for the back. But I'll dress up as Attila, the conqueror of Europe. The front placard will show Hitler with a map of Europe in the form of a globe and this caption: 'I won and lost it.' As for the back, it's going to show Stalin with a similar map and a similar caption: 'I will win and keep it.' And guess what? There's a good caricaturist on board to paint their faces. So, what are you going to do?"

"Well, Hermann, if you're going to wear placards, and if we're to be a team, then I'll do the same thing. Maybe, I'll go as Moses. I could put on a long white beard and a skull cap—and the placards could—hey, I know, the placards could show the Ten Commandments."

"Hmm. But everyone knows about Moses and the Ten Commandments. Jaakob, this has to be—"

"Yes, I know. How about this? Moses would carry not the ordinary Ten Commandments but the Ten Commandments for corporate business. Five prohibitions will be on the front and five admonitions on the back."

"That's more like it. So, what would these commandments be?"

"Well, the front placard will say:
1. Thou shalt not commit adultery with the president's wife or have sex with his secretary.
2. Thou shalt not manipulate company shares.
3. Thou shalt not disclose company secrets.
4. Thou shalt not question suspect financial statements.

5. Thou shalt not oppose questionable mergers.

The back placard will state the admonitions:

1. Thou shalt comply with the good and bad decisions made by the board of directors.
2. Thou shalt tell the press what is obviously true and what is already known.
3. Thou shalt answer telephone calls obliquely. Spies from rival companies might be listening.
4. Thou shalt maintain a well documented office for your successor.
5. Thou shalt wait for the right moment to ask for an exorbitant increase in salary."

"I like that one." Hermann smiled. "You seem to know something about corporate trends."

The captain continued, "Certainly, because I helped in my father's business before the War and he insisted that I learn everything about it, especially the way people take advantage of their positions. It's always hard to control everything in a big company. Dad sent me everywhere, London, Paris, Zürich, and I tried to learn as much as I could. I learned about shenanigans that he could never have imagined. Anyway, he knew that I'd take over the business after he retired."

"Well, Americans are the big boys now. If any American businessmen are on board, they'll be interested in your point of view. I mean, there's irony in your commandments but also truth."

Just then, as the two friends were finishing off their roast beef, Captain Johansson made a welcome announcement.

"Ladies and gentlemen. Due to the storm, it's going to take us two extra days to reach Halifax. The ship suffered minor damage, but is completely seaworthy. And the weather forecast is encouraging: seasonal temperatures but with some light rain. So, everything is back to normal. On behalf of my crew, I want to thank you all for your patience."

"Thank God, Jaakob. I couldn't have survived a repeat of last night's storm."

THE EXPATRIATE

The captain saw no need to answer because he could easily imagine himself in a calm watery grave. "By the way, Hermann, did that notice say anything about going with partners?"

"Not that I can remember. I'd ask Clarice to go with me, but she's on staff and not allowed to compete. But you're in luck Jaakob. You can ask Catherine, your latest conquest."

"Yes, but who knows if her costume would go with mine? You and I will be wearing very similar outfits, yours is a political barb and mine a corporate one."

"Yes, I see what you mean. Then I'll ask Clarice to supply both of us with cardboards, straps and paint."

Next day, preparations began right after breakfast. Most passengers, who had kept their distance from each other until now, began discussing their ideas. Late that afternoon, the stewards distributed a flyer with the event's date, time, place, and official contestants. The theatre's stage would be equipped with a special oval platform. Each contestant would march around it slowly under a spotlight. Everyone in the audience would participate, by applauding and casting a vote for the most imaginative, and ingenious costume.

Next evening, almost everyone had arrived by eight-thirty. The orchestra tried to impress its many American passengers by playing Irving Berlin's most popular songs: "God Bless America" and "Alexander's Ragtime Band," as well as songs from George Gershwin's Porgy and Bess. Many passengers hummed along with the orchestra. When the big lights went out, coloured spotlights replaced them. Each contestant walked around casually and remained standing for a few minutes before stepping behind the curtain.

Two men, dressed as Russian sailors, stood one behind the other. Each held under his outer arm one part of a long, white plank that resembled the side of a sailboat. They moved this plank back and forth to imitate the motion of a vessel at sea. On the plank, they had written in Russian letters *Voine eh Mir* (War and Peace). For good measure, they sang the "Song of the Volga Boatmen." After that, they tugged their plank back and forth a few times and made their exit.

Hermann appeared next, then the captain. Finally, a woman walked onto the stage. She wore a white sheet. Under that, she had put a stuffed cushion over her stomach to simulate pregnancy. Hanging down her back from the neck was a white placard with what she clearly knew was a familiar commercial slogan. "I visited the Chase Manhattan, the friendly bank." That brought down the house. Nonetheless, she came in second. The Volga boatmen came in first. Hermann came in third and the captain fourth. But all four won coupons to use in the ship's stores.

Solédad came over to congratulate the captain and Hermann. Her casual manner suggested disappointment that a budding relationship had ended prematurely. The captain was polite but clearly indifferent. Taking the hint, Solédad left immediately. Later, in the lobby, the captain spotted Catherine with Irene. He was about to avoid them, but Catherine called out to congratulate him.

"Your poster was very clever. I had to laugh. Listen, why don't you join us for a drink."

"Oh, thanks, I'd like to—but I think that I need to get some rest now. I'm exhausted after all this preparing and performing."

A few minutes after returning to his cabin, the captain received a letter. In the envelope was a gold-edged business card from Donald Wilmot, vice-president of Hoodoor Inc. in New York. Also enclosed was an invitation for cocktails and dinner next evening, at six-thirty.

"I want to meet someone," wrote Wilmot, "who knows so much about the shenanigans of corporate life. Please reply to stateroom 2."

The captain read this discreetly worded invitation very carefully and even admired the handwriting. He lay down on the bed and tried to read between the lines. As usual, he was suspicious. The purser had insisted on keeping most of his personal documents during the voyage, but Wilmot might have connections at sea, just as he had on land. Maybe someone on board had become suspicious of "Jaakob" and asked Wilmot to check his passport in the purser's office. But who would have asked Wilmot to do that? The Immigrant Aid Association? They'd always keep an eye on him. They had expedited his visa application, true, but obviously with misgivings. Distraught, he went to the washroom, looked into the full-length mirror and saw someone who looked uneasy. "God, who am I?" But he calmed down staring at his own reflection. "You're Jaakob Kesselmann, a Jew, that's who." He had to admit that this image looked kinder and less rigid than the original one of Captain von Heissel. Refusing Wilmot's invitation would imply that he had something to hide. In that case, Wilmot and his colleagues, whoever they were, might actually redouble their investigations. And they would certainly continue, the captain thought, until they discovered something, no matter how insignificant. He had to accept this invitation, but he would have to be on his guard at all times. This would mean remaining calm and answering all questions without hesitation. If he could not think of an answer, he could always claim to have partial amnesia. Merely repeating all this to himself buoyed his confidence.

Next morning at breakfast, Hermann noticed that his friend looked tense. "Have you met a fellow," the captain asked "by the name of Donald Wilmot?"

"Yes, as a matter of fact, I have. He came around last night, asked me a few questions about myself and about you. Come to think of it, he also wanted to know how you spelled your name."

"He invited me to have dinner with him. Isn't that strange? Out of curiosity, I accepted."

"Why strange?"

"He's an American big wig. Probably, a wheeler dealer. Americans by and large don't hate Jews. They took in millions of Jews between the 1880s and the 1920s. By late 1930, though, things were changing. Even so, they took in some German Jews— the ones who were most likely to help them."

"Which ones?"

"Well, Einstein was one of them. He helped to develop the atom bomb." The captain remained pensive throughout breakfast. That evening, he dressed as usual with great care and appeared punctually at six-thirty. Table 3 was set for two. Donald Wilmot arrived late, at six-thirty five. He wore a plastic smile, which resembled Sunny Jim, the orange juice advertisement. He was well dressed in a gray suit, white silk shirt, sapphire cuff links and tie-tack.

"I'm Donald Wilmot, but please call me Don."

The captain smiled, thinking that this informality was typical American blarney.

"Let's have a *Schnapps*. Isn't that what you Germans say?"

"A martini for me," the captain replied.

Waiting to be served, Don began to explain the purpose of his invitation.

"Here's what this is about, Jaakob. I'm the vice-president of a big company, among the biggest in the world. We're on the New York Stock Exchange and have a very high financial rating. But I'll bet you're wondering what our name means. "Hoodoor" means hoods and doors. We manufacture them for many car companies. And by "we," I mean thirty thousand workers all over the world. In fact, we're expanding."

The captain could not guess why Don was telling him all this. He attributed it to the fact, that as he understood it, Americans were all braggarts. Still sipping his drink, Don scrutinized the captain and continued.

"We've got twenty-four vice-presidents as well as a headhunter."

The captain stopped drinking when he heard an English word that made no sense to him.

"What's a headhunter?"

"Oh, yes, of course," Don replied, "Well, a headhunter searches for intelligent and experienced administrators—heads— for his company. And I, Jaakob, I am one of them. That's my job at Hoodoor. I'm a headhunter. But I'll get to the point. I was intrigued by your poster in the masquerade. Satire is good. It shows that you have insight into corporate life. I'm looking for clever heads. In short, I can offer you $200,000 with special benefits. Also regular increases and a pension, offices in New York and Detroit, a pool of stenographers, a limo at your disposal and—what else?—oh yes, a paid entertainment account."

The captain listened without replying. Was this a ruse to reveal his credentials? Besides, what if Don required his curriculum vitae? From Don's point of view, everything looked somewhat different. He was observant enough to realize, not only that this man was worried about something, but also that he would never reveal what it was. Don suspected that it would be the prospect of working with people who were hostile to Jews and Negroes.

"I think," said Don, "that you'll find our staff very congenial. We have some Jews at the very top, you know. As a matter of fact, some of them are German Jews."

The captain took out his muslin handkerchief and swept it over his forehead. Anxiety always made him sweat. Before he could find a reasonable answer, dinner arrived. Eating gave him time to think.

"You know," the captain said eventually, "we now have people like you in Germany. We have to rebuild the country, after all, and lots of money is flowing in. Business is very brisk. But usually, we find people through ads in newspapers or through employment agencies. The advantage is that we can check everyone's credentials."

"Of, course," Don answered, putting down his knife and fork. "We go through all those procedures once we know that someone is interested in working for us. But ultimately, we rely on the intuition of an experienced headhunter. So, if you're interested to work for us, we'll give you a two-month initiation period. You'll learn all about the Hoodoor team spirit and the way we run things." He paused. "So what do you say, Jaakob. Are you interested?"

"No, not really. Sorry, Don. I'm off to South America. I'll look around for opportunities down there."

"What kind of opportunities?"

"To tell the truth, I haven't thought that far in advance. I don't know yet. Probably in manufacturing."

"Tell me, Jaakob, what did you do in Germany before the War?"

Ah! The captain hesitated. If he said that his parents had owned a big paper mill, he'd have to mention its name. And if he did that, Don might trace it. Anything suspicious or even unusual, no matter how slight, could encourage Don to investigate. It seemed best to combine the truth with exaggeration by answering that the Kesselmanns had owned a stationery store. No, several of them.

"My parents owned stationery stores, but we were planning to manufacture our own paper products."

Don looked pensively at the captain. "And how big was this operation?"

"Well," the captain replied, "you Americans would call it a small cap business."

"What was the name?"

The captain was almost caught, but he had an answer. "Each store had a name to represent its location. It would be too tedious to name each one. Anyway, they were all destroyed during the War. We lost everything."

"But aren't you worried about starting your own business in a foreign country? I mean, every country has its own rules."

"Yes, but if you have business experience, it serves you anywhere. Of course, every country has its own way of controlling business and commerce. But most important is to make good products and market them effectively. Thanks, anyway, for your offer, Don. May I have another one of your business cards?"

The conversation was over. Don knew very well when to stop. This German Jew, he realized was very much on the ball and was very sure of himself. Besides he probably knew that he'd have to work very hard for such a high salary.

"Well, then," said Don, "that's that. If you decide to reconsider, though, just let me know. I'd give you a year to see if things work out."

Don asked the waiter to add one more place for his wife. Irma Wilmot was tall, blond, about forty years old, glamorous and aristocratic, friendly and not at all pretentious. Her black chiffon gown had a sequined bodice and long flowing sleeves. She wore a diamond and ruby necklace with matching earrings and an eight-carat diamond solitaire on her third finger. Born and brought up in Virginia, she spoke with a Southern drawl. Don ordered a special liqueur and the three began to discuss American movies.

In the captain's opinion, Italian movies were more interesting than American ones. He was thinking of an article that he had just read about "neo-realists" such as Roberto Rosselini, who had caused a sensation one year earlier with *Rome: Open City*. Of course, he said nothing like that to these Americans. But if Irma said she liked a movie, then he agreed. Why contradict a beautiful woman, even if she might be wrong? The conversation dragged on aimlessly. After a little while, the captain excused himself on the pretext of having to send an urgent message to his colleague. He said this so earnestly that Don believed him.

Slowly, he made his way to the deck. The ocean was dark and calm, stretching out to what seemed like infinity. At the far end of the horizon, a huge orange gold globe sat watching on her watery nest. A fresh breeze brushed his face. But he could see no one and hear nothing except for the incessant swish of the waves. He walked nearer to the rail, steadied himself and shut his eyes. A moment later, he opened them and looked over the rail. If he jumped, he would fall not into the sea but onto the lowest deck. His body would lie there, his limbs stretched out and his blood spattered everywhere. A gruesome mess! Shutting his eyes again, the captain invoked someone, anyone, who might save him from madness. But as usual, he soon came to his senses.

Thinking about death, was a waste of time. But death made him think of the War. Why had he obeyed orders to send innocent people to deaths for which all Germans were now paying the price? This had been a just war, he believed. To win it, he and many others had had to obey orders. Only a traitor would have undermined the War effort by not doing so. And yet he was now paying a heavy price for his loyalty. The future was another matter. He found it exciting to think of starting a new business, a new life, in a foreign country. In fact, he began to whistle. Just then, he heard cheerful voices calling his name. Hermann and Clarice were holding hands and walking toward him.

"We were just taking a stroll before bedtime," said Hermann. "Hope your dinner with Wilmot turned out well."

The captain snapped out of his reverie. "I'll tell you all about it tomorrow at breakfast. Right now, though, I'll leave you two lovebirds alone. See you tomorrow."

Back in his cabin, the captain drank a cognac then settled into his comfortable bed. Feeling calmer and mellow, sleep came quickly. He woke up late next morning, but Hermann had waited for him. "*Guten Morgen*. I gather that you overslept."

"*Ja*," the captain replied, "but thanks for waiting."

Hermann couldn't wait to tell him the news. "You know what? We're going to land in three days."

"So soon! Now, Hermann, are you going to marry Clarice?"

"No, Jaakob, I can't." And he began to smile.

"Why not?"

"It's hard to explain, but I'll try for you. It would deprive my mother and sisters of their profession. They're matchmakers. You see, since I started university—that was about twenty years ago—they've been looking for eligible girls for me to marry, and they're still trying. If I suddenly got married, well, think how it would disrupt their way of life. They'd be out of work."

"But why didn't you get married years ago?"

"I had always planned to join my father's business, manufacturing medical instruments, but I had to study medicine. So I could hardly consider marriage and university at the same time. Well, I studied medicine for several years but hated every minute. You know—cutting people open and things of that kind. So I switched to accounting and got my diploma three years later. I did sow a few wild oats during my university years. Then my father suggested that I forget about how doctors use medical instruments and consider them nothing more than utensils like any others. 'It's just another business,' he explained, 'and you like business.' My father was right about one thing. I do like doing business, especially in foreign countries. Canada is a stable country. It has plenty of room for everyone and its immigration policy favours entrepreneurs. That's why I'm going to Canada. But what about you? Where are you going to settle?"

"I'm not quite sure yet, Hermann. I want easy access to particular kinds of wood for paper. That would save the cost of transportation. I'd like to try Argentina, because it's a modern country and near Brazil—which is where the wood comes from."

The captain realized immediately that he had made another mistake. Hermann might ask about his choice of Argentina instead of Brazil, the source of wood. He had chosen Argentina because it openly welcomed both German War criminals and skilled Jews with capital. How could he discuss that with Hermann? But Hermann never asked about Brazil.

While the two friends were chatting about their last evening at sea, Don and Irma Wilmot were discussing something quite different. Irma was very sensitive to Don's changing moods. After last night's futile attempts at lovemaking, Don had wondered if he was losing his masculinity. Worse, he had blamed it on her. But at breakfast, Irma had looked as attractive as ever. She understood that he was simply refusing to accept the fact of growing old and slowing down. Some people could admit this, but not Don. He saw himself as an ambitious businessman, someone who would surely never lose his vigour. Irma was realistic. She accepted the facts of life and thought it best to focus on more urgent problems.

"Did you make any headway with those two German Jews?"

"Those two German Jews! What specimens! I couldn't budge them."

"Well," said Irma, "aren't you going to try again?"

"No, it's no use. I know when the game is up."

"Do you really? Here's a trick question, Don. What's the difference between a canoe and a Jew?"

"How the hell should I know?"

"Well, a canoe always tips."

"Says who? Those two Yids do tip, Irma, and believe me they tip handsomely. Besides they're Gerrys."

"What do you mean?"

"They're Germans and quite sophisticated ones. Yesterday I spoke to Kesselmann's friend, Hermann Baumbach. Handsome fellow. Very smooth, too. And he knows about business. He's trained, organized and speaks English well. He's just the kind of man we're looking for. But no dice, Irma. He's on his way to Calgary. I can't budge either one of them."

"Never mind, honey. The world is big. You'll find plenty of others."

That very morning Solédad called Clarice to join her for a leisurely breakfast together. The two women had confided in each other for many years, sometimes irritating each other but remaining friends. Clarice buttered her corn muffin and came straight to the point

"You know, Solédad, Jaakob really likes you. If only Andreev hadn't scared him off."

As for Hermann, Clarice was unsure of him. He had given her a lame excuse about urgent business instead of joining her for the night. Suddenly, he had turned into an ordinary passenger.

"Well, Solédad," Clarice whispered affectionately, "it was nice while it lasted. And now, it's over. So long! Nice knowing you! We were carried away by a couple of handsome Jews. Who knows what's going on with them? I mean, we don't even know if they really are bachelors. Maybe they've got wives and children at home."

Solédad's eyes began to fill with tears. "I don't care about all that. All I know is that we loved each other. If only he'd come back."

"Well, you're on the wrong track, *amiga*. (friend). You and I have to chalk up these affairs to experience. Shipboard romances last as long as the voyages. It's fate."

"You're right, Clarice. You're always right. There's nothing we can do. Nothing at all."

"Oh, yes we can," Clarice smiled. "I'm about to find solace in scrambled eggs and fried onions."

"*Olé*, Clarice. You're beginning to like good Spanish cooking instead of your tasteless English food, especially those muffinosos"

Both laughed, because Solédad liked to add Spanish endings to English words.

A different mood prevailed at the captain's table. He and Hermann were feeling very depressed.

"You know, Jaakob, I feel guilty about Clarice. I hate to leave her with just a cold good-bye. Last night I began the dénouement. My 'goodnight' was lukewarm."

"I know what you mean, Hermann." The captain had more pressing problems to think about, but he continued cautiously.

THE EXPATRIATE

"I was perfectly straight forward. Solédad enjoyed our affair as much as I did. I promised her nothing. She knew what she was getting into."

"Yes, but Jaakob, we sort of used them. And now we're going to leave them flat. I don't know what to do, but we should do something. The proper thing, if there is a proper thing in these situations, might be to give them some mementos."

"When we began this trip, Hermann, I called you a genius. You've proved it again. But if you're so smart, you'll know what to buy them. You do, don't you?"

"Something not too intimate. How about those little hand-carved coral brooches? They're not very expensive here, because no duty is added."

"Hermann, you're terrific. Let's go to the store quickly, because it's going to close before we enter the port."

"And let's have the gifts wrapped nicely. We'll attach cards that say something like 'You made my trip very pleasant' or 'In appreciation' or 'With best wishes' or something like that. Then the store could deliver the packages to their table. Without being invited, I doubt if they'd come to ours."

On their way out after breakfast, the two men passed Don and Irma. They waved but hurried on.

"You know Don, those two Jews are like brothers."

Don snarled. All he cared about was losing his grip on business.

When the captain and Hermann entered the shop, the saleswomen exchanged knowing glances. The reappearance of these two proved not only that their girl friends had been pleased with their previous gifts but also that the men had been satisfied with services rendered. Only satisfied customers returned.

"We'd like to see your collection of brooches," Hermann said. "Those small ones over there."

He picked a linen colored one, intricately carved, for Clarice. The captain chose a watermelon one for Solédad and a lilac one for Catherine. Both men filled out cards, "Thanks for making our trip very pleasant," and left instructions about how and where to deliver them. The saleswomen smiled with satisfaction, because they now knew the women who were going to receive these gifts.

But the captain seemed troubled. "What's the matter with you," Hermann whispered while leaving the store, "depressed about leaving your girlfriends?"

"You know why, Hermann. I'm sad about leaving you, not the girls."

Hermann looked rather puzzled. "You sound as if this were the end. We can write to each other. We can visit each other. We can meet at business conferences. So, cheer up."

But Hermann stopped. The captain's pale face frightened him. And why was he wiping his forehead in this breezy weather?

Hermann's words had deepened the captain's isolation. It would be dangerous for him to communicate with Hermann. If only he could bare his soul even to one person. Hermann was somehow like a brother. If he confessed, Hermann might react with compassion. Or he might not. He might feel betrayed. He might even contact the police. But this moment, like all the others, passed. Slowly, he regained his usual good humour.

"Hermann, I sort of envy you. You know where you're going to live. You know that your risks are negligible. You have ties with your family in Palestine. I know where I'm going to live, but I also know that I'm taking a huge risk. Well, I'll just have to cross that bridge when I come to it."

"I can't give you my address yet, because I don't have one, but I can give you the name of my company: Baumbach & Sons, Medical Instruments. I will probably be listed as soon as I find a place to live in the city of Calgary. You can send me your address as soon as you get settled."

The captain said nothing at first. He knew that writing to anyone from the *Vaterland* would be risky.

"Sure," he finally answered. "Now listen, Hermann, how can I find out which documents I'll need to get off this boat?"

"Can't say," replied Hermann. "But I'll find out for you." He enjoyed hunting down information.

The captain felt relieved. After living in Nazi Germany, he could imagine disembarkation only in connection with suspicious or even sinister bureaucrats. He walked slowly to his cabin and began to pack.

Every deck was crowded with silent but frantic passengers. Many carried briefcases or leather pouches filled with official papers. Deck hands pushed large carts, piled high with suitcases of all colours and sizes, to the lowest deck. And there it was. Land! A jagged shoreline was barely visible through the fog.

While packing, the captain began again to imagine the worst and to prepare alibis. Why, someone might ask, have you chosen Argentina? Why Buenos Aires in particular, which has recently seen outbreaks of anti-Semitism? Isn't it because Nazi war criminals are welcome there? Aren't you a Nazi war criminal? No, no, he would reply. I'm just going to set up a paper mill and sell the products in my own stationery stores. Most of the raw materials come from nearby countries, so I'll be able to save money on transportation. To the captain, this seemed to be a plausible explanation. As for anti-Semitism, he hated even to think about that. He certainly had no answer. And what about his family background? What about names that anyone could trace? Despite his worries, time passed quickly. His hands moved deftly, folding and arranging clothes in suitcases. Soon enough, it was time for lunch.

Hermann had arrived early and ordered an expensive German wine. The captain poured and toasted their health. While drinking, he realized again that Hermann was unlike the stereotypical Jews that he had been led to believe. Hermann was sophisticated. Moreover, he was German. Very German! In fact, he was nicer than most Germans.

"Great wine, Hermann. I haven't had this in years."

Hermann wasted no time and got right down to business. "You need to get your luggage stamped with 'in transit' along with the name of your final destination. Canadian customs won't inspect your bags. Argentine customs will, of course, when you get there. You can buy your plane ticket right here. There is a choice of three airlines. They've set up desks on B deck. Any airline you choose will pick up your bags and stow them on the plane, out of your reach until custom officials have inspected them in Argentina. Oh, and you'll have to declare any valuables or gifts. If you can't get a flight immediately, you'll have to wait for another one in Halifax. So be sure to take one small bag for an overnight stay. As for me, I'm staying in Canada, but I'll be among the first to get off so that I can catch the four o'clock to Calgary."

The captain sat still for a few moments. As usual, he had overreacted. These were all routines. Since he had no valuables to declare and no contraband to hide, he felt more at ease.

"Hermann, I sincerely thank you. You've saved me time and eased my mind. I suppose you managed to ask competent officials, people who really *know* the procedure?"

Hermann put down his drink. "Well, not quite. This is a bureaucratic age. It takes several people to answer every question. And then you have to decide who gave you the right answer. As soon as we finish lunch, I'll say *'auf wiedersehen'* till tonight. I've got to finish my own packing."

"Before you leave Hermann, I'd like to know what you expect from the ladies?"

"I'd like to avoid any personal confrontation, although I expect some form of acknowledgement for my gift. These are women of the world, Jaakob. They know what shipboard romances are: affairs that last from embarkation to disembarkation."

"Well, then, never mind the women. I'll miss you, Hermann. Somehow, I've come to think of you as the brother I should have had."

"Same here, Jaakob. I would have preferred a brother and a sister instead of two sisters. That would have diminished the company of matchmakers."

Both laughed and felt their eyes moisten. "I wish we could have met back home," the captain remarked casually, "and become close friends."

"Oh, never mind 'back home.' We're going to make new homes. Argentina has a lot of Jewish refugees, I hear, although it has a lot of Nazi war criminals as well. I've also heard over the grapevine that someone has established a kind of secret service to hunt down all those Nazis. I'm sure you'll help if you can."

THE EXPATRIATE

The captain was well aware of the haven that Argentina provided for Nazi refugees, but he had not heard of this secret agency.

Their final evening at sea was very festive. The orchestra added a few musicians and played nostalgic songs from several countries. The dance floor was extended. Floating from the ceiling were balloons and spotlights, which projected coloured streaks across the ceiling and walls. Every table had a vase of fresh flowers. The entertainment committee knew that passengers always feel sad on their last night at sea and hoped that a lively atmosphere and music would cheer them up.

As usual, Hermann was early for dinner. When the captain arrived, they toasted each other in German. They hardly heard each other because of all the chattering and the music. The two men embraced and sat down to eat without being able to say anything more. Hermann thought that it would be impossible to meet tomorrow due to the line ups. After relaxing over cognac, they embraced once more and made vague promises to stay in touch. Each rushed to his cabin, finished packing and resolved to be the first in line for disembarkation.

When the captain entered his cabin, he found a blue envelope on the floor.

> *"Querido amigo. I'll never forget you. Thanks for your thoughtful gifts. I'll always treasure them. If you come to Madrid you'll find my name in the phone directory. I plan to open a school for dancing, the Escuela Solédad Perez. In the summertime I plan to dance and sing on ships. Buena suerte, wherever you will be. Solédad."*

He read it carefully, wishing that he could have spent more happy nights with her. He finished packing, lay down and fell asleep almost immediately.

When Hermann reached his cabin, he found a note from Clarice. She asked him to get in touch with her. Later on, he telephoned, hoping she wouldn't be in her cabin. As it happened, she answered.

"Oh, thanks so much for that brooch. It's beautiful. Hermann, did you know that we're going to stay in port for several days?

I'll have nothing to do on board, so I'd like to see something of Canada. If you like—well, why don't you join me? We could—"

Hermann was stunned. Why prolong the agony of parting?

"Well, Clarice that does sound interesting. But I've bought a ticket for Calgary. I brought samples with me, but two other cases of instruments will arrive one day after I reach Calgary. I really have to pay duty on them and fill out declarations, otherwise they'll be returned to Europe. I can't change my schedule now. But I do regret not having had more time with you."

Clarice's voice changed in tone. "I thought that we'd have a lovely time together. And I can't reach you in Calgary because, well, I don't even know your address."

"Oh, that's easy. The name would be Baumbach & Son, Medical Instruments. As soon as I set up my business, it will be listed in the phone book."

Hermann did not ask for her address. Clarice became aware of that immediately. "Well," she said after an awkward moment, "thanks again for your gifts. If your family plans to cross the Atlantic, do book with our line. We offer discounts for those who sail with us more than once."

And then she hung up, not waiting for him to wish her well. Hermann had experienced farewells of this kind several times. He always felt uncomfortable and a little guilty. After sending a telegram to his parents, he began to pack. But his thoughts returned to Jaakob Kesselmann. What a great guy, he thought. Jaakob is smart, nice-looking, educated and yet there is something *goyish* about him. Maybe his education has alienated him from our Jewish roots.

But Hermann had already begun to focus on his new beginning in Canada and imagined himself as a great industrialist in this underdeveloped country. As a subscriber to several Canadian magazines, he knew that Canadians needed professionalism in manufacturing and new ideas in marketing. The population was small, so the domestic market was limited. A big business would have to sell its products in the United States. The market there was big but the competition fierce. Maybe Jaakob had made the right choice. Manufacturing and industry in South America was beginning to expand. High quality instruments would be in great demand there.

Planning his business, daydreaming of success, packing his clothes, organizing his documents, all of these activities energized Hermann but also exhausted him. He fell asleep quickly.

Next morning, according to schedule, Hermann was first in line at the immigration office in the lobby. Officers came on board and cheerfully welcomed passengers to Canada. After a brief check of his passport and bags, they declared that everything was in order and told him to confirm his ticket for Calgary. He did that quickly, which left him enough time to reach the airport and catch his flight. Just as he was leaving, he saw the captain. The two men waved to each other. The captain had just enough time to ask one question.

"*So schnell mit dem Protokol?* (So quick with the protocol?)

"*Viele Gluck.*" (Much luck) replied Hermann while rushing out.

This was it, the captain's moment of truth. A Canadian officer asked for his passport and then disappeared. In no time, he returned the passport.

"Everything is in order, Mr. Kesselmann. Please go upstairs to buy your ticket. If you can't get on a flight today, you'll have to remain overnight in Halifax. Just let us know where you'll be staying."

The captain sighed with relief.

He had already read sketchy descriptions of Canada in travel brochures. These emphasized Canadian courtesy. And so it was, as he soon discovered at the Lord Wilson Hotel in Halifax. Settled in his room, he asked a clerk about important sites to see for a tourist with little time. The clerk suggested a stroll on the "skywalk," which connected the hotel with a big department store.

"What's a skywalk?"

"Oh, it's a bridge with a ceiling and walls of glass. It's suspended in the air, you see, way above the street level. Walking through it is just like walking in the sky."

After the skywalk, which did lead to the department store, he passed through a doorway marked "Exit" and found himself on a wide commercial boulevard. At one end was a small park. Set incongruously in the midst of that park was the public library. Its façade resembled a stage set for *Hansel and Gretel*. The ground floor was architecturally impressive but somewhat shabby.

"I'm not from around here," he told the clerk at the reception desk. "May I enter the stacks and look around?"

"Yes, of course. But only members may take books out of the library."

"Do you by any chance have a few German books?"

"Yes, sir. We keep German books that are on reading lists at our universities. We have the complete works of Goethe, Hesse and Mann."

"Well, then, you have the best ones. Do many people still show an interest in these classics despite, you know, anti-German sentiments?"

"Oh, yes. People want to understand the Germans, and why they were so senselessly cruel. Maybe their greatest authors can give us some clues based on knowledge of their own people."

The captain thanked her and walked out.

At dusk, the streets lights went on. Stores were closing. It was drizzling lightly. The captain returned to his hotel. Sitting in his gloomy room, he ordered a cocktail from the hotel's restaurant and opened *The Jewish Manual* to wile away the time. He noticed it had an addendum. Disregarding the bookmark, he turned to it for the origin and meaning of the swastika and the Nazi slogan "pure Aryan." He should have investigated their origins long ago.

The swastika is a very ancient symbol. No one knows its precise origin. Archaeologists have found swastikas not only in the Old World but also in the New. It is a common artistic motif among Hindus and Buddhists. The symbol appears to "move" clockwise or counter-clockwise, moreover, which might be why the Indians have used it to symbolize the cycle of existence: birth, death, and rebirth. The Nazis adopted it for at least two reasons. They realized that it was very simple yet visually striking. They also realized that no other religion had used it as its central symbol. National Socialism was, in effect, a new religion. Archaeologists had found swastikas in Germany and Greece (among other places). As a result, the Nazis claimed that Germans were directly related to the prestigious ancient Greeks. They ignored the fact that many "primitive" peoples had also used the swastika."

"The Nazis never claimed to have invented the swastika but were merely reviving an ancient symbol on behalf of all Aryans, by which they meant only northern and western Europeans who had not intermarried with other races. Why did the Nazis believe in their racial superiority, a theory that has no scientific legitimacy? They were racist for reasons of their own. They rose to power because of the peculiar conditions in Germany after World War I and drew on racist theories that were already prevalent throughout Europe. Before 1933, the German Jews had good reasons for looking at their history in Germany as one of continuous progress since the eighteenth century. They had indeed become thoroughly integrated into German society. No one, neither Jew nor gentile, could have foreseen what would happen if the state collapsed and social order disintegrated and the criminals took over, because of conditions that were unprecedented in modern times. The rise of Nazism in Germany was anything but inevitable."

Exhausted, the captain dropped *The Jewish Manual*. An ocean breeze seeped through the damp walls of his hotel room. He looked out the window and saw nothing but blackness. It was time for bed, because his flight would leave early next morning. He fell asleep thinking not about fate but about sunny Buenos Aires and freedom.

CANADA

Hermann gazed through the airplane's window, squinted at the jagged streaks of vivid sunshine and pulled down the window shade. Reclining, he began to dream of a cozy future: a home, a family of his own and a profitable business. For all he cared, the outside world with its many problems could glide to its own destruction. Just then, a passenger sat down beside him and introduced himself as Stavros Givakis. Was this trip for business or pleasure he asked his fellow traveler. Hermann replied that he planned to establish a manufacturing plant in Calgary. Mr. Givakis then explained that the Canadian government encouraged immigrants, especially those who planned to establish new enterprises that would create jobs. As for labour, Hermann would have no problem; in Canada, workers were plentiful, except in highly specialized fields. Canadian unions were strong, and respected. Alberta, in particular, was a good place to settle. Its oil fields had made it quite rich. " You've chosen well to settle in Alberta."

Just then, the stewardess came around to ask what each passenger wanted for lunch.

"What," Hermann asked, "is the national specialty?"

"Well, sir, in Quebec, it's pork and beans. On the coasts, of course, it would be some kind of seafood. Our lakes supply a lot of fish. "You're going to Calgary and that's where people really like their beef. They're famous for it."

But Hermann ordered the fish dinner, and in no time, the stewardess gave him a little white tray with a small piece of salmon, boiled carrots, green salad, a small cold bun with a tiny tub of butter and a piece of yellow cake smeared with chocolate frosting. Hermann thought the meal was tasteless, but the other passengers were eating with gusto. After lunch, the stewardess gave him a choice between coffee and tea. Hermann noticed that Stavros poured a lot of cream into his coffee.

"Well, then, how do you like Canadian cuisine?"

"Oh," Hermann replied politely, "it's rather nice."

Just to make conversation with Stavros, Hermann ventured to ask if he was Canadian and what was his business.

"I'm Greek—a Greek Canadian—no, just a Canadian who came from Greece. Anyway, I own a restaurant in Montreal. My parents came here after escaping from Salonika. They built a small restaurant in the east end. Business was good, so we opened more restaurants in Halifax and Toronto. Right now, I'm on my way to look for a site in Calgary."

Hermann never forgot what Stavros said about being Canadian and discovered that it was true. Origins really did not matter very much in this new country.

Over the loudspeaker, someone asked all passengers to fasten their seat belts. They were about to land. Passengers from foreign countries with items to declare would have to prepare their documents for the customs inspectors.

Calgary's airport seemed small and quiet to Hermann. Signs told passengers where to find their luggage: one way for citizens and the other for immigrants or visitors. An officer looked calmly at Hermann's passport, turned a few pages and stamped it.

"Welcome to Canada," he said cheerfully. "You've chosen well to come here. Please go down there, to the end of that corridor, and show the inspector your declaration form."

Chucking his luggage onto a cart, Hermann waited in line at customs.

"Please put your valises on the conveyer belt," someone ordered, "and open them for inspection."

He was about to do so, in fact, when the inspector stopped him.

"Just show me the instruments that you've declared, the ones that you're carrying."

THE EXPATRIATE

Hermann opened a neatly packed box with various compartments, each containing a few medical instruments. The inspector picked up a rather large clipper.

"I suppose this is for pulling teeth."

"Doctors use it for many purposes," Hermann laughed, "but seldom for teeth. Mostly for bones."

"How many of these tools of torture do you have in there?"

"Exactly forty-two. I sent another thirty-three by plane. They'll arrive soon."

"Do you plan to sell these?"

"Of course not. I need them for demonstrations and advertisements."

The inspector examined them again. "Please wait here until I return."

Hermann was left standing, wondering if he should have asked for a special permit to import these instruments. What an inconvenience! Bureaucratic paperwork had taken over the world! He began to worry. In twenty minutes, the inspector returned.

"Okay, sir, you may take your instruments with you. Sorry it took me so long. The airport is quite big, and the supervisor's office is way over there."

Rather taken aback, Hermann heard only the remark about the airport. Canadians, he thought, must be given to overstatement. By comparison, Amsterdam's airport was almost a city.

"I explained to the supervisor of customs," continued the inspector, "that these are samples. They're not for sale, so they're duty free. Now, take your sample case and your luggage over there to lane C. There's a taxi stand there. Welcome to our country and, good luck to you."

"Thanks," said Hermann rather surprised. This cheerful efficiency was a good omen. No one had even hinted about a tip!

Looking out of the taxi, his first impression was that Calgary was spread out and clean. The Tildon Hotel, in the center of the city, was quite large and fairly luxurious. At the registration desk, he learned that a package had arrived from Palestine. No one had detained it, although someone had opened it for inspection, closed it, and stamped it with undecipherable words. Its entry declaration was missing, but this package was obviously duty free. In the hotel room, exhausted after arranging his belongings in proper order, Hermann went straight to bed.

At breakfast the next morning, he was astonished to read in the *Calgary Daily News,* corruption in the cabinet, opposition leaders contesting the new sales tax, murders, rapes, criminal convictions, sales for shoppers, letters to the lovelorn and ads for massage parlours. Newspapers around here followed a fixed formula for their contents. One page, relegated unobtrusively to the end, was for cultural events.

The page that he needed was the classified section for apartments to rent. One of these ads caught his attention:

"Luxuriously appointed apartment in an exclusive residential district, easily accessible to transportation, schools, churches and synagogues. By appointment only."

Compared to the rentals in other ads, this one seemed expensive. What amazed him was its reference to nearby synagogues. He arranged an appointment immediately.

His next priority was to list the local hospitals that might become customers for medical instruments. Near the phone book lay a Bible, which made him wonder how many people read it without questioning not only its legends but also, after the War, its moral efficacy. But he lost no time speculating about morality and began to call prospective customers.

He was pleasantly surprised at the response. Some wanted to see him next day. Others asked him to call again. When he stated that some of the instruments still had to be made in Germany, although most were now manufactured in Palestine, it seemed of no importance to them. After arranging several appointments for the next day, he called room service to order dinner. Knowing what to expect of Canadian food, he ate mechanically.

His mind drifted back to the Atlantic crossing. Jaakob had really become his friend, it was true, but sometimes he had taken on a look that could not be fathomed. On those occasions, Jaakob seemed anxious for no obvious reason; maybe he had recalled some unhappy event. Jaakob had often wiped his forehead, moreover, with an exquisite muslin handkerchief. But this reaction, Hermann believed, seemed normal after the brutality that he had suffered and seen.

Then, the image of Clarice drifted before him. Wonderful lady! She had been reticent, never mentioning her family. If she had been married—if so, why had she never mentioned it? He had never bothered to ask. For a shipboard romance, he was not fussy. Marriage, of course, would have been another matter. For that, education, class, and religion were important matters. Well, he smiled to himself, enough of those prejudices. Jewish or not, he realized suddenly, Clarice would make a good wife. He slipped into bed and put on the radio. The station was broadcasting jazz, which Hermann disliked. He turned it off.

Next morning, he inspected the apartment that had been advertised. It was in a luxurious residential building, on a wide avenue with gardens everywhere. A rental agent greeted him at the door.

"Mr. Baumbach? I'm the agent, Joan Stewart." Without further ado, she began to show him the apartment. "This unit is furnished, as you can see. It has two bedrooms, a dining room, a living room, a very spacious kitchen—with a dinette—and two full bathrooms."

Hermann looked around and admired the style of its furnishings, a somewhat mild imitation of Louis XVI. "Can I rent it for six months instead of a year?" he asked. "And does the rent depend on the length of my lease?"

Mrs. Stewart was prepared. "The lease is for one year, $1500 a month. If that's okay with you, then I'll need to see some credentials and a cheque for one month's rent. If the landlord finds everything in order, then I'll ask you to come and sign the lease. By the way, Mr. Baumbach, there are quite a few Jewish families living around here. The synagogue is within walking distance."

"Yes, I'm a Jew, but—"

"So are the owners. It's all much simpler this way. I mean, if you were German, not German-Jewish, it would be, well, so much more complicated."

"Why do you say that?"

"Well, you see, we Canadians are very tolerant. After all, people from many countries have come here and some of them may be suspect." Hermann disregarded this remark.

"I do like this apartment, although I haven't seen any others. I'll rent it."

"Good, Mr. Baumbach. Now, may I have your credentials and your cheque? I'll contact the owner immediately and I'm sure that they'll agree to rent it to you. How about meeting tomorrow afternoon? Oh, and by the way, the owner's name is Irving Frieden. He's a lawyer."

So, all was arranged quicker than he had anticipated. Feeling pleased, Hermann left the building and took a taxi to the Calgary Public Library.

At the desk, he asked for a book about Calgary's history, architecture, culture and, above all, its economic potential. The librarian scrutinized him for a few moments.

"I don't think that I can find all of that in one book. We have a history of Calgary, which shows some architecture. And we have another one about Calgary's economic growth. But—"

"Good. I'll take both of them."

"Yes, but you must become a member of the library first."

Hermann signed up as a member, while someone went to the stacks for the books. To his amazement, the librarian asked only for his name and address. When he received his books, the librarian told him that he could keep them for two weeks. How very helpful! This, too, he decided, was a good omen.

Back at the hotel, he found a message from Mrs. Stewart. Yes, Mr. Frieden was ready to discuss the lease. He could meet Hermann, at home, tomorrow evening at eight-thirty. Hermann would need his passport, his entry visa to Canada and some bank references.

Lawyer Irving Frieden and his wife had two sons. One was teaching at a university in New York, the other was a corporation lawyer in Toronto. The Friedens were wealthy. As soon as modern bungalows were being built on their street, they bought one in the first phase of construction. This entitled them to a substantial discount for an early down payment. Moreover, they rented their furnished apartment for $1500 a month, which was considered very reasonable. But the Friedens wanted a short-term tenant, hoping that one of their sons would return to live there.

When Hermann arrived next evening, he immediately presented his credentials. Lawyer Frieden was accustomed to scrutinizing his clients. And he could not help but admire this one. Hermann was well dressed; his papers were organized, precisely annotated and filed neatly in a leather briefcase.

Hermann asked for immediate occupancy, so that he could begin his business and use the phone without delay. At Mr. Frieden's request, he presented a picture of his parents and sisters in Tel Aviv. The lawyer sat back, looking first at the pictures and then at his new tenant. His admiration grew. Hermann Baumbach spoke English well, even though it was his third language! Nevertheless, signing the lease would have to wait until he could check the documents for authenticity. He needed to know that they had been registered with immigration officials and that Hermann was a bona fide German Jew and not an imposter. He explained in layman's language the legal terms of the lease to Hermann, especially the respective responsibilities of both owner and tenant. If all went well, they could sign the lease in two days, at seven o'clock. He invited Mr. Baumbach to stay for dinner that evening. Mrs. Frieden would join them. Hermann accepted with pleasure.

As soon as Hermann left, Stella Frieden entered her husband's library and sat down facing him across his desk.

"You know, Irving, we should introduce this Hermann to Rose Waterman. You took care of her divorce, remember? And she went around telling everyone how well you handled her case. She's gorgeous but, unfortunately, she doesn't have much luck with men."

"Stella, haven't you learned anything at all from experience? Your last two introductions were disastrous."

"Oh, Irving, you remember only the mistakes. But what about the Teitelbaums and the Meyers? They're happy as larks. Anyway, Rose is different. She's got a great job, she's president of Calgary Hadassah, she runs Ort—By the way, her latest project is to merge Hadassah with Ort. That might be a good idea, don't you think?

A big organization has much more clout than a small one. You've already invited him for seven, so why not ask if he can make it a bit earlier—say, five-thirty—for cocktails?"

"Okay, okay. But this is against my better judgment. And I still need time to check his credentials. These Germans are tricky dicks. They're excellent imposters."

"Oh, Irving, you're too suspicious—even for a lawyer. I'm convinced that he's legit."

"Remember the gut feeling you had about that—that silk salesman or whatever he was, the one with the continental manners who turned out to be a smuggler. And what about that builder? The one who ran away with those down payments and his fake building plans. It took two years in court to get back even some of the money."

"All right, we all make mistakes."

"Yes, but you make them a little too often—especially—when it comes to matchmaking. Oh well, I'll invite him for cocktails at five-thirty and dinner so you can start your maneuvers. Just the same, I love you with all your *shtik* (devious tricks)."

Hermann was satisfied with his day's work. His apartment was very convenient and the Friedens were a nice middle-class couple. His parents would approve of them, even like them, particularly Irving. After all, he was a respectable lawyer. But it was time to do business, to contact hospitals for appointments to show his medical instruments. Next on the agenda was to open a bank account in the firm's name and transfer his funds from England.

Entering the Queen Bank on Ninth Avenue, he asked to see the manager. Mr. Hycroft welcomed him to Canada, and handed him a form to fill out. The manager carefully read what Hermann had written.

"I see that you're going to transfer funds from a London bank. Are these funds in marks, pounds or American dollars?"

"English pounds, Mr. Hycroft. I'd like one hundred thousand transferred immediately. When I need money for living expenses, of course, I'll convert the pounds to Canadian dollars."

THE EXPATRIATE

"Well, that sounds like good common sense. As you know, the exchange rate fluctuates daily."

"Do you need any references or supporting documents?"

"Just your signature," replied Mr. Hycroft. "Be sure to sign it exactly as you sign your cheques. And if you need cash right away, Mr. Baumbach, we can give you an advance before the transfer goes through."

Once again, Hermann was astonished at the lack of bureaucratic red tape in Canada. In most European countries, he thought, this transaction would have taken days instead of minutes.

Back at the hotel, he wrote to his father in Palestine about everything that he had done so far. Calgary, he wrote, seemed under populated; it had huge open spaces and wide streets. This city has great potential. But, he added, first impressions can be deceiving. After signing and sealing his letter, Hermann asked a hotel clerk to mail it for him by the quickest service available. Losing no time, he opened the city directory to find hospitals and drugstores that would need medical instruments. Suddenly, however, he heard a knock on the door. It was the maid.

"Sorry to bother you, sir. I was hoping that you'd be ready for me to prepare your bed."

"What do you mean by 'prepare the bed?"

"Well, I pull the bedspread down from the pillows."

"Oh, yes, of course. Please go ahead."

After preparing the bed, she placed a gold-covered chocolate on the pillow and left. Hermann looked at it with surprise and shrugged his shoulder.

"Every country, I suppose, has its own quaint customs."

Feeling mellow, he soon fell asleep—but not before regretting the absence of Clarice.

Next day, he met the purchasing agent of a Calgary hospital. His office looked like the storage room of a department store. Mr. Dickson removed some boxes from a chair for Mr. Baumbach to sit down. Hermann asked which instruments the hospital needed urgently. Before answering, Mr. Dickson told his secretary to bring in his inventory list. Studying it carefully, he noticed a shortage of medium-size shears and special steel cutters.

"Every year, many people fall on the icy sidewalks. Our orthopedic department is extremely busy in the winter. That's why we need cutting instruments."

Hermann immediately displayed a red velvet box that held cutting instruments for plaster, nails, bones and teeth.

"How expensive are these?"

"Probably more expensive than the ones that I see lying on your desk. Yours were probably made in India. They're made of a cheaper kind of steel, which bends, blunts or even breaks more easily than ours. We use the best steel and work with the finest machinery. Should I quote our prices in Canadian or American dollars?"

Mr. Dickson shook his head sadly. These prices were twenty percent higher than those of his current supplier. But he said he might be able to justify the higher price if their supplies were not available and needed urgently.

Hermann secretly resented this attitude. Quality was always more important, he believed, than cost and convenience.

"We plan to establish a factory here, and keep most items in stock. Of course, you have to pay a higher price for a better product. In the long run, our instruments will be cheaper, too, because of their durability. So, if you need a few items immediately, we can ship them by air from Tel Aviv to Halifax and then by train to Calgary."

"I'll give a small sample order first to test these instruments before committing myself to a large quantity." Looking at Hermann's list, he continued, "Let's say, oh, a dozen of these 1280s. Send them C.O.D."

Hermann rushed back to the hotel and sent off his first Canadian order. Just then, a message arrived from Mr. Frieden. The lease was ready. The appointment, however, was to be changed to five-thirty instead of seven. Hermann called Mr. Frieden to accept the invitation and then continued to work. He had to hire an agent, quickly, find an office and a large area to build a factory.

Equally important would be finding Canadian machinery. Close to midnight, after a very tiring day, he went to bed.

Meanwhile, Stella Frieden began to make her plans. This was a good time to cultivate a closer friendship with Rose. After resigning from Hadassah, Rose had recommended several women to succeed her as president and even a few to become vice-presidents. Stella was very eager to become a vice-president. The work would be easy, because she'd have a staff to help her. Stella was confident that no one would refuse a recommendation from the former president, especially Rose Waterman.

Rose had a master's degree in sociology and was highly respected for her experience and competence. But on account of her divorce, and being childless, Rose felt a need to "find herself." And the first step in that direction, she believed, was a new career. Fortunately, in addition to doing social work in the Jewish community, she was executive secretary to the president of Alberta's largest investment corporation. To become a broker, all she needed was technical education in business administration and finance. Her personal appearance, moreover, would be an asset. Rose was an attractive woman, of average height, slim, blond, with a fresh-looking complexion and always dressed elegantly. She impressed most who met her as being smart and successful financially. For business purposes, she wore suits and carried a fine black leather briefcase. As for her apartment, it was a luxurious two-bedroom unit. And she could afford it. Why she had married Sam Waterman, a shoe salesman, remained a mystery to most who knew her. They assumed that she had fallen for his extraordinary good looks. He was undeniably a very handsome and sexy man, but an unassuming milk toast. No one could figure out how a man of this kind could ever have become a salesman. Above all, Rose now wanted a new life, and she was very ambitious. In fact, she actually convinced Hadassah to organize a dinner in her honour, to advertise her competency, and as usual, she used this event to raise money for the organization. This would be a valuable addition to her curriculum vitae.

As Irving had done a splendid job for Rose's divorce settlement, particularly in the division of assets, Stella felt free to ask Rose for the vice-presidential nomination. And introducing

Rose to Hermann would support Stella's request. With all this in mind, she called Rose and mentioned that Irving's client, a rich German industrialist, had rented their previous apartment; she asked if Rose would like to meet him over dinner on the following day.

Rose hesitated. Did she really want a German industrialist? She imagined him as a middle-aged, bull-necked and generally a bulky man of average height. He would be wearing thick glasses, and speak with a heavy accent. Worse, he would be arrogant. On the other hand, at the moment there were no men on her horizon. She accepted Stella's invitation, but not without some misgiving.

"Why, of course, I'm free tomorrow evening and will be delighted to come. If you need any help I can come early." Stella thanked her but said their maid would attend to everything.

Stella immediately began the preparations—a special menu, set the table with embroidered place mats and the antique Imari chinaware. She wanted to impress Rose with her savoir-faire, which she would need as vice-president to entertain foreign dignitaries. But if Rose and Hermann failed to attract each other, she could always try again with another of Irving's clients.

Stella was a typical woman of her generation and milieu. She believed that women were the family's homemakers and men its providers and protectors. Few women felt any need to start all over again in mid-life. Some did rebel, though, and Stella's friend, Rose was one of them.

Rose put down the phone and smiled. She knew that Stella wanted the nomination for vice-president. But this invitation came as a surprise. Maybe Stella was not so scatterbrained after all. In any case, she may have finally understood that social life was problematic for some divorced women. Their best friends might desert them, for instance, out of loyalty to their former husbands. And it was not so easy to find new friends at this age. It seemed to Rose that people were always inviting divorced men to parties but not divorced women. Rose told her friends that she wasn't much interested in sex, but secretly she was. Could Stella have discerned that? Sex was one thing, of course, and love another thing. Now Rose wondered if she had ever known what "love" meant. She earned a substantial salary and was financially secure.

THE EXPATRIATE

It was her husband who had had to lower his standard of living after their divorce. But Stella would know all about this, since her husband had handled the divorce settlement. Yes, Rose would consider nominating Stella.

Late in the afternoon, a dozen roses arrived for Stella from Hermann. An attached note, simply stated: "Thanks for inviting me. I look forward with pleasure to this evening." When Hermann arrived, Stella greeted him warmly and apologized that Irving would be a little late—urgent last minute business at the office. The maid brought in a tray of tiny egg rolls with plum sauce. Hermann looked at the plate suspiciously.

"These," explained Stella, "originated in China. They're filled with vegetables. Just dip them in the plum sauce. Now, how about a martini?"

"Yes, I'd like one. Do you know that the martini is more popular in Canada than any other cocktail? I just read it in a book that I borrowed from the library."

"You could be right," Stella replied with a smile, "because I don't know the statistics."

Hermann had expected to find Irving there. He just wanted to sign the lease, make inconsequential small talk over dinner and then leave. When Rose arrived, he was taken aback. In walked an attractive blond lady whose hair did not disguise the fact that previously it had been another colour. Those tanzanite blue eyes might even be the effect of coloured contact lenses. Impeccably dressed in a deep blue silk suit, accessorized with pearl earrings, necklace and bracelet, she stretched out her pearl ringed hand to greet him. Rose in turn, stunned by this fashionably dressed, handsome German, so completely the opposite of her preconceived image, was rendered almost speechless, could barely say, "I'm delighted to meet you. Stella tells me that you've chosen to set up your business here in Calgary. You've made a wise choice."

Before she could continue, Irving walked in. "I'll join you for one cocktail," he said apologetically, "and then Hermann and I will leave you ladies alone. We have some business to discuss."

After a few minutes, the two men entered Irving's home office. It was lined with bookcases and in the centre stood an elaborately carved desk. Irving handed the lease to Hermann, who read every word carefully. Most important to him was the duration: one year with an option for two more years. That will do, thought Hermann as he signed. Both men returned to the dining room where a delicious bouquet of freshly cooked vegetable soup whetted their appetites. Stella wanted to compliment Rose as much as the occasion permitted and coyly boasted.

"I'm so grateful to you, Rose, for giving me this recipe."

Stella was pushing too hard. "Well," said Rose with a trace of irritation, "I'm glad that you like it—but I won't give you another one unless you promise not to advertise it so publicly."

Hermann smiled to himself. Those wily women!

Rose wanted to show an interest in Hermann's business and was astute enough to ask pertinent questions. "What is the nature of your business, manufacturing or distribution of products?"

"As you may have heard, my business isn't exactly glamorous. Medical instruments—some people would say that I manufacture instruments of torture."

"Au contraire," purred Rose. "I'd call them medical healing aids."

"Well, that's another way of putting it," he replied, resting his knife and fork on the plate. "And you're the first person to put it that way."

Hermann did not ask Rose about her family or even if she owned a business. That would have led to personal disclosures, which he wanted to avoid. In fact, he wanted to avoid all personal entanglements.

Rose sensed his reluctance immediately and began to think of subtle ways to change his mind. She could drive him back to the hotel and offer help to move into his new apartment. And if that plan failed, she could invite him later on to a party on the pretext that it would be useful for him to meet important Calgarians.

With Rose cautiously silent, Irving continued the conversation. He mentioned various legal services that Hermann might need, which raised some questions. Was Hermann's business registered in his own name or his father's? How had he arranged to transfer his capital? Did he need to establish a credit rating? Hermann responded slowly. He was not certain that he wanted to hire Irving as his legal advisor, and thought that this landlord should have waited before trying to get his business.

"I'll have to contact my father and his lawyers about all these issues and wait for their instructions."

This ruse would give him time to meet other lawyers and possibly to find someone directly connected with the provincial administration. Yes, that would be a major advantage.

Rose listened politely, but her thoughts were not about business. Was this, she wondered, love at first sight? What was so attractive about this man? He was handsome, charming and sophisticated. But she had resolved not to be swept away for any of those reasons.

After dessert, Hermann excused himself. He planned to move the next day and asked if anyone knew of someone to help him. Stella suggested that her maid might be willing to help. Just before a casual farewell, though, Rose intervened.

"I have my car parked outside, Mr.—I mean, Hermann. Do you need a lift?"

"Sure. Thanks. But I have to get back quickly, so that I can contact my dad in Tel Aviv."

This was to let her know that he had no intention of inviting her up to his hotel room for a drink. Rose understood perfectly.

"Then I'll take the shortest route."

Because Hermann did not know his way around Calgary, she actually followed a longer route.

"By the way, Hermann, I have some spare time tomorrow. I could help you move. Then—well, we could have dinner at my apartment."

Taken by surprise, he was confused. Why would she put herself in a compromising situation? But the reason made no difference. He had no intention of accepting her invitation.

"Thanks. I really appreciate that, but I can manage without someone to help me. I'll call you, Rose, as soon as I can."

Rose understood perfectly the vague timing. "As soon as I can," she repeated under her breath. After a few inconsequential remarks about the size and population of Calgary, they reached the hotel.

"Well, thanks again for offering to help me move."

Without waiting for a parting word from her, he quickly stepped out of the car and into the hotel.

Rose knew that Hermann would soon receive countless invitations from single women. He was a very eligible bachelor, a newcomer at that. She needed to act quickly. His lukewarm attitude indicated little interest in her. Like most bachelors, perhaps, he shunned emotional involvement even before it began. But Rose was a woman of action; his behaviour did not deter her. In fact, she immediately began to make plans. Surely, she thought Hermann would not refuse an invitation to meet Calgary's most prominent businessmen? Besides, this would be an occasion to wear her most becoming outfit and show her skill as a hostess. She liked him and found him exciting. Even as she drove home, Rose was planning her guest list. In the morning, she would phone Bernice, her friend since high school, to discuss this with her.

Bernice Sternthall followed all the rules. As a semi–educated Jewish girl, she had helped her mother with the housework and obeyed her father's curfew. Rather attractive, she wanted to marry only a good provider—handsome if possible—and have two children, a boy and a girl. She married Henry Sternthall who manufactured ties and sold them nationally. Bernice wanted nothing more. In her spare time, she raised funds as one of Rose's volunteers. She was aware that she lacked Rose's prestige, but where did Rose's prestige get her—a divorce, no children, plenty of shame from her handsome bum of a husband.

Rose's voice sounded ominous over the phone. Bernice knew immediately that something had upset her. It was probably, as usual, a romantic fantasy. Bernice listened carefully but knew that what she heard would translate into trouble—unless, of course, she could make Rose realize that Hermann had shown little interest in her. She asked Rose to recall the other men who had disappointed her. What about the one who had posed as an art historian from New Jersey, a good-for-nothing free loader, who told such lies you'd swear it was the truth. What a con man he turned out to be! It was a good thing Irving Frieden had been on to him.

THE EXPATRIATE

"This time," she cautioned, "look before you leap. Ask Irving to check his credentials. And if you don't want to bother him, I'll ask Henry. He has connections with some private detectives."

"Oh, you really think that I'm out of control again? But this guy is different, Bernice. Honest. He's quiet, well educated and sophisticated. Anyway, he says very little about himself, unlike that other phony American. We never could find out what he did for a living. But I think Irving must have already checked Hermann's credentials before renting the apartment. So don't you think that I could make this little party? What could I lose?"

Bernice paused before replying, "I don't know. Well, yes, I suppose so. Make the party. At least it would give you a chance to observe him more closely."

Bernice put down the phone and poured a cup of coffee. If Rose felt strangled by social conventions, especially by a husband and marriage, why would she want to be trapped again in the very things she ran away from? Bernice remembered what her father used to say: "Some people have a '*dybbuk*' in them" (an evil spirit that takes possession of them). Realizing that Rose had no idea what she really wanted, Bernice put down her empty coffee cup and returned to her chores. She was pragmatic and sensible. And she understood herself, wisely dismissing ideas that were beyond her ability to analyze. "The world," she thought, "will take care of itself. But I must attend to my own chores."

At home, Rose entered her office. This room always gave her a warm feeling. It was very modern. One wall was entirely of glass. Its doors, opening onto a veranda, had translucent drapes. In the summer, she opened the glass doors and enjoyed the fresh air. On cool afternoons, she liked to read on the balcony. But not this afternoon. With a sigh, she sat down at the desk. It took her only a few moments to recover. Enough of this mooning around, she thought, I have to attend to my business. She looked at the pile of letters. The first one was about finding a name for the two organizations that she was planning to merge. What about The Jewish International Social Aid? She picked up a few more letters but soon lost interest in them.

A vision of Hermann began to haunt her: his dignified face, his pale manicured hands, the skull cap that he wore unobtrusively while eating, and the puzzled look that crept into his eyes as she explained how synagogues and other institutions supported the local Jewish community. Why was she so acutely aware of his body and his gestures? Dropping her pencil on the desk, she sank into a voluptuous easy chair. Rose's immediate goal was to forget Hermann and concentrate on her future career as a financial broker and advisor.

Dozing off, she dreamed about Hermann embracing and making love to her. The grandfather clock in the dining room chimed, woke her. This must stop! She tried to imagine how her mother would respond to this infatuation. Had she lived, her mother's first words would be: "Roselle, forget this German. They're all punctilious nitpickers. They're the worst kind to marry, even the Jewish ones. I have a feeling that he still believes in *Kinder, Küche und Kirche*. (Children, Kitchen and Church). Dear, you're too smart for that." Rose laughed to herself. Mother was always right. Bernice, too, was always right—or at least realistic. Maybe Rose should listen, this time, and leave well enough alone. Or maybe not.

Hermann, Rose remembered, was interested in synagogues. She was invited to a bar mitzvah that was scheduled for the following Saturday at Beth Tilliph, a Conservative synagogue near his apartment. Everyone was welcome so he needed no invitation. She would send Hermann the bulletin, and if he neither appeared at the synagogue nor called her within a few days, she could still invite him for a party. Feeling relieved after these decisions, she continued in a more tranquil mood with the urgent work on her desk.

Early next morning, Hermann packed his belongings and moved into his new apartment. He had traveled much—Frankfurt, Tel Aviv, Zürich, Paris, Le Havre, London, Calgary, and the peripatetic life was beginning to bore him. He wanted to settle down. By late afternoon, with the help of Stella's maid, all his effects were in the apartment. He felt as if he had lived there for a while.

Losing no time, he began to look through the city directory for general hospitals that could be his potential customers. His work was suddenly interrupted by the shadowy image of a pretty blond.

THE EXPATRIATE

An impish smile hovered on his lips, as he recalled Rose's remark about "instruments of healing." A clever woman, he thought, but an aggressive one. On the other hand, it would be impolite to refuse her invitation. After all, she was trying to be helpful.

But he had work to do and also wanted to find a synagogue within walking distance, call the rabbi and announce himself as a newcomer. On second thoughts, he should attend a service before introducing himself or planning to become a member. After a few days, he found a bulletin from Beth Tilleph Synagogue in his district. He read the liturgical schedule which announced that this coming Saturday's bar mitzvah was for Stephen Weisberg. Hermann recalled Saturday mornings in Frankfurt. Orthodox Jews did not drive to synagogue, because that would mean using "fire" on a holy day. But he and many other Jews had compromised, adapting to modernity but preserving their respectability, by driving half way and walking from there to synagogue. Everyone knew about this subterfuge, but very few were willing to cause communal strife by acknowledging it publicly. Here in Calgary, he could easily walk to the synagogue. Doing so, moreover, would allow him to observe its architecture from a distance.

Walking to the synagogue on Saturday, Hermann discovered that it spread over a short city block. Its exterior was unadorned. Even the entrance was bleak, facing a parking lot with room for five hundred cars. Nowhere did he see trees or flowers. When he arrived at nine-thirty, he took a few minutes to look around. In one sense, seating followed the Orthodox pattern: seats arranged in a semi-circle around the lectern and in front of the holy ark. This massive wooden closet contained several Torah scrolls, each wrapped in blue plush and adorned with silver ornaments. In another sense, seating followed the Conservative and Reform pattern: men and women sitting together. On this one floor, there was room for 1,700 worshipers. Although the walls and seats were pale beige, the stained-glass windows were exuberantly colourful. Most intriguing, thought Hermann, were those on either side of the ark: glass adaptations of paintings by Marc Chagall. These depicted biblical stories, but viewers were usually more fascinated by the brilliant colours than they were with the stories. Coloured light danced over the walls. In the evening, Hermann learned, exterior lights shone through these windows to provide the same effect.

When Hermann was ready to sit down, the sexton led him to a seat near the back. He looked around at the congregation. Men and women had dressed somewhat formally, as if for a special occasion, but they seemed bored and complacent nonetheless. Life in Canada was economically comfortable, after all, and politically stable. Turning another way, he caught sight of the Friedens and Rose Waterman. At that very moment, he decided to avoid them by leaving just before the service ended. But that did not happen.

This particular Saturday morning, Rose came early. She kept looking around to see if Hermann had arrived. After three quarters of an hour, she spotted him and waved. Out of sheer politeness, he acknowledged her greeting. Rose immediately told the Friedens that their new tenant had arrived. She whispered to Bernice to take a look at Hermann, who was sitting in the second seat of the last row.

Rose planned to rush toward Hermann as soon as the liturgy concluded, lead him to the food-laden tables and introduce him to a few members of the congregation. As a community leader, she felt obliged to do so. It never occurred to her that Hermann might find her too forward. But he did. Hermann was embarrassed by her gloved hand waving to him across the aisle and knew that it would continue waving until he showed some sign of recognition. Unfortunately, he would be even more embarrassed by leaving before the service ended. Finally it ended. Hermann rushed to the exit, but Rose was already there and waiting for him. He wanted to tell her about an urgent call from Tel Aviv, which he was expecting at home, but he noticed the eager look on Rose's face and hesitated. She put her hand on his arm and urged him to come with her. "I want to introduce you to our Rabbi and to some members of our congregation."

Rabbi Shloime Zazlove was a tall, handsome man of about fifty. He greeted Hermann with a strong handshake.

"Always good to see newcomers here, Mr. Baumbach. Mrs. Waterman tells me that you're planning to open a factory in Calgary. You should meet some of our members. They're always ready to help newcomers. After all, you're a fellow Landsman. And we Jews—"

"Rabbi," interrupted Rose, "I've added Hermann's name to your phone and mailing list. He won't be hard to reach. Right now, I want to introduce him to some of the members."

She led him first to Bernice and Henry Sternthall. A flash of secret conspiracy passed between the friends, and Rose was instantly aware of Bernice's approval. But did Hermann approve of the Sternthalls? To him, the Sternthalls were perfectly ordinary bourgeois Jews: Henry a businessman, Bernice a housewife. After a brief introduction, Rose led Hermann to the bar for drinks and then to the reception. Wrenching his arm from Rose's grip, he stared silently at one of the tables. Heaped almost obscenely with food, they could have rivaled those of the most ostentatious Roman feast: vast mounds of gefilte fish, smoked salmon, trout, halibut, caviar, eggplant, salads, cheeses and so on. At another table were large glass bowls, each filled with salads, and white baskets of rolls and bagels. On yet another table were huge vats of coffee, tea and hot water.

More fascinating than the food, however, were the people. They were trying to hold their overloaded plates, eat their food and carry on conversations simultaneously. The shy bar mitzvah boy had escaped to his small circle of friends. They were discussing the new baseball season. Stephen disliked all the fuss. It was not primarily for him, after all, but for everyone else. His parents wanted above all to display their wealth and thus impress their envious friends, relatives, even business contacts. Moreover, Stephen disliked the way that people patted his head and plied him with patronizing platitudes.

"Stevie," said one of his father's friends, "you were great up there. You could become a professional singer."

Stephen knew, of course, that he had made a few bad mistakes. And everyone knew that his voice had cracked halfway through his passage from the Torah. In a few hours, though, the fuss would be over. He would open all his presents and then escape to the kitchen for his favourite radio program, the next baseball game.

JEANNETTE MOSCOVITCH

The Friedens joined Rose and Hermann. Chatting aimlessly for a little while, Hermann soon excused himself but promised to return on the following Saturday. Rose offered to drive him home. Taking her aside, though, he explained that it would be inappropriate to leave her friends on his account. Rose did not answer, but was visibly disappointed. This made Hermann feel vaguely guilty. Suddenly, he knew how to soften the rebuff.

"By the way, Rose, I had no idea that your bar mitzvahs were so elaborate. I mean, all that food! I was going to ask you out for dinner tonight. But now, well, I won't be eating very much for the next few days."

Rose stared at him. Was she shocked or just angry? He had to say something.

"But is there an interesting movie tonight?"

"Well," she began cautiously, "we could go to the Glenbow. It's just around the corner from the Tilden. But I don't know what's playing there."

"A Canadian movie, I hope."

"Oh, it won't be Canadian. I don't think there are any Canadian movies. Anyway, I've never seen one. Not unless you count *Rose Marie*. That's American, of course, but the story takes place somewhere in the Rockies. Nelson Eddy plays a Mountie, an officer of the Royal Canadian Mounted Police. You must have seen pictures of them. They dress up in red uniforms and ride around on horseback. Anyway, he and Jeanette Macdonald sing this beautiful song. I can't remember the title. Oh yes, the "Indian Love Call." But that movie was made around ten years ago, and I've seen nothing that was even set in Canada ever since. No, this will be an American movie."

"It doesn't matter, Rose. Anything you say."

"Movies begin at eight. Will that be okay for you?"

"Yes, I know it will. I'll be ready at seven-thirty."

Rose could hardly have planned it better. Hermann left abruptly and she returned to her friends. Bernice glanced at Rose and knew instinctively that Hermann had made some friendly gesture. As for Rose, she remained with her friends to catch up on the gossip and then rushed home.

THE EXPATRIATE

Having left early that morning, she had not taken the time to tidy up. Now, she ran around picking up clothes, purses and shoes, putting them in place and making sure that she had enough fresh fruit in the fridge, enough liquor in the cabinet and fresh flowers in the vases. She wondered what to wear to tempt Hermann. But would it work? Would Hermann stay overnight? If he did remain for the night, he would need pyjamas and a bathrobe. Her husband's bathrobe was still in the drawer which she liked to wear now and then, but not his pyjamas. She rushed out and bought one pair at an exclusive shop in the vicinity. Back home, she unpacked the pyjamas, crumpled them up to make them look used, and then lay down to rest on the chaise longue, shut her eyes and daydreamed about a night of love.

Meanwhile, Hermann felt heavy and sleepy. He would have to fast before going to another Canadian bar mitzvah. He turned on the radio, hoping to hear an opera. Even in Europe, many were aware that New York's Metropolitan Opera had been broadcasting operas every Saturday afternoon since the early 1930s. This time, it was *La Boheme*, which he liked. But he had been hoping for something by Wagner, because the Metropolitan had been among the first to embrace his revolutionary music. On the other hand, anything by Puccini was pleasant. By the time Rodolfo and Mimi had begun their first duet, Hermann was in a comfortable mood between sleep and consciousness. He thought about this prosperous new country, knowing very little about the underlying social, political and economic forces that had created it. All he did know was that here he could live in peace. He now experienced what peace really meant: no more bombs, landmines, anti-Semitic attacks, nor bureaucratic intrusions into private life; no constant inspection of passports or private identification; no fear of foreign attacks. Canada is the biblical lamb, he thought, lying down next to the lion—that is, the United States. If only his family could have come with him. And maybe they would eventually. The effect of overeating eased, as he listened to the opera. The afternoon sunlight shimmered through the curtains, casting a soft shadow on him and lulling him into peaceful slumber.

At seven-thirty sharp, Hermann was waiting downstairs in the lobby. Rose arrived just as promptly. She was dressed in a deep orchid silk ensemble that contrasted with her blond hair. A warm smile graced her pale face as she held out a gloved-hand—a friendly greeting that charmed him. Hermann had to admit that she looked very attractive. "I'm so glad that you could make it, Rose. Otherwise, I would have stayed home and worked on my schedule for next week."

"Same with me," she replied, "but we'd better hurry. They're playing *The Best Years of Our Lives* this week. It's about some soldiers who come back home after the War and try to readjust. Great review in the paper. Did you read it? It's very popular and we'll probably have to wait in line to get in."

"I can buy the tickets," Hermann suggested "while you park the car. The movie sounds interesting. I know something about soldiers coming home in Germany, but I'm sure that the experience of American soldiers has been very different. After all, they won the war. And they were on the right side. But I also see that they are featuring Mann's *Blue Angel*. I think I prefer that."

As soon as they sat down, Hermann glanced again at Rose. She was, indeed, attractive. But what drove her toward him so intensely? Why did she resort to such obvious manipulation? Rose could sense that Hermann was trying to read her mind, and that troubled her. When he took her hand in his, she interpreted this gesture as a sign of sympathy instead of friendship. The situation reminded her of something that Bernice had said.

"Listen," she had begun, "sometimes you use the best ingredients to bake a cake but the cake does not turn out well nor does it taste good. You may have all the sterling qualities and good looks a man wants, yet the sexual and spiritual chemistry does not happen. Hermann is certainly smart enough to appreciate you as a beautiful emancipated woman. Yet love is another area. But please do not invent an image of him and constantly overfeed your imagination. It can only lead to a depression." Recalling Bernice's words depressed her even more. She had no way of knowing that Hermann found her sad expression not merely pretty but beautiful. Breaking his resolution, he squeezed her hand and held it.

"You look so lovely tonight," he whispered. The warmth of his hand and the sincere tone of his voice revived her hopes.

THE EXPATRIATE

After the movie, surprisingly, Hermann felt somewhat hungry. But Rose insisted that she had prepared refreshments at home. Entering her apartment, Hermann was impressed by the elegant décor: the luxurious furniture, Persian rugs, a crystal chandelier, a hand-carved coffee table set for two and with a variety of finger sandwiches. A crystal bowl was filled with fresh fruit. Gazing at the coffee table, he said rather apologetically, "It's very good of you, Rose, to take so much trouble but I can stay only for a little while. I really have to prepare for Monday."

Rose knew that this was an excuse, because he would have Sunday to do that, but she tried to hide her disappointment and smiled again as she brought in the coffee cups. He offered to make the coffee. "No, no, no," she called from the kitchen, "it's almost ready. I'll bring it in a minute."

Rose sat down on the couch, hoping that Hermann would sit next to her. But no, he chose a comfortable chair opposite to hers.

"What did you think of the movie?" She was anxious to hear his reaction to the English version.

"I've seen the original German version of Josef von Sternberg's *Der Blaue Engel.* It came out in 1930, I remember, and made Marlene Dietrich a great star in Germany. That was a long time ago, Rose, before the Nazis. The old Germany, it seems now like a lost paradise. Anyway, the story was written twenty-five years earlier by Heinrich Mann. I read it in college. In those days, there was a strong tendency toward naturalism in the arts. No one wanted any more to repress desires and instincts. Sternberg focused directly on sex and its power to overcome reason. I wonder now if he realized even then the power of another instinct, hatred, to overcome reason."

After asking Hermann a few questions about his family, Rose took his hand and led him to her garden on the balcony. A pale crescent moon and a few stars were fading into obscurity. She lit a yellow light to keep insects away, which cast eerie shadows on her flowers. She caressed them, suggestively, as he watched her. In the moonlight, her porcelain ivory skin looked so fragile, so transparent, that he felt a sudden urge to take her in his arms. But he restrained himself, remaining motionless, thinking that above all he must resist involvement.

"Look there, to the west. See? The Rockies. The snow never melts on those peaks, not even at the height of summer."

Only a faint starlight remained, after the moon sank below the horizon. The snowy peaks, too, grew brighter against the night sky, as if suspended in cosmic infinity. Only a few minutes later, though, the stars began to disappear completely; then thunder cracked, a strong wind hissed, and everything trembled. Wisps of lightning were followed by an instant thick flood of rain. Rose barely had time to turn off the light and roll out a linen canopy to protect her flowers.

"Let's go into the bedroom," Rose urged, with more than a little excitement, "and get into some dry clothes. You can wear my husband's pyjamas and bathrobe, which he left behind in a box. They're in the first drawer of his dresser near the bed. Just hang up your wet things and leave them in the washroom to dry."

Secretly, Rose believed that Fate had decided in her favour. Now, he had to stay until his clothes dried. She changed her dress where he could watch her, putting on a seductive nightgown. Her white silhouette in the semi-darkness kindled something within him. Setting aside his reservations, Hermann took Rose into his arms. Suddenly the thunder roared again and all the lights in the apartment and vicinity went off. They tumbled into bed wordlessly but with warm and tender caresses.

Next morning, Rose looked vibrant. She had a sparkle in her eyes and a delicate outward glow. Hermann sat on the edge of the bed, rubbing his eyes, feeling completely relaxed and refreshed. He felt no trace of the tension that had bothered him all week.

"Rose," he called out over some clattering in the kitchen, "don't trouble yourself to make breakfast. We'll go to my previous hotel. Their food is excellent."

"No," she answered, "breakfast is almost ready. Just tell me what kind of eggs you like. You do like French toast?"

Responding to the aroma of fresh coffee, Hermann said something about scrambled eggs.

THE EXPATRIATE

As soon as they sat down in the kitchen, he asked Rose about Canadian weather.

"Do you often have thunderstorms? And what about the winter? Do you get a lot of snowstorms?"

"Didn't you read about our climate before coming here? The weather around here is very, well, erratic. We can get showers in the spring, summer and fall, but they don't last very long. Winter is another matter. It does get very cold, but we don't get many blizzards."

Who, wondered Hermann, would have thought that Calgary, protected by mountains, had an unstable climate? He must tell his father about this; after all, sudden storms could lead to power failures and slow down production in a factory. As for the Canadian cold winters, he had indeed read and heard about that.

"Not bad, Rose, not bad at all," he tried to compliment her cooking. "I'm a bachelor, so I know how to cook. My mother taught me. Even before I moved away from home, I sometimes had to cook for the whole family."

Not many men could cook, thought Rose, or would admit to it even if they could. Besides, Hermann clearly came from a loving family. This sort of talk was very endearing to her.

Hermann avoided any mention of what had happened the night before. He admitted to himself that they had made love. Nevertheless, he wanted her to know that this had been a one night stand. Rose suspected what he was thinking, and why he was talking about her cooking.

"And you know, Rose, this French toast, it's as good as my sister's. Yet it's different—she put something else into it—but just as good."

"Next time," Rose answered somewhat impatiently, "you can give me her recipe." She decided to take control of the situation. "I loved your gentleness last night, Hermann. I loved even the mumbling in your sleep. You mumbled in German, of course, but I understood one thing very well: '*Ich liebe dich.*' Everyone knows what that means."

"Really," he said, raising one eyebrow in disbelief, "did I really say such foolish things?"

Rose refused to let him help in the kitchen after breakfast. Feeling anxious, left alone, and useless, he excused himself and went toward the door. She went with him, still hoping that he would take her in his arms once more. Hermann gave her a friendly peck on the cheek, said *"auf wiedersehen"* and left.

That cool farewell left Rose feeling depressed. Bernice was right, she thought. It was all a fantasy. What was it about Hermann? She hardly knew the man. How could she be in love with him? Maybe this was all because of the ennui that follows divorce. Worse, maybe it was a sign of the emptiness that childless women sometimes experience. Those who have children running around have no time to feel sad. Rose was alone in the world now, and she was afraid of being alone forever.

Most of Rose's family had died. Only two nephews and a niece were left. But they lived far away in the States. They communicated only by exchanging cards on the Jewish New Year. She had her work, to be sure, which she found satisfying. Otherwise, she would have had to join the rich divorcees and widows who played bridge, listened to soap operas, boasted relentlessly about their grandchildren, gossiped ruthlessly about their friends, and complained incessantly about their aches and pains. No, she was definitely not one of those women. She could expect more from life than that. Thank God, she had enough verve to do what every modern and clever woman should do: increase her skills, learn new ones to improve her professionalism. That's progress. Reflections about aspirations and achievement worked as an immediate catalyst to banish the blues. Besides, she might yet meet someone else. After all, the world was big. So what if Hermann was not deeply interested in her? If not him, then maybe she would meet a man in her newly chosen field of finance. She began to raise her aspirations and hopes of becoming a great financier. Nevertheless, she would call Bernice, describe the weekend events and ask her to assess the situation. And on that thought, making every effort to substitute mind over heart, she began to prepare her week's agenda.

When Hermann reached home, Rose's image began to haunt him. Should he have responded to her with a little more enthusiasm? He did see how hard she had been trying to please him. And he did appreciate her efforts. But experience taught him that most women tried to please at first. In Le Havre, he had met a vivacious redhead with blue eyes, a combination that the Arabs consider an evil omen. She had been fun at first, but soon after! Oh well, he thought, women just disturb my working routine. On the other hand, there was Clarice. She was different. Although experience had proved to her that shipboard romances rarely lead to a permanent relationship, in this instance, she wanted as much from him as Rose did. But she might also have given him more than Rose. He did not doubt, for instance, that Clarice would have converted to Judaism for him. Rose seemed more self-involved than Clarice. He dismissed all thoughts of feminine involvement and began to schedule his agenda for the week.

Good organization, he knew, was the key to success in business. He needed a secretary at once. Among the many applications he had received was one from Miss Margaret Pearson. Her curriculum vitae looked suitable. She had graduated from a secretarial college. For ten years, she worked for the president of a German car company that had an office in Vancouver. Margaret's letters of recommendation praised her meticulous work and her striving for excellence in every way. With that in mind, he arranged to interview her. Then he started to sort letters, read advertisements and answer phone calls. By late evening, exhaustion forced him to stop. Slipping into pyjamas, he sat down and sipped a martini while listening to the news. Then he shut his eyes until pitch-blackness flooded the room. Sleep overcame him. Far away in the dark obscurity, a small reddish gold disk twinkled. Suddenly the disk splits in two and moves apart into green and gold drapes revealing a stage. In front of that stage and high above, is a balcony, whose bottom ledge is heavily carved with gargoyles. On the balcony stand five men. They raise their arms in the Hitler salute. Countless arms, from below, reach up in response. He now sees that the central figure on the balcony is Hitler. His face is angry, his forehead partially obstructed by a patch of black hair on his forehead. One hand points toward the crowd below. Four officers in helmets, two on each side of Hitler, imitate the salute. One of them bends over the balcony and his helmet falls off. He sees the man's face from afar, at first, but then it keeps growing.

JEANNETTE MOSCOVITCH

As the soldier retrieves his helmet his face becomes clearly visible. It is a familiar face. It is the face of Jaakob Kesselmann. The balcony begins to sway. Will it fall on Hermann's chair? He waves at Jaakob. "What are you doing there?" Again and again, he shouts furiously and unintelligibly. Exhausted by the futile effort, one hand falls heavily on the arm of his chair.

Hermann woke up with a shudder. He was sweating and shaking his head. He tried to calm himself by reasoning that dreams are nothing more than frenetic images, jumbled fragments of unformed thoughts or misplaced memories. And yet reason told him also that chaos or coincidence alone could not explain his own mind's link between Jaakob Kesselmann and the Nazis.

On a business trip to Budapest, he had gone to the most famous bistro in town. A Gypsy went around to each table, telling fortunes and interpreting dreams. This was a popular act, because many people believed that dreams really did reflect the past. And some people believed that dreams could help them see into the future. It was amazing how those Magyars had applauded that fortune teller. Hermann did not believe in those things. For him, the act had been nothing more than entertainment.

What disturbed him most was the image of Jaakob as a Nazi. But that was conjecture on his part. At times, to be sure, Jaakob's movements had looked like those of a soldier, even a German soldier, but that was probably true of many other Jews—especially those who had some military training. Jaakob seemed extremely nationalistic, at first, to be sure, but so were many German Jews. Hermann shook his shoulders, trying to banish this nightmare. Usually he slept well even when he was troubled. He believed, that a problem was either solvable or not; if not, then abandon it. Such a formula usually worked very well for him.

He thought of the kind and friendly Jaakob Kesselmann and wondered how he was faring in Argentina. Maybe, once he had established his factory in Calgary, Hermann would visit him in Buenos Aires. Meanwhile, he thought, it was useless to worry about dreams. To induce sleep, he took a swig of whisky and stepped onto his verandah for some fresh air, then returned to bed. He usually slept well. But it was not so with his friend, Jaakob Kesselmann.

ARGENTINA

Captain Yanos von Heissel rose in the middle of the night and lit a lamp on the table near his bed. The Halifax hotel room intensified his gloom: bare walls, old-fashioned furniture, shabby bedspread. In spite of a great effort to remain calm, he became anxious again. By now, the pattern was familiar. Repeatedly, he asked himself the same old question—who was he? This time, the answer was clearer than in the past. Yes, he was a fugitive from society but he would not admit that he was a fugitive from justice. He had acted on orders from the Government. Was he a Christian or a Jew? Was he a Nationalist or a National Socialist? He was, in fact, the former in each case: a Christian and a nationalist. Perhaps, he thought, Hitler should have modified his policy to avoid the death camps. That would have averted universal condemnation. As for himself, his was a guiltless guilt. He remembered conversations with a few of his staunch Nazi friends. Now, their ambiguous answers haunted him. In the damp darkness of his hotel, the captain became fully aware of his isolation. All of his dialogues were interior monologues. He asked and answered his own questions.

But he had more immediate problems. Would anyone interrogate him en route to Buenos Aires? Hermann assured him no one would do so before he had reached his final destination. But anything, he realized, could happen. He wondered how Hermann was doing. Probably very well, because Hermann was practical and adaptable. Jews are like that.

Turning over to find a comfortable position in bed did not help. He tried to apply the old nostrum of thinking about happy times, but this only deepened his nostalgia for home. So far, he had found the best remedy for insomnia was reading a few pages of *The Jewish Manual*. He opened it with little interest, where he had placed his bookmark.

"After the Nicene Creed (325) became official doctrine, all Christians had to accept it. Those who did not were heretics....

By the sixth century, the papacy had grown very powerful both theologically and politically..., those who chose either to leave the Church or not to join in the first place were by definition not only theologically heretical but also politically subversive;... Not surprisingly, the Church tried to stamp out dissident communities. First to go were the pagan infidels..., most through conversion. Next the Christian heretics,...through martyrdom. Finally came the Jewish infidels... forcing them to baptismal fonts... Another solution was driving them away. But where could they go, when most of the known world was part of a Christian empire? Yet another solution was... isolating them. During the three centuries after Constantine had made Christianity the empire's official religion, the Church took legal measures against Jews. Constantius forbade intermarriage between Jewish men and Christian women. Theodosius II passed laws to eliminate Jews from high positions in the government. Justinian prevented Jews from appearing as witnesses in court against Christians. The purpose of these and other measures was to protect the state by supporting the state religion." (1)

The captain was beginning to feel drowsy, but he carefully inserted his bookmark before putting the book down.

"So," he assured himself, "Germans aren't the only ones to have imposed restrictions on Jews." Feeling somewhat justified, he fell asleep.

Next morning, he woke up in time to reach the airport.

At the airline counter, he was asked for his passport and ticket and then told to proceed to the gate where he was given a boarding pass. No one inspected his documents. After half an hour, he boarded the plane. Just before take-off, a disembodied voice asked all passengers to fasten their seat belts and put out their cigarettes. At last, the plane rose up into the air. They would have calm weather and excellent visibility.

A stewardess passed down the aisle, distributing newspapers. The captain asked for an Argentine newspaper, hoping to find a small English section, but only the *Montreal Star* and the *Times of London* were available. He chose the latter and noticed that his fellow passenger, by the window, pulled out of his traveling case what looked like an Arabic newspaper.

"Excuse me. Are you going all the way to Buenos Aires?"

"Yes. I'm Naim Husnani, from Syria. I'm going there to sell oil. We export oil to many parts of the world."

"You speak English very well," the captain remarked.

"I went to primary and secondary school in England. And what's the purpose of your trip, Mr.—?"

The captain stared at Husnani for a few moments and then turned away in embarrassment. The man sitting next to him, unlike Hermann, really did look like a Jew—that is, the Nazi description of a Jew. He had black curly hair, a light brown complexion and irregular features. The captain could not help noticing that he was well-dressed and looked cosmopolitan. Paranoia seldom left him. Was this Arab telling the truth, or was this a ploy to apprehend him? Nevertheless, he had to answer.

"Oh, sorry. Kesselmann is the name, Jaakob Kesselmann. I'm from Düsseldorf. I'm planning to set up a paper mill in Buenos Aires."

"A good idea. I hear that there's a great demand now for paper products. And Buenos Aires is right near the forests that supply the raw material. I've been to Brazil, and I can tell you those forests are very beautiful. I hope they don't destroy them all."

The captain could think of nothing to say, so he remained silent. "Did you know," continued Husnani, just to make conversation, "that Muslims were involved in the early production of paper? I think it was around the year 750 on your calendar that the Chinese attacked Arabs in Samarkand. They were repulsed, and among the prisoners were some Chinese men who had been trained to make paper. They taught us how to make paper, and we taught the Europeans. But they didn't make good paper before the eleventh century, first in Italy and then, by the fourteenth century, in Germany. I believe it's a good field and wish you success."

"Well, thank you, Mr. Husnani."

"By the way, do you know that the Arabs speak a Semitic language that's closely related to Hebrew?"

"Oh, yes, of course."

The captain sat back in his seat. Some of the myths he had heard about Arabs being ignorant and backward did not apply to this gentleman.

During lunch, the captain wondered if his Muslim neighbour would refuse to eat pork or ham. He knew at least that much about Islam. Meanwhile, Husnani wondered if his Jewish neighbour would refuse to eat ham or pork. When the stewardess came to ask what they wanted for lunch, meat or fish, both chose fish. Neither, therefore, would have the answer to his question. The captain thought it best to end this tête-à-tête long before reaching Buenos Aires, because he anticipated embarrassing questions by immigration and customs inspectors. Above all, he wanted to avoid anyone who might be eavesdropping, especially a fellow passenger whom he might meet in Buenos Aires. To indicate that he had some urgent work to do, he took out a pad and began to plan his schedule.

They reached Buenos Aires at dawn, and the plane landed smoothly. Passengers proceeded to a large waiting room in four groups—Argentine citizens, people who were en route to some other place, visitors and immigrants. The captain and other immigrants had to collect their luggage and wait for officials to inspect them for illegal drugs, firearms and planting seeds. Finally, they had to wait for immigration officials' inspection.

The captain was fifth in line. He was surprised that the others were dragging their valises on carts. He did not need to do that, for some reason, because someone had carried them to a special investigation office. This special treatment worried him.

"My name is Fernando Rodriguez and my partner is Hernando Bodega," said one of the two inspectors awaiting him there.

THE EXPATRIATE

"We have checked your luggage and found these blueprints and sketches. Please explain what they represent."

"While I was on the plane," the captain answered with assurance, "I prepared rudimentary sketches for a paper mill that I plan to build here. The blueprints, well, I used them as models for my own plan. And these calculations—see, the ones right down there—those are for how much land I'm going to need."

The inspectors looked at each other knowingly. He was telling the truth. That was because Argentines were always reluctant to sell land to foreigners, even if they became citizens. Had Kesselmann known this, they thought, he would have destroyed the sketches. He had done nothing of the kind, however, so he must have been telling the truth. The sketches did not contravene any law, so they had no legal right to detain him on any pretext. But they did mention these sketches in their report.

Next, they asked the captain how much capital he planned to invest in Argentina. Germans bringing in large sums of money, no matter how desirable that was for Argentina, were always suspected of either stealing it or accepting it from sinister sources. What would happen if, at some future date, the United Nations Commission on Human Rights were to investigate German depositors who had opened large bank accounts in Argentina? It would embarrass the Argentine government, to say the least. The captain was aware of this, therefore avoided specific figures about the capital that he might invest.

"That," he replied, "depends on the rate of exchange from marks to pesos. I can't calculate it in advance."

The full amount, of course, would have included the money in his parents' bank account and the money from the sale of his father's business. He had already converted all of this money into dollars and transferred it in medium-sized deposits from Düsseldorf to Zürich, Amsterdam, New York, and Rio de Janeiro. As the inspectors wrote down "an undisclosed amount," he watched the expressions on their faces. Intuitively, he knew that any disclosure would be detrimental and immediately tried to lessen its impact.

"Of course, with a large factory, I'll hire many Argentines and teach them a trade that will be useful in this country."

The two inspectors looked at each other. This immigrant clearly knew what most immigration officials wanted to hear. But they knew that the mark had little value at the moment, and exchanging it for pesos would bring in far less than Kesselmann had anticipated. His hope of buying lots of land in Argentina was unrealistic and even grandiose. But that was his problem, thought the inspectors, not theirs. They checked his documents, passport, visa and entrance papers.

"Mr. Kesselmann, your documents are in order. Your luggage has been inspected. You may pick it up at the end of this corridor near the exit. After that, give the security guard this pass. According to the agency that issued your permanent residency visa, you must report to the Department of Immigration every six months for the next two years."

"That's no problem for me. I'll be living in Buenos Aires."

"Where will you be staying until you find a place to live?"

"At the Americana on Avenida San Martin."

"Here's your pass, then, and welcome to Argentina."

Both inspectors agreed that this Jew was very wise. Immigrants usually wanted to improve their situation. They talked too much and revealed what was better left unsaid. But this Herr Kesselmann did not say one unnecessary word. They smiled to each other, though, because they knew what was in store for him. To set up a big business under the current regime would be a constant battle with the red tape of petty bureaucracies.

At last, the great moment of relief, the first taste of freedom. The captain took a taxi directly to the Hotel Americana, which faced the Plaza San Martin. The driver spoke English well, explaining that English was the second language in Argentina. Everyone learned English in school. And everyone who worked at a station, port or airport had to know English. The driver was very polite and solicitous, especially to those with reservations at the Hotel Americana. They gave big tips. The captain tipped so well, in fact, that his driver carried the luggage right into the lobby. At the desk, the clerk said nothing. He merely placed a registration form before the captain, who had to fill in his name, the anticipated length of his stay, and where he lived. Next, the clerk asked him for his passport, checked it carefully and returned it. This surprised the captain, because most hotels in Europe held passports until checkout time. The clerk disappeared, but he returned within minutes. Records confirmed the captain's reservation for a business suite, for a stay of at least two weeks, for payment in dollars. Those who stay longer, he told the captain, get a ten percent discount and one of the best suites. Now that, thought the captain, was clever marketing—probably the kind of marketing that originated in the United States.

His suite consisted of a small waiting room and a large bedroom. A colourful bedspread matched the upholstered chairs and the curtains. On the walls were Japanese prints. Behind one curtained wall, glass doors opened onto a balcony. A short corridor led to the business suite, equipped with a desk, typewriter, telephone and filing cabinet.

Before unpacking, he walked onto the balcony and gazed at the city. It was late afternoon. Looking upward, he saw the sun setting to the west and increasing darkness to the east. A fading gold haze moved slowly over a bluish sky, like a picture postcard where time and motion seem to stand still. Down below, traffic was moving slowly. On his left was the silvery Rio de la Plata, on his right the grand Avenida Libertador.

The captain could hardly wait to see the city where he would spend the rest of his life. A few minutes later, walking across the street, he came to the huge Plaza San Martin. For a moment, he stood and stared in amazement at the luxuriant trees. Wandering further on, he came to a bronze statue of General San Martin (1775-1850), a leader in the struggle for Argentina's independence from Spain. The pedestal was surrounded by a wide bronze band of hand-sculpted figures and flowers. The whole statue covered about half a block. Even in the fading sunlight, reflections from it shimmered everywhere. The captain wandered into a park. Scattered there were marble statues of Greek goddesses. Some held small marble bowls in the form of seashells. Such a scene would be rare in a European city: a large park, with trees, flowers, statues, people lying on the grass and sitting on benches, right in the centre of a busy commercial district. Back home, the public squares of commercial districts were full of traffic.

Looking up at the sky, he felt carefree, light headed, even delirious. So this was freedom. He could neither stand still nor sit down. All he wanted to do was jump, run, wave his hands and shout "Freiheit—Freiheit!" Suddenly, three young men, wearing sweatshirts appeared from nowhere. They were running. Stealthily, he ran behind them and imitated them. They continued till the edge of the park, where several steps led down to the sidewalk. After all three young men crossed the street, the captain slowed down. He felt exhilarated but lost. Looking across the street, he recognized the elegant Hotel Americana. Before returning, he sat down on a nearby bench to enjoy the cool, peaceful atmosphere.

Closing his eyes, for the first time in a long while, he felt a sense of freedom and light-headedness. He had found freedom. But what, he began to reflect, does freedom really mean? Have people ever been truly free? Since the remote past, people had come together in groups to protect themselves from predators. As a result of the need for cooperation, they would become conventional creatures. Everyone had to live by communal rules. But where does freedom exist, if we are bound everywhere by social conventions? Personal freedom is ultimately about making choices from the selection that society considers acceptable and makes available. But what governs those choices? What makes someone choose this and someone else choose that? The choices that we make as individuals, thought the captain, are determined by the cultures that shapes us through education, social environment, economic status, political affiliation, religious experience and biological nature. These influences are very strong. Do people actually make crucial choices freely?

In high school, the captain once had to write about Calvin's theory of predestination. Are we really free agents, he had asked in his conclusion, if our freedom is limited by all these external forces? Under the Nazis, many people were so influenced by Hitler's theories or seduced by his personality that they lost the ability to think for themselves. Nevertheless, the captain was still convinced that a united Europe under the domination of Germany and ruled by a German autocrat was the panacea not only for

Germany but for all of Europe. Hitler wanted to make this happen at any cost. The Nazi logic was clear.

The waning sun cast a grayish haze over the park as the captain began walking slowly back to his hotel. Settled comfortably in his suite, he called room service and ordered dinner. A small glass of cognac made him drowsy. For the first time in months, he needed nothing at all to induce sleep. It simply embraced him. The past, present and future slipped away. Only a few comforting memories stirred him gently.

Next morning, sunshine filtered cheerfully through the curtains. Feeling buoyant and enthusiastic, he ate his breakfast with the gusto of someone anticipating a new life. To be happy in this life, he mused over a cup of steaming coffee, you need two basic things. The first is a purpose. The second is a structure within which to attain or fulfill that purpose. That reminded him of his father's reliance on self-discipline and his scorn for self-indulgence.

That morning the captain placed ads in local newspapers, requesting the services of a bilingual secretary, the languages being Spanish and English, and the services of a real-estate agent. The latter would have to find a large space suitable for a paper mill—that is, at the very least, near a source of raw lumber. In addition, he looked at ads for offices in prime commercial buildings. Finally, he placed a notice in the *Argentine Financial Post: "European entrepreneur with capital will establish a business for the manufacture of paper and paper products to be sold worldwide. The corporation requires a board of directors. In your reply, include a curriculum vitae. Preference will be given to those with considerable capital and experience in either this or an allied industry. Mergers with small companies will be considered. Replies may be in English, French or German. Confidentiality will be respected. Box 145."*

Next, he checked the brochure that promoted Spanish for beginners. One advertised an evening course. Its venue was the University of Buenos Aires. According to the brochure, there was a waiting list for the class of Professora Severina Filipovic. Priority would be given to those who were too late to be accepted last semester. New applications were due by September 5 so that classes could begin on September 15. The captain had to hurry.

Replies to his ad for a secretary poured in. After examining these, he arranged for an interview with Carmela Mendoza. Her application was brief and clear. Though a native of Buenos Aires, Miss Mendoza spoke English as well as Spanish, studied for an arts degree at the University of Buenos Aires, then changed to a secretarial program. After graduating with first-class honors, she worked for a government agency. She had resigned two months ago, but had remained until the agency could find a replacement. Miss Mendoza preferred to work in a commercial enterprise. She would bring letters of recommendation and be ready to start immediately. As for her salary, that would be negotiable.

Miss Mendoza came on time, wearing a crisp white blouse with a pink linen suit, her black hair in a pigtail, coiled in a circle on top of her head. Although she was rather plump, the captain found her bright eyes, regular features and pale bronze complexion attractive. More important, she gave the general impression of being intelligent and efficient. He hired her immediately at a higher salary than her previous one. The captain told her to wear business clothes at all times. And, according to the formal protocol of business, he insisted she was to call him Mr. Kesselmann; he would call her Miss Mendoza. She did not mind, even though everyone had used first names in her previous position. The captain explained that she would work at his hotel suite, in an adjoining room, until he found a business location.

On Monday morning at nine, Miss Mendoza arrived for her first day. She carried a large bundle of mail, which the concierge had given to her for Herr Kesselmann. After opening each letter, she stamped it with the date of arrival, using her own stamp, bought locally but made in Germany. She piled the letters neatly and gave them to the captain so that he could sort them in order of priority.

The captain immediately answered the letter from the university, which requested him to register for Spanish language instruction on the following Wednesday at four o'clock. Second was a letter from a real-estate agent, José Perez, who could find space for both an office and a factory. Moreover, he was also a car salesman. No one in Germany would be both an agent and a car salesman, but the captain realized that Argentina was not Germany. He asked Miss Mendoza to arrange an appointment with Señor Perez for the next morning.

After that, the captain began to read the forty-five replies from businessmen. Fifteen were of particular interest. He put their letters into five folders, three in each. Miss Mendoza would schedule two appointments every afternoon and one every evening, so that all fifteen would be interviewed within five days. Of the fifteen, he thought, three or four would probably either, modify his terms or reveal that they were short of investment capital.

The first applicants were two brothers, Kurt and Hans Keunenberg, who had come from Germany in 1936. They owned a logging and paper mill on the outskirts of town and one in Montevideo. Their assets included two hundred million pesos, capital for stock, machinery and operating expenses. And their credit rating was A-1. The brothers would consider merging with another company to cut operating expenses, and hoped to expand sales to the whole of South America and Australia. Their products ranged from medium to high-quality paper for industrial uses.

The captain sat back to evaluate these facts. Would the brothers still subscribe to German newspapers? If so, they might recognize him from pictures of wanted persons? Would the authorities in Germany send his photograph to undercover organizations throughout Europe and America, stating that he might have changed his name and appearance? Might the brothers belong to a German club in town, whose members were either fugitives or refugees? Setting aside these qualms, he realized that the Keunenbergs' company would be an asset. Business could begin without delay, because they had a factory that was already operating. But how modern was their machinery and was it in good working condition? If not, replacement might turn an asset into a liability. He would have to examine their financial statement very closely. The captain could not tell if the brothers were Jews, or if they were single or maybe even homosexuals. Nonetheless, he told Miss Mendoza to arrange an appointment with the Keunenbergs, as quickly as possible.

JEANNETTE MOSCOVITCH

The next letter was from Jorge Valdez, a native of Chile. He was part owner of Argentine Airlines, as well as a large shareholder of Bolivian Airlines. Valdez claimed to have considerable liquid assets in American banks and would invest to become a partner in the new paper company. He was an expert on shipping raw materials around the world. He spoke Spanish, English and a little French. As for his background, his father was an accountant for Argentine Airlines. When young Valdez finished his second year in business administration, he found a clerical job in the same company where his father worked. Over the years, he advanced to part ownership. The enclosed photograph showed a handsome man in his late fifties. He had black hair, white teeth and an engaging smile. Valdez stated that he was a Catholic, that he had been married for twenty-five years and that he had a mistress. The captain shrugged his shoulders. Maybe this country tolerates mistresses, he thought, because the Catholic Church does not permit divorces. He felt relieved. This man would have no interest in his past. Besides, an expert on transportation would be a valuable asset. He told Miss Mendoza to make an appointment with Valdez, as quickly as possible.

The next letter was from Carlos Boisy, president of the most powerful labour union in Argentina—that of the auto industry. He expected that the profits from an investment would provide hedge funds for lost wages due to strikes. The union would approve joint ventures in Argentina, especially if workers learned the skills that they would need in new industries. Many enterprises from Europe and America had established branches in Latin America before, and during, World War II. These had been growing rapidly. Even the unions had grown rich and powerful, though not without a struggle. Boisy emphasized that the capital to be invested, was part of the union's surplus. But he added that the final decision to invest would have to come, through a vote, from the union's members and its executive committee. A Protestant, Boisy had been born in Rio de Janeiro to parents who had emigrated from France in 1890. He had been educated in Paris. Boisy was fifty-two, a widower with two grown children. He had enclosed a photo of himself and his children.

THE EXPATRIATE

For some reason, thought the captain, people around here consider it important to show pictures of themselves, and even their families, to potential business associates. Whether Boisy looked presentable or not was of little or no interest to the captain. Of prime importance was his business acumen, credit rating, liquid capital and his record of success in business. Boisy might prove useful as director of labour relations. And he would probably take no interest in the captain's past. Miss Mendoza was told to schedule an appointment for Señor Boisy.

Another letter, more revealing than most, came from Abogado (lawyer) Francesco Hernandez. He presided over a firm of twelve lawyers, specialists in corporate law. Abogado Hernandez and his colleagues were very interested in this new possibility, because they were certain that a paper company with international scope as well as expertise in both business and marketing would be very successful. Paper was a necessity in daily life, and possibly nowhere more so than in Argentina. As a lawyer, he wrote, he would consider it dishonorable to become the part-owner of a commercial enterprise, but his son-in-law was always looking for opportunities to invest. His name was Armando Muñez, vice-president of a brokerage corporation. Both were natives of Buenos Aires and Catholic. Both spoke English. Hernandez enclosed a picture of himself and his wife Marta, their son Rodrigo, and daughter Elizabeta, along with her husband Armando Muñez.

Imagine, thought the captain, a lawyer using this kind of subterfuge. But having an expert in corporate law would certainly be useful. The captain did not doubt that Hernandez would investigate thoroughly, his background and credentials, especially if his son-in-law were to invest a considerable sum of money. But how far could he go in any investigation of Jaakob Kesselmann? The captain presumed that most of the Kesselmanns had perished during the War. After much deliberation, he decided to take the risk and interview Hernandez.

The next prospect was interesting but threatening. David Fischmann and his family were from Munich, where unfortunately the rest of his relatives had been murdered. They fled to Argentina with little capital. In no time, they had established a dry-cleaning plant, which soon flourished. Now, they owned two plants and had ten outlets in Buenos Aires and Montevideo. They were Jews who practised their religion and attended the oldest synagogue in Buenos Aires. David and Sophia Fischmann had a son, Joseph, whose wife, Sylvie, had converted to Judaism. They had two children. But David and his son Joseph made it clear that being Jewish was important to them. Their business was closed on Saturdays. They included a photograph of the whole family. They were really a handsome family group.

The captain began to realize the importance of having a varied board of directors. Accepting Jews would fortify his own cover-up as one of them. He would certainly arouse suspicion by having no Jews on the board of directors. But would the Fischmanns, who spoke German, reminisce about their harrowing experience under the Nazis? Socializing with them would require a great effort. And their business was not even remotely connected with the paper industry. Being Jews, moreover, they might resort to underhanded tactics—although, the captain had to admit, that could be a useful asset in commerce. He began to think about that. After all, everyone in business sometimes resorted to tricks of one kind or another. He had. Why single out Jews? As he was thinking about that, Miss Mendoza interrupted him with an urgent message from the university.

Professora Severina Filipovic would appraise and register students for her introductory Spanish course. Such appraisals were necessary to find out if they already knew the basic grammatical principles of most European languages. His interview would take place next day at four-thirty, and he would have to confirm that appointment immediately. Without hesitation, the captain told Miss Mendoza to reschedule his appointments.

The captain repeated her name several times. Severina. It sounded like "severe." He imagined that she would be strict, very domineering, old, haggard, but also experienced and a very effective teacher. Filipovic. Was her family from Yugoslavia? In any case, he would insist on being accepted for the coming semester. Even a rudimentary knowledge of Spanish, at first, would be essential for his business.

Next day at four-thirty, he arrived at the university and entered a building with long corridors. Students were everywhere. A few spoke English. One directed him to the end of the corridor and told him how to reach the Professora's office. A black-and-white sign on the door announced Professora Severina Filipovic. He checked his watch. It was four-thirty-three. After knocking on the door, he heard a soft voice:

"Entre usted, por favor."

Behind a large oak desk sat a pretty woman in her late thirties or early forties. The walls of her office were lined with bookcases. After taking a few moments to finish reading an article, Señora Filipovic introduced herself in English.

"I'm pleased to meet you, Mr. Kesselmann. I've studied your application. You learned English and French from a private tutor but prefer to be in an English section. Fortunately, so do most of our Spanish beginners this term. We do have five who speak French and two who speak Italian."

He listened attentively to her voice. What a soft tone! He wondered about its origin, but she interrupted his thoughts by pointing to a registration form.

"I'm glad to know that you studied with a tutor and are familiar with some basic grammatical rules. I'm always amazed at how many students have never heard of a declension or a conjugation, or even a verb. In your class, only two students lack basic grammar, and I'm going to help so they won't slow down the whole class."

"Is there an extra charge for help after class?"

"No, of course not. I give extra help to those who need it because I want all of my students to progress at the same pace. It helps them, and it helps me."

The captain was impressed. He could imagine how tedious it must be to correct the papers of beginners and explain linguistic forms that defied rational explanation. He felt like a schoolboy meeting his teacher for the first time and for a moment, lost his savoir faire.

Unobtrusively, Señora Filipovic observed her student. He was a very handsome man, she thought, and obviously rich. Without further ado, however, she underlined the last paragraph on his registration form. It was a list of required books and recommended a bookstore on Avenida Florida. She smiled and handed him the list.

"*Auf wiedersehen,*" she said as he got up to leave. "Tuesday at seven-thirty."

He could hardly believe this pleasant surprise! She was anything but severe. On the contrary, she was warm, pleasant and very attractive: clean-cut features, bright violet blue eyes, a flawless complexion. He whistled and walked lazily toward Plaza St. Martin.

Gray shadows leaving pink smoky patches were slowly spreading in the sky, as fragmented images of his Spanish teacher crowded other thoughts from his mind. Shops were closing, so it was too late to buy books. The captain trudged back to his hotel, sat down at his desk and began to check the mail. But his mind kept drifting back to his Spanish teacher. Was she really from Yugoslavia? If so, was she a Catholic? He thought of the contrast between his stereotype of a teacher and the reality of this one: old versus young, plain versus pretty, severe versus warm. And her face, it had a peculiar radiance. He had to stop dreaming. There were more urgent matters that required his attention.

The captain rescheduled all interviews to be free for his Spanish class. His first appointment would be with that lawyer, Hernandez, to inform him about the legalities of setting up a company in Argentina.

Next morning, he found it difficult to concentrate on business affairs, and decided that a walk on Avenida Florida to buy the required textbooks would save time later on. The street was narrower than Avenida Libertador, and no traffic was allowed. There was a strange hush: no screeching tires, no honking horns. Shops, restaurants and kiosks lined each side of the street. Most pedestrians wore colourful cotton shirts, some with absurd or even violent designs. When he finally found a store that sold books, someone told him to walk further down the street to one that specialized in university textbooks.

There, the captain looked around. He found not only English and French books but also German ones. In fact, the German section was bigger than any other. This did not surprise him. To be truly educated, he had always thought, meant studying German literature and philosophy. Without doing that, after all, how could anyone understand either the Enlightenment or Romanticism? Even though other countries had originated some great ideas, he believed Germany had developed even those and had taken them to new heights; all the others were derivatives. He passed a store that featured a mirrored wall to glamorize its displayed merchandise. Walking by, he caught a reflection of himself in the mirror. It surprised him to notice that he wore an expression of violent arrogance, an inner consciousness made visible. He shut his eyes and moved on, but not without feeling troubled.

Other windows displayed leather goods, household utensils, antiques, liquor bottles and small paraphernalia. Strikingly different were some extensions of these stores, leading from entrances in the front to commercial malls in the back. A few policemen sauntered up and down the street. When the captain asked one of them why he was on patrol, the answer was not subtle: "To protect tourists like you." But protection from what? The captain suspected that this big city might have many pickpockets and armed gangs.

Sauntering toward the beginning of the street, he stopped to look at a store with an elaborate display of glassware. The entire window represented a theatre stage. On the two sides were glass steps that rose upwards toward the ceiling. On each step stood glass vases in various shapes and colours. Some were Bohemian, others Venetian. Some were Baccarat, others Waterford. In the center were dozens of glass objects. This collection of stemware displayed every conceivable shape, size and colour. Standing proudly in the centre was a huge burnt-orange vase with fine black and green lines etched into it. Sprinkled on the mirrored floor of this improvised stage were tiny Bohemian garnets. There was no awning outside the display window, and the sun shone directly on these crystals, which produced a dazzling rainbow of muted colours. Many passersby stopped to admire the glassware. It reminded the captain of windows on the Kastanienstrasse in Düsseldorf or on the Pariska in Prague. The store's location had been chosen very carefully. Its neighbour across the street, the captain could see immediately, was among the most elegant jewelry stores in town. But he remained fascinated and looked into the store. The inside was decorated in pale olive and pink with gold accents. A chandelier, probably Bohemian, held countless crystal droplets. Above the entrance of the store, the captain noticed a bronze sign with the name: Galina Osteropovic. In one corner of the window was a sign that said, "Aqui se habla English, Français, Deutsch, Czech." He would have preferred to linger, but he had to return to his office.

Entering the hotel, the concierge handed him a message. So, thought the captain while reading it, Hernandez was punctual. Having seen his photo, the captain was not surprised to see a tall, slender, handsome man with black hair, black eyes and light brown skin. They shook hands, and he led Hernandez to the office.

"What do you Porteños (those born in Buenos Aires) usually drink at this hour?"

"As you must know," Abogado Hernandez replied with a smile, "the heat is fiercest in southern countries between noon and two. We take a siesta till, maybe three o'clock. So any mild drink will do. We have supper from eight o'clock to ten. As for that drink, Mr. Kesselmann, I'll drink anything that's available, even a beer."

"Oh, we can do better than that. How about a martini?"

"Sounds good to me."

The captain called room service and ordered two martinis. Hernandez came directly to the purpose of his visit.

"Mr. Kesselmann, what kind of company are you planning to set up?"

"Well, I'm going to manufacture and sell paper for newspapers, magazines, offices supplies, bags, envelopes, cards, wrapping paper and things like that. The plant should be near forests and near transportation, but the office and showroom will be here in Buenos Aires. You're my first contact, actually, because I need some legal advice. How do you incorporate a business down here? And how much will it cost? As for other matters—well, I have a list here somewhere. Yes, here it is. First, is there any limit on the number of directors? And what responsibility do they have when debts occur? Are we allowed to merge with other paper companies? Do we have to specify in our charter that we plan to sell in other countries? What about labour unions?"

Hernandez sat back to think about these questions. This Señor Kesselmann, he thought, was a man who knew what he was doing. He might become a very lucrative client, so as a legal advisor he'd better be certain to give the best studied counsel he could. After all, these Jews are shrewd business men. Hernandez was as meticulous in his work as in his attire. He took out a large writing pad from his briefcase and began to take notes.

"I'm listing your questions, Mr. Kesselmann, and I'll try to answer them—as the Americans say, 'off the cuff.' For the more complicated ones, of course, I'll have to take some time and send you a written report. Now, as for setting up a business, we've been helping companies do that for twenty years. Have you ever heard of Counselors for Business Initiatives? They originated in the States, but they've become very popular here."

"No, never heard of them. But it might interest you to know that my grandfather started the paper business on his own. He chose paper, because it was in short supply. He also planned to expand when his sons were old enough to join him. My father did the same with me. We learned the business by trial and error."

He stopped abruptly, realizing that he was talking about his own family, not the Kesselmann's. The captain's face paled, but he quickly regained control of himself and continued.

"Of course, we were building a family business." He stopped to see the reaction, and then continued. "Unfortunately, though, I'm the only one left. Are there many big family businesses in Argentina?"

"Probably a few. But, as you know, the most innovative people aren't always members of one's own family circle. And if you want to sell products all over the world, well, you have to keep coming up with new and improved ones. But let's get back to the question at hand. As I see it, you have two disadvantages. First, you don't speak Spanish. Second, you're a newcomer. It's going to take you, on your own, twice as long as a local to get even the most basic information. And believe me, there are plenty of con men here. But think it over. Do you need professional and legal consultation?" As soon as Hernandez said that, the captain began to gain confidence. This lawyer was smart enough to let a client make his own choices.

"I guess there's a big difference between starting a small family business at the beginning of this century and establishing, now, a large operation with global distribution. But there is one great advantage here. Labour costs are low."

Abogado Hernandez sat still for a moment. He winced. He knew that foreign investors liked to exploit local labour, taking advantage of conflict between the unions and the government. In this respect, Herr Kesselmann was just like all the others, but he was also open to innovation.

"Mr. Kesselmann, let's get down to brass tacks. If you want to incorporate your business with a special charter, including international rights, then you must pay the going legal rate. You may be charged on an individual case or you may want to hire our firm on a yearly retainer."

The lawyer stopped talking long enough to pull a printed sheet from his folder.

"I'll leave this with you. It's an article printed six months ago in the *Buenos Aires News* that will give you a clear understanding of the work we do and our reputation."

He paused and gazed intently at Herr Kesselmann before speaking again.

"By the way, I must tell you that although I did answer your advertisement, I cannot be involved personally in your business. I can act only as the attorney and legal advisor, otherwise it may involve a conflict of interest. But my son-in-law is another matter entirely. He might want to own shares or be a director. He's well educated, a stock broker and director of one of the most important financial firms in Argentina."

He got up to put on his hat, then stopped.

"Oh, I almost forgot to tell you. If you want the bureaucrats to process your application within a reasonable time frame, you may be obliged to pay a secret gratuity in cash to certain people to speed things up. Otherwise, they'll delay matters indefinitely."

THE EXPATRIATE

The captain stiffened to an upright position, his hands firmly grasping the arms of the chair. But his face remained placid, and he smiled amiably. "Yes of course. Everyone should be compensated for their extra help. This—this payment—I have to pay it in advance and in private, is that right?"

Attorney Hernandez smiled inwardly. His client understood exactly what he meant. He had kept this bit of information to the end, expecting some resistance to graft or at least an explanation for it. Such demands could put a professional and respected lawyer in danger not only of losing his reputation but his license to practise law. But these clever Jews know how to get things done. Well, he thought, that's the world of today."

"In that case, Mr. Kesselmann, I'll think about what we've discussed and have a portfolio delivered to your secretary."

He stood up, an indication that the consultation had ended, shook hands and left. Walking to the lobby and then toward the parking lot, Abogado Hernandez kept thinking about this meeting. Kesselmann is a smart, educated, experienced businessman like any other. Why should he accuse the man and his race of being tricksters. After all, who suggested the graft? Kesselmann knew that such practices exist almost everywhere and accepts that as a fact of life. Who doesn't? He shrugged his shoulders. Prejudice, he thought sadly, makes no sense. By now, the jockey had brought his car. He looked forward to a pleasant family dinner after a busy day's work.

In his room, the captain poured himself a scotch and soda, then ordered dinner. Sitting in his chaise longue, he began to assess his progress so far. Though satisfied with his efforts, he felt vaguely anxious. Seldom could he say aloud what he really thought. What about the freedom that he dreamed of and so recently celebrated? Why was he sweating once again? He remembered his father's business. To make any decision, he would summon a committee consisting of father, son, manager and an account executive. Together, they would examine every aspect of a proposal. And then, accepting their approval, they would go into action. If only Hermann was at his side, he would be the very person with whom to discuss business matters.

Over supper, the captain wondered how Hermann Baumbach was faring. Nice fellow. No doubt, he would soon find another "gentle dove" to replace Clarice. Maybe he'd join the Jewish community. That way, he could not only make friends but also find support for his business. The Jews always helped newcomers, his father had told him, especially if they were "Landsmen" from the same country. If only Hermann were with him. What a great time they would have.

He began to read the leaflet that Hernandez had left behind. It was not only political but also promotional. At the moment, he had no effective way of evaluating the competence of this lawyer or his firm. One thing was certain, though: he needed legal services immediately.

Meanwhile, the captain had some instructions for Miss Mendoza. First, she should set up a joint meeting with Abogado Hernandez and the Hacienda Consulting Company and ask Hernandez to come an hour earlier than the others to arrange for the payment of his legal fee. Second, she should arrange an appointment with the Keunenbergs. Third, she should make an appointment with Perez, the real-estate agent who was going to bring a map and some photos of Buenos Aires. Finally, she should buy some packages of coloured letter-size paper, preferably perforated, and a three-ring folder. From now on, Monday's agenda would be on pink paper, Tuesday's on yellow, Wednesday's on blue, Thursday's on green, and Friday's on gray. Each day's unfinished items are to appear on the back with instructions for postponement. At the end of every day, the sheets were to be placed on his desk.

Returning to his bedroom suite, he turned on the radio to an Argentine station. The news in Spanish, some of which he vaguely understood, reported that a local bank had had to close its doors for the time being because a Brazilian bank had defaulted on its debt payment. He could not catch the name of the bank, but he knew how threatening that was. This news confirmed what the lawyer had said about the need for caution in choosing a bank either for personal or business purposes. Following the local news, he listened to a blues singer on a radio station. It sounded to him like caterwauling, which irritated him so much that he turned to another one. There, another blues singer was whining. He turned off the radio.

Unable to relax, he tried to study the first two lessons in his Spanish primer, *Lengua viva y gramatica*, which stressed everyday expressions. He had encountered the same method many years ago when studying English. In Spanish, it was easy to recognize gender—feminine nouns ended in *A* and masculine ones in *O*. He learned a few phrases, then put away the book. To learn a language properly, he realized, required professional guidance. Besides, Spanish grammar reminded him of his teacher.

To clear his mind and get some fresh air, the captain walked out onto the balcony. It was dark by now. In the distance, he could see the sparkling lights of cars on a highway. Even the *Rio de la Plata* was invisible against the blackness of night. Here he was, alone in a city of eight million. Back inside, he poured himself some cognac and drank it slowly. Then, tired after a working day, he turned off the lights and went to bed. But insomnia, that curse of the aged and the troubled, plagued him unsparingly. Of course, he knew of one remedy and decided to try it. He closed his eyes and thought of a bucolic landscape.

In his dream, the captain found himself back in his grandmother's garden near Düsseldorf. The rose bushes are over two feet high, but the grass is brown and trampled. His grandmother complains that returning German soldiers are responsible for that. But he hardly listens to her. He is dancing with a woman, holding her so close that he can feel the warmth of her breasts and the strong beat of her heart. The face is that of the beautiful Señora Filipovic, but the body that of Lara. She smiles and sings a lullaby: "Do not worry about me. Do not regret to be free. I cannot follow thee, because I belong to my country." The lingering melody floats above the rustle of leaves. Lara moves away from him, but he follows her into the flowered countryside. There, he finds grape pickers in the vineyards and shepherds in the meadows. One shepherd girl sits near a crystal stream. She exchanges passionate kisses with a shepherd boy who is sitting beside her. The captain reaches for her hand but it is Señora Filipovic's hand. They tip-toe into a valley and embrace. Time and space vanish until the golden rays filtered through the gauzy curtains, promising a very sunny day. Startled, the captain felt the mattress of the bed for assurance that he was still on this planet. He sat there, rubbing his eyes, thinking that wishful dreams of utopia were a relief from the harsh realities of daily life.

The captain dressed quickly and went downstairs to the restaurant. At breakfast, the maître'd always handed him the *Buenos Aires Herald*, an English daily. Today, the featured story was about Juan Peron: "Who Is Peron, and What Does He Stand For?" After a brief account of Argentina in the early twentieth century, it continued as follows:

> *"By 1930, President Irigoyen had grown very old and his government very corrupt. The revolution came, with backing from the army, on September 30. Among the officers was Juan Peron. Readers should note something about his military background and that of Argentina in general. In 1900, Germans began to train the Argentine army. But in 1933, when Adolf Hitler came to power back home, they began to indoctrinate the army with National Socialist ideas." (2).*

The captain began to eat his scrambled eggs with greater gusto and continued reading. Evidently, Castillo, who had succeeded the ailing president, wanted Argentina to conquer the whole of South America. The feature story quoted a passage from one of his speeches:

> *"We must inculcate the masses with the spirit necessary to travel the heroic path... We will do this by controlling the press, movies, radio, books and education, and with the collaboration of the Church." (3)*

This, said the feature story, had been Peron's paradigm. The next president, too, had been pro-Fascist. During the military government of Remirez, Peron had headed the Department of Labour. After Farrell's rise to power, Peron had taken on two extra portfolios: the ministry of war and the vice-presidency. Between 1944 and 1945, he had established social security for all workers. But at what cost?

> *"For Christmas, in 1945, Peron ordered all employers to give workers a bonus of twenty-five percent of their*

yearly pay (although he exempted the government). This rallied the working class to vote for Peron. Peron used good jobs, too, in his effort to lure labour leaders into his camp. He gave three of them cabinet posts. When bribery failed, went the rumour, blackmail succeeded. Peron's victory in the election of February 24, 1946, followed the heaviest vote in Argentine history: two thirds of the seats in Argentina's chamber of deputies and all but two seats in its senate." (4)

The captain folded the newspaper in disgust. A mist of fear clouded his eyes. This feature story did not augur well for setting up a business. It was contrary to what he knew about Argentina. He had thought, primarily, that it was quite advanced with social insurance covering virtually all avenues of workers' lives—establishing low-cost housing projects, annual vacation with pay after one year of service, and increased wages, although the cost of living in Argentina remained relatively low. This was certainly, according to the brochures that he had read, a good place to start. Here, in Argentina, he had thought, the cost of labour would be competitive for all business and a contented work force would refrain from striking. He could not remember where he had read that, but he had been convinced that Argentina was a prosperous and well-governed country. He gulped down the coffee, rushed to his suite and concluded he would dismiss these allegations of corruption until someone provided him with proof. After all, spreading sensational material is good fodder for newspapers; yet its contents could not be ignored.

When he entered his office, Miss Mendoza handed him the daily schedule. Before explaining its contents, she cautiously ventured to ask what had been on her mind for the last few days. She wanted to know if he would mind being called 'el patron' which was in common usage. Somehow, her pronunciation of his German name, sounded rather comical. Of course, he agreed.

The first item on his agenda was an interview with Perez, who had left brochures and photographs of residential and business premises ready for immediate inspection and occupancy. The second item was an interview, after a siesta, with the Keunenberg brothers. And the third item, that evening, was his Spanish class. He began to examine the pictures. Maybe an elegant woman such as Señora Filipovic would know which of the forty-seven 'barios' was the most prestigious. Showing the pictures to her would, at the very least, give him a pretext to remain after class.

The brochures that Perez had left promoted the beautiful Plaza de Mayo as the locale of power and prestige in town for an office, and two barrios, Norte Palermo and Belgrano, as the best residential areas in Buenos Aires. The captain picked a few pictures and instructed his secretary to tell Perez that these were the ones he would inspect.

Once again, the captain opened his newspaper and continued to read about Peron.

"Since 1943, the cost of living has risen sixty percent. This led to criticism of government interference in business and industry."(5) But he ignored the warning signals concerning his own factory. On the contrary, he thought, the government would help him because of his potential contribution to the country's economy. He would corner the paper market and be in a position to produce a great quantity of high-quality paper at a lower cost than anyone else. Moreover, he would buy out smaller companies and even purchase a shipping company in order to save money on transportation. His dreams of big business had no measure. Success, he concluded, was the reward for ambition. This vision of dominating and cornering the paper industry buoyed his spirits. Absorbed in all this, he forgot that it was siesta time. Meanwhile, Miss Mendoza had ordered sandwiches and coffee *como à los Americanos.*

Hans and Kurt *Keunenberg*, in their mid-fifties and dressed informally and flamboyantly, arrived on time. Miss Mendoza's first reaction was surprise mingled with amusement. Each gentleman was a rubber stamp of the other. She barely hid her smile while introducing them to 'el patron'. Even in the hottest weather, he wore a suit and tie. The first thing the captain noticed about the brothers, in fact, was their clothing. He assessed them as peasants. Nevertheless, he greeted them politely in English.

"Pleased to meet you, gentlemen. Now, how about a drink to celebrate our first meeting? I recommend one of these European beers." They chose a German brand. Drinking his beer, Hans spoke up in German.

"Since you're German, Herr Kesselmann, why don't we all speak in our mother tongue?"

The captain now knew that the brothers must have come from northern Germany, because Hans spoke Plattdeutsch, a dialect that was still common among peasants in northern Germany. It was certainly not the kind of German that people spoke in Berlin. He turned away slightly to hide his disdain. In any case, he had no intention of speaking German with them. That kind of intimacy might lead to personal questions.

"No," the captain replied, wiping his forehead. "I want my secretary to make a record of our discussion, and she speaks English but not German."

Miss Mendoza came in to take notes. Kurt took some financial statements out of his briefcase.

"We'll begin by showing you a profile of our business. Then you'll be able to consider a merger. Our assets come to about sixty million dollars. We own two buildings: one to store the lumber, the other to manufacture plain paper and paper products. Only our sales office is here in Buenos Aires. Whatever we owe the bank is covered by our accounts receivable as collateral. We have no debts." The captain looked casually over the papers in front of him and nodded in approval.

"How long have you been here in Argentina?"

"Ten years," said Hans proudly. "For the first few months, all we had was what little our parents could send us from Rostock. They owned a tanning factory there. Do you remember how those journalists at the *Munich Post* exposed Hitler for murdering his opponents? In 1931, they told the world what he planned to do. We believed them and decided to leave. The two of us went first. But when our parents finally wound up their business, it was too late for them. In fact, we lost contact with them. Anyway, the only jobs that we could find here were as loggers for a paper mill. We decided to learn the trade. After all, what did we have to lose? We saved much of what we earned, and, by the time that we had learned Spanish, we had enough capital to buy some old plants and renovate them. After that, we did very well. But we're ready to merge with other companies."

Hans stopped speaking. Kurt took documents out of his briefcase and handed them one by one to the captain.

"Here's our latest credit rating, assessed by the largest credit institute in this country. Look here, it says A-1. We don't know exactly what your requirements are, Mr. Kesselmann, but we do know that paper is in great demand."

He stopped abruptly to judge the captain's reaction. The captain did not hide his enthusiasm. "At least we have the same basic concept for global operation. I certainly agree about the demand for paper. As soon as I have a team, we'll all get together with our lawyers and sign the documents. My secretary here, Miss Mendoza, will arrange an appointment."

He was about to get up, when Hans spoke in German.

"Before we leave, Mr. Kesselmann, we have something personal to discuss with you. Would you please ask your secretary to wait in her office?"

The captain tried not to reveal his anxiety.

"Miss Mendoza, would you please type your notes in the office and make copies for these gentlemen." Then, he turned to the brothers.

"Well, gentlemen, what's this all about?"

"You see, Mr. Kesselmann, we noticed the *Buenos Aires News* on your desk. You should be very careful not to leave it lying around where anyone might see it. Now, have you read it?"

"I read part of it, yes, but had no time to finish it."

"Please read it now. It's not very long. But you must already know that Peron admires Hitler and Franco. You've probably already heard that Peron was born in a small town near Buenos Aires. He entered the National Military Academy and became a full lieutenant at the age of twenty. Not long after that, he became a colonel. Meanwhile, he wrote several books on military strategy. No wonder, then, that he joined the *Grupo de officiales unidas*. Read the quotation in paragraph three."

He stopped, as the captain looked at paragraph three and began to read the quotation.

THE EXPATRIATE

"The age of nations is being replaced by the age of continents. Today, nations must unite to form continents. Germany is making a titanic effort to unite the European continent. The biggest and best equipped nation will guide the destiny of Europe. That nation is Germany. Germany has given a new sense of heroism to life. Here, too, continental unity will be the next step. Paraguay is already with us. We will get Bolivia and Chile. Together, we will put pressure on Uruguay. These five nations will attract Brazil. And once Brazil has fallen, the South American continent will be ours. As in Germany, the government will be headed by a supreme leader, although we might have to make concessions at first. (6)

"What worries us most," said Kurt, "is that the Peronista regime has smothered freedom of the press. I mean, how can you expose a bad government without free speech? If Peron gags the press, then we're all lost. This is exactly what happened in Germany. As a Jew, Mr. Kesselmann, you know how dangerous this is. I could go on and on."

He stopped to see the captain's reaction who sat there, looking solemn and rigid.

"Let me give you an example," added Hans, "of how Peron closed down the newspapers that exposed his corruption. It would be excellent material for a movie. You might not know that most newsprint in Argentina is imported, and that two dailies, *La Esperanza* and *La Nacion* imported large stocks of paper.

"Suddenly, the government prevented them from using scarce dollars to import any more newsprint. From then on, it would grant licenses to import newsprint only to newspapers that had very little of it. Moreover, it seized most of what La Esperanza and La Nacion still had and gave it to pro-Peron newspapers. And because newspapers depended heavily on profits from advertisements, the government allowed them to print no more than sixteen pages, which left little room for advertisements. Finally, the government accused La Esperanza of being subsidized by foreigners. This was its

excuse for nationalizing that newspaper and thus taking control of its contents. All in all, the government closed down about sixty-five newspapers." (7)

Hans stopped and looked at Kurt, who understood the signal. Kurt moved closer to the captain, who was just about to wipe his forehead again and was showing visible signs of fatigue.

"Very disturbing," said the captain, "but what does any of this have to do with me?"

Hans stepped on the toe of Kurt's polished shoe, a sign to continue. "You must be aware, Mr. Kesselmann, that we're all hostages without a free press to oppose government corruption or even tyranny. If we sit around and do nothing, then we'll have to relive what happened in Germany and other countries. There were a few newspapers—for instance, the *Munich Post*—that exposed Hitler's ruthless methods, it's true. But even so, not enough people did something about it. Don't you see how serious this problem is?"

He stopped and looked at the captain. When the captain showed no sign of response, Kurt continued.

"By the way, we know the publishers of *La Esperanza*. If they could get hold of more paper for printing, they'd publish it in Montevideo and distribute it here in Argentina. We managed to send them some of our newsprint, but they need a better quality. In fact, they need someone to buy newsprint paper in America. So, Mr. Kesselmann, here's what we'd like you to do. While you're setting up your company, you could easily get a wholesaler's license to buy and sell newsprint paper. Then, you could buy the newsprint paper and send it to *La Esperanza* in Uruguay. Their place of operation has been changed for obvious reasons. May we count on your help?"

The captain remained silent and immobile. A few awkward seconds passed. Kurt's opinion of Peron was not the one that he had heard.

"But I've read that, in only three years, Peron has done a lot of good for this country. He's nationalized railroads, telephones, public services and even agriculture. He's created a merchant marine. He's revitalized industry. He's even paid off the foreign debt. More to the point, I've heard that Peron's five-year development plan gives preferential treatment to new industries. I don't remember the details, of course, but I do remember thinking that he was progressive, at least economically progressive."

"We can't go into details now," Kurt replied immediately, "to show you how those good intentions to stabilize the country's economy were dissipated."

The captain remained silent. Out of the frying pan, he thought, and into the fire. He could hardly help the brothers because of his precarious status. But on the other hand how could he refuse to help. After all, he claims he is a Jew.

"Well, this is certainly a surprise. No foreign newspapers have reported widespread corruption here. But I agree with you in principle. As you say, after all, every country needs freedom of the press. Still, I'm a foreigner here. What if someone were to find out that I'm involved in illegal business? How could I become a citizen? But what I will do, is discuss this with my legal advisor. That's Francesco Hernandez. Oh, by the way, would you gentlemen happen to know where he stands—politically?"

"He's for freedom of the press," said Hans without hesitation. "He's anti-Nazi and anti-Fascist. I've heard him speak many times about freedom under the Constitution. It's safe, I assure you, to tell him that you want to help us."

"In that case, I'll arrange an immediate appointment with him. I'd invite you for dinner, but I have a Spanish class tonight."

They shook hands with the captain and left. When Miss Mendoza came in to say goodnight, she found the captain sitting at his desk with his hands clasped behind his head.

"Are you well, patron? Can I get you something?"

"No, no, I'm fine. I was just thinking what these gentlemen said. And that reminds me of something. May I ask you a personal question?

"You may certainly ask but I don't know if I am able to answer a personal question."

"Miss Mendoza, do businessmen down here wear light-coloured suits with floral shirts and no ties?"

Miss Mendoza could not help smiling, this was a personal question about himself, not about her.

"You know, patron, the weather is warmer and sunnier here than it is in Europe. We can spot northern European types very quickly. They wear dark suits and tight collars and plain ties. We see them on *Avenida Libertador* and *Avenida Neuve de Julio*. That's where Mercedes Benz and all the big foreign companies have their offices."

The captain had been thinking about what to wear for his Spanish teacher, of course, not for business meetings.

"Thanks, Miss Mendoza. I'm beginning to learn all sorts of things. So, how should I dress tonight for my class?"

"Oh, well, how about your light-beige suit? Too bad, though, that your shirt collars close and choke your neck."

Without contradicting her, the captain decided to play it safe and wear a more formal brown suit. After all, he intended to ask Señora Filipovic out to dinner after class. With that in mind, he took along the pictures of houses and office buildings that Perez had sent.

Entering the classroom, he saw that Señora Filipovic had dressed just as formally in a royal-blue silk suit. She greeted him warmly and pointed to the tables and chairs. The classroom had three rows of bridge tables; each had one chair. When twenty of the twenty-one were filled, she closed the door and wrote her name on the blackboard.

"My name is Severina Filipovic, pronounced Fi-li-po-vitch. I'm from Czechoslovakia, but I studied English in London and Spanish both in Madrid and here in Buenos Aires. All of you speak English, so we'll speak English in class."

Without further ado, Professora Filipovic launched into the basics of Spanish. She knew from experience that the first four or five lessons should be very easy to understand and memorize.

"Spanish," she began, "is quite easy to learn. Its spelling is phonetic, so you pronounce words just as they appear in written form. Nouns are either masculine or feminine. Masculine ones end in *o* and feminine in *a*."

THE EXPATRIATE

She continued with the definite article and concluded by asking everyone to learn the simple vocabularies of chapters one and two. As soon as everyone else left, the captain approached her desk and invited her for refreshments.

"Well, yes, I do have some time now. But I must phone Mother and tell her that I'll be late for dinner."

"Dinner," the captain echoed, "but it's nine o'clock already."

"Well, you see, we have dinner late in Argentina. That's because of the mid-day siesta, of course, an interval that makes the working day longer than it is in colder countries."

"Right, then, choose a restaurant. And tell your mother that you'll be thinking of her, even though you won't eat as well tonight as you usually do at home."

"Mother doesn't cook," the Professora laughed. "She has a business of her own, so we hired someone who cleans and cooks."

His heart began to beat a little faster. She was pretty, and intelligent. He could talk to Señora Filipovic. It didn't take long to reach the restaurant, although they had to wait in line before the hostess led them to a table in one corner. He walked behind her. Why did her stride and even her back remind him of Lara? The captain tried to dismiss the resemblance as an illusion. But the past kept intruding. He wanted to hold a woman in his arms, to feel a smooth cheek next to his own. Sadness crept into his eyes. Noticing this, Señora Filipovic suspected that he was remembering something unhappy and tried to divert his attention by asking questions.

"So, Mr. Kesselmann, how are you managing with your business? Are you all set up by now?"

"Call me Jaakob. And I'll call you Severina. I'm not. These things take time. But I'm making progress. In fact, you might be able to help me. Look at these pictures of houses and office buildings. A rental agent left them with me. Which ones would you choose?"

"Well, that would depend on how much I could spend."

"Yes, of course. Well, let's just say that I'm willing to spend enough for the exclusive sections of Buenos Aires."

She smiled discreetly, "I see."

After looking at them carefully, along with the prices, she selected two houses and two office buildings.

"Well, it seems to me, Mr. —I mean, Jaakob, that these prices are ten or fifteen percent higher than they should be. I suggest that you bargain with the owners."

"Did you just say that I should bargain?"

In his circles back home, people would never bargain personally. In most cases, they would hire agents.

"Yes," she replied, "of course."

"In that case, I should ask my secretary to compare prices."

She nodded in approval.

"Now let's forget business. I've been sitting all afternoon and then, again, all evening in class. Let's dance, a little. Those two couples on the floor would appreciate a third."

In the dimly lit dining salon, the dancing floor seemed to move as he floated along, his mind blank, his eyes shut. He had to steady himself. At last, a woman in his arms—the lovely Señora. The past vanished. He was only conscious of the soft warm human near him holding her very close. He kissed her gently, and she automatically returned it with warm abandon. Neither of them spoke a word but kept on dancing cheek to cheek until the orchestra stopped.

"Would you care for a cognac?" the captain asked as they returned to their table.

"That would be nice, but I must warn you that a kiss won't raise your marks."

"Oh, I know that," he quipped. "One kiss isn't enough. A few more should certainly help."

It was midnight, and both were beginning to feel tired. But before parting, he asked if they could meet tomorrow evening.

"I'll have to help out in Mother's store tomorrow before preparing for my class."

"Well then, Severina, how about the day after tomorrow? I have a few more questions to ask you."

THE EXPATRIATE

Arriving at the entrance to his hotel and being unable to find a parking space there, they drove around to the rear entrance. A few cars were lined up on either side of the street. She stopped and bent forward to open the door for him, but he put his hand on hers, drawing her close. She responded, holding him even closer. The whole world disappeared for a few long moments. Gently, almost in unison, both released each other. They sat mute until the full meaning of this passionate embrace betrayed to each of them a deep longing for something not quite defined. For her, it was a yearning, a hunger for a kindred spirit, a mate of the opposite sex. For him, it was a short respite from the constant presence of inner angst, anxiety about his identity, a partial sexual fulfillment for feminine contact. Both became suddenly conscious of the unexpected bond between them.

Severina smiled as she opened the car door.

"Auf wieder sehen bis Mittwoch am Abend." (See you again. Until Wednesday evening.)

"Hasta la vista."

As he entered his room, the captain was humming. He changed into pyjamas, sat down in a comfortable chair, turned on a lamp, and shut his eyes to relive the kiss. After that, he picked up his textbook. For some reason, though, he found it hard to concentrate. Hazy images drifted before his eyes: Lara, then the first meeting in Solédad's bedroom. Then standing near him, almost lifelike was Hermann Baumbach. He shook himself, put away the Spanish primer, poured himself a drink, regained full consciousness to face reality. More alert now to the problems facing him, he asked himself questions which could not be answered. How was Hermann faring in Canada? Was that country as politically unstable, as flooded with flammable propaganda as Argentina? And Hermann? His image reappeared. How was Hermann faring in Canada? Had he found someone to replace Clarice? Probably. Hermann adjusted easily. And he was lucky. Apart from anything else, Hermann did not have to learn a new language.

BUSINESS IN CALGARY

Baumbach & Sons in no time became a noteworthy business establishment. Hermann reluctantly admitted that much of his success was due to Rose Waterman's persistent efforts. She offered useful suggestions and provided influential connections. On the other hand, he resented her conniving ways.

Before Hermann signed the lease for his office, Rose had negotiated a reduced rent. He had hesitated to let her decorate the premises but finally succumbed. Most visitors commented on its avant-garde furnishings and its technological innovations. For instance, two sliding glass doors opened automatically as anyone approached the entrance. On the desk stood two phones and the most avant-garde typewriter. But Hermann became very annoyed when visitors asked for the name of his decorator. Miss Pearson, his secretary, immediately recognized the slight scowl on his face. She was somewhat pleased, of course, because Mrs. Waterman had become a nuisance: phoning at the end of every day, just as Mr. Baumbach was leaving, so that she could drive him to her apartment for a home-cooked supper. Men are always being spoiled by women!

The first letter on Hermann's desk one morning was from Tel Aviv. He ripped it open.

My dear son: Thanks for your recent letter. We're all well and send you our love. We've filled every order according to your instructions, calculating each invoice in both Canadian and American dollars. And yes, you should have a Canadian bank account and an American one. I do believe that we're still wandering Jews. You might have to leave Canada. Who knows?

By the way, I've consulted several experts about selling our plant here in Tel Aviv. They advise me not to sell and to remain in Palestine. In the near future, they say, this is going to become a Jewish state. Also, our sons-in-law, here, like the business. They'll continue it, when I'm too old. That's important to me, because I've always hoped this would remain a family business. But we should expand and set up additional plants in Canada and maybe later in the States.

Thanks for the pictures of your office and of Rose Waterman. She must like you very much to spend her time to help you. Mother and I have often mentioned marriage. It's high time that you married and have children. If you find an educated, attractive Jewish lady about your age who shares similar interests, and a genuine friendship develops, this is the basis for a happy marriage. That's what children need. The irony is that while you're looking for some unattainable jewel, you miss the available gem within your reach. Mrs. Waterman seems to have excellent qualities and both of you appreciate the same lifestyle, which is a good foundation for a happy family life. Your sisters want to know if the dress Mrs. Waterman is wearing in the photo is from Dior or Chanel. Love from all of us. Dad.

It was past lunchtime, when Hermann walked out of his office and saw Miss Pearson still pouring over the books. She was conscientious and a perfectionist who would rather miss lunch than leave the cash book unbalanced. Each day, his admiration for her grew. In fact, he began to compare her with Clarice.

"Miss Pearson, you look tired, take a break and be my guest for lunch. You'll balance the books a little later."

At the restaurant, he asked her to choose from the menu. "Oh, no, Mr. Baumbach. It's your choice. I want to know what Germans like to eat."

"Well, I don't see anything German on the menu—but wait, what's this? Yes, here's something. *Liebfraumilch.* Ever heard of that, Miss Pearson? It's a sweet white wine from the Rhineland.

This isn't the real thing, of course. It's made for export. But even so, I'm surprised to find it here."

As they were enjoying their salmon steaks and green salads, he ventured to ask about her family.

"Well," she hesitated, "I have one brother. He's in the R.C.M.P. I mean, he's a Mountie—you know, the Royal Canadian Mounted Police. My father was an administrator for the Canadian National Railway, and my mother was a school teacher. They retired a few years ago and live in a cottage just outside of town."

She stopped. What was he thinking? Hermann stared at her. Miss Pearson looked as fragile as Clarice. He suddenly wanted to touch her, to hug her. Was he attracted to women who looked fragile? Was that because he preferred submissive women, sensitive ones? His mother had been the submissive type. But some women today, he had read recently, were beginning to assert themselves. Rose, for instance, was obviously the new kind of woman. She was the aggressive type. But this made no difference. The fact was that he did not feel that magic spark of love for Rose. His father would never understand. For him, marriage was about having common backgrounds, mutual likes and dislikes and above all, producing children.

Miss Pearson remained quietly thoughtful. She was not afraid of silence and avoided conversation for its own sake. Studying her employer from across the table, she realized that he was thinking very seriously about something, and looked slightly confused or maybe sad. Dismissing what was on his mind, Hermann tried to concentrate on Miss Pearson.

"I see that you like the American custom—a big cup of hot coffee after lunch."

She did not answer but reminded him, "Well, Mr. Baumbach, we really should get back to the office. The phones must be ringing wildly by now. Yesterday, someone from the Winnipeg General Hospital phoned to ask about an instrument that we don't have in stock, so I suggested an alternative. Is that okay? The one that they actually wanted would take weeks to import."

At the office, Miss Pearson checked the messages that the answering service had taken. One of them was from Mrs.

Waterman, of course, explaining that she had found a jade pen holder for Mr. Baumbach's desk and would bring it over at six o'clock. This annoyed Hermann. After all, she could have mailed it or had a messenger bring it over. Besides, he had been planning to drive Miss Pearson home that evening.

Maybe, it was all for the best. Never be too friendly with your employees and especially with your secretary, his father always cautioned. You could lose a good secretary and get into a bad relationship from which you could not extricate yourself. He looked longingly at Miss Pearson but asked her to tell Mrs. Waterman that he would be ready at six.

"Yes, sir," she answered slowly, "I'll do that right away."

Rose arrived a little after six and carefully opened the package for Hermann. It contained a carved four inch tube of green jade, which stood on tiny curved legs. Hermann examined it carefully. Only the Chinese, he thought, would devote so much effort to such a useless object. But then, what about the Germans? What about Meissen and Dresden figurines? They were just as intricately made and many served only to delight the eye. Rose interrupted his thoughts.

"Well, Hermann, do you like it?"

"Oh, yes, of course. Just tell Miss Pearson how much it cost, and she'll write a cheque. If you prefer American dollars, that's fine."

But Rose was not fond of Americans.

"I'll have you know," she sneered, "that I prefer Canadian dollars. Our banking system is safer than the American one. Anyway, I prefer everything that's Canadian. I just don't trust Americans."

"Okay, okay, Rose. I apologize. I'm looking forward to another one of your Canadian suppers."

Rose's table was set—elaborately, as usual—for two. She lit the coloured candles.

"It's very nice of you, Rose, to take time from your busy schedule just for me."

"Dear Hermann, it's a pleasure. But never mind that. How is business?"

THE EXPATRIATE

"So far, what I like best about doing business in Canada is the lack of bureaucratic interference. But I keep wondering about this. Why the hand's-off policy? I mean, why doesn't the government encourage business? Why doesn't it offer financial incentives to foster manufacturing? After all, more factories would provide more jobs."

"Well, if you're really interested," Rose replied in a tone that made her seem less than interested, "we could write directly to Mr. Torchin. He's our member of parliament, in charge of the department that deals with these issues."

"Do you really think that he'd reply?"

"I don't see why not. This isn't the Soviet Union, you know."

"No, I guess not. Well, then, I'll do just that. I'll write to Mr. Torchin and see what happens."

It was rather late when Hermann helped to clear the dishes. They went into the living room, where Rose turned on the radio. As usual, she suggested that he remain for the night and he agreed.

"I'm so glad now that I kept those pyjamas," she reminded him.

He did not reply and automatically put on the pyjamas, slipped into bed beside her, put his arms around her, kissed her cheek, thanked her again for supper, and quickly fell asleep. Slowly, she removed his arm and lay there in angry silence.

Next morning, she felt no better. What was she doing wrong? Did she look that old? These Germans are cold fish, Rose thought, not like Frenchmen. That was a stereotype remark, she admitted to herself. But all men needed and wanted sex. So why not Hermann? Maybe the War had made him impotent. But in that case, why had he made love to her on the first night? Did he have another woman somewhere in Europe or Palestine? Certainly not here in Calgary. After all, she was with him almost every day. When would he have time to see any other woman?

She dressed quickly and prepared breakfast. When he woke up, Rose was not in bed. He expected to find a note saying that some urgent business had prevented her from joining him for breakfast and, in polite words, adding that it was all over between

171

them. He was rather surprised to find her in the dinette, reading the *Calgary News.*

"You're really spoiling me, Rose. I was so tired last night."

This, she knew, was a hollow excuse. He clearly felt no regret and no need to apologize for a loveless night.

"Rose, how can I show my appreciation for your gracious hospitality? Suppose on Saturday evening you choose a theatre and a restaurant for dinner and then let's spend the weekend at my apartment."

In spite of everything, Rose began to hope again. All was not lost. A weekend in his apartment! What luck!

"Oh, Hermann, that sounds great. Finish your breakfast, while I get my briefcase." She drove Hermann to his office quickly and silently. Her heart seemed to be humming as she maneuvered through the heavy morning traffic.

Miss Pearson greeted him cheerfully, as she always did. Handing him the daily agenda, she noticed his lack of enthusiasm as he hurried into his office without saying a word. He was upset about something but she could not define it. Maybe it was his work. In the future, he told Miss Pearson, there should be fewer items on the daily agenda. That would give him more time for correspondence and interviews with customers and allow him to leave the office a little earlier. Miss Pearson suspected that he wanted more time with that Waterman woman, or someone else whom he'd recently met.

Actually, Hermann really did need more time for research to set up plants in Canada and to consider his father's advice. Should he establish small subsidiaries here? Or should the head office be transferred from Tel Aviv to Calgary? Either way, he was not ready to make an informed decision.

The population of Canada was small. Selling enough instruments to make a profit would require exporting most of them to the States. But that would create other problems. For one thing, it would mean competing with American companies. And these would be protected by import tariffs. To survive, Baumbach & Sons would have to do business with every hospital and drugstore in Canada. But Canada, like the United States, was a very big country. What would transportation cost? Without the actual facts and figures, of course, he had only questions, and needed advice. Even more than advice, he needed government support. At the very least, he wanted the government to reduce its tariffs on imported raw materials. In addition, the government should support a school to train specialists in this new field. The truth was that he had to ask a lawyer to write a request for help from Ottawa. And he knew one lawyer, Irving Frieden.

Hermann asked Miss Pearson to contact Mr. & Mrs. Frieden and invite them for dinner this Saturday at seven at his apartment. Then invite Mrs. Waterman and tell her the Friedens will join us on Saturday. If she calls, say that I'm out with a customer and you don't know when I'll be back. Is that clear?"

Miss Pearson smiled; she understood.

Next, Hermann sent a telegram to his father.

Have received your letter. Stop. Am considering all possibilities for plant location. Stop. Will hire agent to find summer cottage. Stop. Glad you approve of Rose. Stop. Will write soon. Stop. Hermann.

Miss Pearson read the telegram and shrugged her shoulders. Then she conveyed Hermann's message to Mrs. Waterman who insisted that he speak to her personally, but Miss Pearson had been warned. Mr. Baumbach would call her later that evening.

Depressed once more, Rose lay down on her couch. Hermann had invited her to spend the weekend at his place but had now changed his mind. Dinner at seven and then what? Was this just another polite brush-off? And after dinner would he drive her back to her apartment?

Throwing down her magazine, she turned on the radio. At least the news was encouraging. Alberta's budget was balanced. Its deficit would go down, and so would income taxes. That was more than anyone could say about the national deficit. Alberta was the best province in Canada in which to establish a new business. She must mention this to Hermann. Trying to relax, she mixed a cocktail and drank it immediately. Would Hermann ever call? What excuse would he give this time for changing his plans?

Surely, she thought bitterly, he would tell her that he had to meet a buyer on Sunday, who was leaving for Europe next day.

Rose was to graduate in a few months and then set up her own consulting firm. Maybe it was all for the best. Away with love! Away with a domestic world, narrow scope! Replace it with a wider vision: travel to conventions across Canada, giving enlightening presentations about finance, getting rave reviews about her illuminating speeches, having one-night trysts with fascinating men. That would be an exuberant lifestyle instead of mooning about an unresponsive lover. Rose thought about that for a few minutes, and then, as usual, wondered what Bernice would say. She could almost predict what Bernice would say: "Forget it. Move on. You've done all you could, and that's it lady! You're smart and pretty. You'll meet others. In the meantime, just keep busy. Life is a carousel, a merry-go-round of good and bad."

Having finished her cocktail, Rose returned to the magazine that she had been reading. *The Woman's Voice* featured articles on sexual permissiveness. One write-up in this issue told women how to avoid becoming pregnant. The author was an obscure psychologist, evidently looking for publicity. She turned a few pages, looking for something on women at work. What she found, instead, were glossy photographs of semi-nude women in promiscuous positions. God, she thought, this is downright pornography. People were distributing magazines of this kind by throwing them into letter boxes. She flung the magazine into a wastebasket and tried unsuccessfully to study. Exhausted, she eventually fell asleep and was awakened late in the evening, when Hermann finally called.

He launched directly into his schedule for Saturday night. The Friedens were coming for a specific purpose, to give him legal advice. They would call for her on the way over at six-thirty. She would spend the night at his apartment, and he would take her home on Sunday. It was far from the original plan. But maybe, she whispered to herself, all is not lost. Merely being alone with him in his apartment might kindle a spark of love. But his words were so bland that she imagined herself sleeping in his bedroom and he on the living-room couch. In the morning, after a hurried breakfast, Hermann would say apologetically that he had to leave early to meet a buyer who was flying to Europe that morning. He would take her home, and then drive to his office. In any case, his instructions were clear.

"Yes," she replied, trying to hide her disappointment, "thanks for the instructions. I'll arrive with the Friedens on Saturday." The conversation ended.

On Saturday, Hermann greeted his guests warmly, grasping firmly Irving's hand and gently kissing the ladies' hands.

Accustomed to a certain formality, Hermann was dressed in dark attire, while the lawyer, as usual, preferred a banker's grey business suit. Hermann asked Irving to serve the cocktails, while a waitress, dressed in black, with a starched white half-apron, brought in a variety of dainty hors d'oeuvres on a silver tray. After a few remarks about politics and the weather, dinner began. Hermann steered the conversation to his affairs. Business was brisk, now that peace was restored. Trade was increasing with Europe and the United States, and Canadians were selling wheat all over the world.

"In general," Irving interrupted, "business is booming. So is the stock market. You got here at the right time. This is going to be a very prosperous country."

"And it's going to be prosperous for another reason," Hermann ventured, in an effort to make Rose smile. "Here's to our rising authority on investments. Rose tells me that she's going to graduate in a few months. And I'm sure it will be magna cum laude." She blushed slightly, which added colour to her pale face.

"Of course, we're not accustomed to women as investment consultants," Rose interrupted, trying to defuse the compliment. "But I think that we'll have a lot more of them in the years to come."

While waiting for the soup, whose appetizing bouquet made everyone hungry. Hermann began to explain his problems.

"Irving, here's one problem. The duty on imported steel is so high that to manufacture these products in Canada would be more expensive than to import them. And here's another problem. We have few if any skilled workers to produce this type of instruments. And then there is the question of easy availability.

If we were to have distribution outlets in Canada and the price is right, there would be no reason to import these instruments from other countries. Not only would we establish a permanent industry in this country but also train and employ many workers. My father urges me to study these issues very carefully, because he's thinking of relocating one of his plants to Canada. It seems to me, so far, that Canada should reduce the duty on raw materials that are used to make medical instruments. And I think that Canada should establish technical schools and subsidize students to attend."

At this moment, the main course arrived. Irving chose a red wine and began pouring it. Stella, who had listened only to parts of this conversation, was fascinated by a Meissen vase on the sideboard. She was about to interrupt, but Irving gave her a stern look.

Hermann, on the other hand, was delighted that she showed interest in his vase.

"I was downtown, Stella, wandering around an antique store, when I saw some Meissen pieces. They made me feel so nostalgic. My mother still has a few in Palestine. Look at the workmanship on this vase. Look at the details. Who else makes porcelain so fine?"

Irving winced, because he did not believe that any country had a monopoly on good quality.

"Yes, but Hermann, what about the Czechs? I mean, what about their glass? Who makes better glass than they do?"

"Well, no one does. I don't know. But this is porcelain."

Irving tried to hide his irritation.

"Is there a way," Hermann asked, partly to change the subject and avoid any controversy, "to discuss our problems with someone in Ottawa?"

Before Irving could answer, Rose suggested that they arrange an appointment with her own member of parliament. If that fails, she added, they could always write to Ottawa. But Irving quickly intervened to prevent Rose from offering more advice.

"Yes, yes, Rose, your suggestion might work. I'll call this man myself on Monday and try to set up an appointment."

THE EXPATRIATE

Hermann sat there amazed. "So, you can just call for an appointment? You don't have to go through an army of clerks and other underlings? You don't have to pay, *um,* gratuities of some kind?"

"You mean bribes," Irving replied. "No, of course not. But we do have to follow protocol. First, you'll have to submit a written request, a detailed one that outlines the purpose and importance of your request. Then someone will decide if it has any national benefit and, if so, which department should respond to it. Finally, the minister himself or his next in command will ask you to come in for an interview."

Irving was an astute observer of human nature. Facial expressions, hand gestures, voice tonality, all revealed hidden meanings to him. He understood Hermann's disbelief.

"I suppose" Hermann replied "that there will be a considerable delay, a waiting game with the usual, 'our department needs time to study your project.' Every modern country has a big bureaucracy even Canada, I imagine."

Rose remained somewhat listless, rather annoyed at Hermann's preoccupation with business while entertaining guests.

"Anyway," Hermann continued, "are you aware that some metal instruments absorb blood, so we can't sterilize them properly. They could cause infections, which no one would detect quickly. To be on the safe side, we should throw away these instruments after using them once. What I mean is that we need to think about quality, as well as quantity. We could reduce our prices considerably by making and stockpiling our products right here in Calgary. Hospitals wouldn't cut corners by re-using instruments, if they are easily available and costs are reasonable. And, Irving, you realize that if we train young people to make these instruments, we could start a new industry and employ many Canadians."

Irving was impressed. "Yes, Hermann, that's precisely what the government needs to hear. Still, both houses of parliament would have to vote for any change in legislation. That wouldn't happen overnight. Neither would the implementation of any new legislation. Even so, it wouldn't take forever. Laws change all the time, and people do manage to conduct business here."

"Well, Irving, I guess that's it for now. Let's go into the living room and have a drink."

While Hermann was pouring the second round of Grand Marnier, Irving and Stella got up.

"Please excuse us, but we really must leave. I have to be in court on Monday morning, and must prepare your request as quickly as possible. In short, I've got a whole lot of work to do between now and then."

"Well, what can I say to that? You do seem to have a legitimate and judicial excuse for leaving early." All laughed at the legal terminology.

As they prepared to leave, Irving and Stella wondered what to do about Rose. Irving thought of asking her if she'd like to stay, but it might sound indelicate. Before he could say anything, Stella did.

"Rose, may we give you a lift home?" Irving immediately cut her off.

"Stella, why shorten a pleasant evening for Rose and Hermann just because of us? Rose, you remain. I'm sure Hermann would prefer that."

It suddenly dawned on Stella that Irving wanted Rose and Hermann to be alone. He could be so clever. Irving was indeed clever. He had looked at Rose and quickly assessed her relationship with Hermann. She was fighting a losing battle, he surmised. Most men didn't like domineering women, and Rose was nothing if not domineering. Hermann, ever the man of savoir faire and the bon mot, put his arm around Rose's shoulder and cut in, "Of course, a real pleasure to have Rose with me a while longer." When the Friedens left, Hermann slipped his arm around Rose's waist and whispered to her. "Come into the library—that's what I call the extra room over there. I have a surprise for you."

On a side table in the library was a record player. "Since you like dancing, I decided to buy some Canadian dance music. The sales clerk suggested a French Canadian swing band so I chose three of its latest records. At the same time, by the way, I bought an abridged history of Canada."

After dancing for a few minutes, Rose decided she would complain of a headache and call a taxi.

"Mademoiselle," he said in his slightly comical French, "may I have this dance with you?"

Well, thought Rose, why not? "Avec plaisir."

Kissing the nape of her neck as they danced, Hermann began to flatter her.

"You look very lovely tonight."

That was Hermann, she thought. He comes up with all these complimentary expressions and romantic gestures to cover up a multitude of hidden truths. She did look lovely tonight, Rose agreed, but she found it too painful to stay more than a few minutes. He was just playing around with her, and she was making a fool of herself. Meanwhile, they enjoyed dancing. Hermann took her in his arms and pressed her close enough to feel her heart beating. Every now and then, he kissed her with genuine pleasure. When the record ended, he led her into the bedroom.

"I have another surprise for you."

This time, she had high hopes. On the bed lay an oblong box with an attached note: "To a lovely lady who is always in my mind." She opened the box slowly, then gasped. Inside was a set of monogrammed pyjamas.

"Oh, Hermann, how beautiful!"

Instead of thanking him, she threw her arms around him. Hermann was delighted.

"So, will you stay for the rest of the weekend?"

Rose nodded.

"Well, then what are you waiting for? Try on the pyjamas. I hope they fit. When the saleswoman asked me for your size, I had no idea. She told me to look at several ladies in the store and instructed me to point, discreetly, to anyone who looked about the same size as you."

"Now, let's relax in bed," Hermann suggested, "and listen to the radio. The CBC is going to broadcast *Much Ado about Nothing* or *As You Like It* or something else by Shakespeare. You know what? I've heard that Germans read Shakespeare more often than the English do. Maybe that's because of Ludwig Tieck's beautiful translation." But they listened instead to *A Midsummer Night's Dream*—until they were too tired to continue. Hermann encircled Rose in his arms and kissed her tenderly. His silence was eloquent, Rose thought, and his gestures spoke louder than words. Hermann had once told her that words were inadequate to convey the joy of love. It should be nature's response not word exchanges. Rose suddenly became inarticulate, speechless and ecstatic. Was she dreaming or was this reality? She saw nothing, her eyes were closed, and only heard the soft susurrus of throbbing heart beats. Blackness, vaporous blackness circled the room until, much later, an orange golden dawn slowly filtered through the transparent window shades and an unhurried bright sunlight seeped through the apartment. They awakened almost simultaneously and kissed instantly.

"Rose, darling, you're very dear to me. You deserve a good breakfast by chef Hermann of Cordon Bleu."

Rose smiled and moved to the edge of the bed, reliving every gesture, but thinking he never did say, "Rose I love you." "Oh well," she shrugged her shoulders. She no longer cared about the details.

"Is this going to be a German breakfast? I'll eat anything, I'm famished."

Hermann prepared a feast, though not a particularly German one. He turned on the radio.

"You just sit here and listen, Rose. I'll do the serving this time."

"Sounds good to me. I feel content, Hermann, truly content."

"So am I, Rose—at least for the moment. But it won't last. I can't forget the past. Every now and then, it troubles me."

Even as he spoke, Hermann was thinking about his parents. They wanted him to marry. For them, bourgeois to the core, it was not only about children but also about stability, order, security, comfort. This was what "the good life" meant to them. For him, on the other hand, that way of life seemed narrow and confining. He wanted more. Much more. He looked at Rose. Was she observing him too carefully?

"What do you want to do this afternoon? Maybe there's a good movie playing at the Glenbow."

"I don't know. Do you have the newspaper? I'll check. As for tonight, I'll have to go home early. We tend to have a lot of unscheduled exams in economics on Monday mornings."

"Okay, I'll go and clean up the kitchen. Isn't that what Canadian husbands do?"

"Canadian husbands do that or should do that. But you're neither a husband nor a Canadian, so I'll help."

Too late, Hermann realized that he should have avoided the word "husband".

"So, this will be what the American's call a 'joint effort?'"

"What's it like in Europe?"

"I don't know what's changing over there. It's too early for any predictions. They still haven't recovered from the War. But I do know that my father in Tel Aviv would never dare to enter my mother's sole territory, the kitchen. The women in our family spoiled their men. In exchange, the men supported them and provided for all of their needs and desires."

"Yes, that's the tradition. But things have been changing gradually over the past half century. Since the late nineteenth century, the ideal has been what sociologists call 'companionate marriage.' People no longer get married only to have children or to share their labour and resources. They get married to live with their best friends. They cooperate in every way. And if they need more money, the wife might get a job."

Hermann wondered about who would bring up the children, but he dared not say so directly.

"Well, I don't know about all of that. For the time being, though, I do enjoy helping you."

He liked Rose. She was well organized and efficient. She got things done. She might make a good wife for someone. In his case, the enchantment of getting to know her had slowly faded because of her relentless manipulative ways. Besides, living with Rose, even now and then, had taken away the magic of getting to know each other step by step. In the past, men and women had accepted traditional roles without thinking much about them. But those roles had made sense. Most women, for instance, did want children. Rose might or might not have wanted children, but was she too old now? Even if she would have children, Rose probably would not want to put her career on hold to take care of them.

For some reason, he began to think again of Jaakob Kesselmann. Maybe that was because Jaakob, unlike his parents, could probably understand the problem with Rose. Jaakob was like a close friend or even a brother.

"Well, then," he turned to Rose, "what about next weekend? If you're free, we could spend it together again. What do you say? My apartment or yours?"

Moving back and forth between apartments reminded her of a paradox. On the one hand, she thought, absence makes the heart grow fonder. On the other hand, it makes finding a replacement much easier. Suddenly, the meaning of his invitation became clear to her.

"Sure," she replied without much enthusiasm, "let's get together next weekend. We'll stay at my apartment, so you can get acquainted with my kitchen shelves."

This was enough for Hermann. He took Rose in his arms, kissed the nape of her neck and pressed her to his chest. She relaxed in his arms. So what if he wanted to play around with her for another few weeks? The pleasure was hers no less than his. She would deal with the painful withdrawal symptoms later.

That Sunday night, after Rose left, Hermann began to write a letter to his father about Frieden's advice. He added something about Rose. Yes, he was contemplating marriage. But he was not ready to make the final decision. That would satisfy his father, who believed in careful deliberation. Next morning, he gave the letter to Miss Pearson. She gazed at her boss. He looked vibrant, as usual, but also content. Intuitively, she knew that he had enjoyed the weekend with Mrs. Waterman.

"Here's today's agenda, Mr. Baumbach, and one for the rest of the week. You seem to have a good many interviews lined up with customers. And here's the *Calgary World News,* which you requested."

"By the way, Miss Pearson, please order half a dozen long stem roses and send them to Mrs. Waterman."

As soon as he sat down at his desk, he noticed the glaring headline about Juan Peron's victory in Argentina. The story went on and on about the unions, the restriction of freedom, the anti-Semitic demonstrations in Buenos Aires, and so on. Hermann thought immediately of Jaakob. Was there any way to contact him? Why, in any case, had he chosen Buenos Aires? Hermann recalled something that his father had said both during and after the War. If too many Jews migrated to Palestine at one time, the Arabs would resent them. Someone should direct at least some of these Jews to Argentina, which already had an established Jewish community. But, thought Hermann, had his father—or anyone—realized after the War that Argentina approved of Hitler and offered a haven for Nazi war criminals? The article noted that,

> *"Ricardo Staudte, a leading Nazi industrialist, had fled to Argentina even during the War. He was listed in the Blue Book as Nazi number two. The naturalized son of Ludwig Freude, Nazi number one, was now Peron's personal secretary and had authority over the regime's secret police. Also in Argentina was Vittorio Mussolini, son of the Duce. He had publicly commemorated the anniversary of his father's death and disseminated fascist propaganda there. General Mario Roata, one of Mussolini's top military officers, was working for Peron in the Casa Rosada". (1)*

Hermann usually paid little attention to the fragmented news from Brazil and Argentina. But he could no longer ignore stories about Peron. The newly elected president of Argentina had scored such an overwhelming majority that denunciations of his electoral campaign were constantly appearing. Most of these focused on how Peron had usurped power at every level of society. This article, another denunciation, was about how Peron had connived to take control of the unions, the press, and even the Church. He showed all the signs of a dictator. Moreover, he encouraged anti-Semitic violence.

Why did Jaakob choose Argentina? The only reasonable explanation was that he had found it easy to get a permanent visa.

BUSINESS IN BUENOS AIRES

Hermann may have been aware of the political situation in Argentina, but the captain was not. He was too busy to read the daily newspapers. Sitting in his office, he carefully studied the day's agenda. The first appointment was with José Perez, to inspect offices and empty land lots. A disconcerting letter from him explained the lack of large, choice parcels of land that would be suitable for a paper mill. Most owners were reluctant to sell. Those who did sell were able to inflate their prices. The captain had not had time to think about this problem, when Miss Mendoza, smiling, ushered Perez into his office.

She found it amusing to see how this sales agent tried to impress her boss. Obviously, Perez wanted to give the impression of being a successful American businessman and to dress like one. His brown shirt was not properly buttoned, and he had chosen a garish tie with a large yellow daisy covering its length and width. He looked uncomfortable. Miss Mendoza could hardly wait to see the captain's reaction.

Before him stood a rather short, thin man with peering black almond-shaped eyes, light brown skin, and pitch black hair plastered smooth with brilliantine—his hand outstretched to greet his customer. The captain remained rigid. A master of graciousness, however, he reluctantly grasped the man's hand.

"I am Mr. Kesselmann. Delighted to meet you in person, Mr. Perez, after all of our phone conversations."

Perez spoke English reasonably well despite his Spanish accent. Now and then, he anglicized a Spanish word for lack of the English one.

"Muchos thanks. I am pleased to meet you, Mr. Kesselmann. My car is waiting. May we leave immediately? We have much to do."

Seated comfortably in his car, José began to describe the office that they were about to see.

"I have found a large space, where some big international companies have their offices and show rooms. I'm thinking of one on the eighth floor of a modern building. It looks almost like the one I saw in Berlin before the War. I have not been in Berlin since then, but have seen recent pictures. A heap of rubble. Serves them right!"

The captain began to wipe his forehead, a gesture that did not escape Perez.

"Do you find it hot in here? I can put on the fan. We, *Porteños* do not feel the heat as much as the Europeans, because we do not button our shirt collars as tightly as they do."

When Perez opened the office's double door, both men stood motionless on the threshold. It was certainly big and modern enough. Moreover, with its many windows the office was bright and cheerful. The captain examined everything carefully. The office was designed to promote relaxation, he thought, not work. How unlike his father's austere office. Perez knew that this style was too modern for some Europeans. Nonetheless, he motioned the captain to follow him and examine the washroom, the cloak room, and the compact kitchen, then waited for a sign from the captain, who was still looking around.

"Well, it certainly is very carefully planned, but—"

José smiled. "Is there something wrong, Mr. Kesselmann?"

The captain's mind was far away, recalling his father's office which was like a banker's, where one came in, overwhelmed as if begging for a loan. Suddenly, he realized this was a different time and a different place.

"No, I guess not. It's just not like the offices that I'm used to."

"You must realize, Mr. Kesselmann, that our climate is sunnier than that of northern Europe. We like lots of windows and cool, open spaces."

THE EXPATRIATE

"Well, it is beautiful. And it does remind me of some very distinguished new offices in Berlin before the War. How does this add up in dollars?"

"To rent, well, that would be many hundreds of dollars monthly. I do not know the exact amount. If you rent the premises, as is, furniture and decorating included, you pay me one month's rent as a finder's fee, and the landlord pays me two percent of the first year's rent. But if you like, Mr. Kesselmann, you could hire my decorator. I will give you her card, and you can deal with her directly. If you decide to buy these furnishings, however, I would charge you an additional five percent as a finder's fee."

He waited for a response. The captain was amused by this man's simplicity. He had expected a higher price and a bolder sales pitch.

"Mr. Perez, I like the way you do business. I like this office, and the way it is decorated. I'll buy the furnishings, and if some changes are to be made I'll get in touch with your decorator. I'll also arrange an immediate meeting with my lawyer and the landlord. Now, have you been able to find a big lot for my paper mill?"

"Yes, Mr. Kesselmann, but the nearest one is forty-five miles from town. We could drive out there this morning and I'll explain what is involved. But first, you might want some information about this country. Here is something to read. I had my secretary copy it from a book for all of my customers who want to invest in property here."

He handed it to the captain, who read that people had been buying and selling land here since the earliest Spanish settlements.

"As early as 1589, ambitious families claimed land. In 1608, therefore, the cabildo of Buenos Aires ordered a survey to allocate land for farms and ranches. Most of the land went to the richest local families. By the late colonial period, there were only 327 landowners in the jurisdiction of Buenos Aires. Of these, moreover, only 141 lived outside the city. As in Europe, the primary form of wealth was land. Everyone wanted as much of it, as possible.

And nothing has changed. Peron's rise to power has created an economic upheaval. Argentina owes money to many other countries. The British own our railroads. The Americans own our telephone system. Continuous rising prices in all commodities have caused small investors to buy land at any price as a hedge against inflation. Big industries still depend on land, particularly agriculture, ranching, meatpacking, and leatherworking. All in all, the best investment is still in land. Those who own it hold onto it. (1)

The captain returned the folded paper to Perez.

"Thanks, Mr. Perez. As you must know, this is not what the travel brochures advertise. But Argentina is a very big country with lots of land. Is that not so?"

"Oh, yes, Mr. Kesselmann. We cover more than one million square miles. And we have many other resources. Our ports on the Atlantic give us easy access to trade and forests are plentiful. Our hydroelectric potential is very promising."

"But if we can't find suitable land here in Argentina, then what about Uruguay?"

"I don't know, but I will inquire. You want your factory as near to Buenos Aires as possible, is that right?"

"Yes, Mr. Perez, that is correct."

Reaching their destination, Perez pointed to a barren lot. There were no trees, houses, nor any sign of life past or present. The ground was brown from baking in the sun. Both men remained silent, looking at what seemed an infinity of desolation. The captain's first concern was the size of the lot.

"It's fifty thousand square feet. The original owners died three years ago, and the current ones have neglected it. Occasionally, they rent it out for rodeos."

"What about access to water, and transportation?" the captain asked.

"There are plenty of roads and streams nearby, Mr. Kesselmann, but I have to verify the exact distance of each."

"What's the asking price?"

"It is probably several hundred million pesos. In dollars, of course, that would be much lower."

"Do you have a map?"

"No, not with me, but I will ask the owner for one and see if the land is clear of title."

"I also need to know if I can use this as an industrial site."

"Yes, I have checked. But I will ask for confirmation in writing. To get all this information from our bureaucrats will take time so I want to be sure the land is suitable before starting the paper work."

"I'll also need the advice of an architect and an engineer to know if this land has a foundation of rock or water, because it would have to support heavy machinery."

The captain glanced at his watch. It was midday.

"It will take at least an hour and a quarter to get back to town, and I must contact my office. Is there a phone booth around here?"

"Yes. It is on our way about fifteen minutes down the road. There is a gas station with a phone booth."

They immediately headed southward.

"I appreciate your work, especially for telling me how hard it might be to buy land here, even though Argentina is so big."

They reached the gas station, and Perez prudently remained in the car. Miss Mendoza answered. "I am glad that you called. There is a message from Professora Filipovic. She will be in her office one hour before class for pupils who need help with the assignment. She wants to know how many students need help. So, if you do, I'll tell her."

"Call back, and tell her that I'll get there fifteen minutes early. Also, I'd like to see her after class. I have a few important matters to discuss with her. Now, what's my afternoon schedule?"

"Lawyer Hernandez, has prepared some documents that you must sign to incorporate the company. And he has some information about the Keunenbergs' request. He will be here at five-thirty and hopes to leave by six-thirty, just enough time for you to be in class on schedule."

"That's good, Miss Mendoza. I'll be back soon."

The captain was smiling as he returned to the car. The mere thought of seeing Severina buoyed his spirit and distracted him from the urgent decision that he had to make. Señor Perez observed his client. Kesselmann seemed relaxed and cheerful.

"What's our next step, Señor Perez?"

"You tell me when you and your lawyer can come, and I'll arrange to be there with the rental agent of the office. Next, a lawyer and a director of your firm must inspect the land. Allow me two days to answer your questions. Then, we can all meet at the site."

When they reached the Americana Hotel, the captain stepped out briskly and with his best effort to show how much Spanish he had already learned, he articulated with a heavy German accent "*Hasta la vista en dos dias.*" José tipped his hat, a sign of good-bye but he could hardly stifle the invisible and inaudible laugh. "*Caramba*" (confound it) he thought, "a French Spanish accent is more tolerable than a German Spanish one."

The captain entered his office to find Abogado Hernandez sitting at the table, where he had spread out various government forms.

"The first form is to identify the company's president," said Hernandez, pointing to it. "And the name must be the same as on your passport. The second is to identify the secretary. The third is to identify the vice-president. The fourth is to identify everyone on the board of directors. In all, there are ten of these forms. On each, I've left an explanation and translated into English what you need to sign. One form requires a detailed statement about the need in Argentina for your company. If you want any statistics on paper mills and paper products in our country, just call my secretary. We'll check all these forms, then mail them to the various departments. Now, Mr. Kesselmann, you might well ask why the government needs so many of these forms? Otherwise, you see, there would not be enough work for our bloated bureaucracy. But here is my point. At least three or four bureaucrats will handle these documents. So, if you want to speed up the process, you must give each of them at least one thousand pesos—the equivalent of about $450. Of course, you must do it secretly." He said this nonchalantly, as a matter of fact. The captain remained silent, showed no surprise and consented without hesitating. "Of course, if these gentlemen do extra work, they certainly should be paid for it. Who will handle the payment?"

"They will give us instructions."

"Next on the agenda is the lease for an office and the inspection of the land for a factory. I'll tell my secretary to call yours and arrange a convenient time to meet."

"Now," the captain hesitated a little, "there is another problem: how to get newsprint, which we must import from the United States and pay for in American dollars, when the Argentine government prevents us from buying foreign currency. And, as you know, the newsprint is for a newspaper that the Argentine government has harassed, even forced it to close its plant."

"I've checked the credentials of those Keunenberg brothers, the ones who suggested this proposal. Their personal and business records are impeccable, I must say. They have a high credit rating. In short, Mr. Kesselmann, you can trust them. But when I first considered their proposal, my immediate impulse was to advise you against any activities that might seem even remotely political, because you are a recent immigrant and a Jew. Pay your taxes, your bribes, and remain invisible. It would take too long to tell you how the current regime got into power with such a huge majority. Let's just say that it got support from most of the labour unions such as the *Union ferroviaria*, and the *Federation de la industria de la carne*—by resorting to devious methods. Now, if we sit by quietly like lambs and allow ourselves to be flayed, if we don't protect freedom of the press and speech, our country will be in even more serious danger. I mean, look what happened in Germany."

The captain remained silent as Abogado Hernandez went on about the political problems of Argentina.

"Have you heard about the manifesto of 1943? Leaders from all fields—politics, labour, industry, education, social affairs—demanded a return to constitutional government. And not only leaders but The Manifesto got a lot of support from people all over the country; those who actually signed it, of course, took the greatest risks. The government fired all those who were teachers.

At first, we thought that President Ramirez would join the Allied cause. But the government closed down groups—I'm thinking of the *Junta femina para la Victoria*, say, and Action Argentina—they supported the Allies. As for groups that supported the Axis cause, they were free to say whatever they liked."

Crossing his legs and, without glancing at his watch, he continued.

"How Peron forced the press into submission is another long story. I'll mention only one or two newspapers. In preparation for this recent election, the government lifted restrictions on freedom of the press. The most vociferous newspapers were *La Esperanza* and *La Nacional*. They attacked Nazi and Fascist circles in Argentina and exposed government corruption. Readers and advertisers increased. However, as soon as Peron won the election, he began to harass them. Have I told you about this already?"

"Well, you did mention some—"

"But you must know what's going on. It's very important. First of all, the government stopped granting foreign exchange needed to import newsprint. In the next stage, Peron limited newspapers to sixteen pages and allowed only a few of those pages for advertising. How could a newspaper survive without either newsprint or advertising revenue? The third stage was to accuse *La Esperanza* of taking subsidies from foreign interests, particularly American ones, and of financial corruption. He subpoenaed their books and stationed police in their office. Finally, Peron passed a law that nationalized the newspaper. And that, Mr. Kesselmann, was the end of *La Esperanza.*"

"I see," said the captain. "But what—"

"Freedom of the press and freedom of speech, Mr. Kesselmann, these are the most effective ways of protecting democracy. I suggest the following, although I'd welcome other suggestions. This is only for your consideration. *La Esperanza's* problem is to get newsprint paper from its American suppliers and pay for it in dollars. They need a large quantity of newsprint, but also somewhere safe to store it. Our first step, Mr. Kesselmann, would be to move these operations to Uruguay—to Montevideo.

THE EXPATRIATE

It's a beautiful city, by the way, just like Buenos Aires. In fact, it now has a big colony of refugees from Buenos Aires. Anyway, that's where you could set up in your name a wholesale company, *El Papel* to buy newsprint from North America and sell it to South America. Your company, *El Papel* would lease storage and office space from the Keunenbergs in Montevideo. Then the Alarcons, owners of *La Esperanza* could relocate their printing presses to Montevideo."

"You really have thought about all this very carefully" the captain replied with some apprehension.

"Yes, indeed. Now, Mr. Kesselmann, you have an American bank account in New York. That could be very helpful. Invoices calculated in American dollars would be sent to *El Papel,* and *El Papel* would pay from your American bank account. *La Esperanza* would immediately repay you, of course, and add ten percent for your trouble. *La Esperanza* could then continue its good work and make a profit as well. Once the newspapers are printed, they know clandestine methods to send them directly to homesteaders and business owners so as to avoid government confrontation. Why don't we ask our secretaries to arrange a secret meeting for all of us,—including the Keunenbergs and the Alarcons—in Montevideo."

The captain wanted at all costs to avoid involvement in some illegal activity. After all, he was still a guest in Argentina. From his own experiences in Europe, he knew that newspapers could be very effective in exposing government corruption. But he was also aware that they were very effective in making money by sensationalizing or even exaggerating these stories. Hernandez's proposal was clever, but his own personal involvement would be most visible. He would be paying the bills for *El Papel*, a company that had only one customer, *La Esperanza*. It would take very little investigative work to realize that *El Papel* was a front for *La Esperanza*. However, since both companies were registered and operating in Uruguay, they were beyond Argentine jurisdiction. On the other hand, in the future, both countries could sign a mutual extradition treaty. In that event, Uruguay would be obliged upon the request of the Argentine Government to extradite people who disobeyed Argentine law. The captain asked if, at this time, there was an extradition treaty between the two countries. This question puzzled Hernandez. Why would a Jew be so frightened that he hesitated to promote freedom of the press? Perhaps defying the law is frightening no matter how good the reason for doing so.

"Under Spanish domination," replied Hernandez, "freedom was only a word in the dictionary. After the revolution, Argentines expected a lot more and achieved much. But this regime presents us with a big problem. On the surface, it looks like socialistic democracy. In reality, though, it's a dictatorship—one with fascist tendencies. And—"

"But is there an extradition treaty?" The captain had become a little annoyed and alarmed.

"So far, Mr. Kesselmann, no. But there could be in the near future. So, we must act quickly. The public is still angry that *La Esperanza* has disappeared from the newsstands. If it reappears, even if not at the newsstands, people will continue to support it, in spite of its long absence, because it protected their democratic rights."

The captain now realized what this lawyer suggested made a lot of sense. However, he answered slowly, looking directly at him, but without actually committing himself to any specific action. "You've given me many facts to consider, Señor Hernandez. I'll need a few days to think how to arrange everything. As soon as I can, I'll give you my answer and have our secretaries schedule a meeting."

"Thank you, Mr. Kesselmann. I appreciate that you want to consider this very carefully. If you decide to cooperate, we will meet in Montevideo. Meanwhile—well, I would like to have a drink with you, but it's past six o'clock and I must get back to my office."

After Hernandez left, the captain took a few minutes to reconsider the issues, then glanced at his watch. He had only a half hour to review Spanish, but his mind was on the teacher not on grammar. She was unlike Lara in many ways. Lara was seductive and had manipulative affectations. She attended fashion shows, social teas, liked to dance, gossip, to see and be seen. During the War, movies had been very popular, especially musicals and others in which romantic love triumphs against all odds, particularly military losses. In 1942, she saw three times Germany's most popular movie, starring matinée idols Victor Staal and Zara Leander in a shallow propaganda-ridden love story, *Die Grosse Liebe;* its upbeat song *Davon geht die Welt nicht unter* (the world isn't collapsing from this) was her favourite melody. They had realized that some of these movies had political undertones, even though most of them on the surface were merely entertaining confections. During the War, the films produced by UFA, Germany's greatest movie company (1918-1945) controlled by Goebbel's propaganda machine with messages of service to the Reich and victory, took up a good portion of her time and buoyed her spirits. With victory becoming an elusive goal, most people needed encouragement. Now, in retrospect, he could see Lara more objectively than he ever had. Beneath the glamorous charm was a beautiful and frivolous woman. But Severina—which is what he called her in the privacy of his own thoughts—there was something very unusual about her. She was beautiful, intelligent, patient with her students and dedicated to her work. She cared deeply about her mother, and devoted her spare time, helping at the store. The captain daydreamed about courting her as long as necessary to develop her trust in him and then reveal that he, too, was a Catholic. What a relief it would be to shed this cloak of duplicity—to be his true self. Severina would be his soul mate. They would plan a family. He would build a global paper enterprise and become a business mogul like the ones in the United States. After this evening's class he would invite Severina for dinner to discuss *La Esperanza's* problem. Instinctively, he felt she must have been a subscriber to the newspaper and interested in restoring its circulation. She could probably shed some light on how this paper was ruined and the danger in store for those who help newspapers condemned by this Government. Afterwards they would spend the night together, followed by arrangements to see each other on a daily basis. Miss Mendoza interrupted his tender reverie. "Patron, you must leave now. Otherwise, you'll be late for your class."

"Yes, thanks. Please put tomorrow's agenda on the front desk."

Quickly, the captain changed into a less businesslike suit and rushed out to find a taxi. When he arrived, it was late. The class had already begun. He found a seat very near the teacher's desk. At first, her appearance absorbed all his attention. He heard only half of what was said. But she began to speak so sincerely that he listened more attentively. "If you could learn a language in several easy lessons, which is what many advertisements tell you, then almost everyone would be able to speak a few languages. But that, as you now know from personal experience, is not true. You need perseverance and patience."

Like most teachers, she knew when a student was not paying attention and looking at Mr. Kesselmann she suspected that he was daydreaming, probably about business. This continued for an hour. After class, he waited until the other students had left.

"Well," she said, "you must have had a busy and tiring day."

"As a matter of fact, Señora Filipovic, I did. And I'm sure that you did, too. Will you be my guest for dinner, where we can relax?"

She was curious about him. He is very debonair, must have gone out with many women, she thought, and kept most of them at arm's length. What would a relationship with him actually lead to? She was definitely interested.

"Oh, what a shame. I have to rush home. Mother is having a few of her cronies over for dinner tonight, and I must be there to help. I certainly would like to have dinner with you, but not tonight."

His disappointment was visible, so she quickly added "Meanwhile, Mr. Kesselmann, I can give you a lift to your hotel. My car is in the downstairs garage."

"Oh, well, in that case, yes, I wouldn't mind a lift. And we can set an alternative evening when you will be free."

As soon as they got into the car and drove off, the captain ventured to ask her about *La Esperanza*. "You do sympathize with the people who print it, particularly the way they were put out of business?"

THE EXPATRIATE

She answered him hesitantly, rather apprehensively. The captain was very much aware of this. "You are a newcomer here, Mr. Kesselmann. How does the ruin of this newspaper concern you?"

"Well, I'll be frank with you. My lawyer has asked me to help *La Esperanza* start publishing again. It's a matter of freedom of the press. You don't expect the Government to stifle the voice of the people?"

"Well, no, of course not. The Government should welcome public discussion, not try to stifle it. Yes, but that's very idealistic. Some governments tolerate public discussion, it's true, but I doubt that many of them actually welcome criticism." She paused.

"By the way," he interrupted the discussion, "can we meet for supper tomorrow night or Friday night? I want to discuss my participation in Hernandez's proposal."

"No, not tomorrow night. I have a stack of papers to correct. If I don't, then the students won't be able to prepare for their next lesson. As for Friday night, mother and I go to synagogue on Fridays. If you'd like to join us, that would be great. But you'd have to bring your passport if this is the first time in our synagogue. A few years ago, you might have heard about it, a group of anti-Semites attacked us. Some people were injured, so we're very careful now."

The captain was surprised, to say the least. He sat there as if paralyzed, dumbstruck, speechless. Hot and cold flushes in rapid succession seeped through his body. He was tongue-tied. Severina, a Jewish teacher in a Catholic country! Glancing at her finely chiseled profile, beautiful face, a manner free of pretence, he wondered why she was so unlike his notion of Jewish women. And she was a religious one. He had heard that many Jews in Germany and other modern countries were not religious. After wiping his forehead, with that ever-present muslin handkerchief, he slowly regained his composure and absorbed the significance of her words. She was waiting for a reply and could not understand his silence. German Jews, it was rumoured, were not very observant of the rituals of their religion. Perhaps Jaakob was one of those who visited the synagogue once a year on Yom Kippur, the Day of Atonement.

JEANNETTE MOSCOVITCH

By the time they reached the hotel and she had steered the car into the dark empty lot, he'd regained his equilibrium and moved so close to her that their bodies touched. Inflamed with desire, he kissed her fervently, as if to release the pent-up feeling repressed for so long. For the moment he forgot that she was a Jewess. "Saturday at seven for dinner." She shook her head in approval, waited for him to get out of the car and drove off.

He opened the door of his room at approximately nine o'clock, when most Argentines begin dinner, and he too began to feel hungry. This reminded him that he was a foreigner. Although Argentine beef was world famous, for some reason, he wanted his mother's stewed pickled beef and fried potatoes. On a whim, he called the restaurant downstairs, asked for some *sauerbraten* and potatoes, and expected no one to know what that was. To his surprise, though, the restaurant did indeed serve *sauerbraten*. And, he then asked himself, why not? Since the War, after all, thousands of Germans have migrated to Argentina.

While waiting for dinner, the captain sat down on his favourite armchair, shut his eyes, and sipped a cocktail. A ghost of yesteryear kept resurfacing with bittersweet memories of home. Suddenly, he remembered Brigitta and Lara arguing about clothing. "But you're a young lady now," Lara would say. "These pants are not for you. What's wrong with this beautiful dress that Granny bought for you?" Brigitta did look more attractive in the clothes that her grandmother bought for her, but that made no difference. She wanted to make her own choices. Besides, she probably envied her mother's beauty. A smile crossed his face. They must be having the same arguments, he thought, even now. Still reminiscing, he pictured his lovely mother-in-law. The smile faded, however, when he recalled his haughty father-in-law. In one way or another, the captain loved his wife and daughter. But why? He had never understood either. Do you have to understand people to love them? What drove Lara to be such a social butterfly, especially in the Nazi party? He had to stop reminiscing! How many times had he reprimanded himself for dwelling on the past? But how was he to live without a backward glance, to erase a whole part of his life? Of course, the oft-repeated remedy is to keep busy and leave little time for old recollections.

THE EXPATRIATE

A knock on the door interrupted his thoughts. It was the waiter with his dinner. The captain settled down to enjoy the physical comfort of good food. And the *sauerbraten* was delicious, indeed, albeit cooked in the Swiss style. This was probably due to the excellent quality of Argentine beef. After washing down the meal with some red wine, a mellow feeling of well-being suffused his whole body. He stepped out onto the balcony to breathe in the cool night air. The sky was sprinkled with gold specks. The leafy branches of the rows of trees swayed slowly. Below was a motionless stillness. Was the world really at peace now? Yes, the world was at peace at the moment, and so was he. Back inside as he climbed into bed, images of Severina unconsciously blurred his vision of desires without restrictions to be enjoyed on Saturday night.

Soon his mind filled again with questions. Would it be appropriate in this country, he wondered, to send a corsage of orchids? Did she notice how he had hesitated but quickly gave a reasonable excuse after refusing to go to synagogue with her on Friday night? What had made him fall in love with a Jewess? What is her religion all about? He sat up in bed, turned on the light, and reached for The Jewish Manual, opening it where it asked "How did the Jews survive the three centuries between 300 to 600 when there were continuous wars for religious dominance?"

"How did Jews survive during the Dark Ages of political and military chaos in Europe? During the troubled years from 300 to 600, Christians and pagans struggled for dominance. The wonder is not that the Jews survived but that any community survived. On the Christian side were newly converted Gauls, Vandals, Visigoths, Ostrogoths, and Huns. These were vigorous but intellectually unsophisticated communities. The Jews, however, were intellectually sophisticated. Many of them, at least in the early period, had studied Greek philosophy, literature, and science. Most of them were literate. Not surprisingly, Christian regimes needed them and placed them in administrative positions. Some rulers tried legislation to keep Jews from dominating society, but they seldom

enforced the resulting laws. Jews continued as judges and magistrates, scholars, merchants, artisans, and farmers. (2)

The book slid from his hand, and he fell asleep.

Meanwhile, Severina drove home as fast as she could. When she arrived, her mother's guests were still in the living room, enjoying their appetizers.

"Sorry for being late, Galina. I gave one of my students a lift home."

Galina preferred to be addressed by her first name. She and her daughter enjoyed the same camaraderie as with friends of their own age. Instinctively, Galina knew that her daughter's exuberance after a hard day's work must have come from some new interest, perhaps a romantic one.

"I worried, Severina. Something urgent must have detained you. Just help me carry in the salad, and say hello to our guests."

Galina's friends were a coterie of concerned intellectuals. Among the guests tonight were the Groznis, Count Tibor and Countess Marisa, from Hungary; Dr. Igor Herrenkevitch, whose wife Elizabeta had died three years earlier; Julio Narruda, a history professor and wife, Rosia, and an elusive journalist, Henri Pavlosek, just in from Prague.

"Oh, Galina," exclaimed Severina, "what smells so good?"

"Well, let's see. Marisa brought her homemade goulash. I made Russian *haloopzie* (stuffed cabbage with meat and rice). Rosia insisted on bringing her *medialunes* (small crisp croissants), and Igor arrived with *alfajores* (nut and honey confections) for dessert. Henri sent those magnificent flowers over there."

Galina radiated pleasure. As soon as Severina entered the dining room with a salad bowl, Igor began to help her. He had already mixed drinks for everyone. At the table, a few minutes later, Pavlosek began to tell his friends what they were eager to know, but hesitated to ask.

"My supervisor sent me here, to investigate the Peron dictatorship and compare it with that of our Soviet occupiers. Actually, we've recently had two dictatorships in Czechoslovakia. First was the Nazi regime, thanks to Neville Chamberlain, who allowed Hitler to take over in 1939. The Nazis were brutal, of course, but we could at least communicate with them. Most of us had either grown up speaking German or learned it at school. Culturally, we had really been part of Germany. But now, we have another dictatorship. And with the Soviets, everything is different. Even though we're ethnically related to the Russians, as Slavs, we have no connection at all with Russian culture. We want them out of Czechoslovakia. But I'm not sure what the exact focus of my article will be. I'm waiting for specific instructions from my newspapers."

"Don't believe for one moment," said the count, slowly because of a speech impediment, "that you're going to realize the humanitarian ideals of Tomas Masaryk. Do you remember his slogan? 'Truth will conquer.' That was his slogan. But I doubt that anyone still believes that. Well, I don't want to be pessimistic or even cynical. But I do want to be realistic. The world today is just as chaotic as it was before the War. And where can we find a wise leader?"

Severina interrupted the count. She considered him a born doomsayer and a pessimist. "It seems to me," she said impatiently while looking at Henri, "that your supervisor has sent you here for a reason. He must be aware somewhat of our situation and realize that your focus should be on the labour movement, as well as on the suppression of a free press."

"Yes, but I must still wait for specific instructions. In the end, my employer might tell me to write a broad overview of life in Argentina and Brazil—that is, to ignore Peron. Otherwise, if I don't follow instructions my article won't be printed at all. And that would undermine the idea that truth will conquer."

"What should interest most Europeans," Igor suggested, "is an article on what the word 'nation' means. Is it a body of politically organized people under a single government who merely live in the same territory, a counterpoint to the ethnic nationalism that Hitler preached? In fact, I'm thinking of Czechoslovakia. Why shouldn't the Czechs and the Slovaks live together in peace? Or is a nation a group of people who live in the same territory and have the same racial origin? Or perhaps it's a group of citizens who live in the same territory, respect religious and racial differences, and adhere to a common political and social rule? My hope is that we can create liberal democracies based on tolerance for diverse races and religions."

He stopped to fill wine glasses around the table. Taking a sip, Count Grozni broke the silence.

"As I say, that sounds very nice. But is it going to happen?"

Before anyone could answer him, Galina came around with the *goulash*. Igor began to fill the wine glasses again. Taking a large gulp of wine, Henri was the first to respond. "He has a point, you know. Too many of us in Europe hate each other. The Croats hate the Serbs. The Serbs hate the Croats. That's the way it is. That's the way it has been for hundreds of years. How can we fight against it?"

"What Igor says is true," added the count. "Maybe this is a good time for you, Henri, to discuss liberal democracy. Otherwise, the wars will continue."

"Maybe not in Latin America," said Severina." But it will take a long time before we can achieve some kind of liberal democracy."

"Severina," Narruda answered, "why not? Why not? I mean, just examine this regime. It's a dictatorship and fascist as well. But people defeated fascism in Europe. Do you really believe it can't be done here?"

Narruda, a highly qualified history professor and an outspoken liberal humanist, could not find work in his field. Fortunately, his uncle had used some influence to get him a post as a custom official. It was steady work and paid well. But he never missed an opportunity to wake up people politically.

"You probably all know how Peron rose to power. He got his start in the army, which had already been influenced by Nazi advisors and ..."

But Igor interrupted. "When I came to this country and studied its history, I began to see that there was a problem. This movement, its seizure of power, scared me. It reminded me of what I had already seen while studying in Poland and Lithuania. But I came here looking for a peaceful haven to practise my profession. So this really upset me. Sorry for interrupting. Carry on, Julio."

THE EXPATRIATE

"Well, I don't really need to. In fact, you've all seen Peron in action. I'll say this to you, Severina, because you're a teacher. Peron has given us free education, it's true. Are you aware then, that your university chooses teachers for their political views, not their academic expertise? But other people are in much worse trouble than you are. The unions won't do much for their members, because the government controls most unions. So I think that we are heading for unrest in this country. I know it will take a long time to crush the undesirable factions. But I suspect that Henri won't have the courage to expose all this."

Severina sat there, silent and distraught. She was thinking about Jaakob Kesselmann. He had fled from one dictatorship only to face another one. She hoped that people could avoid trouble—could enjoy normal lives—by living unobtrusively, inconspicuously, uninvolved in politics.

"Yes, well," said Igor, "let's have some tea now. Look, I brought my own little samovar."

While brewing the tea, he hesitated, stopped, and then made an announcement. "I've had some news," he said shyly. "You're about to be served tea by the new chief surgeon and director of the Argentine State Hospital's cardiology department."

Galina was the first to applaud. "Oh, Igor, that is good news. We all know how much you deserve that job. You're one of the very few to be rewarded for merit."

Henri remained solemn. Suddenly, he got up, stood behind his chair, facing Narruda, and said what had been on his mind during the past few minutes.

"Well, Julio, you're wrong about me. I'm not going to wait for instructions. I'm going to find out the truth about this regime. My problem is a practical one: how to get the truth, write about it, but avoid the inspectors and censors. So, here's what I'm going to do. I'm going to memorize as much as I can, and smuggle out the rest. You've made me realize that journalists have both a professional and a moral duty to seek the truth no matter what the consequences. And so, I'll be on my way. Sorry to leave early, but my time is more limited than I thought it was only a few minutes ago."

After the other guests had left, mother and daughter agreed to tidy up and leave the kitchen in order for next morning. Then, they sat down and began to chat.

"You looked lovely tonight, Severina. I noticed Igor staring at you several times. Now just listen to me. He's handsome, he's educated, he's intelligent, he's fairly rich—and now, he's an eligible widower. Just think about him, that's all I ask. He would be a very suitable husband for you. And by the way, the Quitos invited us to a garden party on Saturday night, so try to be ready for eight o'clock."

"Oh, Galina, no. Not this Saturday. I'm going out with Jaakob Kesselmann. You know, I told you about him, the German Jew who is setting up a paper mill."

Galina knew her daughter's temperament. Severina would not break an appointment. "Oh, these German Jews—they're not our kind. You know what people say about them. They've absorbed the worst features of German Christians."

"Oh, Mom, you're just as prejudiced as, well, the Nazis. You should know better."

"And, judging from what you've said about this Jaakob," Galina continued, without acknowledging the truth of what her daughter had just said, "I get the idea that he's a wily person. Somehow, I don't trust him. I trust Igor."

"Galina, that's unfair. Jaakob is like Igor in many ways. He just has a different background. As a matter of fact, I'll find out much more about him on Saturday."

She stopped to see her mother's reaction. This, she knew, could provoke a bitter argument. But Galina kept watching her daughter. Any verbal opposition, she had learned from experience, would add fuel to the fire. The best strategy would be an indirect one: merely arousing suspicions. "You know, Severina, most of these Germans, both Christians and Jews, come here under false pretences. They all pretend to be extremely rich. And some of them are, it's true. But they get rich here, I think, because they know how to exploit cheap labour. Jaakob is like a whirlwind: learning Spanish, setting up his business, buying land. He's alone, isn't that what he told you? No living relatives? Well, then, he's free. He can take advantage of women without making any commitment to them. You're old enough to know that."

Severina moved forward and kissed her mother tenderly. "I understand what you're saying. Really, I do. And I love you Mom. You prefer Igor. I'm aware what a wonderful person he is, what a wonderful husband he would be. But at the moment, Jaakob Kesselmann has caught my fancy. It's true, what you keep saying, that most men who come from far away say that they're bachelors or widowers. You are right. But you also add, who knows the truth? I really believe this man is sincere. Somehow I trust Jaakob. Please let me have your blessing until I find out more about him." Galina had the answer to her efforts and the signal—leave well enough alone.

"All right, Severina have a nice time this Saturday and let's go to bed."

Next day, Severina went about her regular routine: preparing her lecture, correcting essays. But uppermost in her mind was Saturday night. Before class, she borrowed a German-Spanish dictionary from the library and memorized a few German words. On Friday morning, she found a note in her mailbox at the university. It was from Jaakob.

Dear Severina: Looking forward to Saturday. How will we arrange this? Will I call for you, or will you call for me? I still don't know the restaurants around here, so I'll let you choose one and make the reservation. You won't be able to reach me at the office, because I have some meetings elsewhere. Leave a message with my secretary. Love Jaakob.

Severina was overjoyed. She could not fathom why these few words brought so much pleasure and excitement. She replied immediately. "Will call for you on Saturday at seven." A note Carmela put on the captain's desk.

Friday was a hectic day for the captain. Abogado Hernandez approved his lease for the office. The captain was very pleased, because the *Avenida Neuve de Julio*—reputedly the world's widest street—would obviously make a good impression on clients. He received a note from the Keunenbergs, regarding a meeting in

Montevideo to inspect their factory. And Valdez, part owner of Chilean Airways, wanted to know if he had made enough progress on the charter to convene a meeting of the board. Carlos Boisy, president of the Car Manufacturers' Union wanted to know how many employees he was expected to hire for the new paper mill. In a folder, finally, he found brochures from factories in Stockholm, Zürich, Berlin and Copenhagen. These showed photographs of the latest machines he would need and instructions on how to use them. The captain suspected that he would not find enough trained mechanics in Argentina to operate these machines and would have to recruit them from the machine manufacturers. Absorbed in all of these matters, time slipped away. When he looked out the window, it was eight-thirty but not yet completely dark.

Exhausted, he put away all these letters and began to think about his date on Saturday. Like a schoolboy, obsessed over his first love, the captain could not get Severina out of his mind. He told himself that his infatuation was the result of their similar European cultural background. But they were different in one way. She, being from Czechoslovakia, would vehemently disagree that a superior capitalistic nation like Germany should control all of Europe. Yet he believed if that did not happen, scrapping nations would separate into small ethnic units. It still had to be proven that a group of small ethnic sovereign nations, each fighting for supremacy of power, would be a feasible solution for Europe. But he vowed never to discuss this with her. It made no difference to him, ultimately, if she was Czech, Jewish or Hindu. He was in love with her.

At the hotel's flower shop, he asked a clerk about the custom of sending a corsage before a rendezvous. After hesitating, she said that yes, women always liked receiving flowers. The captain noticed her vague hesitation, so he ordered a dozen roses instead and wrote a banal sentiment on the card: *"Can hardly wait until seven o'clock tomorrow night. Hasta la vista. Jaakob."*

It was Galina, however, who opened the box of flowers and read the note. Clearly, there was no point in opposing her daughter. As soon as Severina came home and caught sight of the roses, she smiled to herself. So far, she thought, Jaakob was so thoughtful and gracious.

THE EXPATRIATE

On Saturday night, the concierge handed Severina a note from the captain. She was to go directly to his suite. As usual, the captain was impeccably dressed. He looked handsome, she thought, but tired. They sat down and talked for a few minutes.

"Jaakob, this must be champagne, but it tastes unusual. Very good but quite unusual." "Oh, I chose a German one. Let's have a little more, we must finish it before we leave." It did not take long for them to feel the effects.

"I'm rather unsteady, Jaakob, and dizzy. Let's wait until I'm ready to drive."

"That suits me fine. There's no rush." He took her in his arms and kissed her neck, putting one hand on her breast. She pressed against him, inflamed by his nearness. "Shall we relax in the bedroom to hear what's on the radio before going out on the town?" On Saturdays, the chambermaids finished their work before six o'clock because they had to get up early Sundays to attend Church services. All bedrooms were prepared for the night by removing the bedspreads and folding down the bedcovers, ready for slipping into bed.

Both sat down on the bed, and instinctively, they fell into each other's arms, undressed discreetly, and breathlessly tumbled under the bedcover sheets, locking their naked bodies together. Human warmth, kisses and endearing terms were accompanied by rhythmic movements reflected in the mirror hanging on the opposite wall. Soon the stirrings beneath the sheet covers stopped. Silence became eloquent as the orange golden rays of the fading sunset filtered through the half-closed drapes. Then complete darkness. Tension, angst, exhaustion, faded images, all vanished in a dreamless, peaceful slumber.

Fleeting beams of bright sunshine, penetrating through the half-closed drapes, wakened them Sunday morning. The radio clock showed eight-thirty. Severina wakened first but remained motionless in bed until the captain began to stir. For a few minutes he was completely disoriented. Looking at the woman beside him, for an instant he thought he was in a Berlin hotel and his steward had sent him a call girl for the night. Meanwhile, Severina slipped out of bed, put on the blue satin peignoir supplied by the hotel for itinerant female guests, and waited for the captain to speak first.

He got up, sat on the edge of the bed as if lifeless, then stood up mechanically, put on his brown silk housecoat, and peered at the woman clad in blue, standing near the window. Severina, with a look of happy contentment, a little perplexed, watching his movements, waited for him to speak. Suddenly, he became alert, conscious of where he was and with whom. Why he was Jaakob Kesselmann, in love with Severina Filipovic, the lady with whom he had shared such passionate love, all night.

"Good morning, darling. You are wonderful. I love you so much."

She returned his kiss, quietly whispering, "I love you too." It had been a long time since she had experienced such tenderness, and it overwhelmed her.

The Captain had by now regained his full equilibrium. "Shall we have breakfast sent up or would you prefer to eat in the dining room?"

"Perhaps a secluded corner of the dining room would be more comfortable. You mentioned you have important business to discuss with me, especially the *La Esperanza* project."

The Captain agreed. For the first time since his escape from Germany, he felt relaxed and exhilarated. While dressing, he recalled Hermann Baumbach's remark after a night of love with Clarice. Smiling into the mirror while shaving, he muttered to himself, "Jaakob Kesselmann, you now have the same gentle dove Hermann had, only I will not let my dove fly away."

THE MARRIAGE PROPOSAL

While the captain was counting his blessings to have found a gentle dove, a different turn of events was taking place in Calgary, where his friend Hermann Baumbach felt he had a tiger to tame. All he wanted was an efficient, elegant wife to keep his home orderly and his children happy. He kept asking himself if he should continue or not with this good-looking, charming Mrs. Rose Waterman. Perhaps it would be prudent to arrange a trial engagement period, and then decide whether to marry. He told Miss Pearson to send Mrs. Waterman a dozen carnations.

Rose received the bouquet of flowers with mixed feelings. The attached note invited her to spend the next weekend at his apartment. She was ambivalent about this invitation and his true intentions. Nevertheless, she sent a message of acceptance. But this time, there was to be no angst. She would wear simpler clothes, plain, *à l'anglaise*, perhaps that is what he preferred. Then she returned to her studies for next day's exam.

Hermann received her note while writing a letter to his family:

Dear Dad, I hope everyone is well in spite of the political tension in Palestine. Please tell me more about the situation, because our newspaper doesn't say much about it. As for business, our merchandise is very much appreciated, and if this continues, we won't need to expand into the American market. Living here has changed my mind about several things. This country is vast with a sparse population. Instead of setting up plants in several cities, I think it would be more economical to have one large plant here and a few warehouses in cities with at least two hospitals. And here's some good news. Since we will provide many new jobs, the government has decided to give us a special reduction on the import duties for raw materials that are not available in Canada. Also, I am thinking of marrying Rose Waterman. But first we'll become engaged for a year. If compatible, marriage will follow, and if that happens I will write you and invite everyone to the engagement. Love to all, Hermann.

That weekend when Hermann answered the door, he found someone who looked like an old-fashioned English schoolteacher. For once, Rose was dressed very modestly. Since she always took great pains to be fashionably attired, he wondered what had caused the change. Nevertheless, he maintained his savoir faire with a complimentary greeting.

"Rose. How nice to see you. You look charming and kissable as usual." He then proceeded to do so.

She smiled weakly, recognizing from the timbre of his voice a perfunctory compliment. Obviously, she had made too great an effort to achieve the simple look. During dinner, he began to describe his adventure while wondering around downtown Calgary. In a rather shabby district, he had seen a sign advertising: "The Best Delicatessen West Of Montreal."

"As soon as I walked in and smelled the smoked meat, Rose, I felt hungry. And there was a Jewish fellow, sitting at a table nearby. He must have known that I was a newcomer, so he invited me to join him. A friendly guy. He told me about the house specialties, so I bought what he suggested."

"He surely didn't miss anything," Rose could hardly hide her smile. "Let's see: smoked meat, corned beef, stuffed chicken, salami, hot dogs—kosher, I presume—pickles, sauerkraut, enough to feed a Chinese army."

"Well, you always accuse me of eating like a German, so now I'm eating like a Canadian." She did not answer immediately. Hermann's jokes were charming. She gazed at the elegantly appointed dining table with its floral centerpiece. He always tried to be so perfect. How could she temper her affection for him? To crown the delicatessen dinner he had gone out of his way to buy

Jewish wine. She leaned forward and was about to kiss him but laughter overcame her.

"What? What's so funny?"

"You perfect German '*yekke*'. (Teutonic, pedantic, rigid) I bet that was Finkelstien, co-owner of the store who always sits within sight of anyone coming in, eating and enjoying the food. Then, he invites the customer to have a drink with him and suggests that they ask for the many expensive items on the menu."

Hermann shrugged his shoulders, disregarding her remark. "He included a surprise package: thickly sliced rye bread. But I thought that it was sliced too thick for sandwiches, so elsewhere I bought this white English bread. Look how thin the slices are."

Rose couldn't believe what she heard. Whoever ate smoked meat sandwiches on white English bread? She burst out laughing. Those *German Yekkes!* Hermann couldn't understand why she was laughing.

"Let's drink to Palestine, Rose, with this kosher wine." He poured two full glasses, and watched Rose take the first sip.

"M'm" she murmured, "it is absolutely delicious. At least it is not bitter dry. It's wonderfully sweet." Hermann took two sips and stopped. It was unbelievable what the Polish Ashkenazim Jews liked. Everything was over sweetened!"

Rose's family, Hermann knew, came from Poland. His father had often referred to the Polish Jews with disdain, although his mother had reminded him of the yeshiva in Cracow, the oldest and most celebrated in Europe. Hermann put aside the sweet wine and began to make his sandwich taking one slice of white and one slice of thick rye bread, and filled it with a variety of meats. He watched Rose stacking her skyscraper sandwich on two thick slices of rye bread and eating it gustily. "There is nothing like an old-fashioned smoked meat sandwich. Better than a filet mignon." It was useless to contradict her.

"Shall we go dancing after dinner?" she asked suggestively.

"Perhaps we should clear the dishes first, tidy up and then decide. There is a special radio program, featuring a symphony orchestra from Moscow. Would you prefer that instead of going out on the town?" She agreed. At least they enjoyed the same kind of entertainment. In spite of some of her aggressive traits, Rose was charming, clever and someone with whom he could discuss his business. What was he searching for?

"Maybe" he admitted to himself, "I am the kind of person who cannot be swept off my feet, contrary to the romantic lovers, portrayed in the movies and novels. Maybe it's my fault." He gazed at Rose. She looked radiant and beautiful, in spite of her old-fashioned outfit. Rose had similar thoughts about Hermann. He was charming enough. And yet, something was missing. This evening she had a mellow feeling being near the man she loved unequivocally and who, at the moment, was trying so hard to please her. She wanted to enjoy this pleasure and forget the stark reality that Hermann was a part-time lover who avoided any kind of permanent commitment.

After the concert, both sat down in the parlor with a liqueur. Hermann decided it was a good moment to suggest that they become engaged on a trial basis for a year.

"Rose, do you think that we should be engaged?"

It came as a complete surprise. She drank the liqueur too quickly and began to cough. Suddenly, she realized what he had said. "Engaged? You mean engaged, engaged to be married?"

"Of course" he added, "I think that we shouldn't have a long engagement. A year would be just about right, don't you think?"

"But why do we need an engagement? It seems to me that engagements, and especially long ones, are out of date."

She stopped, afraid to bungle everything. Either he wants to get married or not. Hermann did not answer her. He would try again when they were in bed; maybe she would be more receptive to a trial engagement for a year. Both felt a little weary and slipped quietly into bed. Hermann fondled and kissed her gently.

"Now let's plan a little for our future. Will you answer me?" She stopped kissing him and slipped out of his grasp. "What purpose does an engagement serve? It's old fashioned. When people were poor, the custom was to have bridal showers and engagements to which friends and relatives brought gifts to help the young couple set up a household. Today, this is unnecessary.

Why go to the trouble of making two receptions? Either you want to get married or not." She stopped, fearing to hear his response.

"You caught me by surprise." He lied to hide his real motive. "I thought all Jewish girls wanted an engagement. I was under the impression it gave them some sort of status. Both my sisters insisted on engagement parties. In any case, it has a purpose. It gives people time—"

"Time for what?" she interrupted.

"People must adjust to each other and, and—you know, to the whole idea of being married."

"You really don't expect me to swallow that, do you? Haven't we already adjusted to each other?"

Rose knew what was going on in his mind. He was hesitating, and still not sure that he wanted to marry her. Hermann glanced sideways at her saddened expression, and saw that pristine luminous skin, her kissable mouth, feeling the warmth of her lithe body, a yearning like an addictive craving engulfed him. He longed to hold her close, never to let her go—something daemonic possessed him. Man must have a mate. It complements him. He kissed her cheek and whispered, "Rose will you marry me?"

Realizing abruptly what he had said, Rose instantly released her pent-up emotions and her ardour burst forth. She put her arms around his shoulders and kissed him passionately. No more words were needed. They celebrated their honeymoon night before setting the date of their wedding, and woke up next day at noon, embraced and kissed tenderly. The vast blue sky, with its looming radiant golden sunshine reflected their elated spirits. Hermann suggested brunch at a luxury hotel to celebrate the occasion. Rose preferred to remain where they were to have the privacy of discussing details for their wedding.

The first item was to determine the date of the wedding. Rose would graduate at the end of June, so the wedding could be scheduled for early July. But the conversation soon took a peculiar turn from Rose's point of view.

"Rose, I don't know how to ask this, but—do you want to have children? Can you have children?"

"You should have asked last night," said Rose. "But yes, Hermann, I can still have children. And yes, I do want children. I've never wanted to have them with anyone else. But no more than two. Managing a career at the same time, well, I won't have the time or energy for more than two."

Hermann hoped to have at least four children, but wanted to be flexible for the time being.

"Anyway, let's arrange first things first."

"And what," she asked nervously, "is first on your list?"

"Isn't it obvious?" asked Hermann. "Do we need a marriage contract to declare our personal assets? Are we to be married separate or common as to property? What's the general rule?"

Rose jotted all this down on a writing pad.

"And what about the wedding itself. Will it be in a synagogue or a hotel? How many guests will we invite?"

"Wait a minute," said Rose. "There's something on my list, too, you know. What about my engagement ring? I'd like a ruby ring of four karats with a few small diamonds on each side and, a simple diamond circle for the wedding band. I know a few jewelry dealers and will inquire first, make my choice, discuss price and then we will go together to see if you approve."

He knew that Rose would bargain down the price, because she was smart that way.

"As for the wedding, that should take place in a synagogue. I'll invite 450 guests, and expect approximately 400 will come. We'll also have to invite some members of the synagogue, my lawyer, my doctor, my accountant, my close friends, and a few government officials. If I'm to set up a business as a financial advisor, after all, it would make sense to have a big wedding reception. I could use the opportunity to meet potential clients, who will expect their investment advisor to be financially well off and—"

Hermann interrupted with a wave of his hand. "You don't mean to tell me, surely, that you'd turn our wedding into an advertisement for your business?"

"What's wrong with that? It's better than an ad in the newspaper. You show your clients what kind of person you are, that you have assets, that you're stable, that you have friends. What better way to build credibility?"

From a purely business point of view, this made sense. But a wedding for him was a celebration of life to be shared with family and friends and not a sales pitch for self aggrandizement. He wrote something on a pad and asked her to continue.

"Let's see. What else? Oh yes, the invitations. I think that I'd like them to be written in gold on parchment paper, and suggest that our guests make contributions in our names to their favourite charities, not waste money on gifts for us."

"It seems to me that you've been planning this for a very long time."

"Well," she replied shrugging her shoulders, "it's true. I do want my second wedding to be a whole lot better than the first one. But, if you want to change anything—well, I am willing to listen."

She bent forward on the kitchen table, looked at him, and continued.

"I prefer our synagogue, because it would be able to offer services that a hotel couldn't. It has two kosher kitchens. And we also could hire musicians. As for the flowers, there are plenty of florists."

"Is that all?"

"No, we still have to think about what we're going to wear. You're going to wear a light gray tuxedo. I'm going to wear a pale lilac gown, not a white one. And the bridesmaids—we'll have six. Each one will wear a different pastel shade of chiffon. I hate bridesmaids, who look identical, don't you?"

"How can I disagree with you, Rose? I've never been married. But won't all this take a lot of organizing?"

"I'll take care of everything, Hermann. The only thing that you'll have to do is walk down the aisle."

"And what about the cost? This sounds very, very expensive—"

"Don't worry about that. I'll price everything. In fact, I will contribute. That's what my parents would do, if they were alive. Any other questions?"

"No, you're a wonderful lady. It looks as if all I have to do is, have a good appetite for the wedding feast, build up strength for the honeymoon, keep an open cheque book and smile before the cameras. But you still haven't mentioned any legal matters. What is the procedure in this country? If both husbands and wives in Canada have their own assets, do they require legal contracts in addition to religious certifications?"

His father had insisted that each of his daughters have a secular marriage contract. And he had been wise, because one husband had eventually come close to bankruptcy and the creditors were unable to seize his wife's assets. Hermann wanted to be just as careful, because Rose was planning to establish her own business. If she ever ran into trouble, he realized, a marriage contract would protect his assets.

"I certainly agree. That's because of my experience with Sam, my previous husband."

For a moment, she leaned back in the chair, and a sad shadow spread across her face as she recalled all the endearing terms he said during the night—yet never, "Rose I love you." But in a flash her face lit up again. She was certain he would say it when they were married and having a pleasant life together.

"One more thing," Hermann wanted to know, "how will you manage to take care of a husband, children, our house and your business?"

"I've thought of all those things, too." She knew the answer by heart. "We'll hire a housekeeper, of course, and then a nanny for the children. A professional nanny would be better than an overindulgent mother, don't you agree?"

Hermann nodded his head, but Rose could not tell if he did so to agree with her or merely to avoid an argument. "But" he added after thinking a little, "I will insist that you divide your work day, so you'll be able to spend part of the morning with the children we may have."

"Hermann, it's enough for now. Let's relax."

On Monday morning, Hermann prepared a telegram for his parents in Tel Aviv. Miss Pearson read it and congratulated him without much enthusiasm. He nodded, went into his office, and sat down to rethink what had happened over the weekend. As an adolescent, he had wanted a life of adventure and excitement. But now, as an adult, he preferred stability. All he really wanted was to earn a good living, support a family in comfort, and practise his religion. Rose, however, he thought to himself, wants more than being an ordinary *Hausfrau*. She did not seem to need a man at all. He did not doubt that she would become successful in business. But the finance and investment business was not an easy one for a woman to succeed in.

Miss Pearson knocked on the door and said that she had received orders from Winnipeg and Kingston.

"They want immediate delivery, Mr. Baumbach. How soon can we ship the equipment?"

"Call my father in Tel Aviv and ask if he can arrange for an immediate shipment. Also, I need to know about the cost and timing of air-freight to Kingston and Winnipeg. Oh, and send a box of the finest chocolates to Mrs. Waterman with a note. It should say, *"For a sweet beginning. Your Hermann."* Without further ado, he began to check the week's agenda and examine the pile of letters on his desk. But his thoughts returned to Rose. A nagging doubt kept disturbing him. Was he converting lust into love and believing it would last? His parents would no doubt point out, that if two people were culturally and socially compatible, and had the same religious roots, such a combination would be the best foundation for a happy and peaceful marriage. His parents' marriage was proof of that. If only he could speak to Jaakob Kesselmann. But he did not know where Jaakob had settled in Argentina. Besides, Jaakob had been secretive. As a Jew, moreover, he probably wanted to keep a low profile. On the other hand, if Jaakob wanted to get in touch with him, he could do so very easily, merely by checking the Calgary phone book under Baumbach or Baumbach & Sons.

MONTEVIDEO, URUGUAY

Hermann was unaware that Jaakob also wanted to discuss his intimate affairs with him. But it would have been foolhardy for the captain to contact someone outside of Argentina, because he still might be under surveillance by the Argentine Immigration.

For the first time since his escape from Germany, the captain felt almost at ease and exhilarated. After last night, he was certain that Severina loved him and would marry him. They entered the luxurious dining room overlooking a garden of colourful flowers. He picked up the breakfast menu, but waited for her to make the choice. She looked so sympathetic. Would there ever be an occasion he could tell her the truth about himself, and have a soul mate to share his real self? Last night had brought them very close to each other, but would that be enough to forgive him? A sad shadow slowly spread over his face; his lips compressed, motionless, off guard, he seemed lost in thought.

Severina immediately noticed the change and put her hand tenderly on his arm.

"What is it Jaakob? Did something remind you of the past horrors?" Aware of his lapse of consciousness, he tried to cover up the incident by looking at the menu as if to make a choice.

"No, no," he lied, "I was just trying to choose one of these breakfasts."

"Oh, is that all? Try number three: freshly squeezed orange juice, eggs Benedict, Swiss croissants, coffee. And that will be Colombian coffee."

"Sounds great. Make it a double. At least you don't hate everything that is German."

"Jaakob, let's forget Europe. What about *La Esperanza*? You wanted to show me something about restoring its publication."

"Yes, I have the plan with me. But someone might overhear us in this restaurant. Let's finish breakfast first and then discuss it in my suite."

Half an hour later, Severina had read Hernandez's proposal.

"At first, Jaakob, I was against this plan. But I discussed some of it with Galina, and she suggested that I read more about Uruguay. In fact, I've read much about Uruguay and been to Montevideo several times. Anyway, I can now give you a factual answer. Your main concern is the possibility of an extradition treaty between Uruguay and Argentina? And you want to know if it would be legal to set up a buffer company that would buy and sell newsprint only to *La Esperanza* at its new office in Montevideo?"

"I've printed a summary of my findings. I'll read them to you. But first, let's consider the Uruguayan president's slogan: *"The evil, the great evil of this country, is not in its laws; it is in the apathy of its people."* In hindsight, we can see the truth of this very clearly. If we act immediately to protect our civil rights, instead of remaining indifferent, we would have fewer military dictatorships."

Severina began to read her notes. The captain listened with great interest.

"I won't read everything. Let's start here. 'At the turn of the nineteenth century with the coming of many thousands of Europeans, Uruguay developed into the staunch and mature democratic land that it is today—a democratic society. Uruguay is the most politically free country in Latin America. During the War, it openly opposed Nazi Germany.

"On December 12, 1939, the German battleship Graf Spee exchanged fire with the British Ajax, Achille and Exeter. The German ship was badly damaged and sought refuge in the harbour of Montevideo. But the Uruguayan government followed international law and ordered it to leave within three days. After futile protests, the ship did leave. To prevent capture by the British, the captain sank

his own ship with himself in it, just outside the harbour. When Hitler found out, he said that Uruguay would pay for this. But in 1940 evidence came to light that, highly placed Nazi agents were planning to overthrow Uruguay's government and turn the country into a German agricultural colony. When officials found out, they arrested these pro-Nazis. To help out, two American battleships sailed to Montevideo." (1)

So, you see? There was no coup in Uruguay and no popular support for one. Uruguay's free press, especially its hostility to Peron, irritates Argentina. Here's another interesting passage.

"Uruguay... nation of newspaper readers... ten dailies and three weekly papers... Spanish... English... El Dia is the political, social, and economic gospel of the ruling party, which is liberal. It is a living monument to President José Battle y Ordonez, who founded it in 1886. From then until his death forty-three years later, it was his mouthpiece. He used it to publicize his reforms... famous... eight-hour work day, free education, freedom of religion, separation of church and state..."(2)

"You see, Jaakob, it's a real democracy. Not like ours."

The captain remained silent. He took out his handkerchief, which still showed an "H" monogram, and began to wipe his forehead. Silently the familiar refrain echoed in his mind: "I must surrender my identity but not my soul. Surely the basic Nazi tenets were still valid. If Germany which has the best administrators and the most disciplined workforce ruled all Europe as one country, then all would be better off. There would be no escalating ethnic wars constantly erupting here and there. Berlin would be the capital of a united Europe under German domination. What has democracy achieved and was real democracy attainable? But why mix love with politics? he asked himself. He loved Severina, in spite of her religion and idealistic concept of a socialist democracy. Maybe Blaise Pascal's aphorism, which he had not forgotten, still rang true: "The heart has its own reason which reason cannot fathom." But this could be dangerous, he thought. She believed that he supported liberal and democratic ideas. Severina could not understand his obvious reticence. He seemed confused.

"Did you find this disturbing for some reason?"

"Why, no, not at all. I was just surprised that the Nazis had planned to control part of South America. I was not aware of that."

She shook her head slowly. "Your lawyer's plan is feasible, Jaakob. Uruguay really would welcome an Argentine newspaper, one that attacks corruption and dictatorship. I also checked into extradition. There's no treaty of that kind between Uruguay and Argentina at this time. I believe the plan is feasible and realistic, there is nothing to worry about."

Her voice became poignant and her eyes luminous when she was moved by a cause or her work. He restrained himself from bending over to kiss her. He loved her most at times of this kind.

"You've almost convinced me. Abogado Hernandez will give me very specific instructions, how to order the newsprint and how to keep track of these transactions."

With a look of compassion and a heart-warming smile of satisfaction, she moved closer to him with outstretched arms. He anticipated her gesture, and took her in his arms whispering in her ear, "Severina, I love you. Will you marry me?"

"And I love you, too. But before we talk about that, let's settle this matter. I think—let's be engaged for a little while."

"Yes, of course, as you wish. I'll arrange a meeting with Hernandez, the Keunenbergs, and the owners of *La Esperanza*. Would it be possible for you to join us? We'll all be going to Montevideo."

"Yes, as long as I'm not teaching. The earliest for me would be Thursday. I could stay there until Monday."

"In that case, we'll go on Thursday morning and return on Sunday night. By the way, may I introduce you as my fiancée?"

"Actually, I prefer not to do that. In this country, announcing an engagement means a deluge of phone calls, letters and little gifts. And that, in return, means writing notes to thank everyone. It's quite time consuming. These milestones are private, I think, and should stay that way until the wedding. Do you mind?"

THE EXPATRIATE

"No, not at all."

And that was the truth. It was still too soon to publicize his whereabouts by appearing in the social pages of a newspaper.

So many things had happened, and difficult to realize that so much time had slipped by since he left Germany. Becoming engaged to Severina was one step in the right direction. The next was building a paper enterprise, big enough to corner the world market. But first, he'd have to finalize the *La Esperanza* project.

Miss Mendoza, efficient as always, had arranged for everyone to meet on Thursday morning at nine-thirty in the hotel lobby: Mr. Kesselmann, Senora Filipovic, Abogado Hernandez, Armando and Enerique Alarcon, owners of *La Esperanza*. From the hotel, they drove off to Montevideo.

Uruguay, the captain had heard, was the Switzerland of South America. Its best road stretches from Montevideo to Colonia, a small port directly across the river from Buenos Aires. During the ride, the five travelers remained silent. This allowed the captain to admire the scenery. It was not what he had expected. He saw no lush forests. He recognized a eucalyptus tree, but the others were totally unfamiliar to him. It did not take long to reach Montevideo. The city looked attractive enough and deserved the name "City of Roses."

At the Prado Park, the rose garden boasted more than eight hundred varieties. It was November, so these were approaching full bloom. Another big park, Hernandez pointed out, was named after Uruguay's most distinguished author: Jose Enrique Rodo. Rodo Park had a wide range of trees—ombu, palm, eucalyptus—which formed an uneven green wreath around and through it. But the Keunenbergs were waiting for them elsewhere, so they turned northwest and then southeast toward the industrial sector. In the middle of a huge area stood a massive three-storey building. A sign on the roof read: Los Hermanos Keunenberg. The Keunenbergs, as usual wore open-collared shirts and heavy denim pants, led their visitors to a comfortable, informal office. After a few minutes of introductions, Kurt led them to the end of a corridor and into a huge empty room.

"This," he explained, "is where we can store your newsprint. We have nine thousand square feet, enough space for fifteen to twenty tons of newsprint. This building is as fireproof, by the way, as any building can be. But we can do a lot more than store newsprint. It's true that we don't manufacture light-weight paper for software wraps and boxes, but if we team up with Mr. Kesselmann, we would convert our machinery to produce any kind of paper."

"Are you aware," added Heinrich with obvious pride, "of the revolution in paper production? We're using a new micro-flute corrugated sheet instead of cartons. And we're doing research now on thinner but stronger cartons that can be stacked very easily. The thinner the paper, the easier the cartons are to cut. And the easier they are to stack, the cheaper they are to handle. You see, Mr. Kesselmann, we agree with you about the need to diversify production."

The captain understood immediately. They were not too subtle. They wanted to join his company. He responded by reminding them of the business at hand.

"First of all, we should settle this business about storing newsprint. That's between you and the Alarcons. Then we'll think of a way to pay for it. That's between the Alarcons and me."

"We don't lease this space," replied Kurt in his slow drawl reminiscent of *Platsdeutsch,* "because we use it ourselves from time to time. As you know, Mr. Kesselmann, manufacturing paper is a complex process. It involves cutting down trees, pulping the logs, pouring the pulp into thin sheets, then drying and ironing them. We use this space for one part of that process: drying the sheets. But we won't do that for the next eleven months. We could charge you, say, two thousand pesos. That would cover the cost for cleaning up this room. You may use our hoists to haul heavy loads, of course, but you must tell us in advance. By the way, you should take insurance for fire, theft and natural catastrophes."

The captain listened attentively to every word. Obviously, the brothers ran an efficient and profitable operation. The Alarcons agreed and quickly accepted their offer. The only problem was how to get newsprint paper from the United States as quickly as possible. Both Severina and the captain realized that Kurt was taking too much time talking about his business. It was Abogado Hernandez, however, who interrupted before Kurt could begin again.

"Yes, yes, Mr. Keunenberg, this is all very interesting. But we must get on with our business. How can we get the newsprint here quickly? Mr. Kesselmann, do you have any suggestions?"

"You've already made a valid proposal. We'll register *El Papel* as a wholesale distributing company that buys newsprint from the United States and Canada for sale in South America. I'll be the sole owner of this company. It will be a temporary one, until the Alarcons get settled and are able to buy on their own and have their plant here. During this period, the Alarcons will do business with *El Papel*. The American payment will be calculated in pesos, adding ten percent fee as a commission. I'll pay the paper mill in Houston with American dollars, from my bank account in New York. Can anyone think of a more convenient method? I'm open to suggestions."

"That sounds convenient to me," Abogado Hernandez agreed. "I'll have to wait for *El Papel's* legal registration and *La Esperanza's* detailed requirements, before we can do business."

"In that case," the lawyer continued, "I'll rush through the registration and send it directly to Mr. Kesselmann. Meanwhile, the Alarcons can prepare their order, send it to Herr Kesselmann, and get the ball rolling."

The Keunenbergs, delighted to participate in such an important transaction, invited everyone to a local restaurant. The specialty was *carne asada* (barbecued meat) with *maté tea*, the native specialty. They did not linger over lunch, because Abogado Hernandez had to prepare for a difficult court case. Too bad that *La Esperanza* was not yet back in business, he thought, because this case was about freedom of the press. It would have made good copy.

During the return trip to Buenos Aires, the captain announced that he had rented an office on the *Avenida Neuve de Julio*. Furniture was now being installed, and he was planning an opening party. He turned to Abogado Hernandez.

JEANNETTE MOSCOVITCH

"I need a name for my company. The Keunenbergs use their own family name, but I would prefer a title. My company will focus directly on the international market. Maybe it should have a descriptive name of our products."

"Good thinking" the lawyer replied. "Then I suggest one that has the same meaning in English and Spanish."

"Actually, I've been thinking about that. Here's what I've come up with: Atlantic and Pacific Paper Industries. According to my secretary, that would be *Atlantico Pacifico Papel Industria,* in Spanish. A.P.P.I. for short. And it would be the same in English. How does that sound?"

"Splendid, I will register it immediately."

"Now, what about the board of directors?" Abogado Hernandez wanted to know.

"We'll have to agree on how much capital each member is going to invest and then set up another meeting for that. My secretary will get in touch with you. As for buying land for a plant, that could be a problem. If I can't find a vacant lot, I'll have to buy an old building, demolish it and build a new one."

Hernandez smiled. This Kesselmann is shrewd, he thought. Being a Jew, he'll do well in business.

Back in Buenos Aires, the Alarcons got out first. The car took Severina and the captain back to the hotel.

"You look tired, Severina. Shall we go to my suite, have something to drink and relax? She shook her head and smiled. "Won't you stay a little while longer?"

Somehow her presence gave him an indescribable sense of assurance of being safe and a feeling that he was no longer alone in the world.

"Yes," she murmured looking very pleased. "But I must phone Mother to tell her I will be late."

"Then call her immediately while I mix the cocktails."

She shook her head in approval as she held the phone and spoke Czech with her mother.

As they sat down near each other on the silk upholstered love seat, he began to kiss the nape of her neck. She moved away from him slowly.

THE EXPATRIATE

"You know, Jaakob, something about you puzzles me. You're a very rich man. You have millions of American dollars, enough to retire for the rest of your life. Why would you bother to start up a new paper business that will be the largest in the world? And if I understand you correctly, you want to control the prices as well."

He hesitated before answering her. "It's hard to explain. You are partially right. It may be a dream. I believe that one must live with some kind of a dream. I cannot visualize a life without a desire to do things. We must always wish to achieve something. In that respect life is a dream. Did not one of your great Spanish authors, say 'Life is a dream.'"

"Yes, but you do not disclose the essence of your global enterprise. By being the largest manufacturer and controlling the industry you'll create a monopoly—not only dominating the industry, but setting and undercutting competitors' prices."

"You may be right in some respects. But today, paper is a daily necessity. What is so wrong if I try to produce the best, maintain quality, and keep the lid on prices so that this commodity is cheap and accessible even to the poorest? With a more modern operation, I will be able to beat the competition. This is normal dealings in the business world. What is wrong with that?"

He detected a surprised and anguished look on her face. Slowly, she moved and slipped away from him.

"You want to practise totalitarian ideology, like Hitler's scheme to control Europe, and eliminate the weaker people. You want to be the superman of the paper industry. Paper is a necessity. By controlling a necessity you will have created a monopoly and have the power of a dictator. Where have the principles of free enterprise disappeared in your paper scheme?"

He realized immediately that the conversation had taken a dangerous turn. It was a mistake to disclose his desire to dominate the paper industry, which she identified with Hitler.

He continued. "We are now on the threshold of a new industrial revolution. In the nineteenth century and, at the beginning of this century, the small businessman with little capital and some expertise could get ahead. He required only a small market to sell his goods and make a living. Family businesses and family dynasties were the models of the day. Now most heavy industry as well as the banking industry must do volume business in order to survive. Most medium-size businesses are merging—it's the catch word of today. And who knows, some may control prices. So you see, I am not the grasping industrial monster you imagined me to be. My concept is to manufacture an indispensable product that will benefit all. But I admit I am carried away by a vision, a desire to achieve. Is that evil?"

"To achieve something which will benefit everyone is certainly not evil, but what you propose is a monopoly, a stranglehold on the paper industry by one company."

"Yes, but there are newspapers and journalists who are whistle-blowers, who investigate malpractices and report them to society at large. That is why I did not hesitate to help *La Esperanza.*" He was certain she was somewhat convinced since her face had lost its downcast, sad look. Instinctively he moved closer to her, put his arm around her waist and put her gently down on the bed. Then he shut off the lights. Automatically, both undressed in silence. Time became timeless, until the mellow morning sunshine seeped through the gauzy curtains.

Next morning, entering his new luxurious office on the eighth floor of the prestigious building on the *Avenida Neuve de Julio*, he was greeted by his smiling secretary. Carmela was carefully coiffed, beaming, as if she had something special to tell him. Miss Mendoza was always cheerful. The captain valued that as much as her work. But that was not the only thing that he noticed.

"Good morning, patron. Look around you. Everything looks *"esplendido"*, don't you think? But I want to tell you something. This morning, I was walking down *Calle* Florida and passed a newspaper shop. You know, the one that sells foreign newspapers. The headline of an American one caught my attention. I thought of you, so I bought it. The article is about Canadian immigration officials. They've been careless and allowed Nazi war criminals to stay in Canada. But the present government has promised to look into this. As a *Judio*, (Jew) I thought you would be pleased to see this."

"That was very thoughtful of you, Miss Mendoza. Thanks, I'll read it right away."

THE EXPATRIATE

His face had turned slightly pale. After closing the door behind him, he sat down at his desk and held his head. "I should expect such incidents and learn to take them in my stride. Canada, that's where lucky Hermann Baumbach is—and probably surrounded by a bevy of girls."

HONEYMOON IN CANADA

Hermann was not surrounded by a bevy of girls, as his friend in Buenos Aires imagined. On his desk lay a pile of letters. One of these was from Tel Aviv. He read and reread it several times. The unbelievable was becoming a reality. He was getting married. This letter confirmed it.

Dear Son:

We're very excited to hear that you've decided to marry Rose. Mom is already planning what food to bring and what to wear. She and your sisters want to buy dresses in Paris. Miriam suggested Rose send us her measurements and a full-length photograph. With these, a Dior designer will be able to sketch a wedding dress and include swatches of suitable materials. We can safely rely on them. But don't worry about the cost. You know your mother and sisters; they always get the best for their money. But I warned them I am not taking out a mortgage on our house for their dresses. Let us know by return mail because my glamour girls want to go to Paris as soon as possible.

And now down to business. I'll attend to those rush orders. Ship them partly by air and partly by sea. This will save money on transportation. Judging from the number of orders, I'd say that Canadians need our products. If only we could manufacture them in Canada, we'd move there and the whole family could be together again. Looking forward to meet Rose and send her our love. Dad.

Over a drink that night, Rose lost no time in referring to the letter which Miss Pearson had read to her.

"Here you go, Hermann. This is what you need: my measurements along with a photo of myself. I can hardly begin to thank your mother and sisters. And of course, I'll pay for my own dress."

She stopped to see his reaction. He remained silent, waiting for her to continue. When she did, her voice betrayed some anxiety.

"I graduate on June 10, so we can have our wedding on June 25 and honeymoon till July 15. How does that sound? Do you think that June 25 would be convenient for your family to travel to Canada?"

When he failed to reply, she continued. "Will they stay at a hotel or with you?"

"I don't know."

Rose was taken aback by his lack of enthusiasm. Hermann always replied rather cautiously and never did anything spontaneous. However, his indifference was becoming more apparent. Was he ready to back out? That happened in movies, but she had heard about it in real life from one of her friends. A week before the wedding, the fiancé had called it off. Rose realized that she would have to ingratiate herself with his family so they would exert pressure on a reluctant Hermann. Several times he had mentioned to her that his parents were always prompting him to marry, saying he had bachelored long enough; besides, they wanted grandchildren and believed that married men lived longer.

"Now that you've made arrangements for your gown," he said suddenly, "what about my tuxedo?"

"There's a store downtown that rents out formal suits. All you have to do is choose a tux, let someone measure you, and pick it up a few days before the wedding."

He wrote this on a pad and remained silent. She continued.

"By the way, Hermann, I forgot to mention in my letter that I want your sisters to be my bridesmaids. Oh, and one more thing. Give me your guest list. I'll take care of the invitations."

THE EXPATRIATE

"You must have been thinking about this for a long time, Rose. Do you know approximately how much a wedding for 450 people will cost?"

"Something in the vicinity of ten to twenty thousand dollars."

"Well, don't go beyond thirty. Now that all is done for the moment, forget wedding arrangements; let's enjoy our dinner so that afterwards we can celebrate in your apartment, a little advance of our honeymoon." She burst out laughing. Maybe he wasn't such a sour "*Kraut*" after all.

A week after the event, the Calgary Gazette's social page published a detailed description of the elaborate wedding and a large photo of the bridal couple. The bride, a social worker, is prominent in public relations for several organizations, it said, and recently graduated cum laude with a master's degree in finance. The bridegroom, Mr. Hermann Baumbach, a newcomer to Calgary from Frankfurt, Germany, and Tel Aviv, Israel, is president of Baumbach and Son, a company manufacturing medical instruments. The guests celebrated till the early hours of the morning, when the bridal couple left for an extended tour of Canada.

On the trip, Hermann was very impressed with the vastness of the country. In Banff he took every opportunity to compare the mountains with the Alps, which now seemed much smaller than the peaks in Banff. "Why," he asked Rose, "have so few people settled here? People were living in Alpine valleys more than a thousand years ago."

"We don't have enough immigrants for such a huge country, even in the places that settlers would find most convenient. And Canadians, except in Quebec, have few children."

Their trip extended from Vancouver to Halifax. For the first time, Hermann began to understand how vast this country was and why it was so sparsely populated. Did he think Montreal or Toronto were beautiful cities? Yes and no! Both lacked historical and heritage houses and monuments, but they were "nice" cities— a term he applied to most places they visited. The city he preferred most for its natural beauty was Vancouver.

On the way back home, they discussed what they had seen from coast to coast. Rose mentioned nonchalantly, "Let's hope we won't have the bloody heritage the Europeans have." This remark disturbed him deeply. An inexplicable anguish gripped him and a sad shadow spread over his face. He remained silent.

By the time that they reached Rose's apartment, both were exhausted. This, for the time being, would be home. The Friedens had already agreed to cancel Hermann's lease. Meanwhile, just before graduating, Rose had rented impressive commercial space downtown and installed there the furniture from her home office. That had left her apartment with an empty room. It did not stay that way for long.

Eight months later, one evening, when Hermann came home from his office he found Rose looking upset. During supper, she remained sullen. Soon after he approached her tenderly, but she pushed him away angrily.

"You tricked me," she almost screamed.

"What are you talking about?"

"I'm pregnant."

"Oh, that's wonderful news."

She glared at him. "All you think of is yourself. What about me? I'm just starting my business. I need all the time and energy that I can find. How can I work with this—this bulge on my stomach? And who will take care of the baby for the first six months?"

He got up and walked towards the window, trying to avoid her gaze, "Well, I—"

"Never mind you, Hermann. This is about me. I've decided to have an abortion. In two or three years, when I've established my business, we can start a family."

"First," Hermann replied angrily, "you're not going to get an abortion. I won't allow that. No matter how safe this procedure is advertised to be, a mishap may occur and you may never be able to have children again. Second—" She stopped him right there and then.

"How can you dictate to me what I can do?" He disregarded her reply and continued.

THE EXPATRIATE

"Second, I married to have a home and a family, not a full-time business woman. We discussed all this, Rose, before we got married. You know how old you are. Time is running out for—"

"And what do you know about that? I'll have an abortion, and there's nothing you can do about it."

"If you insist, if you have one, Rose, then our marriage is over. I want you to stay at home with the baby until he is old enough to be left with a nanny. I expected this to be the happiest day of my life. I'm disappointed Rose, deeply disappointed. Now, if you'll excuse me, I'm going to listen to the news."

Rose sat there, dazed, looking at Hermann's empty chair. Everything seemed to be falling apart; her dream of having a business of her own, losing the man she loved. All because of that unwanted growth within her. Rose did not call Bernice, who would have offered her nothing but platitudes. "It's a man's world," she would say "so give in and do what he wants." No, this time she would solve her own problem. Certainly not by trying to convince Hermann. How could she argue with a stubborn German? Her mother would have agreed about the Germans. But what if she could find another solution? Some friends had told her about inducing miscarriages—that is, abortions with drugs or exercises. This gave her hope. As for Hermann, he could sleep on the couch if he preferred!

Sleep did not come easily to Hermann. He worried about Rose's health and especially about the baby's. He'd have to inquire about these things.

Next morning, he got up earlier than usual to prepare breakfast without her help. She seemed touched by his solicitude. Meanwhile, she was thinking about how to induce a miscarriage. They ate in silence. Then, Hermann spoke first.

"Did you sleep well?"

"As a matter of fact, I did not. The bed seemed empty without you."

"Well, then, you had plenty of time to think. I'm going to take good care of you, Rose, and of our baby. In fact, I'm going to consult some of my clients. A few of them are gynecologists and I'll ask one of them to examine you."

"So, you're in control of everything. You dictate what to do, with whom and when. I'm supposed to accept your commands whether I want to or not."

"Rose, this is definitely not about me. This is about you and the baby. I'm trying to take care of you. Pregnancy sometimes causes complications. I don't know anything about that, but I'll get a specialist who does." His concern about her health softened her attitude.

"I've thought of an alternative, Hermann. With a healthy regime and cleverly designed clothes, I could work until the eighth month. I could even hire an assistant for the office and interview nannies. When the baby is born, I could stay home every morning. That's a reasonable solution. I think so, don't you?"

She waited, but he did not answer. How could she disregard her own maternal instinct in favour of some business dream? What was at the root of her ambition? Was she looking for some kind of financial security that he could not provide for her? Even now, after starting again in a foreign country, his estate would be enough to live in comfort for the rest of her life. Why would she or any other woman want the burden of running a business? But he was becoming aware of a new change in women's work and attitude. These days women were permitted to set the rules and he must tread lightly. These departures from the solid mores reduce a husband to moral and sexual impotency. Everything that he knew about women and marriage, after all, he had learned from his own mother and sisters. No matter what, he longed for this little baby more than anything else in the world. Children in his own home would bring back those happy times he had enjoyed as a young boy. The best day of the week had been Sunday, and he began to tell Rose about his own childhood.

"In our family the best day of the week was Sunday. Every week, we had a leisurely brunch. Leisurely but rather formal. Mother insisted that we dress properly. We had to comb our hair and shine our shoes. Father sat at the head of the table and handed around the food. And Rose, that food was good: fresh fruit, scrambled eggs, home-baked muffins and marmalade, things like that. Mother brewed Turkish coffee, and its unctuous odour permeated the whole house. Father would always try to tell us interesting stories about what went on in his business. He also talked about German expertness and spoke with pride about Germany's cultural achievements. After a while, though, he changed. Whenever anyone said something about Germany, he turned away. I found out why, of course, when soon enough we read about the anti-Jewish incidents in the newspapers. Anyway, we continued these Sunday brunches after Rebecca and Miriam got married. Nothing changed except the number of chairs increased. We felt so close to each other, Rose. We belonged with each other. That's what I want for my own family."

Rose sat there, bewildered. To him the family was a refuge, and parental love the purest form of affection. He continued. "You said that everyone in your family has died, that you are alone and now my family would be yours. But with children of our own you will never be alone." She sat there bewildered, not knowing what to make of all this, and watched with curiosity the changing expressions on his face. He was eulogizing his family gatherings, trying to escape from a world in turmoil.

"Hermann, you speak with such longing for the life of your past. But today, things are different. Parents have less influence than they used to. Teachers, friends, and movies challenge the old ways. I don't think that we could ever re-create your world for our children. Anyway, make an appointment with one of your gynecologists and let's hear what he says."

Next morning, before opening the mail on his desk, Hermann began to call gynecologists. Someone had told him about Dr. Edward Wong, but mentioned that he was too busy to see new patients. Even so, the doctor agreed to see Hermann and Rose at his office in the hospital three days later, in the evening. Hermann immediately called the doctor to thank him and to ask him not to mention any potential problems to Rose. His task would be merely to offer advice for her daily care. He would discuss any serious problems privately with Dr. Wong, but not in Rose's presence.

Over the following three days, Rose became more and more upset. Her ad for an assistant brought in few replies, and only one looked promising. As for hiring a nanny, a friend told her to wait until the baby was born. So, Rose had nothing to do but worry. One thing, she told herself, was beyond negotiation. If Dr. Wong even hinted at the possibility of a difficult birth, let alone a stillborn or abnormal baby, she would immediately get an abortion. And she knew where to get one. She would explain it as an accidental miscarriage. But Hermann would insist on the truth from Doctor Wong. Then, she knew instinctively, he would carry out his threat to demand a divorce.

Dr. Wong's nurse greeted Rose and Hermann at the door. After a short wait, the doctor examined Rose. A few days later, having received the results from a lab, he asked the Baumbachs to come to his office. The news was good. Rose was going to have a healthy baby. She had every reason to expect a normal delivery.

Later Doctor Wong called Hermann's office. "Mr. Baumbach, your wife is in good condition. But this is her first birth, and she's older than most mothers. We might have to perform a caesarean operation. If so, the delivery won't be normal. But it won't be very unusual, either. And the baby will be perfectly safe."

Hermann was stunned. This was good but also bad news. For a moment, he was confused. "Will it—I mean, the birth—will that be painful?"

"At this stage, I see no reason to think so." With these words, the conversation ended. Hermann immediately called Rose to tell her the good news. "You'll be pleased to know that Doctor Wong said everything is normal."

"I feel very relieved. So, thanks for arranging things." She seemed genuinely happy with the prospect.

"I'm so glad. Everything is going to work out after all."

If only Jaakob were here, he thought. He would know how to tell Rose, without upsetting her, that a caesarean birth is almost a certainty. But he was thousands of miles away and probably very busy.

GREAT EXPECTATIONS

Hermann could not imagine how busy his friend Jaakob was. *La Esperanza* arrangements had taken longer than expected but were now successfully concluded. Everything had been carried out according to plan, and the newspaper was ready for publication in Montevideo. Nothing had gone wrong, but the captain remained apprehensive, as usual. The first letter on the neatly arranged pile on his desk was from the Alarcons.

Dear benefactor:

The initial shipment of newsprint arrived on time. We now have enough in stock for six months. We'll order more in three months. Meanwhile, we've recalled most of our journalists, installed our machinery, set up our presses, and notified our outlets: Chile, Uruguay, Paraguay, and southwestern Argentina. Our final outlet will be in Buenos Aires. Resistance is strong there, and so is fear. We are all very grateful to you, Mr. Kesselmann, and we'll find concrete ways of expressing it. In the meantime, we'll offer you very special rates—below cost—for your advertisements. My brother and I send you our best wishes and warm regards to Señora Filipovic. Signed: The Alarcons.

The captain nodded approvingly. That is the way to do business: simply, clearly, effectively. He asked Miss Mendoza to send this letter to Severina, because it was she who had convinced him to help the Alarcons. It would please her to know that *La Esperanza* was back in circulation.

Next on his urgent list was a letter from Abogado Hernandez, asking him to convene a meeting of the board of directors quickly

239

and to outline the position of everyone. In a separate package, Hernandez enclosed reports on each of his preferred candidates for the board. The first report was about Carlos Boisy, union president of the largest car manufacturer in Argentina. He had at his disposal an undisclosed sum of money, but a recommendation for spending it must be approved by the union's financial committee. However, they usually took his recommendations very seriously. According to the report, moreover, Boisy had settled amicably at least four of the most bitter and knotty labour disputes. Several American companies had tried to hire him, but he had refused to leave Argentina. Finally, the report noted that Boisy was an activist, fighting for human rights. He fought to increase wages for workers and index their old-age pensions. The report recommended Boisy very highly.

The captain read this report twice, focusing his attention on the union and trying to remember the history of labour unions. During the 1820s, England gave workmen the right to collective bargaining. Then, unions began to develop in France and Germany. All that he could remember precisely—because his father had repeated it so often—was that the German union for steel workers had come to control nearly the entire German steel industry by 1904. Neither his grandfather's nor his father's firm allowed their business to be unionized. However, by 1920 there were eight or nine million union members in Germany. Due to their initiatives, wages were increased and the weekly working hours were shortened. The captain carefully considered the consequences of asking Boisy, a traitor in the captain's mind, to sit on his board of directors. Boisy would always favour the needs of workers over those of the company. Nevertheless, being a business partner might change this attitude, but that was unlikely since he seemed to be deeply committed to the union and with great idealistic tendencies. On the other hand, he was experienced in labour disputes, would try to be equitable and now, indirectly, to himself as a partner in the A.P.P.I. It would certainly be useful to have someone who knows how to negotiate with a union. Boisy might even convince the union to invest as much as possible, because he could watch over its assets. The captain began to think that this man would be ideal as a director of personnel. A note to Miss Mendoza: "Advise Señor Boisy to attend the board of directors meeting in two weeks time from today."

The next candidate was Juan Dagunzo, owner and president of the largest leather company in Argentina. He was worth at least thirty million dollars. The report said that he might have started out as a *gaucho* (a cowboy) and become a rancher. At any rate, he was a self-made man with four children and no debts. Dagunzo had no interest in politics. He settled labour disputes by himself and, moreover, had so far avoided strikes. The captain was impressed. This man had worked with common labourers, knew their needs and understood their mentality. Such information is invaluable in establishing harmony between owner and workers. In fact, Dagunzo had probably trained many of his workers. In Argentina, the largest industries were agriculture, ranching, meat packing and railways. Where then would anyone find the skilled workers for a paper mill? And if he brought them in from Europe or the United States, who would train them? Maybe Dagunzo, the captain thought, could be the one to train them. All in all, the captain decided, Dagunzo would be an excellent man for the board.

Next came a report on David Fischmann and his son Joseph. They owned eight dry-cleaning plants and ten outlets. Estimated worth: about ten million dollars. No one knew the family background, but they were Jews and probably from Germany, Poland or Hungary. The report added only that he had come to Buenos Aires in the early 1930s with his wife and son Joseph. Two more children were born in Buenos Aires. The entire family helped to manage the business. The Fischmanns were honest, hardworking, capable, sophisticated, good looking. Strictly orthodox, moreover, they were members of a synagogue on *Cordoba Calle*. Their plants and outlets always closed on Saturdays and for Jewish festivals. The Fischmann males wore skull caps at all times. Even so, customers and workers alike respected them. They avoided all political connections but, once, when the political mafia asked them to contribute financially, they consented, to avoid reprisals. Although the report mentioned some small debts, these were covered by collateral at the bank. The report recommended them highly as potential board members.

JEANNETTE MOSCOVITCH

The captain turned in his chair to face the window. It was a sunny day, and the glare made him shut his eyes. For a few moments, he reminisced peacefully. As usual, though, this evoked less comforting thoughts. He had come a long way from Germany. It had taken longer than expected to set up his business and get all the bureaucratic paper work authorized. He was so busy he'd hardly noticed that almost two years had gone by. During that period he'd set up a business and fallen in love with a Jewish woman—a woman who had shaken his confidence by questioning the moral legitimacy of his business goals. In the distance, he heard church bells. It was time for the siesta, but he remained at his desk long enough to think about the Fischmanns.

The captain tried to evaluate them as dispassionately as possible. Although he was reluctant to choose religious Jews for the board, yet he realized that it would look very odd to have no Jews at all. If the Fischmanns were Germans, they might investigate his background. A simple remark or gesture might give him away or at least provoke suspicion. It was true, moreover, that these people were good businessmen. But was there really any connection between dry cleaning and paper? In the end, he had to admit that he admired the Fischmanns. They had established a large enterprise with little or no capital. His father used to say that the Jews were innately commercial. He smiled to himself. It's so easy to see the faults of others. After all, his grandfather must have had the same innate commercialism. How else could he have established his paper business without capital? The Fischmanns were to attend the board of directors meeting.

The next report was on those Keunenberg brothers, Kurt and Hans, from Montevideo. Their credit rating was A-1. Estimated worth about thirty-five million dollars. As the captain already knew, their company was well managed and they were hoping to expand it. The Keunenbergs were just right for the board.

The report had little to say about Armando Muñez. Abogado Hernandez had mentioned his handsome, hard-working and clever son-in-law Muñez, who was part-owner of a brokerage firm. According to the report, his fortune amounted to at least ten million dollars. The captain hesitated because he was the son-in-law of the A.P.P.I's lawyer, Señor Hernandez. It would be extremely awkward to reject him.

As for Aldo Recardez, he owned one of the largest construction firms in Argentina, although no one knew how much he was worth. According to the report, his family background was hazy. He was divorced, and his children were probably in the United States. Some said that he lived now with one or even two mistresses in a palatial house. Others said that he was a recluse. Some said that he had sold two ranches to repay wages and thus avoid a clash with the government. Others said that he had begun his career with a partner but then, for some reason, either forced him to resign or bought him out. Gossip notwithstanding, everyone considered Recardez an honourable businessman and his credit rating was very high. From a business point of view, though not necessarily a personal one, Recardez would be useful.

The last report was on Jorge Valdez, part owner of Chilean Airways. He owned several thousand shares of Bolivian Airlines. He had liquid assets in a New York bank, but would not disclose their value. His credit rating was A-1. Valdez was middle aged and had an extended family. He wanted to invest in a business that would value his expertise as a consultant on transportation and accept his children as junior executives. Because the captain was planning to ship merchandise all over the world, an expert in transportation would know how to economize. Without further ado, he decided to have Valdez on the board.

Then the captain began to summarize the reports. All candidates had excellent credit ratings. Most had written the truth in their applications, although they were clever enough to know that everything that they had written would be verified. This group represented a cross section of Argentine industry: transportation, manufacturing, finance, unions, and so on. This was a good team. He felt cheerful as he reviewed his future business associates. By luck, or whatever one calls it, it was as good as one could expect. Also, he was in love with a lovely lady, even though she was a Jewess. He was about to call Carmela to take the list when she announced on the telephone that an unexpected visitor was entering his office. His heart began to throb. Was it an immigration inspector? Had they received another list of names and pictures of War criminals in foreign countries? He straightened his tie and told Carmela to allow the visitor to enter. The door opened slowly and in walked Professora Severina Filipovic. She had a mysterious glow about her.

"My darling, what a pleasant surprise. You look radiant. And I know why. Either all of your students did well or you finally have received the grammar books that you ordered last year."

Without waiting for an answer, he kissed her passionately. But she slipped away from him.

"Be serious, Jaakob, I have more important news than that."

"Well, what is it?"

"Sit down, Jaakob." When he did, she continued. "I'm pregnant, two months."

The captain was speechless. Severina waited silently, looking directly at him. His reaction to this news was crucial to her. She was delighted to be expecting a baby. The child would soothe the ache in her heart that had seldom left her since the death of her son in Prague. Besides, she loved the father of this baby. Suddenly, as if some electronic impulse propelled him, he got up brusquely and took her in his arms.

"This is the best news that I've heard in a long time. We must get married immediately. Have you told your mother about this? I'm sure you did. Listen, I'm going to put away all my work and leave early. We'll celebrate and, I hope, discuss our wedding plans."

This time, it was Severina's turn to be speechless. For a few awkward moments, she wondered if Jaakob would take a little time to think about it and then change his mind, even though, he had proposed marriage. But that had been a while ago and he had not mentioned it since. Men often found excuses, she knew, to avoid their responsibilities. But he had not been the only one to surprise her that day. Even Galina had accepted the news without surprise. Severina, she felt, needed another child to replace her little son who had died. Galina would have liked to see her daughter married and having children, but she was still suspicious of the captain.

THE EXPATRIATE

"What would you prefer," the captain asked, "my hotel suite or a restaurant?"

"The hotel, of course. We need privacy for this conversation."

"Of course," he smiled, thinking it would be easier to ask her to stay the night. "By the way, did you cancel your classes for tomorrow?"

"No, it's an official holiday. It's like Spain, these days, with all their saints' days. I've asked the administration to limit these. One for each season would be enough."

In his suite, the captain opened a bottle of champagne and kissed her tenderly. For the first time that day, she felt relieved from anxiety..

"Well," said the captain, "aren't you going to make a toast?"

"Here's to the anxious father. May the little one resemble him."

He recalled a similar toast for the birth of his daughter. How could so many tumultuous years have passed? The entire Third Reich had come and gone since then.

As the champagne touched his lips, the captain's eyes saddened. He recalled the birth of his daughter. It seemed ages since he had seen Brigitta, and now he probably never would. How Lara had hoped she would resemble her. Unfortunately, Brigitta looked like no one in the family, neither her father, mother nor grandparents. For a moment, memories of shadowy ghosts reappeared. Severina was quick to notice that anguished look in his eyes.

"Darling, I think the champagne has affected you."

"No, dear," he lied, "I was just thinking of our future together."

"You looked sad and far away."

He controlled himself and took out that muslin handkerchief to wipe his moistened forehead. "Now," he continued, "let's try some more of this famous Argentine beef and mate, the Uruguayan tea that I couldn't stand at first. Anyway, let's relax and plan our wedding."

He waited.

"Did I hear any objection?"

She smiled contentedly. "No, I have no objection."

"Then," he continued, "should we get married in a civil court, or do we need a religious ceremony. And which do you prefer?"

"Given the circumstances, Jaakob, I'd prefer a civil court. We'll need only a couple of witnesses. But we'll have to put in our request immediately. Oh, and we'll need to get a license"

The captain was relieved to avoid a religious ritual, but he did not say so.

"Yes," he said, "I'm glad that you prefer a civil ceremony, with as little fuss as possible. Now, what about our civil status? Do we need a contract? I mean, does Argentina have community property unless otherwise stated?"

The captain wanted a marriage contract, with a proviso that a considerable sum be set aside as a marriage gift. He had done the same thing with Lara. If he were to die, or if he were to liquidate the company, she would have priority, not the creditors. But he kept this information to himself. "Honey you'd better get some legal advice. Besides, Argentine law would probably be different from the German."

"I'll try to get some legal advice," Severina agreed. "And what about our honeymoon? Will you be able to take a couple weeks off?"

"I certainly will."

"Oh, Jaakob, that would be nice."

"And where are we going to live? An apartment? A house?"

"I don't know. We could rent a house. I'd like that more than an apartment. Building one, though, would be very expensive."

"I would prefer a house. After all, we might want to have a few children."

Severina smiled. The captain could hardly believe his own words. After a long time of loneliness and worry, he was going to have a home and a family. He could not say aloud what he felt and thought. An inexplicable desire overcame him to smother her in his arms. "Shall we have a cognac?" He waited a little until they tasted the drink. "Darling, will you stay tonight?"

"Of course" she whispered and bent forward to kiss him.

THE EXPATRIATE

For the first time after many disturbing incidences, his fear of exposure, and his longing for his own home, for the *Gemütlichkeit* of the kind of life he had had in Düsseldorf, all was now within his reach. No more loneliness, he silently repeated to himself. It gave him peace of mind and intensified his ambition to establish a paper business selling to the whole world. He couldn't believe his own good fortune: a home! a family! He would be a law-abiding *Burger*, not a fugitive from justice. At last, no more loneliness! Love that night was sheer ecstasy.

After days of anxiety and fear that Jaakob would refuse to marry her and her child would be illegitimate, stigmatized by both Christian and Jewish communities, Severina was at last relieved of her secret anguish. The captain without hesitation had suggested marriage and showed his graciousness by asking her preference for all arrangements. She began to feel calm, blissful, and gave herself to him that night as she never had before, even to her deceased husband.

When he arrived at his office next day, Miss Menodoza handed him a message from Abogado Hernandez.

Dear Mr. Kesselmann,
I have invited all candidates to a board meeting five days
from this date at 7:30. Everyone has accepted. I'll need
a chart that shows the company's structure and a list of
duties for each director. If you like, I'll chair the meeting
in English and translate into Spanish if necessary.

He sat back in his chair but could not concentrate on anything except Severina. The wedding, he thought, should take place immediately. He'd need an engagement ring and a wedding band, and knew where to buy them. A luxury jewelry store was located on the corner of Avenida Florida, near his hotel. Instead of consulting Severina, he planned to surprise her with a sapphire engagement ring and a diamond wedding band.

As he stood at the counter, waiting for a saleswoman to make further arrangements, the captain thought of Lara and the world that had disappeared. He longed for the old days, when he had been young and innocent. He longed for, as Goethe had put it "the land where lemon trees bloom, the golden oranges glow amid the dark leaves, and a gentle wind blows from the blue sky." Every day, he tried as much as he could to forget those little wispy incidents of long ago that kept returning and upsetting his composure. But seldom did he recall sitting in his office and signing lists of names, each one consigned to slave labour and certain annihilation. They were merely names. The saleslady noticed that something seemed to have upset her client.

"Sir, are you not feeling well? Would you care for a cup of tea?"

"No thank you. But before I buy this ring I'd like to show it to my fiancée for her approval. I'll arrange for an immediate appointment"

Whistling softly, he turned down the corner of *Avenida Florida* and tried to predict what Severina's reaction would be to such an expensive ring. He missed a bosom pal. What would Hermann be doing now? Probably totally immersed in business. It was hard to believe that time had slipped by so quickly since they left Halifax but still too soon to contact him. According to immigration regulations, it was no longer necessary to report to them. Still, he was not ready to throw caution to the winds.

OTTAWA

Hermann was not the free spirit that the captain imagined him to be. He was about to become a father and preoccupied with his wife's health. His hospital connections enabled him to contact the best gynecologists. Nevertheless, he watched Rose's every move, suspecting that she would try to have an abortion. He even hired a decorator to convert the spare room into a nursery. Rose, was also busy but not on account of the baby's arrival. She had advertised and found an experienced lady for the management of her business.

One morning, her screams woke Hermann. He quickly called an ambulance and her doctor. By the time they arrived at the hospital, the doctor and his assistants were waiting in the delivery room. For a while, they tried to manage without anesthetics and pain relievers. In the end, though, they performed a caesarean section. While Rose was still unconscious, a nurse washed the infant, wrapped him in soft flannel, and held him up to a window. On the other side stood a nervous but proud father. According to the doctor, who shook Hermann's hand, the boy was healthy, weighed seven pounds but the mother was weak and would remain in the hospital for several days. Shaking Hermann's hand again, he excused himself and dashed off to another patient.

Hermann returned to Rose's bedside, waited until she opened her eyes and immediately began to cry.

"We have a beautiful baby boy," he said, bending over to kiss her. In no time, the nurse brought the baby to Rose and she began to cry all over again, almost throwing the baby off the bed. The tiny one began to whimper and kick. Rose tried to cradle him in her arms. Surprisingly, he still whimpered, crying loudly and kicking his chubby little feet. She turned her head away and almost threw the baby off the bed. Hermann caught him just in time and cradled him in his arms, putting his index finger in the baby's hand. The little one stopped moaning and automatically squeezed the finger in his hand. Hermann began to rock him to and fro. The little bundle seemed to be content, his lips spread as if to smile. He showed the baby to Rose, but she turned her head away and remained silent.

Hermann thought that he knew the cause. The majority of babies at birth resemble our nearest ancestors, the monkeys.

"Rose, darling, he will change into a little human being in no time. He'll improve every day. Now we can't even see the colour of his eyes."

Before he could say anything more, the nurse came in to take the baby away for another feeding. "Darling I have good news, the doctor said that you will remain in the hospital only a few days, and then Teresa will come to look after you."

He paused to hear her reaction, but she remained ominously silent. Nonetheless, he continued.

"We'll leave the baby here, until his circumcision."

"Thanks, Hermann."

"Have you thought of a name? Perhaps we should name him after your deceased father?"

"I was hoping that you'd say that. My father's name was Joseph."

"Then it's settled. Should I call my parents, to tell them the good news?"

"Of course. And invite them to the circumcision."

"Yes, but I'm not sure when that will be. Joey will have to gain some weight first."

Hermann was relieved. Rose seemed more cheerful than she had been.

The attending nurse was advised to bring the baby to Rose only if she asked for him. But this did not happen either that day or the next day. On the third day, a nurse came in with a beautiful package from Tel Aviv. When Rose opened it, she was delighted with the blue flannel dress and cap with matching booties. The nurse dressed the baby and the little cap topped his tiny head. The baby looked cute but resembled a miniature monkey. Joey's eyes opened slightly. Rose took one look at his shriveled face, became distraught, screamed unintelligibly and turned away angrily. This made the baby cry, and he waved his little arms so frantically that the nurse had to take him back to the nursery.

That evening, when Hermann came to visit, he heard about the incident. This time, the nurse brought Joey to his father. The infant was screaming and kicking. As soon as Hermann picked him up, Joey opened his eyes as if eyeing his dad curiously. Hermann sat down near Rose and handed the baby to her. Once again, Joey began to whimper.

"Rose, pat his cheek a little. Rub his hand. See how he reacts."

Reluctantly, she did so. And it worked.

"Look," she pointed to his face, "he's examining me."

"Come on Rose, he still can't see much. But he does feel your warmth on his face."

"How do you know so much about babies?"

"Oh, I'm the most experienced pre-circumcision nurse available. You remember my nephews, my sister's sons, I supervised their circumcisions. I learned methods—psychological methods—to keep babies contented." Rose burst out laughing. Maybe it was true. But those nephews must have been beautiful babies, not like this little midget monkey. She cast another look at Joey, who was staring curiously at her. When the nurse arrived to feed him, Rose got out of bed and sat on a comfortable chair near Hermann.

"You look better, Rose."

"I feel better. This morning's check-up was very encouraging. I'll recover sooner than expected. So, let's plan the circumcision reception."

"Reception? Oh yes, the reception. Well, Rose, what have you in mind?"

"We'll have the circumcision right here in the hospital. It has a mohel, who does all the circumcisions. As for the reception, I'll have to think about that. Either breakfast or lunch."

"You decide, Rose, but don't go overboard either with the number of guests or money-wise. In my business I don't need to impress anyone. Our products are the best available and sales are increasing. I make a good living; have a lovely wife, and now a son. I'm happy."

She scowled and he stopped short. This was not her concept of happiness. Her ambition was to be the most successful financial advisor in Canada, maybe internationally. She believed that the first step to be known commercially was to have lavish entertainments, reported in many newspapers, as the basis of public marketing.

"This is a *bris*, Rose, not a sales convention. It's supposed to be a family affair. Unfortunately, my sister and her family won't be here, because the children all have measles, and you have no family. But both of us have friends. Between the two of us, we could invite, I don't know, say fifty guests to a luncheon. You won't have the extra work of calling hundreds of people and giving everyone a pre-sample of a bar mitzvah."

Rose sat up and looked at him scornfully. These damn Germans, she thought, these damn Germans.

"But Hermann, dear, shouldn't we take every opportunity to let people know about our businesses? Our invitation would simply state: Mrs. Rose Waterman Baumbach of Rose Waterman Financial Consultants, Inc., and Mr. Hermann Baumbach of Baumbach & Sons would like the pleasure of your attendance at the circumcision of their son Joseph—What's wrong with that? It's not pretentious and, if the affair is lavish, the impression is that we're successful. People can trust our competence. It's a good credibility pitch."

Hermann did not answer. He was repelled.

"I'll tell you what's wrong. It's vulgar, Rose, horribly vulgar. Why, in Germany, we—" She was, he realized, a modern publicity maniac. The American way! It was totally distasteful to him. The celebration to be used as a cheap commercial!

Before he could finish, Rose stood up and almost fell down. Hermann caught her in his arms and kissed her.

"The house is empty without you."

THE EXPATRIATE

She began to cry but not as a response to that sentiment. Nothing was going her way. She had just given birth to an ugly baby, and her husband was planning a skimpy reception. She felt seedy looking, and now Hermann was thinking like all the bloody Germans still do. They do things best. What had she got herself into?

By this time, Hermann knew that mentioning Germany to Rose was always a mistake.

"Well, never mind Germany. Just think it over. If you insist on a big reception, we'll have one."

Maybe, she thought, he was right. At the moment, anyway, she did not feel strong enough to organize a large reception. Tomorrow, she would discuss it with Bernice.

At home that evening, Hermann found an urgent letter from Mr. Frieden, his lawyer. The member of the provincial parliament, in charge of customs and excise, had suggested an appointment with the federal minister to validate that the Baumbach's medical instruments were needed but are unavailable in Canada. If Hermann could confirm this, the minister would classify these products as "necessity imports" and give them a preferential duty rate.

Hermann replied immediately.

"Thanks, Irving. Just give me a few weeks to be with Rose. She still hasn't recovered."

"All right, but don't wait too long. I'll call the Ministry of Customs for an appointment as soon as you are ready to leave and arrange a personal interview. I don't think I need to accompany you. No one can explain the operation of your firm better than you. And you'll need at least a day for traveling each way."

"I know. And I'd like to see something of Ottawa."

"Sure. Just give me a definite date, and I'll set up an appointment. I'm sure Rose is recovering. Stella sends her regards."

Hermann put down the phone and began to assess his situation. His business was thriving, but his marriage was beginning to be a concern. He was no longer a carefree bachelor, and now he needed approval from a wife for all decisions apart from business ones.

A feeling of uncertainty began to threaten his peace of mind. And yet, for some unfathomable reason, he yearned for a family of his own—a family just like the one in which he had grown up. For him, succeeding in business was important only to the extent that it served the needs of his family. He could not accept Rose's attitude. For her, even family was secondary to business. Shaking his head in exasperation, he poured himself a dose of vodka, sat down and soon was fast asleep. It was dreamless, the sleep of the self-righteous.

Next day, Rose could hardly wait till mid morning to call Bernice who would, at that time, be vacuuming the floors in her cottage. Her voice sounded cheerful as usual.

"Bernice," Rose inquired, after the usual small talk, "what kind of *bris* should I make? You remember the spread you made for Herschel."

"Well, to tell the truth, Rose, if I had to do it over again I would do it differently. Henry thought that we should make a big spread to impress his bank manager. You know, to prove that we have assets and are able to pay back loans. But you know what? It didn't make any difference. Later on, someone offered Henry a low price if he would buy a large quantity of merchandise. I can't remember what it was. Anyway, he had to pay for all of it within two weeks. We were short of cash then, so Henry asked the bank for a loan. But the bank manager would not give him any kind of preferential treatment. He said to him what he told everyone else. Henry would have to put up the standard amount in collateral. So, did it make any difference? But, really, it's up to you and Hermann."

Rose hesitated at first, but then explained her situation in more detail. When she finished, Bernice, as always, did not mince words and replied bluntly. "Rose, listen to me. First of all you chased the guy mad. Either you can be flexible or he'll leave. And he'll find plenty of divorcées to replace you, believe me."

She stopped, waiting for some reaction.

"Rose? Are you still there?"

"Oh, sorry. I was just thinking about what you were saying. But go on."

"I've known you for a long time, and I still don't know what drives you. You have to sort out what's most important to you: business or family."

"So, I should just forget about what I want and do whatever he wants?"

"Well, do as you please, but your ambition to conquer the world will ruin your marriage. Hermann married you to have a home and a family. I don't have to tell you that in the commercial world, it's always a constant struggle to make a living—a continuous battle. Your home should be a haven from all that."

Rose did not reply.

"Of course" Bernice continued, "I'll be on your side whatever you choose. I am your friend."

"Thanks Bernice, I can always count on you to say it as it is."

But in her heart, Rose felt that a person who is not ambitious, not motivated, becomes a "baking-cake lady" for her family, one, who like Bernice, would never understand a desire to rise above the level one was born in and accomplish something worthwhile. Rose believed that ambition was not merely desirable but necessary for those who hoped to rise in the world. No opportunity for advancement was too small. She phoned Hermann's office and asked Miss Pearson about his schedule for that day.

"Your husband is very busy today, as usual, but I'll tell him that you called. He'll put aside everything to speak to you."

"In that case, Miss Pearson, just ask him if he can come to the hospital a little earlier than usual."

"I'll give him that message. I'm so glad to hear you're feeling better."

"Thank you, Miss Pearson."

As soon as Rose put down the phone, Christina, the nurse, came in with Joey.

"He is such a good baby. Just stroke his cheek, and he'll smile. He's gained weight, too, so you can have him circumcised on the eighth day after all."

Christina handed the baby to his mother. Rose took Joey in her arms and began to examine the tiny face and hands. He began to cry.

"Don't worry if he cries, Mrs. Baumbach. It's good for his lungs. Stroke his cheeks and play a little with his hands. He looks so much better now, like a sweet baby doll."

She stopped to see how Mrs. Baumbach was handling the baby.

"You know Mrs. Baumbach, I was once told by a Jewish lady that only Jews circumcise their sons. But that's not true. So do the Muslims. I worked for an African lady, who circumcised her son and told me that many tribes in Africa and India do the same thing. And a rabbi's wife once read me a biblical passage about this. In Genesis 17:10—I can still remember the exact chapter and verse—the Lord says, "This is my covenant…every child among you shall be circumcised." This implied an obligation to live virtuously, according to her, although she never did say what the connection was. I mean, between circumcision and virtue. Anyway, I think that the Lord should have gone a bit further. He should have said that their penises would shrink or fall off if they aren't faithful—you know what I mean—"

Rose interrupted her, "Christina, you're a hundred percent right. I think the Lord made a grave error in this respect. But we women can do the job ourselves if necessary."

Both began to laugh. "I read that one woman was so angry about her husband's whoring around that she bit it off one night. It could not be pieced together and for the rest of his life his intimate friends called him '*El Señor Medio*', Mr. Half.' At this point, Joey began to scream. Christina picked up the baby, rocking him to and fro in her arms.

"Isn't he beautiful? Look at those sweet pudgy hands and how he holds onto my index finger. I wish I had a baby."

She returned Joey to his mother.

"Please try to breast feed him. I have to go now, but I'll check in again after my rounds."

THE EXPATRIATE

As Joey tugged at her breast, Rose examined him closely, "You know what, Joey? You're not a puny monkey after all. Maybe you'll change. Who knows?"

The baby continued to move his lips over her warm flesh, until he fell asleep. Rose wiped his face. Teresa came in for the evening, took the baby in her arms and sat down to keep Rose company.

When Hermann arrived, he was beaming. He kissed Rose, and then produced an elaborately wrapped parcel.

"Open it," he said.

After struggling with the ribbons and paper, she lifted the cover and burst out laughing.

"Hermann, what made you do it?"

"I passed by a toy shop, and this white teddy bear looked so human, almost alive, that I couldn't resist the temptation."

She got out of bed to kiss him. For once, Hermann had acted spontaneously.

"How's the baby?"

"He's gaining weight. In fact, he'll soon be ready for his *bris (act and ceremony of circumcision)* and he already acts just like you, Hermann. Everything must be just so. Christina put on his socks today. One was perfect, the other a bit twisted. You should have seen him throw it off."

"Smart boy, takes after his Dad. But tell me, Rose, what have you decided to do about the bris?"

"I think you're right, Hermann. We'll have a small affair. I've prepared a list of friends and will call them personally. I've booked the *mohel (circumciser)* and the caterer for Sunday, from eleven to two-thirty. It will be the usual, according to the caterer: a buffet of four kinds of fish, a variety of breads, fruits, cheeses, French pastries, tea, coffee, and wines."

"Sounds great to me. How much will this small affair cost?"

"I'll find out tomorrow. If you think it's too expensive, I'll contribute."

"Thanks. That won't be necessary."

This, he thought must be an American custom of sharing. "Oh, I almost forgot to tell you that the decorator finished Joey's room. I'm sure you'll like it."

Next day, Rose was released from the hospital without Joey, who remained for the bris. Hermann reminded Rose again that he preferred to keep the affair private in case a few social reporters came from some newspapers. But in spite of this, Rose informed the social editor of the *Calgary Herald* and gave him a few details. A week later, an elaborate description of the affair appeared. It was clear to everyone that Rose had almost dictated part of it: two sections dealt with her clothing, her status as a business woman, and so on.

When Hermann saw it, by chance, he was furious.

"I thought that we had come to an agreement about this. It was to be our private affair."

"Yes, dear, but I don't see the harm. Besides, I made sure that your name is hardly mentioned. That's what you wanted, right?"

"In the future, I'll have to approve any publicity concerning our family, which now includes Joseph."

"Where the hell do you think you are? In Germany? I must have approval from my master. I see no harm in this write-up."

"That's the trouble. You really don't see how cheap and vulgar such ostentation is." Rose stifled her resentment, ran into Joey's room and picked him up angrily. Not surprisingly, the baby began to scream and kick. By the time she reached the living room, where Hermann was, he had kicked hard enough and almost fell out of her arms. Hermann caught the baby just in time, cradled him in his arms, and began to sing a German lullaby. Joey calmed down, gazed curiously at his father and gurgled with delight.

"Rose, why hasn't someone changed his diapers?"

"You know, Hermann, you're spoiling him."

"Well, you're neglecting him. Do you think that he doesn't feel your resentment? Why do you think that he always cries when you pick him up?"

"Maybe he doesn't like my perfume. Did you ever think of that? I'll change it."

THE EXPATRIATE

Hermann realized that prolonging this kind of argument with Rose would be pointless. It led nowhere. This was a far cry from his idyllic vision of home, wife and adorable little son.

Hermann picked up Joey, "I love you, my own little one. From now on, Teresa will look after you."

That night, Hermann kissed his wife good night and turned his back to her. But he could not sleep. Why did she insist on working relentlessly, neglecting everything and everyone in an effort to build up a business in which the competition is almost insurmountable? Success may not come, no matter how hard she tries.

It was amazing, he thought, how Joey feels her hostility. She obviously harbours a deep resentment because the baby is taking up too much of her time. In a flash, Hermann saw the stark truth. Rose would neglect her own son. An inexplicable fear gripped him. He would ask Teresa to sleep beside his crib for a while.

Next morning, as soon as Miss Pearson greeted him, she knew that all was not well. Mr. Baumbach looked upset. Maybe, she thought, good news would cheer him up.

"Mr. Frieden left a message, Mr. Baumbach. Your appointment in Ottawa can be scheduled when you are free to come but you must advise them two weeks ahead. Mr. Frieden also mentioned that you will not need his presence there, because you are the best one to explain why there should be a preferential duty for materials used in medical instruments." Picking up a pile of papers from her desk, she continued. "These orders came in, sir. I'll check our stock, prices and delivery schedule. Then, I'll send out confirmations."

"Good work, Miss Pearson. Now I'll let you know when to buy my airplane ticket to Ottawa and return. Reserve a hotel for six days. At last I'll have a chance to see the capital of this country."

He turned around briskly and walked into his private office. After closing the door, he called Rose and told her about the news from Ottawa. But he had another matter to discuss with her.

259

"I took a drink last night, a strong one, maybe too strong. I fell asleep in the living room. And this morning, well, I didn't want to wake you."

He stopped, giving her time to react. When she made no response, he continued.

"Listen, Rose, I have good news. Irving made an appointment for me in Ottawa. Do you know what this means? We'll be able to import raw materials cheaply enough to manufacture our instruments right here."

She showed no enthusiasm. He tried another tactic.

"Why don't we go out on the town tonight? We haven't done that for a long time."

"I don't know, Hermann, I—"

"Rose, I just fell asleep on the couch."

"No, it's not that. The baby hasn't stopped crying and kicking since you left this morning. Fortunately, Teresa got him to calm down."

"Well, she's used to handling babies. You'll get the hang of it after a little while. Don't worry about it."

"No, I won't worry. I'll leave it to Teresa, because I have to get back to my office."

Hermann remained silent. Rose had agreed, before their wedding, to stay at home every morning when they began to have a family; Teresa would stay only until she returned in the evening. Now, Rose expected Teresa to stay with the baby all day. Fear gripped him with a sudden threat of an inexplicable danger. What, he thought, if the baby isn't safe with Rose? Perhaps the baby should be with Teresa all day and night. For the time being, it would be best to let Rose go to work and leave the baby with Teresa. Disguising his anxiety, he answered as glibly as he could.

"Yes, maybe that would be best. So ask Teresa to stay for the whole day and for the night as well. Of course, she'll need some time off. No one can work twenty-four hours a day. I'll leave that to you. Now, what about going out on the town?"

"No, I have a better idea. I'll make a special supper."

Rose looked radiant. In fact, she had dressed seductively. After kissing her, Hermann rushed to the baby and fondled him.

Joey seemed to recognize his daddy and gurgled. Gently, he lifted the baby into his arms and sang one of Schubert's lullabies. Rose, who was standing in the doorway, was amazed.

"Hermann, I didn't know that you could sing."

"Well, I never mentioned this, but I used to sing in our synagogue's choir. In fact, I was good enough for free voice training. And I can see that Joey has inherited my love for music."

"I can't imagine that. German sounds so thick and ugly. Please don't sing German songs to him anymore. Besides, I think you are becoming a little dotty about the kid. Put him back in his crib and come for supper before it gets cold."

Hermann obeyed. Together, they walked to the dining room, where supper was waiting for them.

"I appreciate the spread but what is the occasion? Are we celebrating something?"

"Yes, I was given a very large estate to settle. Half the money goes to the heirs, but the other half goes into investments. That's where I come in."

"Congratulations, Rose. But what about other business?"

"The going is tough. I have to convince investors that I'm as good as a man in the financial jungle."

Hermann did not answer nor offer some comforting advice. He knew it takes a while for any business to establish a clientele. But uppermost in his mind was the need to convince her to remain at home in the mornings.

"Have you arranged your schedule so that you'll be with the baby in the mornings as we agreed?"

"No, I haven't. Besides I think Teresa will do just as well, or better, than I would."

"But Rose, no one can replace a mother's love."

"Oh, I don't know about that. That is a centuries' old myth. It is propaganda to keep capable women from invading the work force so that jobs will be available for family men. After all, Hermann, rich women have always had wet nurses and other servants. Only poor women have had to nurse their own children and clean their own houses. Besides, who could do a better job than Teresa? She's had experience with her own kids and with those of others."

Hermann could not articulate what he felt. Gazing at her across the table, he realized that she was completely occupied and obsessed to succeed in her business. Silently he asked himself, was there a substitute for a mother's innate love? What does mother's love mean if it is not an inborn inexplicable tenderness for a part that came from oneself? Perhaps this lack of motherly affection might be due to the pain she had suffered giving birth. But by now, this should have been replaced by a genuine mother's natural love for a part of her own flesh and blood. Gazing at her across the table he had a strange premonition that this would not happen.

"Of course, if you have no feeling to see a little human being grow up before your eyes, I guess I will not be able to convince you. But a baby needs its mother's love just as flowers need water."

She quickly provided an answer. "That is another myth popularized by a certain doctor whose name I have forgotten. Primarily, it was to make women believe that their mission in life was to stay at home, a God-assigned ordinance. Staying at home and devoting one's life to a miniature world was supposed to be woman's earthly duty and destiny. It also stems from children's fairy tales." She filled the wine glasses, sipping contentedly. He ventured again.

"So, you're not going to honour your side of our agreement."

"What agreement? To tell you the truth I hardly remember what we agreed to."

"You promised to stay at home in the morning to be with any children that we might have, and to leave for your business in the afternoons. But, let's leave this now. I need to focus my thoughts on my meeting in Ottawa. And who will show some parental love to the baby?"

"Don't worry. I'll be here. Teresa will be here. Maybe he won't be spoiled for a few days when you're away." He kissed her lightly on the cheek, and lumbered into his favourite armchair to read the stock market. Later on, tired he slumped into bed and fell asleep.

Busy days followed for both. Rose was experimenting with new ways to attract clients, and Hermann was preparing for Ottawa, to meet Minister Jacques Ferland. But in the evening he set aside all business matters, rushed home to embrace the baby and sing German lullabies. Tiny Joseph sensed he would be cuddled and sung to in the evenings and looked toward the door as if to anticipate his father's arrival. Secretly Rose watched Hermann and thought that a sudden baby delirium had afflicted her husband.

While relaxing on the plane to Ottawa, Hermann recalled fragments of the Atlantic crossing and arrival at Halifax. Clarice, his companion on the trip, suggested that they spend a few days in Ottawa. He vaguely recalled her plea, "We'd be together for a few days." The suggestion, if accepted, would probably have led to a deeper involvement for both. But if anything serious had come to pass, it would have been conditional on her conversion to Judaism. Yet, he believed that she would have done so for him. What would his mother have said? Many years ago, she had said that flat-chested English girls made better maiden aunts than wives. But Clarice, he knew, would have convinced her otherwise. He laughed at himself for indulging in memories of outdated prejudices. Clarice worked for a living. Rose, on the other hand, worked for some reason that he could not understand. No two women could be more different, he thought. His random thoughts were interrupted by instructions to fasten seat belts. The Ottawa landing was expected shortly.

At the information desk, he picked up a message that someone had left for him. He read it with curiosity.

"Please go to the main entrance and look for a dark blue limousine. The chauffeur will drive you to your hotel and return two hours later to take you to Parliament Hill. A guide there will direct you to Minister Ferland's office."

A few hours later, Hermann was sitting in an office on Parliament Hill. Near his chair was a table and on it were countless documents. Mr. Ferland entered and pointed to the table.

"Well, sir, there's our research. Your advocate sent a detailed brief of your credentials, your business experience, and your request for federal aid. Now, let me see. Yes. Baumbach and Son are manufacturers and distributors of medical instruments. The price of these instruments is very high due to import duties, brokerage charges, land conveyance costs, special packing expenses for overseas shipping, and your own services. You say that doctors buy only the ones that they can afford. This means that they use them more often than they should. Is this correct so far, Mr. Baumbach?"

"Yes, sir."

"You propose, therefore, to set up a factory in or near Calgary and manufacture the needed instruments. That way, you'll be able to bring down the prices. Is that right?"

"Yes, sir."

"The benefits are obvious: lower prices and immediate availability. Do you have anything to add, Mr. Baumbach?"

"Well, there is one thing. It would take time to set up a factory and train the workers. Meanwhile, we would need to keep importing these instruments. It's the duty on imports, you see, that causes a major problem for us. If it was reduced, we would be able to import these from our own factory in Palestine at a cheaper rate than from the sources in the United States. Here, Mr. Ferland, look at these documents. They show the difference between importing from Palestine and importing from the United States."

"Mr. Baumbach, I'm pleased to tell you that I've presented part of your request to the responsible authorities. And they assure me that only a small fraction of the duties will remain on some articles from Palestine. Moreover, they'll consider reducing the duties on some of the raw materials that you will need for your factory here. This will take a couple of months to pass through the proper channels, and the resulting agreement will be valid for five years. After that, of course, we will have to review them again. As for financial help to set up a factory, I've studied your proposal, and we will remove the duty on all machines that you buy in Europe. Do you understand everything so far?"

"Yes, sir."

"But you also claim that you must hire foreign specialists to work these machines and to teach others. We will facilitate their immigration. As far as the unions are concerned, the Government cannot intervene. Is that clearly understood, Mr. Baumbach?"

"Yes. I understand."

"I've sent copies of your request to the specific departments. So now, Mr. Baumbach, I must only ask for your signature. Sign right there, please."

Hermann was amazed. Everything was far from what he'd expected. No suggestion for a hand out, no bribes! Incredible! This was just like the old Germany, before the Nazis. He took out his gold fountain pen and in admirable calligraphic letters signed his name.

"Well, then, Mr. Baumbach, we have all the information necessary to process your request, and you'll receive as soon as possible the customs permit. As for the other matters, we'll deal with them as quickly as possible." Minister Ferland got up, and so did Hermann. "You've expressed interest in seeing the Parliament buildings, so I asked Marc Corbeil, our chief guide, to show you around."

As they were shaking hands, the guide came in.

"Please follow me, Mr. Baumbach. We'll enter through the main door and look at a display of the world's flags on each side."

They stopped to admire the carefully manicured lawns. In the distance, Hermann saw someone burning the red and yellow leaves that had piled up everywhere. This reminded him of something very tragic. *Kristallnacht* in Berlin, 1938. Flames had roared, a huge bonfire, a tremendous mound of books, some open, others closed, were being thrown into the raging flames by murderous hands; there were shouts and cries of glee, while the limp books crackled in pain. The fire rose in anger and quickly diffused itself in black smoke, while a motley crowd stood by nonchalantly.

"Are you not feeling well, Monsieur Baumbach?"

"What? Oh, yes, thank you."

"In that case, let's move on to the Peace Tower. See? Over there, with the clock that faces all four directions. It was built in

1919 as a memorial for Canadian soldiers who had been killed in World War I. Since then, it has been modified to commemorate Canadian soldiers who have fallen in more recent wars. The tower has a carillon with fifty-three bells, and the carillonneur gives regular recitals." After looking around for several minutes, with Hermann somewhat depressed by his memories, they moved on.

"Here's the most important chamber of all. The House of Commons is where all Canadian legislation originates. Now, look up at the ceiling. It's covered with Irish linen and hand painted. Most people don't bother to look, because they're so impressed by those stained-glass windows over there on the east and west walls. In the sunlight, the colours glow brilliantly. And up there, Mr. Baumbach, are the coats of arms. One for each province or territory, of course, and each one with its emblematic flower."

"Oh, yes, let's see those up close."

The two men took a few minutes to reach them, because other visitors blocked their way.

"Here's New Brunswick. Its floral emblem is the purple violet. Nova Scotia has its mayflower. Prince Edward Island chose the lady's slipper. Quebec's symbol, of course, is the old French fleur-de-lys. Here's Ontario, with its white trillium. Saskatchewan's symbol is the western red lily. And there, Mr. Baumbach, is Alberta. Your province's coat of arms features the wild rose. And look over there. That's British Colombia's white dogwood. They're so beautiful in the early spring. There's Newfoundland's pitcher plant. That was added when Newfoundland joined Canada. Yukon's floral emblem is the fireweed. As for the Northwest Territories, they chose the mountain avens. Now look over there. That huge stained-glass window represents all the provincial emblems together."

Corbeil stopped, eager to see what impression all this was having on his visitor.

"How many seats are in this chamber?"

"That would be 255. But that number keeps changing, Mr. Baumbach, just as the population does. In 1867, when Canada became a united country, there were only 181 seats."

"I see. Now, something else. When we entered, I saw no security guards."

"Well, there are security guards."

"Where I come from, you have to show identification almost everywhere."

"We don't have many security problems in this country. We've been at peace with the Americans since 1815, when the Treaty of Ghent ended the War of 1812. But we have had a few insurrections. One occurred in 1837. It was led by Joseph Papineau. Two others, both led by Louis Riel, occurred in 1869 and 1885. We've had no trouble in this century, but I don't advise you to come around here with a gun. We're relaxed about security, but we're quite vigilant."

"I'll have to remember that."

"It's five o'clock now, Mr. Baumbach. Public buildings are closing. If you come back tomorrow, I'll show you the Senate and the Library of Parliament. It has a very elaborately carved ceiling and some lacy wrought iron."

"Oh, thanks, Mr. Corbeil. Tomorrow, I have several appointments with the local hospitals, and I've left the last day open for a tour of the city. But I intend to return with my wife. I'll be sure to ask for you. Now, is my hotel far from here?"

"Actually, it's just two blocks down this street. I'll drive you there."

A week later, Hermann was back at the Calgary Airport and immediately called his office to see if there was any urgent business which could not be postponed till next day. He longed to see his wife and the baby. Miss Pearson assured him everything could be delayed one day longer. On the way home in the taxi, he thought about how stable this country was compared to so many others. At one corner, he noticed a store that sold Belgian chocolates and asked the driver to stop. One display featured a little black cat with shiny green eyes; trailing behind him was a miniature red barrel filled with multi—coloured balls of chocolate. He couldn't resist that. Joey was much too young to eat chocolate, but he might enjoy the colours. And Rose would appreciate some dark chocolate wafers. Yes, he was anticipating the joy of being home and asked the taxi to speed as quickly as permitted.

Teresa greeted him at the door, but she was agitated.

"You look upset, Teresa. What's wrong?"

She tried to control her tears but could hardly speak.

"The baby—."

"The baby? What's wrong with the baby?"

Hermann dropping his briefcase, flung his hat and coat on a chair, and rushed to Joey's room. There was Rose, sitting in an easy chair. Dr. McDonald was examining the baby. He lay motionless in his crib.

"The baby's temperature has dropped since this morning, Mr. Baumbach. He's stopped crying now and has dozed off."

"What happened, Dr. McDonald? When I left, he was perfectly healthy. What happened?"

Well, Mr. Baumbach, for the first few days after you left, he really was healthy. That's what I guess from what I've been told. The baby did cry a little. Then, he began to kick and scream. Your wife gave him a little wine. When that wore off, he began to kick and scream again. In fact, he tried to get out of the crib. The only thing that calmed him down was a pacifier, but he kept pushing it out of his mouth. Then, your wife thought of something rather ingenious. She taped the pacifier to his mouth. Next morning, Teresa found him lying here. He was hardly breathing. I removed the pacifier and got him breathing again, but he developed a high fever. I gave him a small doze of medication. The fever has gone down a little, but his condition is still serious. He's very dehydrated, so he needs a lot of liquid. Poor little fellow. He opened his eyes only twice."

Hermann could hardly believe what had happened. Worse, he could hardly look at Rose. She had almost killed her son, because he had been disturbing her sleep. Fortunately, Teresa had arrived in time.

The doctor further explained that the baby must have been very frightened in the dark. He couldn't scream, or even breathe properly. "After the medication the fever seemed to subside a little, but his condition is still serious. We must feed him liquids because he is dehydrated."

Hermann stood motionless, speechless, enraged at Rose. He could not articulate what was on his mind. Rose taped the baby's mouth to keep him quiet, so as not to disturb her sleep. The little frightened tyke could have choked to death. There were still marks of the tape on the baby's cheeks. Rose sat in a chair, silent, trying to look blameless quite unperturbed while Teresa, haggard and worried, was gently massaging the baby's feet to restore his circulation. Death might have occurred if Teresa had arrived late that morning. Hermann asked the doctor if he could pick up the baby and sing to him. The doctor nodded approval. Hermann asked no further questions, picked up the baby, wrapped him in a soft blanket, and began to talk and sing.

"Schöne Bube, du wirst glückliche sein." (Beautiful baby, you will be lucky.)

Joey became aware of a familiar voice and started to kick his legs and move his hands. He gurgled, trying to express something. Rose used to remark that the baby found Hermann's German accent very funny.

To annoy Rose, he deliberately began to sing the familiar lullaby, the one that she hated. Joey opened his eyes and gurgled with glee, moving his pudgy arms up and down. The doctor was surprised.

"Well, well. Maybe we can give him a little pablum now. It's about time for him to eat something."

Rose got up from her chair and motioned to Hermann.

"Sit here with the baby, so Teresa can feed him while you keep him steady on your knees."

He sat down with Joey and began to play with him.

"Ah, Joey what do you say to that? Thirsty, are you? *Willst du ein Trunk?*"

Joey smiled again.

"There," said Rose, "you see? What did I tell you? As soon as he hears that German accent, he starts to laugh."

"Rose, let's forget about that for the time being. Bring me that package over there."

He opened the box in front of Joey. Pushing away his drink, Joey poked the cat's green eyes and made them move up and down. Then he examined the eyes more closely and tried to dislodge them from their sockets. Unable to do this, he looked helplessly at Hermann and began to squeeze the little cat, which said "ouch." Confused, Joey picked up the cat and cradled it in his arms. He was imitating his father.

"Doctor, would it be alright for me to give Joey some of these soft chocolates?"

"Yes, Mr. Baumbach. Anything that he can swallow will give him strength. He's old enough now."

Dr. McDonald looked at Joey again, found him considerably improved, and promised to return next day for a check-up.

"If he cries again, just pick him up and sing that German song. He's not frightened anymore. In a day or two, he'll be fine."

After the doctor left, Hermann remained holding the baby. When Teresa cleaned his face, which he had smeared with chocolate, Hermann began to sing some soft Hassidic chants. It had a soothing effect on the little bundle, who dozed off contentedly.

"Well, then," Rose suggested, "let's have supper. I've got something special for you."

"I'm not hungry."

"Then you'll have the salad, or whatever you want. I bought some *Liebfraumilch* for the fish."

"Oh, whatever you have prepared will do. I'll try to eat as much as I can."

He appreciated that Rose had spared no effort to prepare for his homecoming. But sitting at the table, gazing at her, he was troubled and disgusted. For the first time, he wondered if Rose had actually tried to kill the baby. She knew, precisely what she was doing, and might try again. One night, the baby would choke. Before morning, she would remove the tape, clean his cheeks and leave no trace of it. When Teresa arrived, she would find the baby dead. The doctor would explain that infants sometimes died for no obvious reason. All her troubles would be over because she would now be past the child-bearing age. It had now become evident to him that Rose wanted to do away with their baby.

"You look tired, Hermann. Did you have a hard time in Ottawa?"

"No, not at all. The meeting went very smoothly. We'll get our request for a reduced tariff, and we'll be able to set up our own factory. But—"

"But what, Hermann?"

"Rose, why did you tape the baby's mouth? How could you do that? What were you thinking?"

"Hermann, he kept on crying. As soon as I stuck the pacifier in his mouth, he pushed it out. So I taped it on. He stopped crying. I went to bed. It seemed so simple."

"Didn't you even think to check up on him during the night?"

"No, of course not. Why would I have done that? He wasn't crying."

There was no point in arguing about it. She must have rehearsed this many times and come up with a plausible explanation for everything.

"Frankly, Rose, I don't believe—I don't believe—that any reasonable mother wouldn't have checked up on a distressed baby during the night. Most mothers, no doubt, are too indulgent and careful, especially with their first child. But you, Rose, you—"

"But you, Hermann, you're spoiling him. The slightest whimper and you're there to cuddle him. He has to learn self-discipline. How else will he ever eat or sleep on a regular basis? And to think that you Germans are supposed to be models of discipline."

"But there's a big difference between discipline and negligence."

No use arguing, he thought. Rose will use anything to validate her argument.

"Thanks, the dinner was delicious. But tonight I'll sleep in the baby's room. And don't worry about breakfast tomorrow. I'll eat downtown."

Then he hurried to the baby's room. She remained alone. This was the first time he had not kissed her after dinner and the second time that they slept apart since she returned from the hospital. She was losing his love and all on account of that little monkey baby.

She put on a satin nightgown and went into the baby's darkened room.

"Hermann, are you asleep?"

"I was. You'd better get back to your bed. You probably have a big day ahead. And so have I."

A choking sensation rippled through her throat. Her pride was hurt. She almost ran out of the room. This rift must not continue, she thought desperately. At the moment it would be best to accept the terms discussed prior to their engagement: she would stay at home in the mornings and attend to her business in the afternoons. To assure him of her earnest intent, she would put an ad in the newspaper for an extra assistant for her business and show it to him as soon as such an employee was hired. She convinced herself that if she became the little German *Hausfrau* he wanted, the baby incident would fade and be forgotten. Tomorrow evening at dinner would be the propitious moment to tell him about her intentions. She tumbled into bed exhausted; fell asleep, but hardly stirred with remorse. At breakfast, lonely and sad, she had a feeling that something had ended and doubts kept recurring. Perhaps it would be wise to meet him in the garage and, as an expression of her love, kiss him passionately before he drove off. Gulping down the orange juice, barely tasting the croissant, and almost scalding herself with the coffee, she rushed to put on her coat and dashed to the garage. Herman's car was not there.

Entering her office she found the usual, daily tidal wave: inquiries that would lead nowhere, complaints about late payments, demands from small investors who wanted to know what to buy with absolute security, requests for tips on the stock market that would have required a fortune teller. Today, though, confirmations for one major investment and two substantial ones required immediate action. Business had expanded far beyond her initial expectations. In no time, Rose had organized the daily mail. Her secretary came in holding a heavily embossed envelope.

"It's an invitation to a fund-raising dinner, which would be useful for you and your husband to attend. It will certainly be an opportunity to make contacts. The tickets are $250 per person."

"Get two tickets immediately—specify for seats as near the head table as possible."

Then, Rose picked up a letter from Tel Aviv. She opened it with some apprehension. It was from her mother-in-law.

Dearest Rose:

We've heard about your success in business and are very proud of you. Hermann also told us about his good news, and we're very pleased. If we can build a factory in Canada, then we can be together again: parents, children and grandchildren, aunts and uncles, cousins. It would be like returning to Germany, where we lived so happily until a devil from hell descended on us. Rebecca and Miriam went on a shopping spree in Paris and bought two beautiful scarves and a skirt for you. I never question their buying rationale and sometimes wonder if they have one, but you'll like these. Hermann mentioned that it might be a while before you can visit us in Palestine. Perhaps we can come to Canada for a short visit. Love from everyone, Mother.

Rose read the letter twice. If they were to visit, she would have to entertain them and neglect her business. She put the letter away, meaning to discuss it with Hermann.

Entering his office that morning, Hermann found Miss Pearson typing. She was clearly unaware that he was standing right behind her and watching. Suddenly, she became conscious of his presence.

"Good morning Miss Pearson. If you're ready with the work sheets, please bring them into my office."

"Yes, sir, as soon as I finish typing this paragraph."

He paused to look at her again. Her natural ash blond hair, bundled into a pigtail, was held together with a pearl barrette, placed at the nape of her neck. She was wearing a dark royal blue suit with a snow-white blouse. As he stood watching her, she reminded him of Clarice. Same finely chiseled features, the rosy clear complexion of a matured youth. In fact, she resembled Clarice not only in appearance but in gentleness and intelligence. He wondered if she had a steady gentleman friend? No one had ever called to take her home.

Miss Pearson finished typing, walked into his office with the day's agenda, and asked for further instructions. He caught sight of those soulful eyes that now seemed beautiful. Why had he never noticed them before?

"The mail hasn't arrived, Mr. Baumbach. As soon as it does, I'll look for the letters that require your immediate attention."

"Good," he answered.

As she stepped out, he went toward the door and opened it wide enough to see her from his desk. When the mail arrived, she returned with a pile of letters.

"Here's a letter that you should see, Mr. Baumbach. It's from a hospital in Toronto. They need a half dozen B-model scissors, and we have four in stock. We'll have to order the others from overseas. And they'll take several weeks to get here. I'll wire the hospital and ask if the delay will be acceptable. As for the other orders, I'll have to check because I'm still not quite familiar with all of the stock numbers. I'll answer each letter, state delivery dates and possible delays."

Hermann glanced at Miss Pearson holding the stack of letters. Before he could think clearly some words escaped, "Miss Pearson are you busy this evening?"

"No, sir, not really."

"Would you stay a little later than usual? We could attend to these urgent letters."

"Oh, yes, of course, Mr. Baumbach."

"We'll take a little break and go out for supper before returning to work, if it's all right with you. And now call my wife to tell her that I have to work late and won't be home for dinner tonight."

She smiled inwardly. "I'll phone your wife immediately. By the way, the latest issue of *World Finance News* came in today. I put it in the top drawer of your desk."

Hermann examined the pile of letters, dictated some short replies, and calculated that Miss Pearson would finish her typing by six-thirty. They would spend two hours at a nearby restaurant and then return at eight for another two hours. At six-forty, she came in with the typed letters for his signature. When he asked where she would like go for supper, her reply surprised him.

"We don't really have to go out, Mr. Baumbach. There's a new little Chinese restaurant just down the street. They deliver. Have you ever had chop suey? I tried it a few weeks ago, and it's delicious. So are the egg rolls and vegetables or fried chicken with rice. It would save time and parking. Would that be all right?"

"Why not? Sure, then phone them to deliver as soon as possible and set the table, in our reception room."

Within half an hour, they were eating food that Hermann had never tasted.

"You know, Miss Pearson, this is excellent. What is it, chop suey? You must write down the name of everything that we've ordered. And I've just remembered something. We have some red wine in the liquor cabinet. I'll be right back with it."

When they were almost finished eating, Miss Pearson seemed eager to hear his impression of Ottawa. "How was your trip to Ottawa?"

"I was very impressed. I cannot forget Confederation Hall with its centre rotunda pole and its top spread of branches touching the ceiling. The city itself is quite different from those in Europe. You get a feeling that everything is very recent."

"Yes, that's just what I thought. But we are a fairly new country, and everyone continually reminds us how small our population is and how empty our country looks. But what country would permit immigrants to settle without screening them? Of course, the newcomers must be healthy and have a trade or skill before they are given permanent residence and citizenship status. Although many learn the new language and acquire skills or a trade, and by sheer determination work hard to succeed, yet a number of them remain dependent on our welfare system."

Hermann looked at her with mild disbelief. She seemed so earnest and genuinely interested in social issues.

"Miss Pearson, do you belong to a political party? Or do you support one without joining it?"

"Actually, I joined the Liberal Party. It's a tradition in my family, like drinking orange juice in the morning. Sometimes it's sweet, sometimes it's flat. But morning juice is an irrefutable habit."

"Are there many political parties in Canada?"

"No more than three or four, and the extreme ones never get elected."

"Extreme ones?"

"Yes, we have some socialists and even a few communists."

"I see. In Europe, they do get elected. Maybe things will be different now that the War is over and the Nazis are gone. But the Soviets are still there. Right now, though, Miss Pearson, they seem very far away." They were drinking, chatting and, unobtrusively, Hermann checked his watch. It was eight o'clock. They returned to their desks. A few minutes after nine, the lights suddenly went out. Hermann rushed to the window to see if the lights were on elsewhere. No, there was a total blackout.

"Miss Pearson," he called. "Are you alright?"

"Yes, I think so."

"Put your hand on the wall and walk slowly toward the door of my office. We can wait here until the lights come on again."

"Okay, I'm walking along the wall."

"Fine, but watch out for the filing cabinet on that wall."

He met her at the threshold of his office.

"Hold onto me, so you won't fall. I'll escort you to the couch on the right and—we'll just wait, I guess. How long can a power failure last?"

They sat down quite close to each other without saying a word.

"Mr. Baumbach, do you think that the elevators are working?"

"No, I don't."

"What about those small medical flashlights? They run on batteries. They're in the new cabinet. I'll go and get them."

But they were too small.

THE EXPATRIATE

"It's strange that the building administration did not advise the tenants of the blackout, especially if the housekeeping staff come after midnight to clean the offices." Miss Pearson moved a little nervously, but remained silent, instinctively fearing to respond too quickly.

"Come to think of it," she said, " I now remember we did get a notice this morning that the electrical connections were to be repaired and that there would be a complete blackout from nine to two. I thought nothing of it because I had no idea we would work late—so I threw out the notice."

This gave Hermann pause to think. Miss Pearson had a photographic memory. She never forgot anything, not even the most trivial facts; she even could remember dates of delivery on orders that had come in months earlier, and could easily have remembered to tell him about this. But she had not done so.

The darkness in the office accentuated her smooth white cheek and chiseled chin line. He craved to touch it. Why had she not warned him of the blackout? Suddenly the answer flashed through his mind, and with one hand he unbuttoned her blouse. She did not resist but passionately returned his kisses.

At two-thirty, all the lights went on. They dressed silently and prepared to leave.

"I'll drive you home, Miss Pearson. You'll never find a cab at this hour." Seated near her in the car, he felt some kind words were appropriate. "If you want to come in late tomorrow or take the day off, I'll agree."

"No, I'll come in as usual, maybe a little late. There is too much work. While you were away many orders came in, and I know we should not delay."

He looked at her sideways as she said this, thinking that no matter what, she is a competent and conscientious secretary. When they reached her residence, he stepped out of the car first, escorted her to the door, stooped a little, kissed her very lightly on one cheek and left quickly.

As soon as he got home, Hermann tip-toed to the baby's room. Joey was sleeping soundly. Then, he slid quietly to the bedroom and lay down beside Rose.

"Hermann, what on earth kept you so late?"

What a foolish question, he thought. Most husbands respond with one word: "work" The other activities require a special descriptive flair. But he should explain a little. "We had a blackout. No power until two-thirty. Something about the city fixing electrical connections."

"I see. But the phone wouldn't have gone off. You could have called me."

"I didn't want to disturb you," he was about to reply. But she interrupted him.

"Did you put on some new kind of after-shave lotion?"

He did not answer. Suddenly he realized Miss Pearson's cologne had left its scent. " Please, Rose, go to sleep. I need some rest after a heavy day's work."

Without touching her, Hermann turned around to face the wall and fell asleep. Rose, however, felt quite disturbed. Certainly he could have called to say not to worry, he would be delayed. She was not certain if he worked alone or with Miss Pearson. One thing was certain; the perfume scent was not his usual eau de cologne. She spent the next few hours trying to reconstruct what Hermann had been doing at the office, and asked herself again, if Miss Pearson was with him in the blackout. Tomorrow morning, she would not question him but leave his mother's letter on the breakfast table.

Next morning, Rose dashed off without breakfast and without saying good-bye. Hermann picked up the letter from his mother without reading it but found time to play with Joey. The little one raised his hands to say that he wanted to be picked up. Hermann was holding him, when Teresa arrived for the day.

SUCCESS IN BUENOS AIRES

Hermann arrived late to find Miss Pearson busy typing letters. The morning greeting showed no evidence of last night's affair. As usual, he asked if the day's agenda was ready and without interrupting her typing, she said, "Yes." But Hermann could not concentrate. To forget last night's affair and relax, he searched for the issue of *The World Financial News* and found it where Miss Pearson had put it. Its contents had the usual list of shares on the market, their prices, and some mavens who had set themselves up to predict the future. Will the market be bullish or bearish? All based their predictions on the booming American economy. But of particular interest to Hermann was South America where, in the future he might want to affiliate with a local company to sell his instruments. A while ago he had sent a letter to his friend, Jaakob and could not understand why he did not reply. Hermann began to search for an article about the paper industry and perhaps some news about Jaakob's company. But there was no such article. He continued to be a subscriber and only several years later, on the second page, of *The World Financial News,* he was surprised to read in large black headlines:

"GERMAN REFUGEE, IN SEVERAL
YEARS TIME BUILT A WORLD WIDE
BUSINESS EMPIRE."

"Herr Jaakob Kesselmann, the founder and president refused to speak about himself and his distinguished wife, Professora Severina Filipovic. The company's directors, the most powerful industrialists in Argentina manage this huge business. But what accounts for the rapid rise of the

JEANNETTE MOSCOVITCH

Atlantic and Pacific Paper Industries (A.P.P.I)? How has it become one of the largest paper manufacturer in the world controlling much of the world's paper market? It was the founder's belief in progress and innovation. The first thing he did, in fact, was to eliminate the axe and chain, once central to the logging industry. Instead, he introduced new ways of tracking forest growth. His pulp mills use new systems to select the best wood chips, and innovative optical sensors to monitor paper thickness, opacity and moisture. Herr Kesselmann has gone even further, setting up a research institute.

Paper manufacturing is a complex process and an expensive one. It involves cutting down trees, pulping them, using the wet mixture to form thin sheets, and drying them to form paper. Drying alone requires an area the size of a football field. And the drying machines consume tremendous quantities of energy. The research institute is now developing new ways of drying, which will save about thirty percent of the current cost and, if successful, will revolutionize the industry.

President Kesselmann has several additional aces up his sleeve. One is still experimental: using grass to make paper. The advantages would be incalculable. Grass grows quickly. And it is easy to cut, transport, liquefy, and dry. Some tests have already been successful. Further details, he says, will remain secret. Herr Kesselmann says that he will travel to Switzerland to promote the development of a small dryer which would be easy to handle and require much less energy than the dryers currently in use. At the same time, he plans to promote modern methods to manufacture boxes of all sizes. Shares of A.P.P.I. have been trading briskly in markets throughout Europe and the Americas.

Herr Kesselmann shuns publicity. He refuses to discuss himself or his wife. Photographers are not permitted anywhere near his mansion in Buenos Aires. It is now

THE EXPATRIATE

common knowledge that he is a survivor of the Nazi regime." (1)

Hermann had never doubted that Jaakob would be a great success. He put away *The World Financial News* and began to work on his daily agenda. At the same time, in Buenos Aires, his friend had read the same article and was reacting to it in his own way.

The captain was well aware that journalists relied on sensationalism. And in this postwar world, even industrial news had become sensational. The A.P.P.I. was a prime target, because of its mysterious foreign president. Many of those who met the captain were somewhat suspicious of his past.

After reading the article in his office, he walked over to the window, pulled aside the drapes and looked down at Buenos Aires. It was a sunny day. The air seemed to be floating on the pale orange golden haze shading the soft blue sky. Looking toward the west, he could see the majestic Plaza San Martin, with its tall green overgrown trees whose drooping and sprawling branches cast shadows on the naked white marble statues sunning themselves shamelessly near carved shell basins. They looked so serene. Down below on the *Avenida Neuve de Julio*, the moving cars resembled toy boxes dashing quickly, as if propelled by demons. Despite the rush of commerce, all seemed so peaceful. After a few minutes, the captain sat down again at his desk.

He tried to concentrate on business but could not. He kept thinking about the troubling conversation over breakfast. At first, Severina had presented him with a gossipy tabloid that Galina had given her. It featured an article that was ostensibly about his business but actually about him and his family. "Zvi, his son," it remarked, "had flaxen hair, a rarity in Latin America." And Zvi, of course, was the exact image of the captain as a young boy. This is what provoked his conversation with Severina.

"See, Jaakob, our beautiful son looks Germanic."

"And how would you define Germanic?"

"Oh," she waved her hand a little, "never mind. He's just beautiful. And he's smart, too. He loves to learn. But I have better news to tell you. This is very confidential, Jaakob, strictly between us. Galina tells me secret Jewish agents have come to Buenos Aires. They're going to arrest some top-ranking Nazi, and are on the trail of some other suspects hiding in disguise. Galina knew that you'd be pleased to know about all this."

The captain continued to drink his coffee, but the news affected him. Severina noticed this immediately.

"Jaakob, what's wrong? Are you not feeling well? I thought that you would be pleased to know that the guilty ones will be punished for what we suffered."

"Why, yes, I am pleased but a sudden recollection has turned my stomach."

"Yes, of course. I understand. Thanks darling, for telling me."

"How long will the agents stay?"

"I don't know. For a little while, I guess, because they're looking for a few more men who are hiding under false names: they won't be easy to find." Without replying, he had gulped down his coffee.

An hour later, at the office, Miss Mendoza brought in the daily agenda, the mail and a newspaper.

"Patron, you asked me to look for companies that manufacture vacuums and all kinds of equipment. So, I called the Swiss embassy. They'll send me a list of Swiss factories along with their brochures. Also, I went to the newsstand on *Avenida Florida*, the one that sells foreign papers and magazines, and I found this one: *Der Schweizer Tagesblatt*. In one section, there's a list of major factories and their products. It's in German, of course, so underline the ones that you want me to contact."

"Thanks, Miss Mendoza. That was very clever of you. Before you leave, please inquire at all the airlines how soon a place is available to fly to Switzerland. Then contact the Research Department to ask which engineer in charge of pulp-drying equipment is free to travel immediately to Switzerland."

"Right, patron. I'll do this immediately."

The captain pushed away all the papers on his desk except the list of Swiss manufacturers. He was about to throw away the newspaper, when an illustrated section fell to the floor. One headline caught his attention. It was about the social scene in Zürich. Just under the headline were two photographs. On one side were Count and Countess Friederich von Fürstenburger. On the other side were their daughter, Brigitta, and Heinrich Kreuzer, her fiancé. The captain took out his magnifying glass. Lara looked beautiful even with a fuller figure. Her husband appeared pleasant enough but much older. Brigitta is still plain, he thought wistfully, but intelligent and much slimmer. Her fiancé looked like a bright and clean-cut young man. No mention of the von Heissel name. Had the Count legally adopted Brigitta? He could find out, but it would be dangerous to meddle now. The announcement added that the bride-to-be had graduated cum laude in anthropology from the local university. The groom was a graduate engineer, cum laude from Berne. Among the prominent guests would be the bride's maternal grandparents, Count and Countess von Stradta, who had left Germany many years ago to reside in a neutral country. An elaborate wedding would take place at the cathedral, and a reception would follow in the park. Authorities had already given the Count permission to cordon off a large area for this event. A canopy has been erected, and special flooring was put down connecting the front door of the cathedral to the outside park area. Below the article was a photograph of the cathedral, at the edge of a park filled with colourful flowers which gave it an aura of pastoral solitude.

The captain sat down at his desk again. Brigitta a bride! Old enough to marry? How could it be? Had so many years fled by already? But as an educated and mature person would she now begin to question her roots? She certainly knows that her birthplace was Düsseldorf, Germany. Does she realize what a catastrophe befell their country with the defeat? What did she know or suspect about her father's disappearance? No doubt she was told he died in action on foreign territory. Tired of speculating, he put away the newspaper and pulled out his handkerchief, with its monogram that always reminded him of his previous mother-in-law. Reclining in his chair, the captain felt a deep longing to see his daughter again, no matter what the risk. This business trip to Switzerland would provide a convenient, though dangerous, opportunity—the only one that he might ever have. In fact, this trip to evade the Nazi-hunters who had just arrived in Buenos Aires would now serve a double purpose.

Galina, no doubt, would meet these Nazi hunters. Her daughter and son-in-law would have to participate in any plans she made. If Severina showed up without her husband, she would have an alibi for doing so. Urgent business was a convincing excuse. It might work. But leaving immediately would be hard to explain because Severina was by now pregnant with their second child. She was in good health. Travel would pose no problem, and she might even insist on accompanying him to Switzerland. But he must convince her it would be wiser to remain at home with Zvi, that he would be away at most ten days. In addition, his Swiss schedule would be so busy that they would have very little time to be together. Certainly his preference would be to travel with her, but not under these circumstances. It's wiser to go alone and return as soon as possible. Then, suddenly, another problem occurred to him. Would his passport still be valid? Would requesting a renewal mean a new investigation?

As usual when facing several problems, the captain made a list of priorities and then acted on each in the proper order. First, he'd instruct Miss Mendoza to buy an air ticket for departure in two days' time for Switzerland and date of return to Buenos Aires to be left open. This would allow him to stay in Switzerland as long as he needed. All telephone calls and meetings for the day were to be cancelled. Also she should inquire which of the engineers can leave immediately to accompany him to Zürich.

An hour later, while working feverishly, he was interrupted by a flash on his private phone.

"But, I warned you, Miss Mendoza, not to transfer calls."

"Please, patron, just for a minute, take this one."

He picked up the phone reluctantly and heard a small voice. "Hello Dad. Mom said that I should phone you right away."

"Zvi, has something happened? Is mother ill?"

"No. I just got my report card for the year and I'm head of my class. I got ninety-two in Spanish and ninety percent in Hebrew. Mom wanted you to know before Grandma."

THE EXPATRIATE

"I'm so proud of you," the captain answered, while glancing at the boy's photograph on his desk. It was an exact image of him at primary school age, but his son's was much more beautiful, the perfect German: flaxen hair, blue eyes, straight features, an upright and agile body. "This deserves a special gift. What would you like? Roller skates? A baseball and bat? I know, how about a scooter?"

"A scooter? I don't know. But come home early, Dad, so that we can all have dinner together. Grandma will be here."

"Is Mom at home? I'd like to speak to her."

"No, Dad, she's teaching. But she'll be home early tonight."

"Now, what about that scooter?"

"Well, maybe. But you know what I really want? A dictionary"

"A dictionary?"

"Sure. A Spanish-German dictionary. Mom says that you speak German. You still speak German, don't you?"

Where did this come from? He seldom spoke German in front of Zvi. At first, he and Severina had spoken only English. By the time that Zvi had begun to talk, the captain had learned enough Spanish to speak it easily at home.

"Well, Zvi, if that's what you really want then I'll get one for you. Give mother a kiss for me. And I'll certainly be early for dinner so we can celebrate."

"Thanks, Dad. See you soon."

The captain tried to concentrate on urgent tasks, but his thoughts drifted to the children. Both were true Germans at heart. Brigitta was a serious anthropologist. Zvi wanted nothing more than to study German. No one, to his knowledge, had prompted the boy. Again he caught himself returning to the past but resumed feverishly his urgent tasks of replying to important letters. Again a red flash appeared on his phone. "Patron, another urgent call. It's Kurt Keunenberg in Montevideo. He sounds very anxious."

"Hello, Kurt. What's the problem?"

"It's the strike. I thought that we could avoid one, but I was wrong. The loggers and dryers just walked out. I'm afraid that they're going to riot."

"Kurt, stop here! I'll call you right back on a better phone. *Verstehen* Sie?" (Do you understand?)

"Ja."

He put on his coat, checked Keunenberg's phone number, and ran out of the office. From a public phone across the street, he asked the operator to put through a long-distance call to Montevideo.

"Kurt, get out of your office immediately. Use a public phone to call me back at this number. I am in a booth on *Avenida Libertador.*"

"Why not use your office phone?"

"Because it's probably tapped especially for conversations about the strike."

"Right. I'll leave right away. I know where to find a phone and will be there in five minutes."

A few minutes later Kurt was explaining the situation very quickly. The captain replied without hesitation. "We had an exceptionally profitable year. News spread like wildfire. Shares went up, way up, and shareholders are very satisfied. You must have read about all this in *The World Financial News*. Everyone knows about our success. But our workers have plenty of benefits, as well."

"Yes, but the Union got hold of our financial statements. The leaders are demanding a wage increase of ten percent. I checked with our controller—"

"Good."

"And if we give them more than four percent, we'll have to raise our prices and expect fewer orders. As it is, Jaakob, our margin of profit is about average. But only if we can keep up the volume of orders. We have to be very cautious."

"You still don't know what's going on behind the closed doors of unions under this regime," he continued. " I keep hearing government officials blaming the Communists and Jews for every problem. I strongly suspect that the government has incited our workers. Maybe it wants a piece of the pie. Maybe it wants to take over. You also should know what is common knowledge. The Peron Regime expanded the trade union movement by giving attractive welfare pensions. But at whose expense? Merchants and manufacturers were ordered to give employees bonuses and paid holidays beyond their capacity, which forced many to close their businesses and declare bankruptcy. When Peron came to power, the only major industry the Government owned was petroleum. Then he began to nationalize industries. A.P.P.I. is a huge company. Peron would consider it a great prize. Of course, Peron wants a state dictatorship and it is common knowledge that he has strong Nazi and Fascist leanings."

The captain listened politely. He had already heard these comments countless times.

But Kurt did not stop talking "Worse, Peron's regime incited people to participate in public demonstrations that involved violence."

The captain had no time to become involved in political controversy.

"Kurt," he said abruptly, "tell Boisy about all this. A surplus this year is no guarantee of a surplus next year. He knows how volatile the market is. At the moment, our priority must be to buy better machines. Apart from anything else, these will make the workers' jobs easier. Besides, if we don't innovate, most of them will have to retire early. That's because the older workers find it harder than younger ones to operate our heavy machines. Tell Boisy that our best offer is three percent. We can offer nine or ten paid holidays, instead of only seven. And—"

"Wait, I can't write all this down fast enough."

"I've already written down most of what I'm suggesting. I'll send a copy to you immediately. And don't forget to discuss everything with Boisy. If both of you like my suggestions, or even if both of you can think of ways to improve them, go ahead."

"Boisy, he's the key figure and I'm sure he'll know what to do," Kurt replied.

"Yes, that's why he's on our board. Oh, and one more thing. I'm leaving for Switzerland in two days, not two weeks. If you have to reach me there, Miss Mendoza will tell you how."

"Thanks, Jaakob. You're a genius, as many of you Jews are in business. I think this is very convincing. I have a hunch they will accept your terms. But I'll get in touch with Boisy right away."

The captain smiled. A genius! He remembered calling Hermann Baumbach a genius when selecting gifts for those two ladies on the ship. But what was Hermann doing these days? Was Canada a favourable country in which to establish his business? If the captain could look through a telescope, he would have found Hermann absorbed reading his father's telegram.

Dear Son: We received an order from Caracas. We couldn't fill it ourselves, so we bought the instruments from another company and the shipment arrived today. They're made of good metal and are well constructed, but they're not sharp enough. I'll send you a few samples. On your way to Tel Aviv, please stop off in Basel or Zürich to find a factory that would hone these instruments properly. All of us are looking forward to your visit. Love, Dad.

The captain walked slowly out of the telephone booth and wearily trudged back as fast as he could. Entering his office he sank down in an easy chair and gazed idly through the glass wall. The orange golden sun was slipping into eternity. He too was a speck on the infinity. What was the struggle all about? Existence! A peaceful existence! How to attain it and as quickly as possible? Half of his life had passed and no sign of it! Again the red light flashes on his phone and Carmela rushed in.

"Patron, I have your ticket and your reservation. And I asked about your passport. You don't have to renew it. Your first call is from Abogado Hernandez."

She left quickly to send his instructions to Kurt Keunenberg. The captain dialed a private number. Abogado Hernandez answered.

"Your secretary told me about the trip. But before you go, the signature of your previous Will should be updated. I'm sending over a person authorized to witness signatures and he'll return the document to me. Now, we have some problems. Your factories aren't the only ones on strike or threatening to go on strike. I expect to read about violence in the days to come. Anyway, I've contacted the directors. They've agreed unanimously that you and your family need protection at all times, so I've hired two bodyguards for you, two for your wife, and two for your son. They'll—"

"Bodyguards? Senior Hernandez, are you sure?"

"Yes, I am. They'll follow you around on foot or in cars. They're experienced and discreet. In fact, you'll never even know that they're nearby. And of course, all the directors approved that such expenses are to be charged to the business. I forgot to mention, four men will guard your home, two in the daytime and two at night."

"Then I must thank you. But I don't want anyone in my family to know about all this. I'll be in Switzerland for about ten days. As soon as I get back, I'll call you."

"*Buena suerte, el Presidente*" and the conversation ended.

Almost immediately, another urgent call came from David Fischmann.

"Jaakob, do you know that secret Jewish agents have caught another Nazi? They're extraditing him, probably to Israel. According to rumour, they're closing in on someone else in Buenos Aires. That's good news. But hoodlums are planning to attack a synagogue. Maybe the one on Cordoba street. We'll have to warn the Rabbi. This is a very serious situation."

"But, David, is there no government protection at all? Is there no rule of law? "

"Jaakob, how can you be so naïve? Where was the rule of law on *Kristallnacht*? Our government probably instigates attacks but looks the other way when things get out of control. Maybe we are going to have another election, who knows? But I'll tell you this. The synagogues unlike the churches won't bow to Peron's tactics." The captain became momentarily terrified, knowing from experience where all this could lead. Severina and her mother attend that very synagogue. Real harm could come to them.

"So, what do you suggest?"

"First, we're going to hire twenty-four goons, twelve for each side of the synagogue. Some of them work at slaughter houses. Others are gauchos. They're out of work now that their season is over and need money. Also, we're going to hire three guards for the front door. They'll identify members of the congregation and prevent others from entering. So every member will need proper identification."

"To think that it's come to this."

"I don't know if the synagogue can pay for these goons."

"David don't worry. I'll pay. Just get started right away."

"I knew that we could count on you, Jaakob, but let's split the cost. By the way, I've heard about your labour problems. But with Boisy on our side, I'm sure a compromise will be found. You chose well. If this guy can't find a solution, no one can. Anyway, have a good trip."

Miss Mendoza came in just as he hung up.

"Remember, Patron, you promised your son to be home early."

His limousine sped northward on *Avenida Neuve de Julio*, one of the widest streets in the world. Dusk began to shade the tall buildings gaping in the sky, then spread to drain the sunset. The captain resolved to forget about his problems at least until the next morning. But moments of uncontrollable anxiety burdened him again. Would Boisy convince the men to go back to work? Who is the mysterious fugitive from justice hiding in disguise? Could the finger be pointing at him? How would he break the news to Severina that he must leave for Switzerland in two days' time?

Stepping out of the limousine at the entrance of his home, he heard a rustling sound coming from behind the hedges. The captain thought that it must be one of his bodyguards. He straightened his shoulders, tried to conceal his weariness under an air of serenity and, with a cheerful smile, rang the bell. Zvi was sitting nearby, waiting for him.

"Hi, Dad."

"Hi, professor. Here are your favorite chocolates. I'll look around for your dictionary and hope to find one soon. I promise. Has Mom come home yet?"

"No, she went to pick up Grandma."

The captain went into the salon, poured himself a cocktail, sat down in an easy chair and looked around. Everything was so gracious, so '*gemütlich*'. This house, let alone the people who lived there, was everything that he had hoped for. Shutting his eyes, contentedly sipping his drink, the persistent demons slowly returned. He was free! Yet Heinrich Heine had once said, there is something unsatisfying about attaining freedom through disguise. He had become used to his disguise but not to his identity. Who was he now? Brigitta's *Vater* or Zvi's *padre*? Was he still a Christian or a half Jew? Can one be both? The silent question remained unanswered, interrupted by the doorbell. In the distance, he heard Severina and Galina. They came into the living room, laden with colourful packages. He walked over to help them. Galina was the first to notice the roses that he had sent to Severina.

"Jaakob, you must stop spoiling my daughter. You're undoing all of my good work."

"But I love spoiled women and that includes you. But what smells so good in those packages?"

"Galina cooked some Czech food, Jaakob, so that Zvi will know at least something about his ancestors. But she didn't forget you. She made *Sauerbraten* just for you. Now, please wait here until supper is on the table."

Mother and daughter, speaking to each other in Czech as usual, hurried into the kitchen. In a few minutes, the table was ready. Like a queen, Galina took her place at the head of the table. Severina had always insisted on giving her mother this honour.

"Zvi, before I begin to explain some of these Czech dishes, I'd like to tell you something about Czech history."

"Fine Grandma. The food smells so good. It makes me hungry."

"I'll be brief. Long ago, pagans began to invade Eastern Europe. They attacked over and over again for many centuries. Eventually, though, they became Christians and settled down. One family, the Hapsburgs, supplied most of the rulers. And they did so, by and large, without wars. By 1522, Emperor Charles V controlled much of Europe. So much, in fact, that he gave Austria to his brother Ferdinand I. The secret of the Hapsburg success was very simple. They married the leaders of other powerful families, which made their countries allies. Eventually, most of them were marrying each other, which meant that their lands stayed in the family from one generation to another. In 1526, due to one of these marriages, Ferdinand became the king of Bohemia and—"

"But you just said that he was an emperor."

"Yes, but he was also an emperor. He ruled as king over Bohemia, which is part of what we now call Czechoslovakia, and Hungary. But he also ruled the Austrian Empire, not only Bohemia and Hungary. He and his descendents ruled that empire from Vienna for about four hundred years. The Hapsburgs and their ruling classes spoke German. But time was running out on the empire. Nationalism was growing. People who spoke other languages wanted their own independent countries. The Hapsburgs tried to solve this problem in 1867 by dividing the empire in two. One capital was Vienna. From there, they ruled Bohemia and many other places. The other capital was Budapest, in Hungary. This was the Austro-Hungarian Empire, which collapsed at the end of World War I much before your time, in 1918. The Versailles peace conference created a new country in the middle of that lost empire. The people who lived there, in Czechoslovakia, included not only Czechs and Slovaks but also Bohemians, Moravians, Ruthenians, and several other groups. So, you can see why our folklore and food ways originated in many places." (2)

"That's very complicated, Grandma."

"Yes, but it's not so complicated when you think of it in connection with foods and drinks. Poles are famous for their vodka, because their land is good for growing what they need to produce vodka: grain and potatoes. Czechs and many Germans like beer, because their lands have excellent sources of water and fields for fine hops. Hungarians and many other Germans prefer wine, because they have the sunny hillsides that produce fine grapes." (2)

"So what kind of food is ours?"

"Actually, Zvi, my parents claimed that they were Russians. So, we had a lot of Russian food. But we changed it a bit, because we were living among Czechs. Look over there. That's beluga caviar, and it's very popular in Russia. It's really just the eggs from a fish, a sturgeon. These are bigger than the ones in some kinds of caviar. Over here, we have another kind of caviar. And this is *malosol*, which in Russian means little salt. In a few minutes, we're going to have Russian *blinis*. They're little pancakes. We'll spread the caviar on them."

"Let's eat."

"In a minute, Zvi. Look in that tureen near Dad. It's hot *koulibiaka*. That's a kind of meat loaf that contains minced beef and walnuts."

Galina stopped to take a breath. "And you know what? I made that according to a recipe that came down from my great-grandmother. For the crust, I used what everyone uses: flour, margarine, salt, and water. But I used ice water. It makes a difference. For the filling, I used chopped onions and beef. But I fried the onions in olive oil. And I added ground almonds, chopped hard-boiled eggs, parsley, salt, and pepper. It's the almonds that make all the difference. The whole thing is easy. You just spread cooked rice on one half of the pastry, add the filling, and cook it all for about forty-five minutes." She turned to Severina, "You should learn how to make this."

"Grandma, you always say that the Russians are poor. Do they get to eat this stuff? Mom says that they usually eat borsch and potatoes."

"Oh, she's right. That's what they usually eat. But not on special occasions. And today is a special occasion. How often does anyone come home with such a fine report card? And wait. There's more. I baked your favourite Russian cherry pie."

"So, Grandma, Russians are good people? That's not what Carlos tells me."

Who's Carlos?"

"He's my friend at school. He says that Russians are bad. So are Germans. They kill people."

The captain flinched but remained silent. Severina was quick to answer.

"Well, Zvi, Carlos is wrong. He must have misunderstood what someone told him. There are good people and bad people everywhere. No, wait, I'll explain that better. There are no good or bad people, Zvi. There are just ordinary people, like you and me, who sometimes do good things and sometimes do bad things."

Galina smiled. "Well said, Severina. Now, before we begin to eat, I have a present for Zvi from Uncle Igor Herrenkevitch. He could not come because he had to perform a heart operation. It's really for your birthday next month, but we want you to have it now. Well, go on, open the box."

It was a boy's prayer shawl of finely hand-woven silk and wool.

"What is it?"

"It's a *talit*," explained Severina. "You wear it, like a shawl, in synagogue—but only on the Sabbath and festivals."

The captain fingered the shawl, concealing his anguish but he could not utter a word.

The meal was excellent, especially Galina's sauerbraten. The captain tried to be chatty and jovial. Now and then, however, he betrayed anxiety. Severina was quick to sense this, but she had no way of knowing he was anxious about his imminent departure for Switzerland. And she could never have imagined that he had another family over there. After a while, she realized that he had to rest.

Before they slipped into bed, the captain put his arms around Severina and kissed her.

"Did I forget to tell you how much I love you?"

"No, darling, you never do forget. I can imagine what an effort it must have been to come home early and listen to your mother-in- law."

"No, not really. Now I know a little more about Czech history, and the food was super."

"But something is worrying you."

"Yes there is. The board wants me to leave for Switzerland early, to inspect new types of machines for drying pulp paper. I hesitated to accept because it meant leaving you for a few days." He stopped to see her reaction.

Severina smiled sympathetically, putting her arms around his shoulder. "So that was it? That's why all of a sudden you looked so sad and preoccupied. I was hoping Galina would not notice.

Why of course you must go, darling. It's very important that lumber work be made easier. When will you leave?"

"In two days. On the fourteenth. But what worries me most is that you are pregnant."

"I'm in good hands. My doctor knows much more than you do about bringing babies into this world. Besides, Igor is watching me like a hawk. He reports everything to Galina." The captain was somewhat relieved.

"Then it's settled. I'll leave in two days and return in two weeks, at the end of May. By the way, has Galina heard via the grapevine that someone has threatened to attack the synagogue? Fischmann called me about it. He's got a plan: hiring twenty-four goons to beat off the hooligans. I offered to pay for the whole thing, but he insisted on paying for half."

"He's one of your directors, right? I hear good things about him and his dry-cleaning business. He keeps everything closed on the Sabbath."

"Yes, he mentioned that in his initial letter of application to join the firm. By the way, here's something else that I keep hearing, that Jewish secret agents are still in town."

"They were. Only two of them remain here." What a relief, he almost said it out loud.

"I suppose that you and Galina wanted to meet them. Were you hoping to entertain them?"

"Yes, of course. I'm not sure that entertain is the right word. They didn't come here to be entertained. They came to find Nazi war criminals. Anyway, they'll be back."

"I guess so. There must be plenty of old Nazis in this city."

"Never mind the Nazis. Let's get down to practical matters. You'll need clothes for at least ten days, is that right?"

"Yes, but you, too, have a busy schedule."

"No matter what, I'll pack your clothes. All kinds of emergencies may crop up in your business and you'll be strapped for time to do it properly."

"Darling, you think of everything. What would I do without you?" They kissed and tumbled into bed as if on their honeymoon.

ZÜRICH, SWITZERLAND

Aboard *Aerolineas Argentinas*, flight 22, the captain had a window seat in full view of the majestic infinity looming above. In no time, the lush green square patches of Argentina disappeared, replaced by a silver black undulating watery expanse, only to be changed again into a haze as the plane rose into the clouds. Pulling down the blind, shutting his eyes and reclining in his chair, he began to reconsider recent events. A few of his fears had not materialized. There was no news about the strike, which meant Boisy was still negotiating. And no newspaper had reported a riot. He could count his blessings: Severina had taken the news of his early departure in her stride; even the mother-in-law, sometimes overbearing, was likeable; and his beautiful son was an exact image of himself as a boy, and so clever. What do Jews say about clever kids? "He has a *Judische Kopf.*" A German dictionary he wanted! If Lara saw him she would smother him with love. But would he be interested in the history of his father's country? Would he understand that the Germany of the future must be a united country, and that it would be, in the interest of all the small underling European nations, to unite under the leadership of Germany? German culture is the best; its administration is well organized and functions efficiently. Germany would formulate a democracy—its language first, native tongues second, religion of one's choice—but remain *"Deutschland über Alles"* Otherwise, what is the alternative? There would be constant bickering among the pigmy nations, incited by religious bigotry and overzealous nationalistic fervour, as they claimed little pieces of territory here and there. These petty animosities would burst into wars with neighbouring nations and sometimes within themselves. The map of Europe is divided into small nations. But who knows what can happen?

His reverie was interrupted by the steward, who asked if he would like a drink. After sipping a whisky and soda, the captain leaned back in the seat and shut his eyes. Suddenly phantoms paraded before him: strange places, black seas, new countries, inspectors checking, prying—weddings, births, a soft plea from nowhere. Yanos come home! It was his mother's voice.

He was startled by a shrieking sound coming over the intercom system. "Fasten seat belts immediately. Violent turbulence expected." Then all lights went out. The engines roared. Flashes of golden wisps careened on the horizon. Torrents of rain pelted the windows. Hours of fear glided by agonizingly, slowly. And then an unexpected grey dawn, a dark pewter sky, an ominous hush in the plane! The stewardesses sat at their stations, resting a little after easing the fears of the passengers. Slowly daylight filtered in, and soon over the microphone the pilot announced in a soothing voice, "Release safety belts for the time being. Expected landing in Zürich airport in three hours. The weather there is a balmy seventy degrees Fahrenheit." Everyone breathed a sigh of relief. To walk on solid ground at last after twelve hours in the air!

The passengers were escorted by guards to pick up their luggage and then led to customs and immigration. Two inspectors glanced briefly at the captain's luggage and passport. The purpose of his visit, he told them, was to buy machinery. Without further questions he was permitted to enter the city.

An intercom announcement informed Hotel Schwyzhof Continental guests that a few limousines were waiting at exit four to drive them to the hotel. In no time, the captain was settled in a luxury suite. The bellhop insisted on removing the clothes from his suitcases; he hung them neatly in the armoire, its rococo ornamentation sparingly carved to fit in with the modern furniture. Then leading his guest to the bathroom, he proudly pointed to all the features there: a telephone with an intercom system, a mini radio, and a marble bathtub with a hand shower on a movable rod adjustable to anyone's height. All was white, shiny nickel and plexiglass. On top of a large writing desk lay a leather hand-tooled book of white, blue, and gold trim, explaining the amenities available for the hotel's guests. The captain was amused. It was evident that after the War, many establishments imitated the glitz of American styles. Yet in the Swiss surroundings such décor overshadowed the native charm. The ultra modern clashed with the surrounding ambience. Something solid and eternal was projected by the white caps of the Alps seen through the large picture windows in each room. By contrast, everything inside appeared temporal. The plexiglass would crack, the silver trimmings would tarnish, the marble discolour but the awesome Alps with their white caps were timeless.

Before he had time to settle in comfortably, there was a red flicker on the phone indicating a long-distance call. It could only be a message from Buenos Aires.

"Patron." It was Carmela's voice after a long-distance operator had put the call through. "Gonzales Pozas, the engineer, will arrive in Zürich in two days' time. Boisy is still negotiating, but expects the strike will be settled soon. Most agree to a three and a half percent increase in wages and some minor changes to the other conditions you suggested. Anyway, there won't be any violence, so don't worry."

"Thank you, Miss Mendoza. Just keep me posted, and call me whenever you need to."

He put down the phone, greatly relieved. His first priority was to rent a tuxedo for his daughter's wedding, which had to be done before the arrival of the engineer. Pozas must not suspect the purpose of the president's extended stay in Zürich. He would certainly not find a rental outlet in the hotel, but a pamphlet on the desk informed him of the elegant shopping district on the *Bahnhofstrasse*. Sipping a glass of refreshing orange juice, he began to read.

"Your hotel, far from the bustling center of town is situated in one of our highest valleys. Our country is small and is nestled between France in the west, Austria in the east, Germany in the north, and Italy in the south. How have we managed to stay neutral? We took matters into our own hands and were inspired to action by England's Magna Carta of 1215. We rejected monarchy and set up a

republic. In 1648, the Peace of Westphalia recognized the
independence of both the Netherlands and Switzerland.
It recognized Swiss neutrality as an obligation for the
preservation of peace. In 1920, moreover, the League of
Nations again recognized our permanent neutrality and
guaranteed our territorial integrity. Its aim was to foster
peace in the region. In fact, American President Woodrow
Wilson established the League's headquarters in one of
our cities: Geneva." (1)

The captain knew most of this, but what interested him about
Zürich was that it was the commercial and cultural centre of that
country. Its train station was among the busiest in Europe. It also
had a heavy concentration of banks and some of the most renowned
industrial firms in the world. The Oerlikon-Buhrle established in
1906 had its headquarters here to manufacture anti-aircraft guns,
machines tools, components for automotive industries and the
world-famous Bally shoes.

For the convenience of its guests, the hotel provided a shuttle
service to the *Hauptbahnhof.* That left the captain right where he
needed to be: on the grand *Bahnhofstrasse.* After walking for a
few minutes, he entered an exclusive haberdashery and explained
that he needed a tuxedo within two days time. Instantly, two clerks
brought four light-weight black tuxedos with grosgrain silk lapels.
While one tailor was adjusting the suit to fit, another clerk went
searching for accessories, a third one brought a few cummerbunds
and bow ties, and another displayed silk scarves and white gloves.
By the time he had tried on various sizes and examined all the
accessories, no fewer than four clerks had served him. The captain
was impressed and curious to know how these sales clerks knew
to select the proper choice and exact size.

"In our country" one of them explained, "before anyone can
become a salesman, he must take a course on the merchandise that
he intends to sell."

"Please return tomorrow," said another, "for your final
fitting."

And then, suddenly, all four clerks disappeared behind a
closed door. A moment later, someone else appeared, leading him

THE EXPATRIATE

to the cashier who handed him a beautifully written invoice. It ended with a thank-you for shopping in our store, signed "The Establishment." The amount was staggering, but the captain knew if one wanted first-class merchandise and service, one had to pay for it.

Next day, the captain went back for the final fitting, which proved faultless. His package arrived at the hotel a few hours later. Inside a gray box with gold lettering were reams and reams of fine gray tissue paper, with his tuxedo professionally folded to avoid creasing. The accessories were individually wrapped in the same gray tissue and tied with an overabundance of fine gold ribbons. The Swiss have a special penchant for ribbon-wrapped packages.

Next day's agenda was scheduled for meetings with manufacturers of machinery. First on the list was Schubert, Seltzer, & Zeigelhaus, specialists in equipment for the paper industry. The current president's father had founded the company in 1890. After World War I, Seltzer had joined. Still later, the company merged with Zeigelhaus. The captain scheduled an appointment for the next morning at nine-thirty.

Pozas arrived from Argentina that very afternoon. The captain arranged to meet him for dinner at seven o'clock. They agreed to spend the evening together, to discuss the blue prints, drawn up by the A.P.P.I.'s engineers, and then compare them with those prepared in advance by Schubert, Seltzer & Zeigelhaus, which showed meticulous attention to details and had clear explanations. The captain was impressed, but Pozas was not. He did not like to waste time on minutiae. After all, blueprints were always modified several times.

At first sight, the captain thought, Pozas looked like a sloppy fellow, wearing a rather badly fitted hunter green suit and matching tie. His black almond-shaped eyes sparkled behind gold-rimmed eyeglasses. His handwriting, almost calligraphic in its script, neatly matched the clarity and brevity of what he wrote. He carried an attaché case which was much admired. Even the captain asked where he bought it.

"Why, Mr. Kesselmann, don't you recognize merchandise from one of our company's directors? I mean Juan Dagunzo, the one who owns what he calls 'the largest leather business in

Argentina.' When I mentioned that I was looking for a case with many compartments, he made this one especially for me. Look how light it is. And imagine, he refused to take any payment from me."

This did not surprise the captain. Dagunzo knew from experience with employees that the cost of this gift would be repaid tenfold, not only in loyalty, but in the good will such a gesture would generate among the employees.

Next morning, Pozas and the captain arrived on time at Schubert, Seltzer & Zeigelhaus. A secretary ushered them into an austerely furnished conference room. Fritz Gruntag introduced the chief engineer, Johann Steiger, and his two assistants, Heinrich Hüber and Kurt Morgenstern. Then Walther Freulich, the chief accountant, came in. His sad demeanor contrasted sharply with the happy meaning of his name.

In the centre of the room stood a huge table and on it was a miniature replica of the proposed lumber mashing and drying machine for A.P.P.I. It looked very complicated, but when Steiger pushed one button it went immediately into action. All the various parts were folded into a cylinder under its top wagon. The first part to move was a miniature shovel, ejected from the cylinder. The little shovel moved backward and forward, picking up all the little logs lying in front of it on the table. It stopped automatically when it had picked up all the logs. At another push of a button, the shovel full of logs heaved itself up and threw its load into a bin on top in the wagon. As soon as it was filled, automatically a cover rose from its side, and closed the bin which instantly began to churn round and round to grind its content into pulp and stopped when it was all ground. Another push of a button, and the mushy pulp spilled into a container placed in front of it. This would eventually be dried, pressed and become paper. The chief engineer then began to explain how much such an automatic operation would save in time, labour and money. The captain thought this would be a delight to a young boy, mechanically inclined. Only the Swiss would have the patience to make such a miniscule reproduction.

It took two hours for the engineers to explain this model and discuss their blueprint. Finally, Pozas rolled up the blueprint to study it more closely that afternoon. All stood up, shook hands and were ushered out by Herr Gruntag through the reception room. There another client was waiting for him. The gentleman sat bent forward, reading a newspaper.

As the captain passed by, this man stood up and stared at him. The captain stared back. Both men remained standing, startled, speechless, and both said the same thing at the same time.

"What are you doing here?"

"I'm on my way," Hermann replied first, "to visit my family in Tel Aviv. I had to stop off at this firm to ask if they could hone some of the instruments we bought in Pakistan. But I know why you are here. To buy machinery for your paper mills, right? I read all about you in *The World Finance News.*"

"Good, then you know my purpose. I said it before and now say it again, Hermann you are a genius." Both began to laugh at their secret joke, recalling the incidents of buying gifts for the ladies on the Atlantic crossing. Herr Grüntag stood by watching silently, impatiently, as the two friends continued. "Anyway, how long are you staying in Zürich?"

"I have to leave tomorrow evening for Tel Aviv."

"Hermann, I can't tell you how glad I am to see you. Never thought that I would. Listen, can you meet me for dinner tonight? I'm staying at the Continental Schwyzhof and—"

"I am staying with friends."

"Good, well how about seven o'clock in the hotel's restaurant? The one that faces the garden in the back."

"I'll be there,—*Bestimmt, glückliche begegnung"* (certainly, lucky meeting) Hermann agreed and then rushed off with Grüntag. The captain was elated, and he knew why,—nostalgia for something really German. People spoke German here, to be sure, but not like Hermann, a Jew, from Frankfurt. In some way, he had returned to his native land.

Pozas overheard the plans of the two friends and later at the hotel, he excused himself for the evening. This, he said, would be a good time to visit the Zürich *Kunsthaus*. Before leaving, he showed the captain a brochure that he had picked up at the hotel. What attracted him was a photograph of Karl Moser, the architect who had designed this museum in 1910. The *Kunsthaus* was best known for its collection of Swiss paintings, of course, and these ranged from the fifteenth century to the present day. Most famous of all were the pre-Romantic paintings of Johann Heinrich Fuseli. Also on display were assorted works that included seventeenth-century Dutch, nineteenth-century French and contemporary art.

The captain was surprised that such a pragmatic fellow was interested in art.

"Thanks for showing me the brochure. I'll be sure to go there."

Hermann arrived punctually. The captain thought his friend looked extremely well, impeccably dressed as usual, but almost on the point of getting stout. Hermann had the look, he thought with some disappointment, of a complacent, jaded bourgeois. To Hermann, the captain was slightly thinner, slightly harassed, but his Teutonic features were as pronounced as before. His hair was graying visibly; a rather worried, tragic look hovered in his eyes. Almost a decade or more had flipped by very quickly, and things do change.

"Well, old chap," the captain began, "I bet Canadian girls would not let you remain a bachelor for long and you're no longer a roving Romeo."

"Jaakob, I may be a genius but you're clairvoyant. I am married. Here's a picture of my wife Rose and my son Joey. How about you?"

"Well I'm just as proud. Look at these pictures, Hermann. There's my wife, Severina. God, I miss her even after less than a week away from her. And there, that's my son, Zvi. He's playing with his model plane."

"Look at him, Hermann. He's a real blonde, '*echt Deutsch*' (genuinely German). And my wife is now pregnant with our second child. We hope it will be a girl."

"Well, then," said Hermann, "let's drink to beautiful families."

"Prost!"

"Now, let's do something about this food." The dinner whetted their appetites, and the conversation ceased for a little while.

THE EXPATRIATE

The captain was anxious to ask, in an oblique way, if Hermann had any recent news about the rebuilding and welfare of their *Vaterland* and about West Germany's "economic miracle."

"Oh, they're doing very well. Can't say as much for East Germany. But, Jaakob, I'm surprised that you even care about Germany. For me, that country is as closed as an unnamed grave."

"But, Hermann, we were born in Germany. We belong there no matter how we lost the victory."

"You astound me, Jaakob, you really do. The 'victory'—?" He put down his fork and knife. "How can you even utter such a word? We were betrayed by our own colleagues. Not only betrayed but persecuted through the ages and the final criminal act was *Kristallnacht.* Our culture, our education and the Christianity of Christians did not save the lives of our innocent citizens. Yes, we belonged there. But Germany betrayed us in the end and persecuted us. Civilization is just a veneer. Underneath, people are primitive barbarians."

The captain became visibly upset, wiping his forehead with the muslin handkerchief and carelessly dropping his fork on the floor, which the waiter quickly replaced with a clean one. He already had divulged too much, but continued heedlessly, not knowing what possessed him.

"But Germany was never a united country and the Socialist Party was trying to eliminate obstacles to its unification."

"What obstacles?" Hermann's voice became strained. "Did not the Jewish community contribute to the greatness of German culture? That such a disaster should befall us for our loyalty!"

The captain realized he was treading on dangerous ground. Besides, what was he trying to prove? There was much truth in what Hermann said.

"Yes, everything that you say makes sense. Trouble is, not everything about people makes sense. Underneath reason there lies a little emotion. As for me, I feel nostalgic. I can't help it. Sometimes don't you have "*Sehnsucht für die Heimat?*" (a yearning for your country) and the old times?"

"Oh, yes, for the old times but not what we suffered and we'll never forget that, Jaakob. But too much has happened between then and now. It's almost a new country now. I hear that unemployment is at its lowest level and the government was obliged to bring in workers from other countries. But never mind the old. How about Argentina? Is Buenos Aires as beautiful as the travel brochures say it is?"

"Yes, it is. Buenos Aires reminds me of a large European capital. What else? Oh, it has a wonderful climate. Unfortunately, it has a corrupt government. But what strikes me most, is that, in spite of the troubled times and corrupt government, the people seem happy-go-lucky. In northern countries the cold climate seems to breed serious and solemn faces. Of course, that is my personal observation." But Hermann was particularly interested in the status of women in South America.

"Yes, I've heard about Peron. Tell me, Jaakob, what are the women like down there? I mean, are they traditional? My wife Rose is not the traditional type. She insists on having her own business. Did I mention that she has her own financial consulting firm?"

"Why complain," the captain asked. "You have two breadwinners instead of one."

"Yes, but we don't need two. And it costs a lot to hire people for work that most wives do. We have a nanny for Joey, a maid who cooks for us, even a part-time secretary to manage the household expenses. I don't know, Jaakob. I wonder if this is good for us and especially for children. There is such blarney propaganda for the Equality Movement for Women. I saw such an article in one of the popular American magazines which my wife reads. I do not know to what extent the women's movement has succeeded. My wife is an example of it. She was smitten with this vogue and insists on earning her own living at the cost of family and home care. As for me, I'm doing quite well in business. It's because I find new ways to satisfy customers."

The captain smiled. The Jews do well in business, he thought. Even his father used to say so.

"I agree with you completely. And, as you read in that article, I'm an innovator in my own right. By the way, Hermann, what happened at Schubert, Seltzer, & Zeigelhaus? Were they interested in sharpening your instruments?"

"Yes, of course, they were. My father tried several other firms, but all were reluctant to do the job. One did show interest but quoted such a high price that we would have had to sell below cost. But when Grüntag heard that we had ten thousand instruments, he realized that the volume would reduce costs to make it profitable."

"If you are planning to do business in Argentina, I think it would be a good market for your medical instruments."

"Yes, I know. But not right away. First, my father is going to settle in Canada. He wants our family business to continue, and Canada will make that possible. I like Canada, Jaakob. They've fought in wars overseas, but they haven't had to defend their own land since the early nineteenth century. They have everything: wood, water, electricity, food and, above all, no great devastating wars compared to what Europeans have suffered. It's a safe place. But now, I am not so sure this War is to be the end of it."

The captain remained silent for a few solemn moments. "I agree with you Hermann. I foresee ethnic wars breaking out all over the world. But for Europe, would it not be better to have one strong country govern the whole?" He stopped short. Hermann's kind face showed signs of anger.

"Jaakob, if you are suggesting that Germany should rule the roost, you are basically wrong. How can you even think that? We had better hope for a new concept of democracy, a better system of free trade and cooperation, and stop exploiting unfortunate beings for cheap labor."

"I don't know about all this, Hermann. All I do know is that we've had many empires, and all of them have ended up exploiting the cheap labor in conquered countries." The captain thought he should add some words of appeasement. "Yes, we Jews are known to be humanitarians. We never had a chance to strike back."

"No, Jaakob, we do not want to strike back. We just don't want to be the scapegoats forever."

The captain did not understand. After all, there were great Jewish dynasties in banking and other industries. But he decided to avoid politics with Hermann.

Hermann was beginning to have mixed feelings about Jaakob. Maybe his wife was not Jewish.

"What does your wife do, Jaakob?"

"Severina teaches Spanish to immigrants at the University of Buenos Aires. She and her mother fled from Prague. They're not Orthodox, but they take our son to synagogue every Friday night and Saturday morning."

"Well, Jaakob, you should be proud." Hermann replied. "They're maintaining the Jewish traditions. But will that help us socially or economically. It certainly will not. Did going to church help Christians. When I think of all the wars that have been waged by Christians against us, I wonder about the persuasiveness of Christian principles."

The captain remained silent. Even years ago, his mother had warned him to avoid controversies about religion and politics. Under the best of circumstances, he was very vulnerable. He knew a little about both topics. Religion for him was a kind of aphrodisiac, a feeling that after confession and absolution, an invisible Mighty Spirit would forgive the evil committed during one's life. But, at the moment he had to find an evasive answer.

"These universal problems—theologians and philosophers have been thinking about them for thousands of years. We're not going to solve them over dinner tonight."

"Agreed, that's true." Hermann glanced at his watch and said that he would have to leave. They embraced in a spirit of genuine friendship and promised to communicate with each other again.

As soon as the captain left, Hermann began to think about some of Jaakob's remarks. He found them disconcerting. Jaakob suggested that losing the War was a tragedy for Germany. Losing any war is a tragedy, even victory is hollow. But in this instance, because of the unnecessary brutal murders committed by the Nazis, a victory for them would have been a calamity for mankind. Such a world ruled by a few ruthless and powerful men with misguided principles who for their own purpose, brutalized people into submission, a country where neither the law of habeas corpus nor freedom of speech or press existed—that would be a living death. His thoughts were interrupted when the taxi reached the destination of his Frankfurt friends who lived in Zürich. There, standing on the porch, were Martin and Soshana Kleinberg.

They had a son of school age. Martin was a craftsman who worked at a famous toy factory. Later, over coffee, he began telling Hermann about his work.

"I'm so happy making toys. It allows me to daydream about the toy figures coming to life and living in a juvenile, naïve world where no evil or wars exist."

"I don't think that would last very long."

"Oh, I know what you mean. Even in peace, we are at war with ourselves and want to escape from ourselves."

Shoshana came in and led them to the dining room. Lying on the table were thirty toys. She asked Hermann to pick as many as he could carry for his nephews and nieces in Tel Aviv.

The next morning was sunny and mild as Hermann walked across the runway and climbed up into the El Al plane. He settled in an aisle seat, relaxed but kept thinking what Jaakob had said the night before. Why had he expressed so much nostalgia for Germany? Hermann's father had often said that the Germanness of German Jews was innate. Maybe, he now thought, there was a grain of truth in that. He, too, felt some nostalgia for his childhood.

After many uncomfortable hours in the air, he looked down and saw the Mediterranean coast. The plane landed at Lod Airport, near Tel Aviv. Coming out of the customs and immigration offices, he heard a thunderous chorus of voices behind a fence separating visitors from the native hosts. Hermann almost tripped as he ran toward them. Afterwards he kidded Rose, who had arrived earlier, that it took almost a half hour to kiss the entire tribe of Baumbachs.

On the way home, Rose whispered to him. "I hope you are hungry. You'd better be, for the sake of your mother and sisters. They've prepared a feast for you as if it were for your bar mitzvah, and your father brewed the same kind of wine as in Frankfurt."

Dinner began at six-thirty and lasted until long after midnight. Although it was Wednesday, not Friday, the women had spent days preparing the food. Mother Baumbach had prepared gefilte fish with homemade horseradish, home-baked challeh, chicken soup with matzo balls, and three kinds of roasted meats. Then a Russian apple cake for which Miriam boasted to have taken three cooking lessons. Finally Hinda Baumbach brewed '*chai*' (tea) like her Russian mother. After supper, they listened to records. The highlight was a new record. Richard Tucker sang Hasidic songs instead of operatic arias, but there was so much talking and laughter that Father Baumbach shut off the recording. Hermann had good news: he was able to prolong his stay for a few days, so Miriam suggested that they go to the beach next day.

At bedtime, Rose cuddled up in Hermann's arms and coyly remarked how much she appreciated being part of such a loving family.

"Tomorrow," Hermann said "we're all going to the beach. You'll enjoy yourself and forget about business."

"Hermann, I wanted to discuss that with you. What if I don't join you tomorrow? I mean, if we're going to stay for a few more days, I'll have to reschedule my appointments. And some of them are so important that I must speak to the principals myself. It takes a long time to get through by phone, but that's the only way to contact them quickly. Then I'll follow up with letters."

"But can't that wait? We're going to have perfect weather for swimming, and—"

"I'm afraid it can't wait. I have to take time to prepare a legal document, double check it and try to send it by phone in the evening—if I get the connection. As you yourself always say, business before pleasure. I'm sorry, I'll miss being with the family." Hermann shrugged his shoulders. It did take a while to get a trans-Atlantic connection, and in any case, if she made up her mind, it was useless discussing it further.

"By the way," he added, "did you notice how well Joey gets along with his cousins? He's even trying to learn Hebrew."

She did not answer. In her eyes, Joey would always be an ugly child. Clever but ugly. His cousins, on the other hand, were attractive. She got out of bed and walked toward the window. An orange gold crescent moon was poised motionless in the black sky. Heavy with silence, the desert air kindled desires felt by both. In her flimsy nightgown, she flung her arms passionately around her husband, and they slipped quickly into bed.

Next day, Hinda Baumbach led her family to the beach. She pointed to a spot where to place their blankets, spread towels, put their clothing and baskets of refreshments. While everyone else frolicked on the beach, she waited for her friend, Shura Landofsky, and her seven-year-old granddaughter, Hannahele, who immediately ran off to swim with the other Baumbachs, leaving the two women alone. Mother Baumbach pointed to Hermann, standing in the water.

"Look, Shura, over there. See the tall handsome one? That's my son Hermann. And that little boy beside him? That's Joey, my grandson. They're visiting from Canada."

"You didn't have to point him out. Everyone is looking at him."

"I'm not talking about his looks. I'm talking about the good soul that he is. His little boy is a darling as well. You should see how he tries to speak Hebrew and does everything his cousins order him to do without arguing. Like his father, a dear angel."

"Well, what about my sweet Hannahele? At her age she already is a real little housekeeper. She should only have *mazel* (luck) after what we suffered. I still can't believe my daughter and son-in-law died in that horrible accident. At least Hannahele was saved."

"Don't worry, Shura. I'll see to it that she has luck. Now let's take a dip in the ocean. And remember, you and Hannahele are coming over tonight for supper. You'll meet Rose, Hermann's wife. You know, she's like us. I mean, she's an *Ashkenazi* from somewhere in Lithuania. But not a word about what we discussed. Leave it all to me."

"Yes, I understand."

As they were wading out to sea, Shura signaled to her granddaughter to come near her. The child obeyed and waited for instructions.

"Hannahele, I want you to play with Joseph. Poor child, he doesn't understand Hebrew, only English, so be near him all the time. You're lucky you learned English from your mother. And remember we are going over to Mrs. Baumbach's for supper tonight so help to bring in the dishes and clear the table. Now don't forget."

"I won't forget."

She ran off to find Joey, who was resting with his father near the shore.

Hours later, with the approach of dusk, they dressed and headed home. Rebecca and Miriam left earlier to prepare supper. When the others arrived, they went straight to the dining room. For the first time, everyone had an assigned seat.

Meanwhile, Rose was still working upstairs. As soon as she heard voices, she went down to the dining room.

"Rose, you look stunning tonight. Rebecca, come quick. Take a look at this suit."

Rebecca asked Rose to turn around.

"Oh, Rose, is it a Dior? Did you get it in Paris?"

Hinda saw the three huddled together and joined them.

"Hmm. Chanel."

"As a matter of fact," Rose replied," it is a Chanel and I bought it in Calgary."

"You know, Rosele, when I get sales advertisements from Paris, I hide them from Miriam. She is the one for sales. Whether we need it or not, if it's on sale and a bargain Miriam writes to the advertiser to send it to us. She has an eye like a hawk for colour and size."

"Enough about my clothes, can I be of help in the kitchen or dining room?"

"Thanks, Rosele. Everything is ready. Let's go into the dining room."

On the large table were platters filled with mounds of gefilte fish, cheese blintzes, Mother Baumbach's homemade Kaffir (yogurt) prepared according to a Russian recipe, rich sour cream, pure honey, peaches, mangos, apricots, strawberries, and cherries,

THE EXPATRIATE

Turkish delight, halvah, special moon cookies baked by Rebecca and Mother Baumbach's famous Turkish coffee.

They were seated as planned, so that Hannahele sat between Rose and Hermann and Joey sat beside him. Rose tried to be friendly with the little girl beside her. "Do you speak English?"

"Oh yes, a little. I learned it from my mother and father."

"And where did they learn it?"

"In London."

"Well, where are they now?"

"In heaven, my granny says."

"I see. Well, I'm sorry to hear that. Your uncle Hermann tells me that you've taught Joey a few Hebrew words. Is that right?"

"Yes, but Mr. Hermann is not my uncle. My grandmother says that I have no one except, maybe, an aunt in England."

Rose wanted to be helpful, but she found it difficult to carry on a conversation with any child—including her own son. She seldom spoke to Joey except to order him what to do or what not to do. But why, she wondered, was Hannahele sitting between her and Hermann? Meantime, Hannahele looked around, saw a few empty dirty plates, took them into the kitchen and brought in clean ones. Rose watched her and remarked to Hermann that she was remarkably mature for her age.

"That's because she's an orphan, living with her elderly grandmother. They have no relatives. By the way, did you notice how well she gets along with Joey?"

"So I hear."

Hinda overheard the end of this conversation and smiled at Hermann. Rose noticed and suspected a complicity of mother and son in some plot, but dismissed the idea.

After supper, Miriam's husband suggested that they all go to the garden. He played his accordion, and the others—including the neighbours—began to sing. One neighbour accompanied him on the violin and then played a few solos. All sang and danced, and the merriment lasted till midnight.

Hermann got to bed after twelve o'clock and spent a restless night, planning how to propose a contentious issue to Rose. He suspected she would not approve his proposal to adopt Hannahele.

Finally, he decided it should take place away from the family home. Two days later, he and Rose were relaxing on a bench in *Dizengoff* Square. Hermann began the conversation.

"Rose, let's leave in ten days."

"What? Ten days? But I need to leave in seven days. I can't postpone some of my appointments. You remember my bid to settle that huge estate? If I'm not back in Calgary, I'll lose my chance. If the situation were reversed, Hermann, and you had to leave earlier, I would not object."

"Well, of course, if it's that important to you, then leave. I'll stay on with Joey."

Thank God, thought Rose. He'll take care of Joey and find out for himself how tedious it is take care of children.

They moved to another park bench near a huge tree. Its branches waved against each other as if conversing in muted sounds. All was peaceful in this shaded spot. Hermann broached the serious problem which often troubled him.

"Rose, Joey is now old enough to have a sibling. Have you thought about having another child?"

She became rigid, replying slowly, "God, Hermann, you know what a hard time I had with Joey's birth. I doubt if my doctor would approve. Besides, I have enough on my hands with one child."

"I suppose my help doesn't count for much."

Rose said nothing.

"Well, I don't think that one child is enough for a family. Children should have brothers and sisters."

"You're obsessed with this. You must have a big family. Otherwise, you feel deprived of something. Is that it? Well, you should know that I'm satisfied. One child is enough for me."

"Actually, I have an alternative which would save you from going through the pains of childbirth. We could adopt Hannahele. You must admit, she's beautiful, clever, polite and would be an ideal companion for Joey. And here's something else, Rose. Her grandmother is very worried that she might die suddenly and Hannahele would be left to the mercy of some public orphanage."

"But why us? There must be couples in Israel who have no children but want them. And why does the grandmother think that she's going to die?"

"She doesn't look it Rose, but she's seventy-eight. And she has some heart problem. Her doctor has been telling her to sell the house and move into a nursing home. Her great worry is for Hannahele."

"How do you know her?"

"She and my mother were childhood friends. And Mother knew her daughter and son-in-law. They were highly respected school teachers, educated in Israel and England. So, when mother mentioned the circumstances, I thought that this would be a perfect opportunity for us. We are sure of the child's background and we'll avoid finder fees and all kinds of red tape for adoption procedures. The only problem, as I see it, is that Hannahele might not want to leave her grandmother. We'd have to convince her, Rose."

"You'd have to convince me first, because I don't want to take care of another child."

"Rose! When we decided to marry, I distinctly told you that I wanted a family. But you were devious. You didn't tell me that you were past child-bearing age, which is why you had such a hard time giving birth."

As soon as he uttered these words, he regretted it. In seconds, her most cherished image of herself, that of perpetual youth and unfading beauty, was shattered. The façade was off, and he saw before him a middle-aged woman, slightly wrinkled, dabbing a trickle of tears from her eyes. Where was the chic, confident woman, armed with a volley of facile answers? She sat there without answering, searching in her purse for a compact to powder her nose.

Rose looked at him contemptuously and dismissed what he had just said. She had more pressing business problems. Her first worry was the unexpected bankruptcy in one of the investments she had highly recommended to her clients. She would have to compensate them in some way and find new lucrative investments to maintain the integrity of her good reputation. To add to her troubles, this year, for the first time, her company had a loss instead of a profit. Moreover, she still needed spare time to find someone to take care of Joey. And on top of it all, the cook wanted a month's leave of absence. And now Hermann wanted to burden her with another child.

Hermann liked to resolve domestic problems as quickly as at his office. He moved closer to Rose and whispered to her.

"Now, wipe those tears away. I have an alternative solution. Let's get a one-year visa for Hannahele. We'll see how things work out. I think that's a reasonable compromise."

"No, it's not reasonable at all. It's putting off the basic problem. I can hardly take care of one child, and you want to saddle me with another one."

"But Rose, dear, we can hire more servants. We can buy a bigger house."

"But Hermann, what's the rush? Let's wait a little while."

She was hoping, of course, that Hermann would return to Canada and lose interest in this child.

"No, I don't want to drag this on any longer. You know very well that time is running out for both of us to be bringing up a family. If you refuse, Rose, I want a divorce."

Rose sat up straight, pushing away his arm from her waist. She remained rigid, stunned. After last night's lovemaking how could he so cold heartedly suggest a divorce? But she knew he would carry out his threat. Hermann sat there, silent, scrutinizing her. Her decision was important to him, because it could mean breaking up their home. It seemed like an eternity waiting for her answer. After a few minutes she flung her arms around him, almost violently, looked at his handsome, unhappy face, and smiling slightly, kissed him passionately. She whispered, "Oh, Hermann, why do I love you so much? You stubborn German lug! Alright, we'll take her in on trial period." He kissed her cheek.

"Now you're being sensible, like all Canadians. But what makes you think Germans are stubborn? Is it only a German characteristic to want a wife and a family?"

"I guess," Rose answered timidly, "we all have our unsubstantiated prejudices." Both laughed and arm in arm headed for the Baumbach family home.

Hinda Baumbach opened the door. A glance at Hermann and she knew that her strategy had been successful. Hermann made Churchill's V for victory, but for Hinda it meant that Rose accepted the second option, trial for a year. Hermann truly believed that Rose would get accustomed to Hannahele, and he would do everything to nurture love between mother and step-daughter.

Mother Baumbach went quickly to her husband with the good news.

"Thank God," he whistled loudly. At least for the time being the conspiracy and whispering in the corridors had ended.

Later on, he overheard Hinda on the phone.

"What did I tell you, Shura! She is going to have luck. They'll keep her for a year, and my son said not to worry because he is taking immediate steps to adopt her legally."

"Thanks, Hinda. You've always been a good friend. I'll sleep better tonight than I have for months knowing that Hannahele will be taken care of." Hinda was very happy as well. She had performed her '*mitzvah*' (good deed) for the day and went singing into the kitchen to prepare for the evening meal. The clang of pots and pans blended with the tunes of her songs.

That evening, Hermann phoned Zürich to ask how long Jaakob was planning to stay there before returning to Buenos Airs. As soon as the captain answered, Hermann apologized for calling so late at night.

"Jaakob, I hope that I didn't wake you up. During the day, phone connections are almost impossible."

"Oh, don't worry about that. It's great to hear from you. I was busy all day tying up odds and ends."

"How long are you going to be in Zürich? Because on my way back to Calgary, I can stop off there for a day or two."

"That would be '*herrlich*'. I'll finish my business tomorrow morning. Tomorrow afternoon and evening, I'll be at a wedding. Friday is free, but I must leave at around nine o'clock in the evening to arrive in New York next morning. That way, I can make the afternoon flight to Rio and then on to Buenos Aires. We can spend Friday together."

"What a shame. I can't leave before Sunday morning. But we'll have other opportunities now that we know how to get in touch with each other. So, I'll let you get back to sleep. I promise to write."

That night, the captain worried about his daughter's wedding. With no formal invitation his name would not appear on the guest list so he had to plan his strategy carefully. To impress the guards, he would arrive in a limousine, and ask the driver to wait for him, a precaution in case he had to rush back for whatever reason. At the entrance, he would give the guard his calling card with its Argentine address. Being a foreign visitor would provide him with an excuse for missing his invitation. He could have mislaid it easily, anywhere between Buenos Aires and Zürich. As for his written acceptance of the invitation, he might have sent it too late. Besides, the Argentine postal service was notoriously inefficient. In fact, the captain could add, he was a native of Düsseldorf. So were the bride's parents and grandparents. They had all been friends for many years. If all this failed, he would sit in the park until the entourage emerged from the church and into the park. At the very least, he would be able to see Briggita from outside the gate.

Eventually, he did fall asleep, but was sporadically disturbed by nightmarish visions. One was that Lara would recognize him in the church and after the ceremony, when cocktails were being served in the park, she would walk up to him and lash out. Everyone would listen.

"How dare you come here after abandoning us. We almost went insane with worry during the first six months. There was no trace of you. About ten months later, the police arrested Gustav Rundels. The judge sentenced him to ten years. But you got away. All you did was to sneak away, you coward! You swine! You're dead as far as I'm concerned. So stay dead! Stay dead!"

"I did it for you as well as for myself. I saved your reputation and assumed a double identity." But words would not come, nor could he be heard above the shrieking, "Stay dead!"

THE EXPATRIATE

He was moving his arm as if to avoid something when it hit the edge of the bed and he awakened, startled. The pillow was drenched with perspiration. He sat upright for a few minutes, shook his head, felt dizzy and slowly turned the pillow to the dry side. Exhausted, he fell into a deep, soundless netherworld, to awaken late next morning.

Next day according to his plan, the captain got out of the limousine at the entrance of the church, paid the chauffeur and told him to wait until given a signal to leave. He found a lineup at the gate. Two guards, one on either side of the entrance, examined names on the personal invitations the guests received and checked them off from their list. When the captain's turn came, he was asked for his invitation. Instead, he handed the guard his calling card showing an Argentine address. He spoke German, looked very distinguished, and seemed genuinely sorry to have mislaid the invitation among his numerous documents or forgotten it at home. His excuses sounded perfectly plausible. One guard suggested going inside the church to show the calling card to the bride's mother. However, if one guard left his post, only one of them would be standing at the gate. According to their instructions, neither was to leave his post for any reason until he had checked off every name on his list. They decided to let this visitor enter, but instructed him to sit in the last pew, near the doors of the church. Of course they did not explain that this was a precautionary measure, where he would be easy to watch and be evicted quickly if necessary. For the captain this was a good choice because the bridal procession would start from the entrance and remain standing right next to his pew before marching down the aisle, towards the altar. He accepted their suggestion, thanked them, signaled the chauffeur to leave, then went inside to sit down. The organist was playing a familiar prelude, but the captain could not remember which one.

The church, a baroque jewel, was unlike the other churches in this Protestant canton. The others were austere, with whitewashed walls, clear windows and ministers dressed soberly in black. This Catholic Church was splendid, by contrast, almost giddy in the exuberance of its paintings, statues, tapestries and stained-glass windows. The priest, wearing richly embroidered vestments, stood before an elaborately carved and gilded altar. But the captain was not looking at any of the ornaments. He was watching the pews as guests filed in, knelt for a moment of prayer, and sat down.

And then the ceremony began. Twenty-four choir boys, dressed in red gowns, entered from a side door and sang one of Bach's Coffee and Peasant cantatas. Then, the main doors opened. Count and Countess von Fürstenburger walked in. They remained standing next to the captain's pew before proceeding down the aisle. If he stretched out his hand he would be able to touch Lara's dress. Her gaze was directed towards the alter and did not notice how intently he was staring at her. She looked fuller and somewhat older, charming and beautiful in a pink chiffon dress. The chorus continued to sing as the Fürstenburgers walked down the aisle and remained standing on either side of the officiating prelate. Six bridesmaids wearing pale green chiffon dresses took their places along the isles, three on each side. Then the organ began to play the Bridal Chorus from Wagner's *Lohengrin*. When the doors opened again, the bride and groom, clasping each other's hand, stopped for a few moments at the last pew and the captain had enough time to glance at the décolleté neckline of the bride. There around her young healthy neck, hung the shining cross he had given her years ago. The bridal couple was followed by the groom's parents. Then the bride's grandparents, Count and Countess von Stradta, walked slowly down the aisle. *Schwiegermutter* was a little more bent but still regal with cascades of pearls around her neck and wrist. *Schwiegervater* seemed to have aged noticeably as he walked hesitatingly down the aisle. Some of his proud arrogance had disappeared with the passage of time.

As soon as the wedding ceremony ended, the bridal couple, their families and friends proceeded to the reception area outside the church. He followed the last guest and began to look for a seat in some obscure place yet still in view of the bridal table. Unfortunately, his choice was limited. Every table had a place card with a name at each setting. One old gentleman was sitting alone at a table for four. He greeted the captain and explained that he expected his brother shortly. The other two seats had no place cards. The brother came just in time for the toast. Meanwhile, the young couple stepped down from the head table to greet and thank their guests.

The two brothers were friends of the groom's family. The bride and groom knew them, but not the stranger sitting with them. The bride introduced herself and waited for him to do the same thing. He stood up, shook her hand, and introduced himself as Jaakob Kesselmann from Düsseldorf.

"I knew your grandparents on the paternal side."

He realized he should not have divulged this information but she could not possibly have recognized him. Unwittingly, he stared at the golden cross around her neck, which made her self-conscious. She touched it gently. If she recognized something about him, there was no sign of it. She simply replied, "It's good of you to come to share our joy."

At last, the captain was able to take a good look at his daughter. She speaks *Schweizerdeutsch*, he thought with a pang, not *Hochdeutsch*. Her face was slimmer than it was when he had last seen her, and well proportioned. Her freckles had disappeared. Her hair seemed brighter, too, and her eyes bluer. Her mother must have convinced her to "do something." But the result, he had to admit, was a great improvement. Brigitta looked lovely and was as gracious as she sounded. Moreover, she was well educated. The future for the young couple looked bright. Their little country had world protection to remain neutral if war erupted. The people seemed to be embalmed in their habits and mores, which hadn't changed much since the thirteenth century and everybody, is busy with their industries, very unlike Argentina, a political boiling cauldron about to explode. The captain was proud of his daughter and happy for her.

Next, Lara and her husband went around to each table and greeted their guests. When the Fürstenburgers came to his table, the brothers stood up. So did the captain. Lara shook hands with the brothers, thanked them for the generous gift, and then held out her hand to the captain.

"Mr. Kesselmann," she said with a gracious smile, "thank you for coming. After the ceremony, one of the guards gave me your name. He says that you come from Düsseldorf. My late husband came from Düsseldorf. Did you know him?"

"Well, I know that my parents knew his parents."

Lara began to look at him more closely and curiously, as if some startling revelation had suddenly dawned on her. She controlled herself and remained calm. "I do not remember the name but your voice sounds exactly like someone I knew very well, long ago."

The captain turned slightly pale. Only a very severe accident can alter the voice's timbre. He searched for something to say, but he found no words. A sad look spread across her lovely face, as she thanked him again.

The small orchestra played Viennese waltzes, as waiters brought out the main course. But the captain did not wait for it. He slipped out in a hurry, afraid that Lara would ask her mother to meet the stranger from Düsseldorf. At the hotel's flower shop, he ordered some red roses for Countess Fürstenburger and enclosed a typewritten note of thanks for her hospitality. Lara would find that it was from J. Kesselmann, formerly of Düsseldorf. But she would find no hand written signature.

Back at the suite in his hotel, the old feeling of loneliness returned—of being alone in the world, away from his homeland, his roots, and with no familiar faces from his youth. He recalled an English word, "estrangement." For him, this meant the inability to find substitutes for old values. What could ever replace what he had lost? Maybe the love for his new family.

When in Buenos Aires, for long intervals he would forget Lara and Brigitta. He was so busy. If only Severina were with him now. How he would love to caress her and feel the smooth warmth of her body near him. His family in Buenos Aires was as pleasant as could be expected but it was rootless. Would it ever be possible to tell her the truth? At the moment, he urgently needed to speak to her, to hear her voice, to ask if she was well, to remind her how much he loved her and missed her. She would know how to take away the emptiness, so he called her.

"How are you, darling?"

"I'm fine, Jaakob. So are Zvi and Galina. They keep asking when you're coming home. The ten days are longer without you. I can't wait to see you."

"Neither can I, darling, neither can I. And guess what? I'll be back this Saturday, late Saturday night. But how are you feeling? I mean, well, you know,—"

"I'm just going to give birth again, dear, not having a major operation. It's perfectly natural. Galina has been with me since you left. I should be ready in a few weeks. But please don't worry."

She sounded very weak, but she did assure him that all was well.

The next day, Friday, was full of chores. He had to return the tuxedo and buy gifts for everyone back home. Fortunately, Pozas had returned to Argentina the day before. He would arrive in Buenos Aires a day ahead of the captain and announce that "the President" would return to business as usual next Monday. The captain looked forward to a full day, Sunday, with his family.

SEVERINA

Mild temperatures were predicted for the night flight and balmy weather on landing. Nevertheless, the flight was long and tedious, somewhat relieved by the excellent Swiss service and delicious food. The captain was certain his limousine and chauffeur would be waiting for him at the airport. Maybe Galina and Zvi would be there as well. After luggage pickup, customs and immigration inspection, he searched for a member of his family or his chauffeur but could not find them. Perhaps there was a mix-up in timetables, an all too familiar occurrence with schedules. He hired a limousine and drove home, suspecting something was amiss. As soon as the bell rang, Zvi opened the door. The housekeeper was standing behind him. "Zvi, how are you? You look as if you've been crying. Where is mother?"

"Dad, she was taken to the hospital this morning. Granny went with her and said I must wait for you."

"Señora Campana, take care of my luggage. Zvi, get dressed, we're going to the hospital. Don't cry. Mother is having a baby. You will soon have a little sister and all will be well." Secretly, he suspected there must have been some mishap if Severina had been rushed to the hospital.

At the hospital's information desk, an attendant led them to the private lounge where Galina was waiting. She immediately explained that "Severina had a nightmare about an airplane crash and that you were either burnt or thrown out of the plane. At night I heard her screaming, "Help, fire!" so I ran into the bedroom and found her half asleep, half way out of the side of the bed. I woke her, gave her a soothing drink and called Igor to come. He got up in the middle of the night, called an ambulance, and gave instructions to have a surgery room and doctors prepared for an emergency operation. A few hours later he said he was not sure what procedure would be taken—either an abortion or a caesarian birth. But first they had to give her a sedative."

Just then Dr. Herrenkevitch, dressed in a surgical gown, greeted the captain. "Don't worry, Jaakob. The crisis is over. She seems calmer, alert, just recuperating from the strong sedation. Scans and X-rays are being taken to see if the baby is normal. The results will show if we have to abort or induce pregnancy or do a caesarian. But for the time being the danger is over. I have to run back and will return as soon as the X-rays are examined."

The delay had lasted an agonizing half hour when Igor reappeared. "The baby is well. All vital signs are normal. But Severina will have a difficult time. We proposed a caesarian but she refused. Her preference is to suffer a few days more and have the baby in the normal way. We will keep her sedated for a little longer and instruct the nurse to let you in as soon as she wakes up. But now, I must rush to my hospital because in two hours time I have to perform an open heart operation."

Galina aged years listening to Dr. Herrenkevitch, who was trying to lessen the tension by assuring them that all was under control. She still wondered why a dream or a nightmare should have caused such a physical disturbance. The family waited anxiously another half hour, when the nurse finally permitted them to enter. Severina was sitting up in bed, dressed in a silk and lace bed jacket, obviously trying to be cheerful. The captain kissed her, and she beckoned Zvi, "Hop on the bed, Zvi, and give mother a kiss."

"Mom, Uncle Igor said you will be well and the baby too."

"I never doubted it, but I'll stay in the hospital a few days longer and then bring home a little sister for you." Zvi smiled but was unable to say a word. Severina whispered in her native Czechoslovakian to her mother to take Zvi to the cafeteria because she had to discuss something with her husband.

"I suppose," she began, "Igor mentioned that I prefer a natural birth to a caesarian. I'll bear the pain if the baby is born normal and healthy."

"I agree with you. But I'll instruct the doctors if at any moment your life is in danger, you are the one to be saved. I am confident it will not go as far as that." She held back her tears.

"Thanks, Jaakob. I read somewhere or heard that in such cases German men opt for the children rather than the mothers."

"Oh, well," he answered with some irritation, "You hear and read a lot of things these days about the Germans which are not true. Now let's attend to happier things. What shall we name the little newcomer? Last time we had such a hassle. You said Heinrich was too German, although Heinrich Heine was a great German Jewish poet. When I suggested we shorten it to Hans, you objected again that it was too German. So I left it to you. 'Zvi' is adorable in all ways."

"Perhaps we should ask Galina. She knows all the names of the French romantic idols. My own name refers to one of Stendhal's heroines."

"You know what, darling, I could tolerate any French name except Victor Hugo's 'Esmeralda' or the Italian coquette 'Musetta' from opera *La Boheme.*"

"Something just occurred to me. How about some name from Greek mythology. I know Galina would love that. How about 'Ariadne', daughter of Minos (king of Crete), who gave Theseus the thread by which he found his way out of the Minotaur's labyrinth? To me this means that Ariadne stands for help to the stricken."

The captain hesitated. He hated the name Ariadne as much as that of Brigitta, daughter of his first marriage. At that time, he had had little say about it. This time it was to be a mutual decision. The name was far-fetched and rather peculiar. But how could he avoid offending her and causing a rift with his mother-in-law?

"Weren't the Greeks pagans?"

"Why yes," she answered promptly, realizing this had escaped her.

"Then do you think a Jewish daughter should have a pagan name? Besides let's hear how the names of our children sound together: Zvi and Ariadne?"

"My, you're right. They sound strange. What would you suggest?"

"I love names of flowers." He recalled the beautiful lilac trees in his grandmother's garden. "How about Lila. Zvi and Lila sound appropriate. Lila reminds one of lilacs."

"I agree."

"I'm glad you did not consider 'Rebecca,' ' Miriam,' or 'Ruth' because Israel is full of girls with these names."

"Then it's settled. I feel better."

"Now what about the caesarian? You insist on carrying the baby till the time comes, even if you have a great deal of pain?" She nodded her head in approval. "Well, I don't agree. If at any moment your life is in danger, I will order a caesarian if the child is normal or an abortion if it is not. We can have another child or adopt one." She sat up abruptly and looked at him with an inexplicable bitterness.

"Yes, that's quite Germanic thinking, commanding. You said quite earnestly, 'I will order' as if to command an order in the German army and all must obey. In this case I will give the command. If the pain becomes unbearable then I will decide one way or another."

Realizing he may have sounded domineering, he decided it would be best to temper the argument. "Oh, I would never give these instructions unless I consulted with you." Her demeanor softened, a smile lingered on her face.

"Maybe I misunderstood. But the tone of your voice sounded as if you were giving a command to the army. Now please call in Galina and Zvi, and we'll tell them the name for the baby." He walked slowly to the lounge where Galina was talking to Zvi and holding a lunch box for her son-in-law, since he had no time to eat breakfast. The captain was drinking the orange juice when Igor Herrenkevitch returned, dressed in green hospital clothes underneath his dark navy cashmere topcoat.

"I rushed here to check Severina and prescribe a special sedative to be taken immediately after supper. She must have a full night's sleep. All seems well for the time being and the sedative will keep her sleeping all night without pain. I'll come by tomorrow, late afternoon. I must hurry back quickly because the open heart surgery did not turn out as we anticipated. In this profession, surprises are almost the norm. See you tomorrow evening."

"Igor, my chauffeur will take you back to your hospital."

"Thanks, Jaakob. The hospital's taxi is waiting for me." He dashed out.

They entered Severina's room. She seemed to have lost some of her pallor and looked quite cheerful. When Galina was told the name of the baby, she approved without hesitation. Zvi said it was easy to pronounce.

"By the way, I almost forgot to tell you. Carmela called to say Pozas arrived and showed the sketches of the machinery to the other engineers for approval. And I was to tell you as soon as you returned that two of the company's ships full of A.P.P.I. products left yesterday for Holland and Germany and that the declaration documents are in German and Dutch. The chief of the shipping department wants you to check the translation before signing them."

"Thanks Severina, but I distinctly told them not to worry you about my business."

"Oh that's all right. I know so little about your business. As a matter of fact, what did you do in Germany?"

"About the same as here." Just then supper was brought in for Severina. All were exhausted, especially the captain who had had little time to rest after his flight from Zürich.

While chatting at home, the captain asked Galina if she would remain with her daughter for a few days after the birth of the child. He knew she would be comfortable in the guest room with its separate washroom, radio and telephone. Secretly, she had hoped that as soon as Severina retuned home with the baby, he would invite her to stay for a while. This invitation was very welcome. In case of an emergency, the hospital would first call the husband, and in such an event she would be there to help. In spite of all the assurances, she remained uneasy. The captain led Galina and Zvi to the dining room, where the housekeeper had laid out the presents from Zürich. First he gave a gold Pathek Phillip watch to Zvi, who was so delighted words failed him—he just ran to his father and kissed him. Then, in a light blue-and-gold box lay Galina's present—a brown alligator purse with a chaste gold bar across the top, which served as an opening for the purse. Galina was delighted and promised to cook all his favorite German dishes as soon as Severina returned. For his wife, he had bought a maroon-coloured baby alligator purse with a mother-of-pearl and ruby clasp. Schwiegermutter was so delighted, she even kissed her son-in-law.

Next morning, at the office, it was busier than usual. Carmela had divided the mail in three sections: very urgent, immediate, and short postponements. The first urgent letter was from Abogado Hernandez. It explained that documents attached to a cargo, sent from the Keunenberg factories, had not been accepted by the Berlin customs office. The documents in German were returned to be signed by the president and vice-president of the A.P.P.I. This unusual procedure was at the request of the German officials. Abogado's letter continued: *"I was advised that after clandestine inquiries and inspection there were grounds for suspicion that hidden between the bales of matted paper packages were countless smooth packets of clear plastic envelopes containing illicit drugs. I believe they intend to lay charges of smuggling and the Company's two chief executives are to be held responsible. I suggest a tracer be sent to check all employees who handled the shipment ABY-122-118. The tracer must state the names of all the Ship's stevedores who handled and transported these cases across the Atlantic. This must be done immediately. The Company's officers should sign the documents and include a special request to release the merchandise to the consignees."*

The captain immediately phoned Abogado Hernandez to confirm that his instructions would be fulfilled to the letter. Putting down the phone, a sharp stinging pain in his left armpit prevented him from continuing to work. He sat down in the reclining chair and tried to relax and take a nap. But as usual slumber would not come. Glancing at the second pile of letters, his attention was drawn to a long gray envelope, protruding from the stack. It resembled the kind Dr. Middler had in his office. A smile crossed his face, perhaps it was from a secret source informing him that

THE EXPATRIATE

Dr. Middler had died. The pain subsided a little, and he pulled the letter from the stack. The return address was Canada, from the company of Baumbach & Sons.

My dear Jaakob,

I cannot describe the joy I felt when we met in Zürich, and the pleasure of reminiscing. You seemed so happy. Now that you've reached home I hope all is well and that you are anxiously waiting for the new arrival. If you plan to have a reception, do not hesitate to invite us. We would like to visit South America. You may recall I mentioned that my wife cannot have any more children, so we found in Tel Aviv a delightful Jewish orphan girl of seven and brought her to Canada. After a short period of homesickness, she began to change, eat better, smile and is now teaching our son Hebrew. She is a joy to all of us. The problem was my wife. She resented the child because it meant more responsibility and less time for her business. In a short while, the little waif had wormed herself into our hearts. She started school and had no problem with the language. Her teacher told us that after a few days of sitting alone, meekly and quietly at her desk, she decided to make friends with her schoolmates, who used to snicker when she spoke with a foreign accent. But in no time a small group had gathered around her and during recess she began to tell stories about Tel Aviv and amused them all with Hebrew songs. Suddenly, those who were afraid to approach her became friendly, and now she is the centre of attention in her group. As we watch our two children, we see clearly that some are born extroverts, like this little girl, and some are introverts. Such characteristics are even revealed in early childhood. Our son, Joseph is very reserved, shuns people, is always reading and trying to solve the special puzzles we buy for him. I doubt if either of them will lose these traits as they mature. I suppose we all have inherent characteristics. In one Canadian newspaper I read this headline written by Allan Hall of the London Times. "No jokes, please, we're German." The story went on to say that one of the country's few famous comedy actors was axed when researchers discovered only 2 million of Germany's 89 million residents found the programs amusing...The television station SAT is also ditching [German] comedy series." Well, it is the old conundrum—inherent or acquired.

You asked about my wife. She is very different from the docile Clarice of my Atlantic crossing escapade. Women, here, smitten by the emancipation bug, put careers ahead of homemaking. Some believe they can manage both. I am sure that in South America, women know their place is in the home and women's emancipation has not yet invaded that continent. But I doubt if that will continue for long. We hear that Evita Peron's involvement in her husband's politics is unique.

If you plan to visit Canada, you will find this country very beautiful, and profitable as well. You are probably aware that Canada sells a great deal of lumber to the U.S.A., which is used for housing and paper products. It would be our pleasure to have you and your family as our guest. All the best. Viele Gluck. Hermann.

The captain put the letter in his pocket. Slowly, a gentle sense of compassion and affection stirred him for his Jewish friend. The letter was written in impeccable Berliner Deutsch. A feeling of *"Sehnsucht"* (yearning) for the *"Heimat"* (native land) gripped him. The letter's tone of geniality, home, children, wife and family life rekindled memories of the past. Hermann spoke of his wife who put her career above homemaking—at least that was preferable to Lara's pastime of afternoon teas, gossip, clothes and movies. In that distant past, it had seemed chic, trendy to have a wife of leisure. He'd approved. At night she inflamed him with her love and tenderness. Their home in Düsseldorf, what a pleasure! Could he ever be free from remembering the past or would he forever be its vassal? Would forgetting the past give him freedom? Is happiness an unrealistic illusion in the present chaotic world of power politics, nationalism, ethnic hatred, diverse religions and weapons of destruction? Am I a criminal, he asked himself, or a victim of an historical epoch?

THE EXPATRIATE

He shut his eyes and leaned back on the reclining chair, hoping to relax a little. The golden southern morning sun penetrated his office, and the coloured figures on the stained-glass wall grew larger and smaller. Their shadows fell on the carpet. They seemed to dance gaily but were soon swept away by the gauzy side drapes moving lazily to and fro in the filtered sunlight.

No sooner had he shut his eyes then Carmela burst in, "Patron, sorry to disturb you but Jorge Valdez is on the phone. He's extremely agitated."

The captain answered.

"Jaakob, may I see you right away? My wife and children are threatened."

The captain recalled that word "threatened" and recognized the panicky, pleading tones, reminiscent of times in Berlin when some father or mother would beg for his help to postpone the conscription call to labour camps.

"Come immediately. I'll be waiting."

In no time Señor Valdez came rushing into the office.

"Calm down, Jorge. What happened?"

"I received a threat that my wife, children and mistress will be kidnapped and held for ransom if I do not comply with the terms of nationalization of *Aréas Transportes*, which I helped to establish and now own fifty percent. Of course, the offer is ridiculously low, but I must accept or else! I am bloody fed up with the myth of Evita and Peron. You may not be aware of what is going on. The Government does not bother you because of a favourable clause in Peron's Economic Plan that provided for legislation giving exemptions and preferential customs treatment to those establishing new industries."

"You are the ideal immigrant. You brought capital, established a global business offering a product needed in our country, and give employment to many. But when Peron became president, the only major industry the Government owned was petroleum. Then the Central Bank was nationalized followed by railways, telecommunications, part of central electricity, sea shipping, and air transport. *Fabricas Militares,* run by the Armed Forces, took control of exports of all major commodities."

Jorge continued. "My son sent me from London a quote he found in Lawrence Durrell's novel which is appropriate to our situation. It says, *"They are now going to nationalize everything including joy, sex, and sleep. There will be enough for everybody because the Government will control it."* (1)

"Smart boy, your son."

"Yes I have three. One is in London and one in Paris, both studying commerce and business administration. The youngest one is in Japan, also studying business and commerce. My immediate problem is to get my wife and two daughters out of Buenos Aires, and settle them somewhere in a mountain resort in Argentina where they cannot be found. Will you permit me to rent a cottage in your name and with your phone number so that tracing them will be impossible? My wife does not want to go to any country where Spanish is not spoken. My mistress is on her way to New York, and I've advised her to limit her extravagant ways."

"Well, you may use my name to hide their whereabouts. Perhaps I can offer another suggestion. I know the Keunenbergs have a lovely summer cottage in northern Uruguay, which they seldom use. I'll phone them immediately to ask if your family could take refuge there till this affair is settled."

Jorge Valdez was overjoyed. "Capital! If they consent, my family would be better off in Uruguay than somewhere in Argentina." The captain phoned Kurt Keunenberg on his private line and began the conversation in German. Kurt immediately sensed this was a distress call. When the German explanation ended, both men remained silent, waiting for a reply. Kurt contacted Hans to ask if the cottage had been cleaned recently and where the keys were. The keys were in the office safe, the cottage was clean and Jorge could go immediately to pick them up at the Keunenberg plant. Furthermore, either he or Heinrich would accompany the Valdez family to the cottage.

"Thanks a million, Jaakob. I'll run off, settle my family in Uruguay and be back as soon as possible. Hernandez called me about the A.P.P.I. shipment held up at the Berlin customs." He waved, rushed out and, passing by Carmela's desk, remarked that Herr Kesselmann looked very tired and should rest.

THE EXPATRIATE

The captain stretched out on the huge couch. Maybe the pain in his left shoulder and under the armpit would subside with a little rest. But he could not relax. It meant wasting time. A personal problem that had never occurred before troubled him now. Putting his hand in his pocket he took out Hermann's letter. Hermann had a family, one son and an adopted daughter. Would he begin to think about making a Will in case of accidental death? Is it not the duty of the head of a family, to have such a document as a protection for his heirs? Hermann being a good burgher and a German, brought up with the old customs, would certainly have prepared such a document. He would write his friend and in a subtle way broach the subject. Hermann would know the Jewish tradition and some clever ways to cut inheritance taxes, levied in most countries. What tormented him most was that he wanted to leave Brigitta some funds to have as her own. Her stepfather, Count Fürstenburger, would probably leave the bulk of his fortune to the children of his deceased wife and little, if anything, to his stepdaughter, Brigitta. Lara would need all the money she had to maintain her extravagant lifestyle after the Count's death. He was definitely an aged gentleman. But he, as Jaakob Kesselmann, could not under any circumstances expose himself by leaving, even a small legacy to anyone but his present wife and children. He could not predict what repercussions would occur if it were discovered that he had left a legacy to a lady by the name of Brigitta von Heissel, her maiden name. To ease his conscience he thought of another option.

He wondered if, in this letter to Hermann, it would be appropriate to unburden his secret, to hint that he was a Christian by birth but a Jew by choice? As for his involvement in the War, as a true German, he had been motivated by an altruistic patriotic *'Trieb'* (inner drive) to save German nationalism in the hope that Germany would govern in harmony the whole of Europe. Should he mention his real name, Heissel, or just another German name? He was uncertain if, after all these years, the list of wanted War criminals was still in circulation. After considering all options, he decided to ask what essentials should be included in a Will by the head of a Jewish family. It seemed simple. Hermann would know the essential rules for a Jewish family and how to reduce estate taxes to a minimum. The Jews were so plucky in this respect, his father used to say. Relieved to have finally decided what to do, he shut his eyes and stretched out on the couch to rest. Sleep overcame him as if drugged. Carmela knocked on the door. There was no response. She stepped in cautiously only to find the President, one of the richest industrialists in Argentina, stretched out on the couch, sleeping, wearing only his pants and shirt. She shut the door quietly, after tip-toeing out of the office, and left a note on his desk, saying that, Señora Kesselmann had phoned to say that the latest diagnosis was excellent. She was well. All was normal, and delivery was expected at the latest in a week's time. Patron need not visit this evening because Galina and Zvi would be there. He should go home to rest.

Next morning, when Carmela arrived earlier than usual to prepare the daily agenda, she found the captain sitting on the couch rubbing his eyes as if to shield them from the sunlight. She realized he'd slept all night in the office. Would he like breakfast sent in? He thanked her but decided to go home, change clothes, visit his wife and then return to work. Were there any urgent calls? Yes, from Abogado Hernandez about the shipment in Berlin, which was still not cleared by customs. He would be back after his visit to the hospital and attend to it.

Entering the room he found Severina looking peaceful, as lovely as ever, with a book in her hands. She got up to greet him. "Carmela gave me your message, but I had to see for myself how you were, darling."

"I'm quite well. You needn't worry about me being alone. Galina opens her shop in the morning, comes here in the late afternoon and stays till I am ordered to bed. Zvi comes after school. He's such a joy. He wants to know all about Germany, and more. He told me at school his buddies call him 'el blanco' because he is the only one with blond hair and blue eyes. All the others have black hair and eyes. I asked if they made any bad remarks or teased him. Not really, but if they did he had an answer. His father, a ' Judio', was born far away where many people have all colours of hair, even red. He said the kids were so surprised because they'd never seen red hair and all laughed because they didn't believe him. But please don't worry about me." An amiable smile passed his lips.

"Well, now that you have told me all, I've stopped worrying as of this moment. How is Galina?"

"You should know Galina by now. She is always involved in some freedom movement. You never met her friend, the Czech journalist who works for the Prague and Paris newspapers. He was here several years ago. Now that Evita Peron is dead, he's asked Galina to ferret out any inside gossip, as well as true facts, to expose the false myth Evita presented to the world as another charitable Mother Teresa, especially since he heard a movie is to be made in Hollywood eulogizing her as a modern Lady Robin Hood. He is particularly angry because he believes she was responsible for the demise of the free press in Argentina. Galina wrote this small resumé, asked me to check it. Here it is."

The captain took the sheets of paper. Their bouquet of Chanel V perfume reminded him of his previous *Schwiegermutter; *Galina was also the best example of total "chic."

"It is known that Eva Duarte, born in 1919, was the illegitimate daughter of a small provincial landowner. She got a job as a sustaining artist on Radio Belgrano, one of Buenos Aires' principal radio stations. There she met Juan Peron and took a leading part in the organization of radio employees. In October 1945, she was fired from Radio Belgrano and then helped to organize the workers' movement for the October 17, 1945, events. A few days later she married Juan Peron who was 50 years old. On February 24, 1946, trade unions supported the Peron ticket and three of the Peronists Labour Union Leaders were rewarded with cabinet posts. Peron's 1946 victory had the largest electoral vote in history. By 1947 Evita began buying out, at forced bargain prices, all the newspapers that were openly antagonistic to the Peron Government. If newspapers refused to sell, they were shut down on the grounds that they had insulted the national honour. Sixty-five newspapers were closed. Also in 1947, she established the Evita Peron Foundation with money from the trade unions. The Opposition claimed that

JEANNETTE MOSCOVITCH

Banco Central requested all employees to give one day's pay to the Foundation. Any employees not wishing to do so were asked to notify their employer. (2)

Fleur Cowles, a prominent American, in her book, Bloody Precedent, has this to say:

"The influence of Nazi terrorist methods on the police system should not be underestimated. When I (Mrs. Cowles) was in Brazil in 1951, reporters, some from Buenos Aires, brought me names on the suspect list of those former Nazis who masterminded the brutality; it is commonly known that torture is regularly applied to victims to force confession. Leading Nazis, Fascists and very questionable collaborators have penetrated key political arenas—No.1 Nazi in Argentina, Ludwig Freude (his son had also been useful to Peron as one of his personal secretaries)—as head of the dread Secret Service Police. The President's wife no doubt was aware of all this. Peron had a special corps of strong men. Some are included in the police force: others are given quasi-military status." (3)

Mrs. Cowles met Evita Peron in person and described how she was dressed.

"At one appointment she wore a large diamond pin in the form of an orchid…studded completely with diamonds. Its size was about five inches wide and seven long. This was supposed to be the image of a lady who helps the poor. The Perons live like potentates in a palatial mansion on Avenida Alvear, one of the most beautiful streets in the world. What happens to the money in Evita's Foundation (about 100 millions of dollars are funneled into it yearly) is known only to Evita. I asked her if she made any record of these monies. I put the query to her carefully, saying I presumed she kept a very strict accounting of every dollar spent. "How else will history give you credit for your charitable efforts?" was the way I put it. She brushed history and the accountants aside without blinking an eye. "Keeping books on charity is capital nonsense! I just

use the money for the poor. I can't stop to count it."(4*)
Peron was re-elected in 1951 and Evita died of colon
cancer in 1952.

Slowly, the captain returned the sheet to his wife. It would be extremely dangerous for him to be implicated in a government investigation about subversive information, smuggled to the foreign international press, concerning corruption in the present regime. It was sufficiently incriminating that his company was under investigation for cocaine smuggling, found in an A.P.P.I. shipment consigned to a firm in Berlin. The captain stood there, quite worried, wiping his forehead with the ever-present muslin handkerchief. What could he say to his pregnant wife to convince her mother not to send this scathing article to Pavlosek?

"Well, Galina did a splendid job of organizing and writing this article. But isn't she taking a great risk? I read that there is absolute censorship of mail, especially from those opposed to the Government. All mail is opened at the post office and suspicious ones seized. Critical mention of official acts are denied transmission. Don't you think that under such strict surveillance, it is risky to attempt mailing this information? They could even send hoodlums to Galina's store and attack her personally."

"Galina is willing to take the risk. Past experience has taught her that indifference and complacency are the easiest way out but the most dangerous. If the Czechs had not been so frightened when Chamberlain handed over the Sudetenland to Hitler, maybe the course of history would have taken a different turn."

"But how is she going to get this out of the country without being caught?"

"Last time Pavlosek was here, he had to memorize all the facts. There was no other way out. Now he has contrived a good scheme. Galina was given eight names and addresses of his friends in England, France, Spain, Switzerland and Italy. She is to write to each, a simple gossipy chit-chat letter and insert, in an innocuous way, relevant remarks about Evita. The recipient of each letter in Europe where there is no censorship will forward it to Pavlosek, and when he receives these letters from his friends, he will decode the remarks that contain special information relevant to his articles. The return address on each envelope from Buenos Aires will be different so that the sender cannot be traced. "

"A very ingenious plan! I hope it succeeds." He stopped to wipe his forehead with his muslin handkerchief.

Severina noticed the handkerchief and looked tenderly at her husband. He appeared tired, pale and thinner, with dark circles under his eyes. "Darling, don't worry. Galina has many friends in the right places. If anything goes wrong she knows where and how to remedy it." She presumed this reminded him of Germany, particularly the treatment of Jews, and that's what worried him. "Why don't you go home and rest a little. You look so tired." He did feel exhausted, and was very touched by her concern. He left shortly, walked a few short blocks, and took a taxi to his office.

As soon as he settled down to work there was an urgent call from Abogado Hernandez. He had received a notice from the German customs which required immediate attention. "Berlin officials say that if we do not set an immediate date for the president and the vice-president to come personally to identify the merchandise of the A.P.P.I. and check the statements on the bills of lading, they will simply confiscate the shipment as smuggled merchandise. I will be at your office within a half hour."

Carmela brought in the itinerary of the ship in question for the captain to examine. The *Agila* did not have enough cargo of its own to warrant a cross-Atlantic trip. Advertisements had been placed in various cities, inquiring if companies needed overseas Atlantic transportation. Replies were to be sent to the shipping departments of the A.P.P.I in Buenos Aires or Montevideo. Three companies had responded. Shipments were to be picked up at Recife, Brazil, Georgetown, British Guiana with a final stop at Port of Spain, Trinidad, where they were to wait for a shipment from Bogota, Colombia. At Port of Spain there would be a final inspection to see if the *Agila* was sufficiently seaworthy to cross the Atlantic. Such an inspection usually took about twenty-four to thirty hours. During this interval, it was hoped the shipment from Bogota would arrive. The itinerary was well organized and profitable for the company. The A.P.P.I's Berlin shipment consisted of four wooden crates, each a meter and a half square and about the same height. The four cases were exactly the same and strapped around with a thin metal band. Each case had its own bill of lading, and each varied slightly in weight. The captain had just finished examining the file when Abogado came into the office.

Seating himself opposite the captain the lawyer pulled out a letter from his briefcase and handed it to the captain. "Read this letter in German which came from the Berlin customs, and then our Spanish translation to see if we really understood exactly what it says."

"This translation is quite correct. They claim that an examination of the bills of lading showed that the weights might have been slightly changed, having increased on two of the cases. Under a powerful microscope that proved to be so. The inspectors became suspicious: if clerks had made an error on the bills of lading why did they not make new ones, knowing how strict the inspectors are about changes or erasures. A company as large as the A.P.P.I. surely has spare bills of lading. The next step was to have dogs sniff to identify if there were drugs in these cases. On two of the cases the response was positive. Now the question was, who put the drug, and how, into the cases? Before they proceed with charges of illegal smuggling, the customs officials want to confront the president and vice-president to judge if the A.P.P.I is a front for a smuggling cartel." The captain remained silent. He looked calm but began to feel a hammering sensation in his heart. Was he going to be caught in a trap, not of his own making? Why this is preposterous! He, a smuggler of drugs! Someone was putting him up as a scapegoat. Quickly, he regained his composure.

"This is unbelievable! Why should a prosperous company like ours be mixed up in drugs?" he asked Abogado Hernandez.

"Precisely. That is why the German officials are being patient and want cooperation rather than taking immediate action to confiscate the shipment. They want to be certain that your company is not a front for drug smuggling and that you are not involved. Let's trace back where the *Agila* stopped long enough to put in the cocaine."

"The only usual stopover was Port of Spain, Trinidad, where a second complete inspection is made before crossing the Atlantic. But how was the cocaine put in the sealed cases?"

"I see the loophole clearly. The smugglers had a full day and night to do their job. There probably was an inside collaborator from the *Agila*, who gave them the dimensions of the cases and knew that the ship would remain at anchor in Trinidad. From what I can gather it was the old technique of fitting on a false bottom, no more than two inches high by seventy-two inches square, which is large enough to hide many plastic flat bags of powdered cocaine. All four cases had false bottoms nailed to them, but only two had cocaine. The smugglers took pot luck, hoping that if a false bottom was checked and found empty, inspectors would search no further in spite of the changed bill of lading. Of course, the inspectors all wondered why the cases should have false bottoms. Some said that the shippers wanted to protect the paper packages inside. One layer of wood, standing on a wet or even a moistened floor was not sufficient to protect the merchandise inside the cases from becoming wet and mildewed."

"Did they say how many kilos of cocaine were found?"

"Our German representative in Berlin asked the same question, but they only mentioned that on the open market it would bring in millions of Deutsch Marks." The captain could not restrain himself from asking why they should insist that the president and vice-president go to Germany to be investigated? Why not send an investigating drug squad here to find out who the culprit is, how this drug got on our ship, and who in Berlin is waiting to pick up this shipment. Abogado Hernandez moved back in his chair and looked enquiringly at his client.

"Do you know anything about Colombian cocaine smuggling?"

The captain was rather surprised. Why should he know, or have any reason to know, something about drug smuggling in Colombia? Abogado Hernandez pulled a sheet of paper from his briefcase and handed it to the captain.

"While I was doing research for this case, I came across information about drugs in South America. Read it, you may get a better idea why your company is being investigated."

The captain began to read.

"Drug trafficking is a $500 billion a year industry worldwide and the largest drug trafficking cartel in the world is in Colombia. It is one of the most violent countries in the world. Murder is the primary cause of death for men ages 15 to 44—Smugglers also pirate boats on high seas. Traffickers—use cargo containers and ship waterproof cocaine base on the bottom of the ships. Many smugglers leave from countries other than Colombia for their final run—. Colombian smugglers are inventive—The false wall of a cargo may contain as much as thousands of pounds of cocaine—Smugglers attach nets full of drugs—to the underside of cargo ships with powerful magnets and suction cups. Scuba divers slash the net off when the ship docks and swim away with the drugs." (5*)

The captain returned the sheet to Abogado Hernandez. "This is very disturbing, yet interesting. But what is our position now?"

"You and one of the Keunenberg Brothers must leave immediately for Berlin to meet the chief custom's investigator, primarily to allay suspicions that the Atlantic and Pacific Paper Industries is not a front for a cartel that sells drugs. You must also impress upon them that your company is investigating every detail of the *Agila's* itinerary, especially who and how the cases were handled. We must avoid giving the authorities grounds for suing the company as an accessory to a smuggling ring. If that happens, we will be obliged to hire detectives and do extensive research to defend ourselves in the law courts. This is a very serious matter. Then newspapers may see it as a good smear tactic, and who knows how they will exploit the facts and what they will print. So, it is very important that the emissaries we send should convince the inspectors that we are victims of a drug gang's illicit smuggling. If they are not convinced, then the burden of proof is on us and, at best, we may be charged with gross negligence."

"I will call Kurt and Hans to ask how soon one of them can leave. As for myself, my wife is expected to give birth any day now, and I don't want to leave her alone. She has no family except for an old mother. If this can be postponed a week or two, after the birth, then I wouldn't hesitate to go." The expected birth gave him a good excuse for refusing to go to Berlin. He still feared extensive passport inspection and interrogation.

"Well, I can appreciate the circumstances. Who would be a good replacement?"

"I'll try David Fischmann. He has lived here longer than I have and would be familiar with South American drug smuggling. This may be a welcome opportunity for him to visit Munich as well. He speaks Berliner Deutsch. Maybe the investigators will be sympathetic toward him because he is a Jew."

"Yes, that is a good point. Like you, he is a Jew but from Austria and, although it's quite a while now, most Germans still have guilty feelings and some sympathy for Jews."

The captain asked Carmela to contact the Keunenbergs first and then Fischmann.

Kurt answered the phone. The captain explained what was involved. Yes, he and his brother had discussed this as soon as Abogado Hernandez asked them to send a complete list of the *Agila's* personnel and its detailed itinerary. He would be prepared to go. Hans would remain at the paper mills. Kurt asked Abogado Hernandez to determine the date and advise him in advance so that all arrangements could be made.

The second call was not as simple. After a careful explanation, Fischmann remained indifferent and gave no indication that he would consider it. The captain further justified his request, "With a Jew who speaks German and the Germans' sympathy toward us now, we have a better chance of being cleared, especially since we are not guilty. If my wife were not expecting to give birth any day now, I would go."

David Fischmann seldom traveled anywhere without his wife. He and his family had escaped from the War zone just in time, but his wife's relatives lived in Poland and were trapped there. When Irena read about the atrocities there, visions of horrible beatings and screaming haunted her. Strange tales mingled with clear images of bodies burning in smoky fires. The mere mention of going to Germany or Poland agitated her for days. He knew that it would be wiser to say he had to go to Switzerland to find innovative methods for their dry-cleaning business. This would be a clever stratagem. Secretly, he had a yearning to see beautiful Munich, and harboured a romantic, elegiac vision of the city of his birth. Misrepresenting the trip to his wife seemed justified because it spared her unpleasant recollections. He yearned to see the city of his birth and to reminisce about his youth there. Now the opportunity had arisen. By plane, Munich is a short distance from Berlin. "Yes, I'll go. But I would like a briefing with Abogado Hernandez. When are we expected in Berlin and whom are we to contact?"

"All the information will be sent to you tomorrow. Thank you very much for accepting."

Carmela walked in with a list of telephone calls and stopped short before giving it to him. "Patron, you look so tired. You should go home and rest."

"You may be right. I'll leave the office, take a little walk in St. Martin Square, visit my wife briefly then go home."

At the hospital he found mother and daughter laughing. What a lovely portrait they would have made for Renoir! "What's so funny?"

"Galina read a joke in Czechoslovakian and I translated it into Spanish. It sounded doubly funny." Severina stopped.

"Jaakob, you look ill, and tired. You really shouldn't have come today. I'm doing fine, maybe another week or so. But you must rest."

"Yes, as soon as I give you this." She opened the beautifully wrapped package. It was a baby's diary in white leather, gold trimmed, complete with compartments for photographs. Severina was delighted.

"Thank you darling." She got up to kiss him but had to bend over to touch his face, she was so fully pregnant. He left immediately, arrived home, undressed when he noticed an envelope protruding from a jacket pocket. Suddenly he remembered it was Hermann's letter which he had hoped to reread. He wondered how his friend was faring in Canada.

BANKRUPTCY

One evening Hermann arrived home and found Rose sitting in the dining room with a mass of papers spread out on the table. At a glance he knew something unpleasant had happened. She stared at the table as if paralyzed. He sat down and pointed to the stack of papers.

"What's this all about?" She could hardly speak and began to sob.

"Calm down, darling, and tell me what happened. Maybe I can help?"

"About a year and a half ago, the president of one of the largest brokerage firms approached me and explained that a new issue of 200 million dollars of shares at $25 per share were to be sold on the open market. Only special brokers were chosen to sell these. A quarterly dividend of ten percent was projected, with an assurance that shareholders might expect to double their investment within a very short period. The capital was needed by a South African diamond company to invest in a Canadian mining company that had discovered gold in the Northwest Territories. The African company claimed they had been operating successfully for sometime and were interested in a partnership to expand their operations. Colourful pamphlets and brochures displayed dredging and other kinds of machinery on the ground sites, together with impressive accountants' statements showing the cost of operations and, of course, glowing anticipated profits. As an added incentive, the African company stated that they would provide cheap and experienced labourers eager to emigrate to Canada. This would be easy to arrange, because Canada needed such workmen. The brochure further explained, that as soon as the capital is available,

347

the partnership agreement would be signed and that, after one year of operation, the first payment would be sent, followed by quarterly dividends. My commission was to be twenty percent if I contracted to sell $500,000. I accepted and began to market the stock. To encourage me, after I sold $200,000, the company promptly sent me my commission of forty thousand dollars and the balance on the completion of my quota. This cheque was paid by their bank so I continued to sell more shares."

"Sounds good, so far. What went wrong?"

"Well, the shareholders got their first two dividends. When they didn't get a third one, they began to call the company's Calgary office. But they couldn't get through and were told the phone was disconnected, the office was vacated, and the space was up for rent. The principals absconded. The South African company does not exist. If it did ever exist, it was only a registered name. The shareholders hired the most prestigious law firm to take a class action for fraud, but first we must find the principals. How long it will take to find these con artists is anyone's guess."

"What are you going to do?'

"Well, no one on our side can do anything, not until the police find the culprits. Meanwhile, many of my clients who have bought the shares of this company on my strong recommendation have closed their accounts with me. Some have taken out mortgages on their homes and cannot afford to lose their investments. My business and reputation are ruined." She began to sob. He sat there impassive, silent, and did not utter a word of comfort.

"First of all, clear the table so the housekeeper can serve dinner. I may have a practical solution. Meantime, I'll go downstairs to see the children."

As usual Joey and Hannahele were delighted to see their Dad. Both vied with each other to show him how smart they were in school. Hannahele had been chosen to head the school choir and had earned an A in spelling, while Joey showed him his mathematics exam with its mark of ninety-six percent. "You deserve something special for being such good students. What would you like?"

This question did not surprise them.

"Dad," said Joey, "take us to the zoo."

"Yes, Miss Lane says that it's going to open this Sunday."

Hermann was relieved to know that his children were interested in more than hockey and dolls. "If that's what you want, then that's what we'll do. Now, go eat your supper. Mother and I will come in later to tuck you in at bedtime."

Rose looked anguished and defeated during supper, although she made an effort to hide her feelings from the children.

"Cheer up, Rose. You're not the first victim of con men. As of this date, how much cash is left after paying all your expenses?"

"About $70,000."

"And how much do you owe?"

"Only the rent on my office."

"Okay, here's my plan. I'll give you $130,000. That'll give you $200,000 in the bank. If you sold shares worth $400,000 and returned $200,000, this would be fifty percent of the total investment. I mean, your clients would get back at least fifty percent of their initial investment. This would prove that you're acting in good faith. You'd forfeit your commission, in the end, and lose a lot of your own money. But if the case goes to court and a judge finds these crooks guilty, then they'll have to return some of the money they embezzled. In that case, your clients would get back at least a good portion of their investment."

"But not all of it."

"No, not all of it. All investors take risks. You know that, Rose. Anyway, this would be a step in the right direction. But you need to hurry before the gossip spreads that you pressured your clients to invest. That would be their strategy to exonerate themselves for their greedy and unwise investment. The dividends promised were highly exaggerated. The greed of the investors is quite evident and common."

"I must admit, Hermann, it might work. How can I ever thank you? It's an excellent solution. Whoever heard of a broker repaying his clients fifty percent of their investments from his own pocket? I'll get the best publicity available and attend to this first thing in the morning."

"Your reputation will be somewhat restored, but," he hesitated a little, "will they return to give you their business? That, you realize will take time." He stopped, hoping this bit of evidence would have its intended impact.

"If they do," Rose sighed, "they'll take their time."

During dinner he continued. "You may have a tough road ahead to regain your business and pay your bills. At the moment your only expenses are rent and secretarial work." He did not continue. After a little delay, he broached the subject again while both were sipping wine. "You know what they say, Rose, 'If you can't stand the heat, keep away from the fire.' And here's another cliché. 'People in your field are always playing with fire.' The finance advice business is not only a dangerous game but a gamble in many aspects. In your case, you are playing with people's life earnings. It's fortunate I have the money to bail you out."

"I know darling." She began to whimper.

"If you really want to save money, you'll have to cut your overhead and cancel your lease on the office. We have an extra room here. You can run your business right here at home. And, for the time being, you'll need only a part-time secretary."

His ulterior motive was very clear. Secretly, he wanted her to stay at home with the children.

"Well, I can hardly argue with the logic of your solution. I guess you are right. I have no operating capital because I must return $70,000, and I doubt if I can get a large enough bank loan to be able to continue. My only alternative is to cut expenses and work from home. I am grateful to you, darling, for sacrificing $130,000 for my mistake. Working from home sounds like a feasible solution for the time being."

Rose was relieved but not happy. This sudden change meant she was in a cottage industry. Her office was no longer in a prestigious building; there was no smart looking secretary to answer phone calls and usher in clients. Hermann could only conjecture what was going on in her mind. A few minutes later, he left the room and reappeared almost immediately.

"Here's my cheque, Rose. Now, start repaying your clients as quickly as possible. Don't give them time to spread rumours that you misled them. In many cases, you minimized the risks and enhanced the facts by promising high profits. I must say, though, that you really were ambitious and greedy. Otherwise, you would have been much more careful."

"You think of everything, Hermann, don't you?" Both finished dinner in silence.

"Oh, I promised that we'd tuck the children into bed. So let's kiss them good night and then relax. Shall I bring you a cognac?"

"Yes please," she accepted humbly.

Sitting in the bedroom, she shut her eyes and an imaginary tableau took shape in her mind: the perpetual cliché of the good bourgeois way of life—the kittenish pretty female, lying near her big, strong, handsome, money-earning husband; two, three or four little, well-behaved waifs, sleeping soundly in large comfortable beds. Ideal peace of a bourgeois! What could be more idyllic, romantic! By chance, Hermann had got what he wanted. Her failure was his success. But she was responsible for her own undoing. Rose sat there thinking about her new life. She had never embraced the middle-class suburban ideal, and she could not bring herself to do so now. On the other hand, she could hardly blame Hermann for her failure. It would be impossible, at any rate, to continue as a financial advisor. Her recent clients would never regain their confidence in her, and new ones would be hard to find. Starting over again was for young people with the bravado of the uninitiated. She would remain in business, but now her activities would involve nothing more than small estates for ignorant widows or childless widowers. Yet she was grateful to her husband. He had lost quite a sum of money because of her mistake. Hermann sat near her, observing her closely, and knew instinctively she was beginning to realize that, from now on, she was, if not a full-time housewife, certainly a part-time one. Her ambition to conquer the investment market had vanished, evaporated,—*sic transit Gloria mundi* (so passes the glory of the world) for those who make fatal errors. Somehow, in her misery she looked lovelier than ever. A surge of mixed love and compassion stirred him. He put his arm around her, kissed her and whispered, "Do you know who is the prettiest in the world and whom I love most?"

"I love you too, you big German lug." Both undressed, tumbled into bed, mesmerized with each other. His dream fulfilled: a wife, a family, a home! And she—loved this man who had proved he truly loved her. Which is what she really wanted.

Next morning, Hermann entered his office whistling, feeling buoyant. He had thoroughly enjoyed the night with 'his tiger,' a term Jaakob Kesselmann used to describe the love tryst with his girl friend, Solédad Perez, the dancer on the ship crossing the Atlantic. Family was everything, he thought. This reminded him of something that he had been putting off: writing to Jaakob, in Buenos Aires, about the addition to his family.

LILA KESSELMANN

Dusk was lingering in the sky and the warm Buenos Aires breezes calmed the captain as he walked toward the hospital. When he entered, Severina was alone with Zvi. Both were laughing.

"May I share the joke?"

"Zvi wanted to feel the baby moving, so I put his hand on my stomach and the baby poked back. But now he wants to know if the baby will be '*blanca*' like he is '*blanco*' ('white')?"

"Well, Zvi," the captain explained, "we'll just have to wait until she is born." He smiled and glanced around. "Where's Galina?"

"Mother couldn't come. She's unpacking a shipment of glassware from Prague. The insurance company insists on immediate reports of damage. She'll come as soon as she can."

"And what about you? How are you feeling?"

"Quite well, actually. The doctors say that I'll be able to have a natural birth, if I just stay off my feet for a while longer." He kissed her passionately.

"That's great news."

Back home at around eight o'clock, he phoned Galina.

"Dear Galina, forgive me for being blunt, but I don't believe the story that you told Severina. All the broken glass in the world wouldn't keep you away from your daughter. Something must have happened. You're not sick, are you?"

"No, no, of course not. You know, Jaakob, you have a real 'jüdisher *Kopf*' (Jewish head). I can't speak on the phone. Do you mind if I come over right away?"

The captain suspected that this was not some minor business problem. Galina wasn't likely to overlook anything on her tax forms. All her private and business records were meticulously kept. He strongly suspected that she was worried about the political project that Severina had discussed with him.

A half hour later, she arrived, impeccably dressed like a duchess from the imperial Russian palace. Sitting in the salon, the captain offered her a cognac and cautiously asked, "Now, what's this all about?"

"A little while ago, Severina told you about the letters that I was going to send out for Henri Pavlosek. The one I sent to Madrid was detained in Buenos Aires by the censorship department. I heard this today from my grapevine connection."

"And who is that?"

"It's my friend. She works in the censorship department. Anyway, one of the inspectors checked the return address and told the police to investigate. And they did send someone. He found the house vacant. One neighbour told him that the owner had died. But he didn't know when."

"But Galina, why use a return address of a house that you knew was vacant?"

"Because I thought that an investigator would want to know who lives at the return address. Anyone who did live there would deny knowing who had sent the letter or deny knowing anyone in Madrid or—"

"Yes, I understand. Please continue."

"I wanted to avoid any full-scale investigation. Anyway, my friend told me that an inspector was going to contact the Madrid address. That doesn't worry me, Jaakob, because Henri had already briefed the people in Madrid for all eventualities. They're his friends, of course."

"How did you sign the letter?"

"I was cautious, Jaakob. I used 'Helen' for every letter, not my own name."

"Good. Now, has anyone questioned your friend about this letter?"

"So far, no. And no one even suspects our connection. Some of the inspectors said that the letter is just idle gossip. But others said that it could have a coded message. Even so, it's in the 'not urgent' basket."

"What does your friend suggest? Surely they're going to make some kind of investigation."

"She says that the two baskets for letters of this kind are already full. She's going to stay late one day, find the letter, and put it at the very bottom."

"Why not just tear it up?"

"She can't do that, because every item is named, numbered and registered as either 'urgent' or 'not urgent.' They investigate the urgent ones, of course, before those that aren't. It could take six months before they examine my letter. But the rules keep changing. By that time, they might consider my letter urgent so I had to meet my friend tonight. That is why I could not go to the hospital."

"You won't really be in the clear, though, until someone destroys that letter."

"Yes, I know. But I have to wait for further news from my friend. I am confident she knows what to do. But now, I must rewrite the Madrid letter. Otherwise, Henri will miss an important part of the whole picture. I cannot phone from here so I'll go to Montevideo, contact him, get the information, and then mail the letter from there because Uruguay has no censorship."

"That might work, but how will you explain your absence to Severina?"

"She already knows that I've just received a shipment of glass from Prague and that I'm holding a sale next week. You'll see her on the weekend, Jaakob, when I'm in Montevideo. I'll return early on Sunday night and go directly to the hospital."

"Yes, let's keep this to ourselves. We don't want to worry her. By the way, do you want my secretary to make your travel arrangements?"

"No, Jaakob. No one must know about this. I'd better leave now to get some sleep."

"Wait, Galina. Let's have some coffee. This Colombian stuff is quite good."

Over coffee, Galina brought up a topic that had been on her mind for some time.

"Jaakob, have you ever tried to trace your relatives in Europe? Some of them might still be alive?" He went rigid, remaining impassive, as if an electric current had passed through his body that immobilized all movement and speech.

Why would she ask him that after so many years? He took a few sips of coffee before answering.

"Before leaving Düsseldorf, I made extensive inquiries but all research led nowhere. I thought it best to forget the past."

"Yes, but can you forget?" When he began to wipe his forehead with the white muslin handkerchief, she added. "You are right Jaakob, we who are alive must make as good a life for ourselves as we can." She put down her cup. "I must go now. Call Zvi. I'll kiss him good-night."

Early next morning, the captain took a walk in Plaza St. Martin. The weather was caressingly warm, and the greenery seemed alive as if wishing well to all passers-by. He sat down on an empty bench and recalled Galina's remarks. Why would she suddenly ask about his relatives? And why had he always felt some tension in her presence? He had never consciously offended her. On the contrary, he had gone out of his way to be friendly and helpful. She must resent the fact that Severina had moved out, leaving her alone. Thanks to him, though, she'd soon have not one but two grandchildren to carry on her tradition.

The next morning, Miss Mendoza cheerfully handed him the daily agenda. He was reading the fifth item, when Abogado Hernandez called.

"It's about Berlin. They're still suspicious and are detaining Keunenberg and Fischmann for further questioning."

"You mean they're in jail?"

"No, but they're not allowed to leave Berlin. Customs officials expect them to identify those who put the illegal drugs on the ship. If you were there, of course, you might be able to convince them that no one at A.P.P.I would ever have anything to do with smugglers. But you're not there. Anyway," he continued, "the Germans are worried about a new trend: smugglers who hide drugs in commercial shipments and who rely on volume. The inspectors can't possibly go through everything in a ship's cargo because of the shortage of staff and due to the great volume of shipments. They only spot-check the incoming cargos. It's just bad luck for those that are spot-checked and caught. Here's the point. We need to supply the name of every stevedore who worked on that ship."

"But meanwhile," the captain replied, "they're holding Keunenberg and Fischmann. Please send me the transcript of the interrogation of our men. Then, I'll telephone Berlin Customs to let them know that we're also very anxious to find any stevedore who allowed the smugglers to use our ship. And I'll suggest that they hire two undercover agents: one to work in the Keunenberg's plant and the other to work on the *Agila*. If we can give them the names of the stevedores that manned the ship during that voyage, perhaps a thorough interrogation would lead to the cartel that furnished the drugs. All expenses in American money will be paid by us. We are also anxious to stop smugglers from using our ships. Meanwhile, Abogado Hernandez, ask them to keep the contraband but clear our merchandise and permit Keunenberg and Fischmann to return to Argentina. If they agree, I'll send an American money order to cover all of their costs. This should convince them that we're the victims. Explain all this to the board and get them to approve these expenses."

"I'll do what I can. As soon as I get the board's approval, I'll call you." The lawyer put down his phone. It's just as they say, he muttered to himself "*se dice que los Judios son sabios, eso es verdad.*" (It is said that the Jews are wise, that is true.) Señor Kesselmann without much ado had had a solution for the problem and went right to the heart of the matter.

As soon as the captain put down his phone, Jorge stormed in, followed by Miss Mendoza.

"Patron, I couldn't stop him."

"That's alright, Miss Mendoza. Sit down, Jorge, and catch your breath. Then, tell me what's going on."

"You wouldn't believe what they've offered me for my half-ownership of the airline. And they've hinted what would happen if I refuse their offer. Thank God, Jaakob, that my family is safe in Uruguay."

"Have they given you any other choices?"

"So far, no."

"And what do you want?"

"I want to remain in some administrative capacity and get fifty percent of my initial investment but I want it in dollars, not pesos. They refuse to let me remain in any capacity, and offer only thirty percent of my investment and will pay it in pesos, not dollars. If I don't accept, I have a hunch, threats will increase and there will be further restrictions on the purchase of fuel. If we have no fuel, we cannot function."

"But can they really carry out that threat?"

"They can probably go as far as they went with the press, and bring the airline to its knees until it cannot function."

"Have you given them a counter offer?"

"My share is worth eighty million dollars, and they are offering me thirty million pesos. If I refuse, they can wait and they'll continue to threaten me."

"But here's one suggestion. Ask for 45 million in dollars, which they can pay in installments over a period of two years. Another alternative would be to bribe the official you are dealing with. Let him know you are prepared to give someone a generous commission if he manages to get the payment in dollars—but not for less than 45 million."

"But that's dangerous. What if I contact a staunch Peronista? He'd arrest me right away. And I'd never get a fair trial around here."

"But Jorge, do you have an acceptable alternative?"

"No. Maybe I'll get in touch with one of my wife's cousins and invite him for lunch. Then make a few hints and ask him to suggest someone he knows."

"It's worth a try."

THE EXPATRIATE

"Thanks Jaakob. You're a real friend. I can hardly tell you how anxious I am to settle this. I can't live without my mistress and my family."

Energetically, as usual, he rushed out of the office and almost collided with Miss Mendoza on her way in.

Carmela came in carrying a pack of papers. "No, Miss Mendoza, I'm not taking any more calls."

"But you must give me instructions for Schubert, Seltzer & Zeigelhaus. They've made an urgent request. It's about their model of the machine that you ordered. They want you and Pozas to travel there and check everything."

"Well, call Pozas and tell him to get in touch with Zeigelhaus. Those two are engineers. I'm not. They can send us pictures with explanations. Now, I'm off to my wife."

Waiting for a taxi, he began to feel very warm and took out his handkerchief. The corner caught his attention. For the first time in a long while, he noticed the monogram: Y v H. (Yanos von Heissel). When would the past disappear once and for all?

By now, the captain was a familiar figure in the maternity ward. A nurse told him to remain in the waiting room and when Zvi arrived he was to wait as well. Father and son waited for almost an hour. Suddenly, a commotion shattered the silence. Two nurses and a doctor rushed into Severina's room. The captain asked for some explanation, but they ignored him and rushed by. He listened at the door but heard nothing and after a few minutes he opened the door; no one was there, not even Severina. Only then did he notice, next to the cupboard another door. Clearly, they had taken her through that door to the operating room. He could do nothing but wait. The captain recalled Brigitta's birth. Female relatives and friends had convened in the waiting room to keep him company. He had been the only man there. And yet he had not been the first to see his daughter. That honour went to his mother-in-law.

By the time that he entered Lara's room, the new-born had been washed and dressed for show. He would have preferred some time alone with his first child, but Lara was surrounded by her admirers and he had accepted it.

As for Severina, she was alone. She had asked the nurses not to involve either her mother or her husband until after the delivery. A few minutes after midnight, the nurse woke them.

"She's waiting for you. The baby—"

"Is it a boy?"

"The baby is a girl, a very beautiful girl."

"They're both doing well?"

"Yes, of course. Your wife looks happy but very tired. Come with me."

Severina was holding a little bundle. The captain could hardly wait to kiss his wife and look at his daughter. Severina asked Zvi to look first.

"Is she white?"

"Yes, of course. She's your sister. Her name is Lila."

Severina pulled back the flannel covering Lila's head to reveal a little tuft of glistening blond hair. Zvi examined her closely.

"Isn't she going to open her eyes?"

"She will if you just give her a slight nudge. There, you see?"

The captain looked on happily.

"Severina, why didn't you call me as soon as you went into labour?"

"Why? What could you have done except worry? By the way, I'm glad that Galina won't be here before Sunday. This saved her a great deal of anxiety. But as soon as she comes, you may be sure she will bake up a feast the minute we get home."

"And when will that be?"

"The doctors say that I should be able to leave in the middle of next week."

"Well, then, it's over. The baby is really beautiful and *blanca* because Zvi ordered it." At this, she tweaked his ear lovingly, and he smiled. The captain sat there speechless, admiring his wife, unable to express the joy in his heart. Where was the past? It had vanished with this little bundle. A rosy lump of humanity was the future.

THE EXPATRIATE

He bent over to kiss his wife just as the nurse came in. "I'll have to ask you to leave. It's late and the Señora and the little *'hermosa'* (beautiful one) need to rest and sleep. You can come tomorrow afternoon."

Galina returned on Sunday afternoon, rushed home to leave her luggage, checked the mailbox, and then hurried to the hospital. When she arrived, the captain and Zvi were waiting. After they told her the good news, the captain took her aside. He wanted to hear if her trip to Montevideo was successful.

"The whole thing worked according to plan. Before leaving, I found an agitated message from my friend. Her department had just hired new employees. They were turning everything upside down. The chief is fierce about organization. There must be something brewing in government circles, Jaakob. He wants my friend to file every 'detained letter' with a note attached to it. She doesn't know how many men were hired. From what she can tell, though, the ones in her office have Peronist connections."

"What does she suggest now?"

"She's going to find the letter, read the note on it, and then figure out something."

"She needs to destroy that letter, Galina."

"She must have that in mind. But every file has both a numerical index and an alphabetical one. So, it wouldn't be hard to notice that one letter is missing. It's wait and see, until I hear from her."

For the captain, this was bad news. Any investigation of Galina would immediately place her daughter and her son-in-law under suspicion. Just then, the nurse entered and asked all visitors to leave. Mother and baby needed to rest.

As they were leaving, the captain invited Galina for supper. She had not even unpacked after returning from Montevideo but accepted, because she had important news.

"You're too busy to read the newspapers, I suppose. It's just as well, because most newspapers in Buenos Aires would not disclose anything negative about Peron and his regime. All news is still controlled by the Government. But the papers in Rio and Montevideo are filled with the truth about all that has been muffled for years. Evita Peron has been dead for some time now so the truth is beginning to be exposed. Wages fell in 1951, before she died, and have now fallen by an additional twenty percent. This is a controlled economy, just like the economy of a communist country."

"That's not exactly news to me, Galina. After all, I lived and worked in a controlled economy and dictatorial state for twelve years. Sorry to interrupt."

"Another interesting story wasn't actually in the papers. It was about this colonel, J.F Suarez. He and some friends were planning an insurrection for February 1952. They planned to seize government buildings. At the same time, they were going to batter their way into the presidential residence and kill Peron. But the plan fell apart, because a government spy had infiltrated the group. Peron arrested hundreds of people but said nothing at all to the press. In fact, he ordered an investigation and put General Bengos in charge. Bengos actually looked into the business affairs of Peron's own brother and Evita's brother. Everyone suspected them of plundering the country. Evita's brother, Juan Duarte, lost his job as Peron's secretary and shot himself. And that was the end of this investigation. But people suspect now that someone murdered Duarte. After all, he knew too much. But here's the twist, Jaakob. Duarte didn't die in his apartment, which is where they found his body. He died in the Casa Rosada. The staff there worried that they might fall under suspicion, so they took the body to his apartment. (1*)

The captain listened politely, but he was not really very interested in political corruption and patronage scandals—not unless they affected his own business.

"But now," Galina continued, "I have some news that should interest you. It's about Peron's preoccupation with economic nationalism. You know that he expropriated and nationalized many huge industries. Peron expropriated the British-owned railways at a cost of 150 million pounds. He bought out the American Telephone interest for $100 million pounds and nationalized the shipping and local transportation and the airlines—and he instituted severe legislation against treason; that is, anything with which he disagreed. Hundreds of citizens went to jail—and the behaviour of the police was barbarous." (2*) She stopped there, as the white handkerchief began to sweep the captain's forehead. Perhaps this reminded him of events in his own country.

"Why are you telling me all this, Galina? Do you expect some kind of war?"

"Not exactly. But I do expect a revolution and wonder what will happen to our economy?"

"You know, Galina, I have enough to worry about with my own business. I don't have time to think about the Government. This is a rich country, richer in resources than Germany."

She was watching him intently.

"Well, I just thought you might need to know about some of these things. Severina mentioned that you're having some difficulties with the Government, and—"

"I'm certainly grateful to you, Galina. Generally speaking, your information could be helpful to me. I'm just very anxious about my own problems right now."

"I understand, Jaakob." She thought it best to leave now. "Thanks for the dinner and the best coffee in Argentina. Don't bother the chauffeur. I'll take a taxi home."

He went to bed but was unable to sleep, thinking of the new baby, the amount of work at the office, the danger facing Jorge Valdez. What had become of *Freiheit*, (freedom) and Peace? They were just nebulous illusions!

Next morning, the captain learned that Keunenberg and Fischmann were still detained in Berlin. Should he take a chance, fly to Berlin and speak to the customs officials? Was the Hague Tribunal still examining War crimes to track down criminals? He called Abogado Hernandez who was in court and would return the call as soon as possible. There was news from Berlin and from Armando Munez, director of the accountancy department.

According to Munez, sales had dropped by ten percent. But the captain knew what he had to do. New markets were needed, possibly in Asia. But Asia would be very risky. He would have to launch a study. Apart from anything else, he could ask customers about their satisfaction with his products. He would write a letter and have customers send their comments directly to him. With this in mind, he asked Miss Mendoza to arrange a general meeting: board members, sales agents, advertising staff, and managers. But suddenly, once again, Valdez rushed into the office.

"Sorry to barge in again, but I need advice about the final settlement. I did follow your suggestion, Jaakob, you're a genius." The captain smiled inwardly. Where had he heard that word? Of course, he'd called Hermann Baumbach a genius. "I found someone with influence and offered him a million pesos to get my payment raised and in American dollars."

"Good. Seal the deal quickly, before someone else gets the job in his place. By the way, did you hear the latest? Our sales have dropped by ten percent. I'm calling a general meeting for the end of the month."

"I'll be there. You can count on me."

"I know that…"

As he left, Miss Mendoza came in once more.

"I can't reach Pozas. No one knows where he is."

"Send messages to all of our plants, asking him to call us here immediately. By the way, Miss Mendoza, I won't be here tomorrow. I'm going to bring my wife and daughter home. That reminds me, please call my son's school and tell his teacher that he'll be with his family tomorrow. As for Abogado Hernandez, he can come whenever he wants as long as it's after tomorrow. He gets priority."

The captain woke up early and roused Zvi. Then, he dressed carefully. So did Zvi, who had begun to imitate his father's habits. They arrived at the hospital early but still had to wait for the doctor in charge to finish his examination. Finally, the long days of waiting were over. Mother and daughter were free to go home. Back home, Lila's nurse took her to the room that the captain had prepared over the past few weeks.

"Jaakob, it's wonderful. But you're spoiling her already. You did the same thing with Zvi."

Zvi spoke up in his own self-defense. "I'm not spoiled. Look, she is kicking the little teddy bear." All began to laugh while the nurse picked up the baby for all to admire.

THE EXPATRIATE

The dining-room table was spread with a variety of baked and cooked dishes, ready for dinner. They stood admiring the elegantly decorated display, fit for a king. Galina was the first to speak. "All these are Czechoslovakian dishes, a good beginning for the addition to our family."

The captain tried to tease her a little. "At first glance, most of these resemble German dishes." Severina shot him a look of caution.

"Galina is very touchy about Czech and German comparisons." The captain was quick to catch on.

"Well, *Schwiegermutter*, the Czechoslovakian looks more delectable." And indeed they were to her and Severina.

Severina lost no time next morning to prepare for a new term at the university. Long ago, Peron had abolished some of the tuition fees. As usual, though, political considerations had corrupted his good intentions. He hired only teachers who supported his regime, which angered Severina. But she was eager to avoid conflict, and worried only about her assigned curriculum. Fortunately, she did not have to take more time off for a celebration. Jaakob had suggested that they announce Lila's arrival without fanfare in the newspaper. This was a private affair.

Next morning, Miss Mendoza noticed that Patron looked refreshed, ready for a busy day's work. His lawyer arrived on schedule at ten o'clock and wasted no time in stating the purpose of his visit. And he had good news.

"Berlin has released Keunenberg and Fischmann. It's now clear that A.P.P.I. has never colluded with any smugglers. The German officials welcomed the suggestion that an undercover agent be hired to investigate the head office in Buenos Aires. So we will have a gentleman, working under the assumed name of Stanford Smythe, who speaks English, Spanish and German. His first assignment, disguised as a personnel manager, will be to investigate the president, the board of directors as well as the staff, engineers and all employees. Only the captain and the lawyer are to be told of his real name. Under his assumed identity, he'll also inspect our shipping departments. Finally, disguised as a stevedore, he will work on the company's ships *Agila and*

Contessa, tracking down how and where cargos are picked up and delivered. This, it was estimated, will take a year and we are to pay his annual salary and expenses."

Despite the good news, an investigation made the captain uncomfortable. He worried about a personal interrogation for reasons known only to him. The lawyer noticed his discomfort, and believed this investigation might remind him of Gestapo tactics.

"By the way," the captain added, "his English name intrigues me. What's his real German name?"

"His real name is Heinrich Sprügel. He looks and speaks just like a real Englishman. That's what I hear, anyway. One more thing: I heard the news about sales from my son-in-law. How could sales go down like that when we've been selling in all of South America?"

"Yes, but sales over there were minimal. Besides, consider what's going on here in Argentina. This is a very unstable country, Señor Hernandez. So far, we've been less affected than many other industries. But instability is never good for business."

"As you say. But we're going to hear lots of proposals at the next meeting."

"Well, I should hope so."

A GERMAN DICTIONARY

During the next few years, the captain made a special effort to leave his office early so that he could see Lila before her bedtime. He was never disappointed. Lila was beautiful, lively and very responsive to him.

One afternoon, Zvi called during office hours. He sounded very surprised.

"Dad, I received a German dictionary. Did you order one for me?"

"Well, I did promise to do that. I keep my promises. You know that."

"Dad, I checked the package and it comes from a store in Buenos Aires. It has coloured pictures of national flags and the salutes past and present of all countries."

"Oh yes, now I remember. I was always looking for a dictionary for you. By chance, I passed by an antique store, browsed around and to my surprise found this unique dictionary with coloured illustrations. I'll be home even earlier than usual today, and we'll both look through it."

That evening when he reached Zvi's room, he found his son poring over the dictionary. Enclosed on the first page was a note in German, which he could not read. "A special German dictionary for our German customers."

"German looks hard to pronounce."

"So does any language, Zvi, before you learn it."

He opened the dictionary and began to pronounce one of the long words that had puzzled Zvi.

"That's all one word?"

"It's really three short words but Germans write them all together as one word. Zvi, do you expect your mother soon?"

"Probably a little later than usual because she wanted to finish correcting some exam papers."

"Dad look, here are two pages of flags and military salutes from every country in the world. Show me how the Germans saluted when you lived there."

"Certainly, let's move the mirror to the centre of the room so you can see yourself make the salutes. Now stand in front of the mirror and first try to imitate the American salute."

"How's this?"

"Not bad, son, not bad at all. Did they teach you in school how to salute Peron? Is there a picture of the Argentine salute in here?"

"Yes, here it is, at the bottom of the page."

"Now, try to imitate him."

"How's that?"

"Pretty good."

"What's that one?"

"That's a German salute, one of two."

"Two? Why not one?"

"Because the Germans changed their salute for a while and then returned to it again. This one is called the Nazi salute. No one uses it any more."

The captain stood there, stiffly, his back facing the opened door of the room, and showed Zvi how to make the Nazi salute. Just then, Severina walked in. She stood there thunderstruck, unable to speak. Then she burst out, almost shrieking, "Jaakob, how dare you teach Zvi the Nazi salute. I never want to see this again." Her voice was shrill and angry as she pulled Zvi away from his father.

"Oh, no! Darling, you don't understand. I found this German dictionary in an antique store here in Buenos Aires. It has pictures of flags and salutes from everywhere. Zvi noticed this Nazi one just as you walked in."

"It's true, Mom, I learned the American one, too."

THE EXPATRIATE

"Well, I never want this repeated in our house or anywhere. Don't ever do this again. Do you understand me?" She wiped the tears from her eyes and tried to control her anger. The captain moved close to kiss her but she pushed him away, and the three walked silently into the dining room.

"What did we do wrong, Dad? Why is Mom so angry?"

"She's right, Zvi, but it's not your fault." Suddenly he realized his indiscretion. A sudden impulse! A fleeting memory of the good old, old times! A hidden longing for the country of those wonderful times when Germany was winning the War! A vanished lifestyle! He'd lost his bearings!

"Dinner is ready. Let's not keep the maid waiting." Severina wiped the tears from her eyes and controlled her anger. They walked downstairs in silence. During dinner, the captain tried to minimize his indiscretion and moved his chair closer to hers to kiss her cheek. She turned away quickly, to let him know she was still angry. He tried another tactic.

"A few days ago, I received a letter from the Rabbi. He wanted a contribution to fix the roof of the synagogue, which was urgently needed. I told him I'd pay immediately for all expenses so that no additional donations will be asked from the members."

"I'm sure that he'll appreciate the gesture." She still sounded angry. To change the subject he asked if there was any news about Galina's letters.

"Any news from Galina?"

"Yes," she said without looking at him. "Galina met her friend for lunch yesterday. She retrieved the letter from the 'not too urgent basket' and so far, she says it had been regulated. But she did not give me the details."

"So, she's in the clear now."

"Not quite. Galina hasn't heard from Henri."

"He has to be cautious, Severina, but I'm sure he'll get in touch with her."

"I think so, but her friend also mentioned that there is some disconcerting news in her department, because of rumours and upheavals in the present government, which will affect her and the whole staff. It is said that the Government's fall is not merely probable but imminent. There's a story circulating in her department. Some of my students have also heard it. It may be a smear tactic but some say it is true. It's about a young girl who attends a school in Olivos where Peron often visited. He sometimes has lunch with the school girls, one at a time, and tries to win their approval. Anyway, one young girl's name was mentioned very often. It was the name of Nelly Rivas. One morning, she learned that Peron wanted to join her for lunch. Some people thought this was funny, but I didn't. Imagine, a man of fifty-eight taking on a mistress of fourteen. He behaves like a Roman emperor with one of his slave girls. And the Church takes my point of view. The bishops think that he's decadent, or depraved. At least the Church has plenty of motivation to get rid of him."(1*)

"One thing Severina, I don't want to get involved in political conflicts. I have enough to do just to stay in business."

It was the first time she'd heard him raise his voice to her in such a commanding tone. After supper, they remained with the children until bedtime. The captain tried repeatedly to embrace his wife, but she brushed him aside. Once the children were in bed, he tried again, with the same result.

"I have some extra papers to correct. You go to bed. I'll be there later."

He admired her devotion to the students, but this seething anger had nothing to do with that. It was the first time, she had rejected him. In some ways, Severina was not particularly Jewish, but when it came to enemies of the Jews, she was viscerally Jewish. He would wait. The whole night passed, but Severina did not join him.

As usual, both came down for breakfast at the same time as Zvi and Lila. The captain kissed Severina but said nothing about sleeping alone. Instead, he pretended that he had not noticed her absence. But his haggard face betrayed him. He was about to leave, when she walked toward him and put one hand on his shoulder. There was a tender light in her eyes.

"You didn't knot your tie properly."

She began to adjust it. He put his arms around her. She responded, but not as warmly as usual.

THE EXPATRIATE

"Why don't we go out tonight? They're playing Handel over at Santa Maria's. And ask Galina to be our guest."

Severina smiled. He was trying so hard to make up with her.

"Yes, I'd like that. So will Galina."

As usual, back at his office he found a pile of paperwork on his desk. Some had red stickers. The workload never diminished, even though his vice-presidents did take care of many business tasks.

First on the agenda was a note from "Stanford Smythe" (alias Heinrich Sprügel). He must see Mr. Kesselmann at two o'clock and arrived on schedule.

A tall lanky gentleman sat down facing the captain, who could not help noticing the visitor's large Adam's apple and the slender strong hands. For a few minutes, they chatted in Berliner Deutsch about West German prosperity, the Berlin Wall, and the Eastern Russian side, which was faring very badly. The captain suspected that the visitor was playing his cards very carefully, knowing that for a Jew it might be painful to hear about prosperity in any part of Germany; in a fit of anger, the captain might reveal something of his true identity.

"I understand, Mr. Kesselmann that you are Jewish and were born in Düsseldorf."

"That is correct."

"Is it true your folks had stationery stores in Düsseldorf?"

"That is correct. Why do you ask?"

The captain began to show some irritation.

"No particular reason, Mr. Kesselmann."

"Then let's get to the real purpose of our meeting. What have you found out about these smugglers?"

"I came here primarily to meet you and your board of directors," said Smythe—that is, Sprügel—without answering the captain's question, "and I'm convinced that neither you nor your directors are actually connected in any way with smugglers. I'll let Berlin know about that. But I'm also convinced that this was an inside job by one of your employees."

"What? An inside job? How?"

"Yes, Mr. Kesselmann, one of your employees. As for our procedure, I usually hire a small team of undercover men to gather little bits of information. We put them together for the big picture. But in this case, working with a team could be dangerous. I'll work alone in various disguises. But you must not communicate with me directly, not under any circumstances. If you need to reach me, use this address in Bonn."

Sprügel's lean hand wrote the address on a nondescript card, which bore a woman's name and address, and gave it to the captain. Then, he got up, straightened his jacket, and stated sincerely that it was inspiring to find a German who had been so successful abroad. He left immediately.

A few months later, Francesco Hernandez sent the captain his report. Posing as a stevedore, Sprügel had talked to one steward of the *Contessa* (the second ship owned by the A.P.P.I), who had maintained a connection with one of the shipping clerks in A.P.P.I.'s plant 4. This clerk had stashed the contraband. Next, Sprügel had discovered the source of the contraband and reported his findings to the proper custom officials. The case was coming to a close. Officials in Berlin were still searching for those who were hoping to receive the contraband but the original shipment from A.P.P.I. had finally reached its buyers, and the captain's two envoys had returned safely to Buenos Aires.

"But A.P.PI still has one problem," wrote Abogado Hernandez, *"and that is what to do with the clerk in Plant 4. You must fire him, of course, but you must not let the local police get involved or let on to anyone that you know about his activities. That would provoke reprisals from the cartel in some form or another. Advise by return your suggestions in this matter."*

A few minutes later Miss Mendoza was asked to send the reply message to Abogado Hernandez.

Dear Señor Hernandez, tell Boisy about all this. If necessary, he can make up some story about the clerk's incompetence and dismiss him. This must be done quickly. Kesselmann.

On the other side of his desk, lay a pile of letters from customers. Most reported they were satisfied with the quality, the price and the services. The drop in sales, therefore, must have been due to political upheaval. The captain stretched his legs and began to think about that more carefully. Why, he asked himself, would political unrest affect the paper industry? Everyone needs paper products to carry on their daily life. Few could get along without writing paper, for instance, and no one could get by without washroom tissues. Suddenly, a headline in the newspaper on his desk caught the captain's attention: "Attack on Peronistas."

"By now, said the article, *the Peronistas were on the way out."* The captain knew, from Galina and her "sources," that this event was somehow connected with a relentless attack on Peron by the Church. After Peron had expelled two bishops, the Vatican had retaliated by excommunicating him. But the Church was by no means alone in its opposition to Peron's regime. His financial shenanigans had become well known, and the economic effects on the whole country were too devastating for people to continue supporting him. Argentine navel planes had already bombed the Casa Rosada (the presidential residence), while troops had stormed it from the streets. Three hundred people had been killed in the crossfire, but the coup had failed. According to the article, Peron had left his study shortly before the attack and escaped unharmed. But the situation continued to disintegrate. The last act came in 1955. Naval forces moved down the river against him, and he surrendered office without a fight. He fled to a Paraguayan gunboat, so shaken that he slipped and fell into the water, and made his way abroad. Then his long exile began. (2*)

The captain threw down the newspaper in disgust. Long ago, he had come to a country in the midst of a massive reform movement. Peron had been a symbol of the future. The economy was growing quickly. The captain had ignored the signs of unrest and had not taken much personal interest in *La Esperanza* or even in Galina's letters. But now his civil liberties were threatened. The newspapers predicted a coup. Nothing ever really changes, he thought. Germany had failed and Argentina was failing him now. He saw no evidence for freedom, only for the instinctive need to survive.

The captain pushed aside the newspaper and called Severina to say that he would have to work late. Next, he checked his daily agenda. The first item was about selling products in India. After Miss Mendoza left for the day, he continued to work and was about to finish a list of proposals for improvements when Severina called to remind him that it was almost midnight and she was coming to his office to drive him home. He decided, however, to take a taxi instead.

In the taxi, he tried to doze off but found that impossible. The driver took a shortcut that led through the café district. In Buenos Aires the *Porteños* dine late, the city lights up, and the people dance till three in the morning or later. You hear the *milonga* or the happy traditional tango dance of the Creoles, or the *condome,* which has Afro Brazilian characteristics. Both, he thought were barbaric. When the noise subsided, he closed his eyes and finally dozed off. But he did not stay asleep for long. The driver took a wrong turn, realized it, and began to turn around. An abrupt jolt woke up the captain, leaving him with a slight pain under his left arm.

Severina was waiting for him. As usual, they embraced, kissed, and went directly to the bedroom. But he felt listless, distressed and in no mood to make love.

"Did you read today's paper? I kept it for you in case you did not see it."

"No, I was correcting exams. But the students told me what's going on. They're ready to march in the streets."

"Well, today's headline caught my attention. Things are going from bad to worse. Look here is what it says:

"After Peron's fall in 1955 there followed a series of Presidential successors. None could hold unto power very long. During Aramburu's reign, he arrested 40 Peron leaders and shot them." Then the newspaper warned, *"Argentines by and large distrust the American Alianza—but welcome foreign investments, which have fallen off."*

"Meantime," the newspaper cautioned, *"Trouble [is stirring] between President Illia and General Ongania, commander-in-chief of the Army—The newspaper predicted a coup and that Ongania could succeed, and*

he did. On assuming power, Ongania acted swiftly. There were a number of political arrests—Several Jewish shops were closed and the very large Jewish community became understandably very nervous."(3)

"Reminds me of what happened in Germany."

Severina had seldom asked him about his past in Germany or how he understood what had brought the Nazis to power. Her own concept was that the super Nazi propaganda machine directed their hatred on the Jews and Stalin, and by eliminating both, Germany would be the most powerful country in the world.

Again and again, she had refrained from asking Jaakob about his family. He had never mentioned a wife nor relatives. She knew surprisingly little about him but admired his zeal for work, his gentleness, his kindness, and the many ways he proved that he loved her. They were blessed with two beautiful children and, due to his work, they were extremely wealthy. Severina kissed him passionately and spread the blanket over him. "Try to sleep, dear."

Feeling a little relieved, he slept well and woke up in a cheerful mood. Before going to his office, he decided to get a haircut at a hotel across the street. Only two other men had arrived ahead of him, and his own barber, José, was busy with one of them. While waiting, the captain picked up the local newspaper and read the front-page article, headlined "Inside Buenos Aires".

"Visitors often say that Buenos Aires, with impressive plazas and mansard roofs, is the Paris of South America. But is it? Buenos Aires is in many ways more like a Mediterranean city, like Marseilles or Barcelona. Like them, its walls in some districts are covered with graffiti. You may see signs on walls—Contra Oligarquia, Yanqui Go Home. Abajo el Imperialismo. (Down with Imerialism). Those who care to explore these districts will find a city that eludes the tourists. This is a hidden city of poverty and violence. Why doesn't someone do anything about it? The answer is that no on knows what to do."(4*)

The captain turned a few pages of the newspaper and another column attracted his attention.

"What about the Jews of our city? Anti-Semitism is a rising force in Buenos Aires. It is sometimes hard to remember that our country has offered hospitality to Jews since 1891. Many Jews fled from Eastern Europe and found refuge here. Anti-Semitism is a recent phenomenon in this country. It began after World War II, when immigrants brought it with them from Germany and other European countries—A certain amount of swastika daubing and similar infantilism still goes on and has led to more violent outrages in the recent past." (5*)

He would have preferred to continue reading, but the barber beckoned him. This information must be brought to Severina's attention. More specifically, he wanted to suggest the possibility of moving to Montevideo. He recalled reading that many Jews had left Germany just after Hitler took power in 1933. Jews in Argentina must be worried. The captain found it almost unbearable even to imagine that any harm might come to his Jewish family. He left in a hurry, went to his office, and called Severina to tell her that he would be home early that night.

Miss Mendoza came in, cheerful as usual. "Patron, you had a haircut."

"Is it that obvious?" he grinned.

"Yes," she answered, shaking her head, and handed him the daily agenda while explaining the work sheets.

"I have some news for you. Here's a list of potential customers in India. At the moment, they buy their paper in the United States. The next few sheets are self-explanatory."

She put down the pack of papers and returned to her office. The first sheet listed Indian dealers and their financial assets. Only some of them had good credit ratings. He barely had time to examine a list of salesmen who spoke Hindi or Bengali, when Miss Mendoza rushed into his office.

"It's Armando Muñez on line two."

The captain dropped what he was doing and picked up the phone. Muñez sounded agitated.

"Señor Kesselmann, have you read today's *Asuntos Monetaries?* Our customer is filing for bankruptcy. Yes, it's about

Alpara. Just a year and a half ago, they had an A1 credit rating. Now, it's confirmed, they're bankrupt. We're all stunned."

"What does that mean for A.P.P.I.?"

"They owe us half a million dollars, so we'll have to file our claim immediately as a preferred creditor. We need your signature on the documents."

"Come right over."

"I'm leaving my office." Señor Muñez was tall, dark and very handsome. He always made Miss Mendoza blush, which is why he often flirted with her. But today he rushed right into the captain's office, unannounced.

"As I mentioned, Señor Kesselmann, we're all stunned. Who could have predicted this? But I suspect foul play. Someone gave false financial statements to the creditors." He moved to the edge of the chair as if to utter something very confidential.

"We have a lien, on the personal assets of the president and his two vice-presidents. Here are the legal documents, an injunction to prevent the *Alpara's* president and his two vice-presidents from leaving Argentina. But I suspect that they've already moved most of their assets to some other country where no one can seize them."

The captain knew that good accountants might not be fortune tellers, but they should at least be able to spot irregularities in financial statements. It was too late now, though, for accusations. "Can we absorb this loss?"

"At first, it may be difficult, but in the long run, we'll be able to absorb it. At any rate half a million is negligible considering our assets."

"Thanks for assessing the situation. But in the future, let's try to prevent this kind of thing in the first place."

An intensive frown on the accountant's face changed his demeanor to one of ferocious exasperation. "How could we have done that? No, Señor, you can't control everything. It is simply, as the Spaniards say *'La Fatalidad.'*

Secretly, in German, he muttered to himself *'das Shicksal'* (fate, destiny). Those Spaniards believe in the inevitability of destiny. Fate, he thought, what nonsense! This problem could easily have been prevented. The accounting department should have made frequent credit checks on large accounts. Three months ago, *Alpara* had failed to pay on time. Even so, according to the report, A.P.P.I. had sent them a shipment four weeks ago. To avoid any delay, the captain signed the documents without reading them. Armando Muñez quickly dashed out of the office.

The captain began to prepare for tomorrow's meetings by making a list of products to be sold at discount if ordered in bulk. He had barely finished, when Miss Mendoza reminded him that he had promised to leave early.

"Is it five-thirty already?"

"It certainly is. You hardly notice the time even on quiet days, so I do that for you."

She called a taxi for him and half an hour later, he was approaching his home. A few hundred yards away, he noticed two police cars parked at the front entrance. Terror gripped him. He told the driver to stop, paid his fare, went quickly to the garden in the back of his mansion, and sat down to speculate why the police cars were there. Were the police after him? Were Wiesenthal's agents back in Buenos Aires asking about German residents in Argentina, and was he a suspect? What about Galina's letters? Was she a suspect? Were they after Jews? He recalled how it had all started in Germany. What if the children were harmed? Were they waiting for his arrival to take him to the police station for interrogation? Hiding in the garden, he felt somewhat safe. No one apparently had heard the arrival of his taxi. For the moment the best course was patience. He would only enter the house when the police cars left. No one would suspect he was sitting in the back garden. Dusk was beginning to shed its faint glow of colours: pale blue changing into mauve pink, all gliding somewhere into a dark grey infinity. Severina had landscaped the garden, planted a variety of trees and colourful flowers. He sat there admiring the garden and planning a strategy to get his family out of Argentina. He wasn't going to wait until it was too late to escape, as some Jews had in Germany. But another thought occurred to him. Maybe a relative of the Kesselmann's family had come to the city and sworn that it was not confirmed that Jaakob Kesselmann had died in a labour camp in northern Germany.

THE EXPATRIATE

He sat there apprehensive, looking at the drooping branches of the trees. Where and when had his dream of *"Freiheit"* disappeared? An illusionary myth! He was now beginning to reminisce about those by-gone days, even though he had vowed to shut out the past, live in the present and prepare for the future. But memories kept creeping up, like hidden snakes crawling to the surface from a deep pit. This garden reminded him of Brigitta's garden wedding in Zürich. When she approached his table to thank the guests, she stopped long enough to say that he resembled faintly someone she knew in Düsseldorf. Then came Lara with an unforgettable remark, "Your voice and eyes are very like someone I knew long ago in Düsseldorf." His reverie was interrupted. Muffled sounds, then the clear voices of two policemen.

"Thanks, Mrs. Kesselmann. You've been as helpful as you could be. We'll be in touch with you."

A car door closed, then another. The two cars drove off. He waited for a moment before going inside. A glance at Severina told him that she was upset. Trying to keep calm, he kissed her and asked for the children. Everyone was in the dining room, as usual, and so was Galina. At first, Severina said nothing about the police. He waited until she gradually told him the story.

At three o'clock, Galina had called to say that a few rowdy hoodlums were walking up and down *Avenida* Florida, throwing stones into windows. Policemen were watching but had allowed most of them to get away. After Galina's call, however, the local police precinct agreed to send an officer to investigate. The gang had targeted Jewish shops and left swastikas on the sidewalk. Two stones had shattered Galina's store windows, so she boarded them up and sent her saleswomen home. Money was not the problem, because Galina had insured her store against vandalism. The problem was fear.

"Two policemen left just before you got here," Severina continued. "They seemed quite cooperative and promised to make a thorough investigation."

She stopped talking after noticing that Jaakob was in pain, physical pain. It was his left side again. This was not the first time that she had seen him suddenly grow pale and hold his right hand over his left side. She decided that this episode had brought back memories of riots against the Jews in Germany, causing chest pains.

"Darling, we're all upset. But there's nothing to worry about. This isn't Nazi Germany. Let's eat later. In the meantime, a drink will help you relax."

"Severina," he said, "come and sit over here, next to me. There's something I want to discuss with you."

She welcomed his invitation and sat by his side, holding his hand. He outlined his plan.

"We need to arrange things right away, Severina, before it's too late."

"Too late? Jaakob, do you really think that the situation is so threatening?"

"I don't know. It might be. I'm worried."

"A single incident! We should at least wait for some word from the police. And things have already changed for the better since we got rid of Peron. At the university, I notice that more and more of my colleagues are working with the new government."

"Yes, but will things change for Jews? I mean, will things get better for Jews or worse?"

Almost two decades had passed. Jaakob had prospered. Galina had her friends and contacts. Severina had never experienced any hostility at the university.

"Jaakob, the world isn't the same as it was before the War. Jews have a state now. We need to stop running, even running to Israel."

"But Severina, we have to consider the children."

"Yes, of course. Let's wait just a bit longer and see who gets elected next month, and hear what the police say about the incident at Galina's store."

"Alright, Severina. But we should use the time to make plans. We'd have to sell the house, and maybe some of the furniture."

"But Jaakob, you're a very well-known Jew. Wouldn't we arouse suspicion by suddenly selling the house?"

"I hadn't thought of that."

THE EXPATRIATE

Selling the house might arouse suspicion, but he was even more worried about another source of suspicion which would follow directly from the first one. Anyone who began to investigate the imminent departure of a wealthy citizen would want to know about his past.

"Jaakob, I'm more worried about you than anything else. You look terrible. I'm going to call Igor tomorrow."

She was planning to take action before then. A sedative in his drink before bed-time would be a good remedy for the time being and kept thinking that running away might not be the best solution. Jaakob was too cautious because of his experience in Germany. But what if and when they decided to leave, it would be too late, just as it was in Czechoslovakia when Galina and she only managed to escape with the help of influential friends? Finally she replied. "Let's wait just a little. Maybe things will improve. At any rate we must remain for the police report about the stone throwing. This will give us a little time to decide what to do."

Next morning, at the office, it was busy as usual. No sooner had the captain sat down to check the daily agenda when accountant Muñez burst into the office. "Here are some more documents for you to sign, Señor Kesselmann. One of them is an injunction against *Alpara's* officers to keep them from leaving the country; the other documents state that under oath they must disclose their assets. They've publicly declared bankruptcy and are probably planning to leave the country quickly—unless, of course, they've already left. These documents will immediately prevent them from leaving Argentina."

The captain signed both documents without checking them, a very unusual procedure for him. As soon as Muñez left, he sent a telegram to the Keunenbergs, asking if some accounts receivable amounting to half a million dollars could be put up as security at the Central Bank of Buenos Aires to replace Alpara's invalidated collateral. A prompt response, he added, would be appreciated.

The reply came back quickly.

"Yes, but it will take a few days to do the paperwork."

"I'll call the bank," he replied, "and tell them we have the collateral. Thanks, Kurt." Ten minutes later, Galina called to give him some news about the stone-throwing incident.

"The police questioned some hoodlums last night and found the ones who broke my windows. I'll bet some government office hired them for precisely this purpose. Anyway, the police want to interview all of us. They need to keep an eye on German Jewish immigrants, particularly rich ones, because they may be targeted for the gang's next violent attack. I did try to dissuade them, explaining that any interrogation of your past would be very upsetting. But they insisted that the department must have this information and photos of the family for their records." This, the captain believed, was a ruse on their part but he had no choice.

"What? You mean the government is targeting Jews?"

"No, Jaakob, not targeting. Protecting. They want to protect Jews, especially rich ones, from future attacks by this gang—or some other gang."

"But I don't have time for an interrogation, Galina. Can't you and Severina tell them what they need to know?"

"Well, I tried, but they insisted. And it won't take long, Jaakob. After all, how long could it take to ask a few personal questions?"

Refusing to be questioned by the police would immediately imply that he had something to hide. The captain thanked Galina for calling. He hung up and lay down on the couch for a little while and then continued to work. The inspectors came an hour after Galina's phone call and asked to see Herr Kesselmann. Miss Mendoza rang the captain's phone over and over again but received no reply. Perhaps, she wondered, he might be in the washroom? She had not seen him leave. On the other hand, he might have left while she was on her coffee break. Even so, she knocked on his door twice. Still no response! Now frightened and apprehensive, she opened the door cautiously. And there he was, slumped over, his head on the desk. Miss Mendoza was not a woman who gave in easily to fear, and went immediately into action. She pulled his head up, slapped his cheeks, poured a little water into his mouth, took off his tie, and unbuttoned his shirt collar. Once he regained consciousness, she called the emergency clinic on the ground floor. After examining him very briefly, two nurses took him in an ambulance to the emergency ward of the Buenos Aires General Hospital. He was admitted as a cardiac patient. As soon as Señor Kesselmann, president founder of the international firm of A.P.P.I, was registered, he was given preferential treatment and assigned to the special section reserved for C.E.O.'s of the state. The chief cardiologist monitored all examinations. The diagnosis, when he heard it, was that he had just had a heart attack. Immediate steps were taken to stabilize his condition.

Meanwhile, Miss Mendoza called Severina. Her husband was now, after four hours, in stable condition. Severina left immediately for the hospital, even though she was not permitted to enter his suite immediately.

After waiting two hours, she finally entered the special executive suite and stood on the threshold, astonished. Before her was a large salon lounge with a marble tapestry floor, near both walls were placed mahogany coffee tables with shapely legs. The huge room was divided by an opaque glass wall that missed the ceiling by two feet. The smoked glass partition was decorated with a variety of large hand-painted flowers in soft greens, pinks and blues. As one approached the centre of this wall, it opened automatically, leaving a space wide enough for two people to enter. Once someone stepped over the threshold, the opened parts closed automatically. When Severina finally entered his room, she found her husband dressed in a patient's gown and resting comfortably. She walked toward the bed, put her cheek against his then kissed him.

"Considering this ordeal," she said with a smile, "you look pretty good. Igor tells me that you're doing quite well after a mild heart attack which is easily treated."

"Yes, that's what he told me but they still insist they must take further X-rays of the heart and every part of my body, not only to determine the source of the attack but to keep a record. This will take a few days. Then I'll need a couple of days rest. So I expect to be back at work within a week's time."

Severina bit her lip. This was characteristic of him: barely out of danger yet thinking about work. "What about advising your partners, especially the vice-presidents, to take over while you are recuperating?"

"No, that won't be necessary. I asked my secretary to come here early every morning with the mail. Then she can return to the office and I'll dictate my replies by phone."

"But Jaakob—" she interrupted, a little irritated.

"As soon as I know how long I have to stay in the hospital, I'll arrange for someone to take over some of my work for a while." Just then the nurse came in announcing that visitors must leave in fifteen minutes.

"Severina, will you bring the children tomorrow?" She smiled, and nodded yes.

"You know, dear, I almost forgot to tell you about a notice that I saw on the bulletin board downstairs. It's hard to believe, really. This hospital permits a Rabbi Shumansky to visit and bless the Jewish patients. We should send a donation to support his work."

Before she could explain further, the nurse reappeared with some medication and, with regret, asked the visitor to leave. But the family might visit next day if the doctors approved. Severina suggested she would bring special food that her husband preferred. "No, that is not permitted because patients in the executive suites have special meals prepared by a gourmet chef."

The captain kissed his wife good-night but his mind was elsewhere. If a rabbi is permitted to make the rounds, blessing the sick, what about a priest? He ventured to ask the nurse in attendance. "I was told that there is a rabbi coming here to bless the sick. Is there a priest as well?" he asked timidly.

"Why, of course, Señor Kesselmann. Padre Marcos Rodriguez also visits. He has been with us much longer than Rabbi Shumansky."

After taking a sedative, the captain fell quickly into a dreamless sleep.

As soon as Severina reached home, she phoned Galina and told her what had happened to Jaakob.

"I'll tell you when to visit him. But what have you heard from the police? They went to his office, didn't they?"

"Yes, two policemen went there to get information for the dossier on our family. He could not be interviewed at that time so they found some other source of information about him. At some government office, perhaps the immigration department, they found the date of Jaakob's arrival in this country and even a copy of his passport. That's all the police needed. But at the end, the inspector made a baffling remark about Jaakob's passport. The picture didn't look quite like Jaakob and the face seemed bigger. Of course, I said he was younger then."

Early next morning, a nurse wheeled the captain out of his room for a series of tests. On the way, he inquired about the padre's visiting hours.

"He's here every second day and always on Fridays but the Rabbi does not come on Fridays."

"Would it be possible for the padre to drop in to see me on Friday? I am sure Rabbi Shumansky will visit me during the week. I'd like to meet both men."

"Of course, I'll ask him to put you on his list. But I can't tell you exactly when he'll come, because he doesn't make personal appointments. He just makes his regular rounds every second day and stays with patients as long as they need him."

The captain was told that his family would visit him on Wednesday evening. When the children saw him, they jumped on his bed and kissed him. Zvi brought his most recent report card and pointed to the gold stars for composition and history. Lila, not to be outdone by her brother, shouted "me too, I'll bring my report card when I get it next week." For a moment, the image of Brigitta's school days drifted before his eyes, the day when she brought her report card with the teacher's note, "Your daughter needs some help in several subjects. Please speak to the head mistress immediately after Christmas." But Brigitta had worked hard, obtained a university degree and was now married to an educated and fine fellow. He could not forget the past. It still haunted him. Yet sitting in his reclining chair, the captain beamed with pleasure as the children hovered to embrace and kiss him. Severina and Galina stood by, admiring. After a little while, Severina cautioned the children not to tire their dad and asked them to leave while she gave him a few important messages. Time slipped by unnoticed, until the nurse signaled that all must leave. They could come again Thursday evening.

The captain was tense on Thursday morning, when he greeted the doctors expecting them to tell him about the results of all those tests he had. Doctors Armando Dominico and Merlo Limon, chief cardiologists at the hospital, carried large files under their arms and with their business suits resembled executives about to announce a huge decline in profits or accountants who had checked and realigned profit-and-loss figures. Accustomed to communicating good and bad news, they had standard soothing formulas for opening the conversation.

"Señor Kesselmann, we have made a thorough examination and analysis of your heart condition." Dr. Limon sat down, while, Dr. Dominico continued with what most patients want to hear first. "You do not need a heart operation or a by-pass. With proper medication, you can continue to live many years. But we warn you again, the heart is an unpredictable organ." He sat down and shifted a few pages in his file, then continued, "If you abuse or strain yourself beyond your capacity you risk cardiac arrest and probable death. Recently, you must have experienced shortness of breath, gasping or some chest pains. They did not last long, so you ignored the symptoms." He bent forward, took the patient's wrist to check his pulse and kept on talking. "The medication we are prescribing will keep you going for many years." He stopped to glance at Dr. Limon. Both knew that Señor Kesselmann was an inveterate workaholic and only a strong warning might force him to reduce his work load. "Much depends on the management of your lifestyle. You must avoid stress and reduce your work load. The nurse will bring your daily medication and leave a packet of mild sedatives to be taken, one before bedtime. This will give you a full night's sleep and a good rest." He bent over and took the patient's hand to check his pulse again. "We will return in a few days to get the nurse's report on the effectiveness of the medication. It's a standard remedy for your type of problem. This combination has helped millions around the world with similar ailments." Dr. Limon got up and pointed to his wrist watch. Dr. Dominico was talking too much with this patient because he was an important businessman. "You will be permitted to leave the hospital by the end of next week. After that, I expect to examine you in my private office every six months to monitor the effectiveness of the medication." Dr. Limon joined Dr. Dominico in a quick handshake with a "Buenos *Dias et Buena Suerte"* (good luck), they rushed out. Their schedule was completely booked, hour by hour.

The captain considered every word of the doctors' warning. He was pleased with the prospect of returning to work next week and began to prepare his agenda. An extra assistant would be hired, which would permit him to leave the office a little earlier each day and at noon on Fridays. His Will and Testament are in Abogado Hernandez's hands, and no changes were necessary. Padre Rodriguez was to come on Friday, and he would make his confession to him. He, Captain Yanos von Heissel, would be prepared for any eventuality, including sudden death—which could happen sooner or later. If, as Socrates said, "an unexamined life is not worth living," he should have added an "unorganized life" as well.

THE HOMECOMING

Relieved that the prognosis was very optimistic—certainly not as serious as he had believed, the captain felt very cheerful. He lost no time in calling his secretary to come the next morning with the most urgent files. Good news came from other sources as well. Business was beginning to pick up since Argentine president, Umberto Illia, in the second year of his presidency, had achieved some degree of economic stability and prosperity. Sales were up. Abogado Hernandez had called with more good news. Alpara had agreed to settle out of court and pay most of its creditors in return for preventing a public scandal. All that was now needed was Herr Kesselman's signature on the approval. As well, there was a huge stack of speedy recovery wishes from almost every employee of the company and friends.

Next morning as requested, Carmela came with a briefcase full of files. While they were checking the agenda, Rabbi Shumansky poked his head through the half-open doors, saw the two at work, and merely stood on the threshold of the opened doors. "Shalom brother Kesselmann. I see you are busy so I'll drop in on Monday. Speedy recovery. God bless." And with this he fled. Carmela remained till the nurse came in with some medication.

That evening Severina arrived alone. As she walked down the corridor, nurse Inez Ramon, rushed towards her. "I'm so glad to meet you. We are extremely busy tonight with critical emergencies. Would you save me a trip down this long corridor? Take this packet of pills for your husband. They are only mild sleeping pills, and he knows that he has to take one dissolved in half a glass of water before bedtime. It's only to give him a good night's sleep. It will save me time because I must rush to help the doctor in room 3B. This evening we are terribly short of nurses because of the many emergency cases."

"You say there are no specific instructions, only one pill dissolved in half a glass of water before bedtime."

"Yes, they are quite harmless. You may take the balance of the packet home and give him one every night for a week. He may sleep better at home and will probably not need them." Before Severina could say another word, the nurse rushed off.

Severina smiled happily and kissed her husband. He looked so attractive, so dignified, wearing a brown silk lounge coat, reclining in the chair. She showed him the packet of pills, explained the instructions and put them in the medicine cabinet. "It's easy enough to remember." Both laughed. "The children wanted to come but they have to go to bed early. Their exams begin early next week." He was disappointed but tried to hide it. She made herself comfortable, moved her chair nearer to him and continued "Mother could not come. One of her sales ladies was sick today. But business, she told me, is brisk with many tourists in Buenos Aires, surprisingly some from Australia. Then I had a special message from a friend of yours in Canada. Can you guess who?"

A broad smile covered his face. "Of course, my landsman, Hermann Baumbach."

"Yes, he mentioned that he subscribes to the *World Financial News*, which had huge headlines stating that a mogul of the Argentine paper industry had had a heart attack. Nevertheless, the paper noted, business goes on as usual. The president is to return to his duties shortly."

"I wonder how they got the information about my leaving the hospital before I did."

"Probably there are a few journalists always snooping around in hospitals for news. But I almost forgot to tell you that your friend also mentioned that he plans to visit Buenos Aires to make some business contacts and remain for a few days to tour the country. His wife will accompany him. They will send a telegram to tell us when they expect to arrive. I hope by then you will be home."

"That sounds nice. I would like to meet Hermann's wife." A sly smile crossed his lips as he wondered if Rose, Hermann's wife, resembled Clarice, the gentle dove on their Atlantic crossing.

Severina took his hand and held it tightly. "Galina called to say the inspectors who came to your office, the day you had the heart attack, have decided to get the information from the Immigration Department." The captain's face paled. He shifted in his chair. She wondered if she should tell him what ensued. Apparently, this reminded him of some unbearable incident in his past. But she continued, "They checked all the documents, date of your arrival, declaration and your passport. They made a foolish remark that the face on the passport looked broader, the eyes narrower and the nose thicker. But Galina laughed and told them what should have been obvious, that everyone changes a little and you were younger then. They agreed. The necessary information about our family is complete, and all is in order now." The captain looked relieved. But he was a little doubtful if that remark about the passport picture was as innocent as they wished him to believe. "Galina also called again to Igor and he will be here to examine you tomorrow."

Both sat back, held hands and watched television contentedly. Time seemed timeless until the loudspeaker announced that visiting hours were over. Before leaving, Severina opened a neatly wrapped package. "I thought you needed another pair of pyjamas so I rummaged around in your cabinet at home and found at the very bottom these lovely silk ones. They look new, as if you've never worn them. Not only is the beige silk satin of the finest quality but the brown piping matches the hand-embroidered brown initial H. You probably bought it and ignored the H, which resembles a K." He sat there motionless, speechless. Slowly he reached for the glass of water on the little table near him, remaining silent. He fingered the pyjamas. They had been Lara's gift.

"To tell the truth, darling, I don't remember where or when I bought them. I even forgot I had them."

She smiled, patting his hand, "Never mind, handsome, put them on tonight." Soon the bell rang, announcing that visitors' hours were over.

JEANNETTE MOSCOVITCH

Severina had had a busy day: lecturing in the morning, correcting exams in the afternoon, rushing home for the children, listening to Galina's problems, and then rushing to the hospital to see Jaakob. Exhausted, she tumbled into bed and only glimpsed at the newspapers lying on the end tables near her bed. The front page showed a pit with naked bodies, atrocities somewhere in Africa. She turned the newspaper over to hide the revealing pictures and, without even turning out the lights, fell asleep, sinking into a shadowy abyss of unconsciousness. From the gray shadows, a huge box-like train moves slowly, like a snake on giant wheels, chugging along, then stopping. She stands near the railroad tracks. Large doors with large iron bars are lifted and the inside of the train gapes open. On the platform, long lines of gray-clad human beings, carrying small ragged valises are being shouted at and pushed by sturdy Nazi S.S. officers to enter the cavernous train quickly. A thunderous whistling, doors close, the heavy bars clamp on the locks, the train chugs and clanks on. Severina awakened, startled to find herself in a luxurious bedroom and not trudging with a small bundle to the train. Years had elapsed but, at intervals, images of the tragedies she'd witnessed in Czechoslovakia still haunted her.

It was late. No time for breakfast. A cup of coffee would have to do. And no time to call Jaakob to tell him when she would visit, although he knew it should be sometime after her lectures at the university. She did call Galina to tell her that she'd work through the lunch hour, then rush to the hospital to be there as early as she could to pack Jaakob's effects. He was to be released from the hospital tomorrow. She'd eat supper in the hospital's cafeteria and remain until visiting hours were over in the evening. Would Galina take the children for dinner and to the Friday evening services at the Synagogue? Early Saturday afternoon they'd go together to the hospital to accompany Jaakob home.

PADRE MARCOS RODRIGUEZ

Padre Marcos Rodgriguez was a middle-aged man whose black almond eyes and tobacco-coloured complexion betrayed an Indian ancestry. Tall, slim, clean-shaven, with a generous crop of black hair, he had a kind and sympathetic appearance. Far from being a pulpit priest, he ardently championed social issues, especially help for the impoverished. "The Church," he constantly repeated, "should play a greater role in the welfare activities of the community. Man is surrounded by greed and corruption everywhere, and his soul is torn between good and evil. This makes him unfaithful to the divine call of remaining truly humane."

He emphasized that the Gospel does not solve all of man's problems in advance. It leaves many moral and intellectual questions unsolved. What the Gospel lays bare are the forces that could destroy, what it offers as a remedy are the sources that enable man to become a listener, to enter into dialogue, to be ready for conversion and growth and to participate in the life of the community. This is the present salvation brought by Christ. (1)

He deplored Peron's incursions into ecclesiastical affairs, particularly his methods of bribing priests and placing them in important positions so as to gain votes for himself and his party. He thanked the Lord that the late Evita Peron's tactics had been exposed and that Peron, himself, was exiled. Now at last, in 1965, with President Umberto Illia, hope was revived. Hope, but not certainty. After all, Peronistas still controlled the labour unions.

The Church's role in society troubled the padre constantly. To him the overwhelming powers of evil that pervaded human life today showed that the Church had become meaningless and was losing independence in the community. Have we failed to assess the gravity of the situation, he asked, recalling Nietzsche's dictum, *"The Christian myth has lost its redemptive power."(2)* He acknowledged that we have not eliminated drug smuggling in the world, nor corruption in our Church. We have not spoken when millions of Jews were exterminated. What did St. Paul say? *"man is a sinner and hence in need of redemption. Man tends to evil. To sin comes natural to him. But man cannot become a sinner without consenting to it."(3)* What was his mission now? Who are we, as mankind? Consider—*"the forces that pit men against men, class against class, many as we have seen, pathological, [that] have gained such power… cause misery in unprecedented proportions and may even provoke a catastrophe that could destroy life altogether."(4)*

The padre kept wiping his hands with a large white handkerchief as if to eliminate menacing thoughts and germs. It had been an exhausting day, and it was almost three o'clock when he remembered that Nurse Inez had asked him to see a Jewish patient, one Jaakob Kesselmann. He was rather intrigued by the request. Why should a Jewish patient wish to see him? Without further hesitation, he headed for Señor Kesselmann's room.

As he stepped on the threshold to enter, the glass doors opened, shutting automatically behind him after he entered. Señor Kesselmann was sitting in his reclining chair. They greeted each other courteously and the conversation began. Just a few minutes later, Severina arrived and heard voices coming from behind the closed doors. Assuming it was the doctor, about to examine Jaakob, she decided to remain seated in the outside lounge, very near to the closed glass doors where she could hear clearly.

Jaakob was straightforward and unpretentious. "Padre Rodriguez, it was good of you to come. I know how busy you are, but I have some urgent matters to discuss with you." He began to move nervously in his chair and sat up very erect, a posture reminiscent of his military days. On the other side of the room's partition, Severina moved even closer to the glass doors, so as to hear better what was being said.

"Padre Rodriguez, the doctors say I am in a stable condition and well. With medication, my heart will function properly for many years. But we know that the heart is unpredictable and an unexpected attack could cause instant death."

The padre had heard this argument many times before. Patients usually rambled on before they came to the point.

"Death, Señor Kesselmann, is inevitable and unpredictable for all of us. But how can I be of any help to you?"

Severina shifted her position to hear exactly what was being said. Jaakob's vibrant voice now sounded strained.

"Padre, all is not what it seems. I was born a Christian Catholic and baptized in Düsseldorf, Germany. During the War, I served in the Fuhrer's bureaucracy. After the War, to escape prosecution for crimes to humanity, I had to assume the identity of a Jew in order to obtain a Jewish refugee visa to immigrate to Argentina. This was the only way I could escape detection. You, of course, may know Germans in Argentina, who escaped without having to change their identity so drastically." He paused, and out came the muslin handkerchief to wipe his forehead while waiting to hear the padre's reaction.

Severina heard this quite clearly and almost fell to the floor, gripped by fear, anger and disbelief. She was overcome by a wave of biliousness. Jaakob, the father of her children, a disguised Nazi criminal, a German Catholic! She gripped the arms of the chair, wiped her face with a handkerchief moistened in the glass of water standing on the coffee table and listened. Perhaps! Maybe! It's not true! She had not heard clearly!

The captain continued, "I have done my penance, secretly and unobtrusively, for obvious reasons. I have fulfilled the conditions for atonement and the requirements necessary for absolution. This is a very appropriate moment, padre, to give me absolution because I may not have the opportunity to be alone again. If you grant me this, I shall live untroubled with myself for the rest of my days and if death suddenly overtakes me, then I die in peace. I believe you have the authority to—" He stopped, moved nervously in his chair and looked directly at the padre, waiting for his response.

JEANNETTE MOSCOVITCH

Padre Rodriguez remained silent for what seemed like a century, stretched a little in his chair and, in typical clerical fashion, folded his hands on his lap. He struggled, hesitating with his words, "Señor Kesselmann, to hear a confession from an ordinary baptized Catholic person and listen to his misdemeanors, which are mostly not serious or inconsequential, is simple. Your request poses quite a dilemma for me and the Church. Since you adopted the Jewish disguise and all these years have practised somewhat the Jewish rituals and services in a synagogue with your wife and children, you may possibly, possibly, be deemed an adherent to the Jewish Faith. Your children are considered Jewish. Your wife will, confirm that. All this then, opens the question of how valid now is your Christian affiliation. You have somewhat, and I repeat somewhat, stepped over to the other side. In view of the many German criminal fugitives in this country, my colleagues and superiors have been reviewing the concept of Penance and Auricular Confession." He pulled out a little black book from his pocket, opening it at a designated page and began to read.

> *"There were some sins called capital (murder, adultery and apostasy) for which local churches at times did not perform the rite: this did not mean that God did not forgive but that good standing in the Church was permanently lost." From what you told me you have committed murder and apostasy. "However," he continued, "the penitential rite...has endured into modern times.... no quality or quantity of sin was too great for sacramental absolution. But today the Roman Catholic theologians have not arrived at an explanation of the process of absolution. They do not admit that absolution is merely a recognition by the priest of dispositions on the part of the penitent that merit forgiveness, nor that it is merely a process whereby the penitent is reconciled with the church. There seems to be an unspoken belief that it is a rare person who is really sorry for his sins..." (5)*

"Before I can accept your confession and admit absolution," continued the padre, "I have to examine and discuss this dilemma with my colleagues. I shall get in touch with you as soon as I have some answers." The padre stood up. "Bless you my son, but I must leave, pressing affairs await me at my church."

The padre fumbled to push the right button for the doors to open. But Severina did not wait. She ran to the nearest washroom and sat down in the little waiting room provided for visitors. Leaning back in the chair, shutting her eyes, she could not help recalling some occasions, particularly those when she'd asked about his past. His elliptical answers now began to reveal their hidden meaning. She began to understand his confession to the padre—that the change from his Catholic identity to a Jewish one, had been in order to escape criminal prosecution for crimes against humanity. Many of his inexplicable gestures became even clearer. It had seemed strange that, when Simon Wiesenthal's agent came to Buenos Aires, Jaakob instantly had to leave for Switzerland. It had been inexplicable that he rarely joined the family for Friday night or Saturday services at the Synagogue. However, he did donate considerable sums to the synagogue's maintenance. Probably to ease his conscience! And that unforgettable Nazi salute he had been teaching Zvi. How well that was explained away! Then there were the initials Y.H. on his handkerchiefs and pyjamas. His explanation was that these were bought at a luxury estate sale. The articles were so well priced for their superior quality that, despite of the wrong initials, he could not resist buying them. All his rigid manners were remnants of military training and those fearful facial expressions were not due, as she had presumed, to sad memories but to fears of being detected for his duplicity. He always had a plausible explanation and she'd believed him and trusted him.

The years passed before Severina's eyes: the death of her father, husband and son, the painful escape from Prague. Once in Buenos Aires, mother and daughter had reestablished themselves and life resumed a normal bourgeois pattern. But Severina had felt she could never love again nor want children. Then along came this educated, cosmopolitan handsome man, with whom she fell madly in love. The married years were happy, gracious and pleasant. It was Galina who had sensed something amiss from the very beginning. However, she could neither pinpoint it, nor put it into words.

JEANNETTE MOSCOVITCH

In the dimly lit washroom lounge, Severina shut her eyes, silently repeated to herself what she had heard. She began to comprehend its full impact. Jaakob was a Nazi war murderer! That is why he had had to change his identity—to escape life imprisonment or execution, verdicts certain to be given by the Nuremberg Court. She recalled a paragraph in the lengthy description of the Nuremberg Trials, written by Rebecca West, who was the official reporter. The article referred to the extermination of the Jews.

> *"Riots were organized by [Nazi] Party leaders to loot Jewish business places and burn synagogues. Jewish property was confiscated....The program progressed in fury...sending all Jews who were fit to work in concentration camps as slave laborers and all who were not fit, which included children under 12, people over 50 as well as any others judged unfit by an S.S. doctor, to concentration camps for extermination."(6)*

She moved her chair away from the light to be in semi-darkness, bent her head backward and shut her eyes tightly to avoid thinking. But slowly the images of last night's dream became visible once more. Those frightened faces begging for mercy, dressed in gray tattered clothes, being pushed with large batons by hefty S.S. troops to enter the box trains. And those inside were seen alive for the last time!

Severina sat there, pale, traumatized. A lady entered the washroom lounge. Seeing Severina looking rather ill, she touched her shoulder. "Are you not well, Señora? May I get you something to drink?"

Severina opened her eyes slowly, then realized she had lapsed into a dream, that she had been living in Prague. "No thank you so much. I am well. I just dozed off a little."

"Are you sure you are all right. There are some nurses around. Perhaps you need a mild sedative?"

"No, thank you for your kindness. I am well. As a matter of fact, I'm leaving now." Both ladies left the washroom lounge.

Slowly Severina walked a short way to a small café, ordered a strong coffee and tried to repeat again what she had heard.

One thing was absolutely clear. This must be locked forever in her heart. Gazing listlessly for something to give her momentary relief, she picked up the *Buenos Aires News,* lying on the table near her.

"*Inflation is raging. The Government is unstable. The Unions threaten a country-wide strike. How safe are the Banks?*" asked the editorial essay. Why did everything suddenly point to destruction and annihilation? Usually, she bought this newspaper because of its candidness and gave it to Galina, who would communicate its contents to Pavlosek in Prague. Listless and troubled, she began to walk back slowly to the hospital while repeating the exact words she had heard Jaakob say to the padre. Not once did he say, "I may have been wrong and beg forgiveness for my part in the brutality." No, he clearly intimated that he now lived a moral life, was a '*guter Burger,*' that confession and absolution were his right according to the Catholic religion. Slackening her pace, she mulled over what to do and how to face him.

Back at the hospital, she walked down the long hallway and entered the washroom to powder her nose, put on fresh lipstick and comb her hair. She braced herself and entered the captain's room. He was sitting as usual in his recliner, looking very handsome, and in fairly good spirits. There was no trace of anxiety about the padre's visit. As soon as he saw her, he beamed with pleasure, got up to kiss and embrace her. She stood impassive, accepting coldly his warm greeting. "You look as beautiful as usual, darling, but tired. I expected you a little earlier. Will the children come?"

"No, they are going with Galina to the Synagogue for Friday night services. They will come tomorrow, after Saturday morning services."

"Come and sit beside me and tell me what's new." She obeyed, wondering how he could continue as if nothing had happened even though the padre had rejected his confession and probably would refuse absolution after consulting with his colleagues. Did it not have any meaning to him that he had aided and abetted the murder of innocent people?

He sensed that she was not her usual cheerful self. She didn't tell him about her students and the smart remarks the children had made, or about Galina's exquisite glassware which had just come from Czechoslovakia. No, this evening she began by commenting about the political news.

"Have you read today's newspaper? It's the usual in Argentina—after hoping for better times, the economy is heading for a crisis, and the unions are relentless." He interrupted her.

"Is that why you seem a little upset and tired? Don't worry. I have foreseen the economic downturn, and the amount of foreign business we have developed in India will by far cover our domestic loss. I did read today's gloomy news. But never mind that. What's new at home?"

She answered with guarded pauses. "Igor phoned. He'll be here tomorrow and will give you a final check-up. The housekeeper called to say that a telegram came from a Mr. Hermann Baumbach in Canada. It says he will arrive in Buenos Aires on Sunday or Monday, if no delays occur. Then Carmela phoned to say that urgent matters have been taken care of by the directors. She asked if there was anything special she could prepare to welcome you back. I just said no, but to keep everything as normal as usual. The children are well and doing great in school." She stopped abruptly. Why take up so much time with domestic trivia?

"Is that it?"

"Yes," she answered, trying to stay as calm as possible.

"Then all seems as usual. Shall I call the cafeteria for some fruit and coffee?"

"Alright."

As soon as the refreshments arrived, he sat down beside her, kissed her neck, and settled down comfortably to watch a Spanish melodrama on television. Both smiled and agreed the ending was quite romantic, but unrealistic. Soon the bell rang for all visitors to leave. She removed his hand from her shoulder and helped him get into bed.

"Now my dear, you mustn't forget your sleeping pill like you did last time. I'll get it from the cabinet, let it dissolve in a glass of water and bring it to you."

In the washroom, Severina took the packet of pills from the shelf where she had put it last night, emptied almost half of the packet into the water and put the other half in her purse. Then she mixed the pills in the glass until the cloudiness disappeared, and brought it to him. Her hand was a little shaky, but he did not notice. Before leaving, she tucked the blanket around his neck and kissed him. It was eight-fifty.

Severina wandered distractedly along *Avenida Florida*, trudging wearily as far as her mother's store, where she stopped to gaze at the window display of exquisite Bohemian glassware. Then, she trailed along as if sleepwalking, until she reached *Avenida Libertador.* She was startled out of her reverie only when a loud screech and a honk from a car saved her from being run over. She stopped and hailed a taxi.

At home all was calm. The servants were asleep in their quarters. The children were with their grandmother. Her bed was prepared, and the telephone stood on the night table. She undressed slowly, automatically, and climbed into bed. But she could not sleep and decided to drink a few ounces of vodka. That was certain to induce slumber.

She did not hear the first telephone call from the hospital at five o'clock in the morning. When the second call came at nine, she picked up the receiver. "Señora Kesselmann" a sad voice continued, "we regret to inform you that your husband passed away at 4:50 this morning. He had an unexpected cardiac arrest. Needless to say, we tried to revive him. His body will be in the room until the cause of death is verified, and then your family will be permitted to see him for the last time before he is taken away for burial. Doctor Herrenkevitch called seconds after you left last night to say he will come to the hospital early Saturday morning to examine your husband. We will permit him to do that and to give us his report because we are extremely busy, as I mentioned to you last night. When this is completed, you may come and make arrangements for the body to be taken away for burial. Please wait for our next call."

Severina began to dress slowly, listlessly, in a dark navy blue silk suit and a navy blue large organza hat with a veil to cover her face. At 10:30 the second phone call came. "Doctor Herrenkevitch arrived, examined the body and left his report. He had to return to his cardiology department and left a message to say he'll get in touch with you as soon as he can."

She immediately called the Jewish funeral parlor but a message stated their offices were closed on Saturday. She left a message, asking if arrangements could be made on Sunday for a funeral to be scheduled as soon as Monday. Her intention was to avoid any delay and prevent many from attending. The servants were told the sad news. Then she summoned the chauffeur to drive her to the hospital, where she waited for the arrival of Galina and the children after attending the Saturday services at the Synagogue.

Severina entered the captain's suite where he lay on the bed as if asleep. She gathered all his belongings. Then called Carmela, instructed her to advise Abogado Hernandez and the board of directors that the funeral would be held on Monday at two o'clock. It would take place at the Beth Funeral Parlor and then proceed to the Jewish Cemetery. The nurses brought in a carafe of strong coffee and asked if they could remove the body. "Not until my mother and the children arrive to have a last look at Herr Kesselmann and then the hospital can proceed with the usual arrangements" she replied.

Galina and the children arrived as previously scheduled and at the reception desk were told the sad news. As soon as Galina saw her daughter, she kissed her, whispering that for the children's sake she must be brave. As for herself, she took the news with inexplicable equanimity. The children sobbed with heartfelt sorrow. Severina remained calm and unperturbed. Galina glanced unobtrusively several times at her daughter, but kept her silence. No condolences! No sympathies!

That evening mother and daughter planned the funeral. Both agreed that it should be in keeping with Jaakob's status as one of the richest and most successful businessmen in Buenos Aires. All day Sunday, they attended to the sumptuous and elaborate funeral arrangements. Radio announcements were made, detailing a funeral service on Monday at two o'clock at the Beth Funeral Parlor, followed by a burial procession to the Jewish Cemetery. Shiva, strictly private.

Igor Herrenkevitch came early to help in any way he could. He was a pallbearer and sat with the family in the limousine following the hearse. At the burial ground he stood on Severina's right, with Galina and the children on her left. Galina looked very composed in her dark royal blue suit, with a large brimmed hat to match—the regal, matriarchal bearing of an aging, beautiful Russian queen who has overcome much grief in her life. Her eyes darted ever so often to Severina and Igor. The children were weeping silently. Severina stood dry-eyed, worried and tragic. Igor, standing at her side, moved still closer and grasped her hand in his large, strong one. At one point when the Rabbi was eulogizing loudly, he whispered in her ear. "Don't worry. I was the only one who signed the death certificate. The other doctors were busy and in a hurry so they left all matters to me. I stated that he died of an unpredictable acute cardiac arrest." Severina remained erect, impassive and unmoved. Galina, glancing sideways at her daughter, noticed Igor holding Severina's hand tightly. The ghost of a sly tiger's smile grazed her lips: "Severina, her dear daughter, was at home at last, with her own kind."

SOURCES OF REFERENCE

Chapter I
1. F. Nietzsche from The Age of Ideology by Henry D. Aiken (A Mentor Book published by The New American Library of World Literature N.Y. 1956) 211
2. Ibid 211-215

Chapter II
1. "Goethe: A Critical Introduction by H.C.Hatfield Norfolk Conn. 1963) 177
2. Ibid. 180
3. Johann Wolfgang von Goethe, Faust translated by Barker Fairley (University of Toronto Press, 1970) 7
4. Ibid. 23
5. Goethe by Hatfield-Eckermann's Gesprache

Chapter III
1. Jews, God and History by Max I. Dimont (Signet Books, New American Library Inc. N.Y. 1962) 14, 15,18
2. How the Great Religions Began by Joseph Gaer (Signet Books, The New American Library, N.Y. 1954) 145
3. Ibid. 155, 156 somewhat transcribed.

Chapter IV
1. Jews, God and History by Max I.Dimont (Signet Books, New American Library Inc. N.Y. 1962) 113
2. Ibid. 148
3. Ibid. 141
4. Ibid. 143
5. Ibid. 144
6. Ibid. 174

Chapter VI
1. Jews, God and History by Max I. Dimont (Signet Books, New American Library Inc. N.Y. 1962) 148, 149
2. The Peron Era by Robert J. Alexander (Columbia University Press.N.Y. 1951) 4

3. Ibid. 12, 13, 33
4. Ibid. 64, 65
5. Ibid. l2, 13
6. Ibid. 64
7. Ibid. 65

Chapter VII
1. The Peron Era by Robert J.Alexander (Columbia University P. N.Y. 1952) 213, 214

Chapter VIII
1. History of Argentina by H.S. Ferns (Ernest Benn, London, 1969) 29
2. Jews, God and History by Max I.Dimont (The New York Library, N.Y. 1962) l55, l56

Chapter X
1. Portrait of Democracy by Russel H. Fitzgibbon (Rutgers U. Press, N.B. 1954) 256
2. Ibid. 257

Chapter XIV
1. Information about the paper industry summarized from the Montreal Gazette's article in the Business Section, by P. J. Greenbaum. (Jan 23, l999, Montreal, Que. Canada.)

2. Information about the Hapsburgs and others from Life World Library, Eastern Europe---Czechoslovakia, Hungary, Poland (Godfrey Blunden, U.S.A) l3

Chapter XV
1. Switzerland---Land, People, Economy by Aubrey Diem (published by Media International, Waterloo Ont. 1960) 22

Chapter XVI
1. The Dark Labyrinth by L.Durell (Faber & Faber, London Eng. 1969) 78

2. The Peron Era by A.J. Alexander (Columbia U. N.Y. 1951) 66
3. Bloody Precedent by Fleur Cowles (Columbia U. Press.N.Y. 1952) 206
4. Ibid. 109
5. Good Guy Bad Guy by Yves Lavigne (Random House, Toronto 1991) 1, 184, 277

Chapter XVIII
1. Peron and the Enigmas of Argentina by R.Crassweller (W.W.Norton Co.N.Y. 1986) 253, 254, 255
2. Inside South America by J. Gunther (Harper Row 1967) 182, 183

Chapter XIX
1. Peron and Enigmas of Argentina by R. Crassweller (W.W.Norton Co. N.Y. 1976) 274
2. Ibid. 275
3. Ibid. 276
4. Ibid. 276
5. Ibid. 183

Chapter XXI
1. Credibility of the Church Today: a reply to Charles Davies by Gregory Baum (Herder and Herder. N.Y. 1968) 186
2. The Age of Ideology by Henry D.Aiken (A Mentor Book. New American Library, 1956) 211
3. Credibility of the Church Today by Gregory Baum (Herder and Herder 1956) 159
4. Roman Catholicism, (Encyclopedia Britannica, volume 26) 908, 909
5. Ibid. 908, 909
6. Nuremberg Trials, in Law and Literature excerpt by Rebecca West (Simon Shuster N.Y. 1966) 476